Time's Paradox

The sequel to

Time Portals of Norwich

and

Time's Revenge

David Viner

Published by
Viva Djinn (Horde) Publishing
vivadjinn.com
Norwich, UK

ISBN: 978-1-913873-12-7

British Library Cataloguing in Publication Data available.

Design and layout: David Viner

Time's Paradox

Garden

"How's it going?" Cassie asked her companion as they sat on wooden chairs outside the back of the cottage. They were drinking wine grown from grapes that wouldn't be harvested for another hundred and sixty years.

In the west, the sun was slowly sinking towards the woods. Above the trees, birds circled and called to each other before departing to find somewhere to roost for the night. Up closer, the garden hummed to the tune of some late evening bees and the occasional clatter of a dragonfly's wings.

Cassie's companion smiled, the sun painting her face orange. "I could ask you the same thing," came the reply. "Especially your hair. It's lovely. You never did tell me what made you go back to being curly. I thought you hated it."

"Hah, yes. I did. Long story. Maybe later."

"Tell me about something shorter but not hair-related, then."

"Okay. Well, I got through my exams. I don't think I did too badly in history and English. Not sure about sociology, though."

"What about Georgia?"

"I bet she aces sports. She's talking about getting engaged to Mark over the summer."

"Hmm, if they're both sure. Still a bit young, though."

"Maybe. Talking of which, I've got a proper boyfriend now," Cassie grinned.

"Oh. Do I know him?"

Cassie shook her head as she breathed in air that held little of the taint of the twenty-first century. This wasn't surprising as the year was 1856. Although the Industrial Revolution had already taken place and the railway mania of the eighteen-forties was long past, the number of metal tracks cutting their way across the countryside was still a fraction of what would evolve. Steam engines belching smoke were still quite a rare sight. Such roads as already existed were mere tracks and the traffic on them was mostly by foot, horse or, upon the rare occasion, solid heavy bicycle.

Also permeating the air was the scent of freshly baked bread. It emanated from the back door of the cottage.

"No," Cassie said. "I first met him in early 2019 when I was still seventeen. Then I bumped into him a few months later when I was twenty-two or whatever age I was."

"What's his name?"

Cassie told her.

"How old is he?"

"Twenty-one."

"So, he's both older and younger than you," she laughed.

"Yes, at the moment, I haven't told him my real age as I don't know for certain myself."

There was a knowing chuckle from her companion.

"He used to have a limp, you know," Cassie added.

"Used to?"

"Yes."

"You fixed it?"

Cassie nodded.

"Did he know it was you?"

Cassie nodded again.

"And you really like him?"

"Yes."

"A lot?"

After a short pause, Cassie nodded yet again, adding, "Yeah, he might even be, you know… the one. I really hope so."

"I'd like to meet him. Does he know about all the things you can do?"

"A few. Actually, we both have something unusual in common."

"Oh? What's that?"

Cassie spent several minutes explaining what had happened on their first proper date a few weeks previously.

"That will probably make things easier when he gets to find out everything about you… and what you've been through over the past few years."

"Yes, that is going to be an interesting conversation."

"But only if he really is the one?"

"Yeah, my lips are sealed until I'm certain."

"This is the happiest I've seen you since… well, you know…"

"You're definitely right there."

"Mind you, when he sees those scars on your leg from the wolf and the fire, then he'll really start asking questions."

Cassie grinned, saying, "Already sorted."

"Oh? You mean he's already seen them?"

"No, and he never will. I, er, got rid of them a while back."

"Really? Got rid of them? How?"

"Ah, it's all part of that long story…"

"Well, there's still a good half hour before the sun sets."

"Okay," Cassie said, pouring more wine from the bottle and raising her glass. "At least we have enough wine to just about last."

Cassie told her story. Her companion's mouth opened wide in surprise several times before the tale had ended.

"Wow. I hadn't realised it had got as bad as all that. I still feel you're not telling me everything, though."

Cassie grinned. "Yes – I can't yet. So, how are you getting on with all this?"

"Not having electricity takes a lot of getting used to. I really miss instant hot water and decent lighting. Candles and oil lamps are no substitute. And boiling up enough water for a bath seems to take all day."

"Sorry," Cassie said. "But, it has to be this place, this cottage."

"You know exactly what's coming, don't you?"

Cassie nodded. "At least, it's not actually haunted."

"Yes, I heard a number of stories about that. I hear it was bought for a song because of its reputation."

"Yeah, that was fun to sort out."

"Why was that?"

"The law changes in a few years but, in this time, married women don't really own property. It all gets passed to their husbands when they marry."

"But you're not married."

"No, but the, um, person who bought it was. Or had been – she was a widow by that point."

"Oh yes, I heard that. And who exactly was this Boardal woman and why is she happy to let me live here, rent-free?"

Cassie grinned, shook her head and said, "Not yet."

"Ah, another one of your secrets."

Cassie nodded and stared past the garden at the countryside beyond. She was intrigued at the way the land undulated with hills and dales in a manner that would never be encountered in Norfolk. For Sussex, however, this was normality. Towards the south, a valley would allow the occasional glimpse of the English Channel if both the weather and light were just right.

"The garden looks fantastic," Cassie said, glancing over the late summer flowers, few of which she could name. She could only identify lavender, lupins, helenium and golden rod, remembering them from the garden of her childhood.

"Well, I don't exactly have too much else to do at the moment," came the reply. "I do need some new gardening gloves, though," she said gazing at her hands, which were red and scratched in places. She picked at a mark on one of her fingers and, squinting close, extracted a small thorn with her fingernails. "Gardening has its downsides," she added.

"Ah," Cassie grinned, "I'll hunt down some new ones for you." She placed her half-finished glass of wine on the wooden table. Standing, she held her companion's hands and, seconds later, the scratches were gone.

"Make the most of it," Cassie said, indicating the garden with a wave of her hand. "Things will change soon enough and you will find your hands full."

"I'm not sure whether that's bad or good news."

"It'll all work out well in the end. I have it on good authority."

"Hmm, well, you're the expert in such matters."

"Not sure about that. Actually, I think the next time you see me I definitely won't be the expert and I might just be rather surprised to see you, instead."

"All this time travelling does get rather confusing."

"Yes, just like how complicated it got after I returned from the Stone Age. I was confusing everyone back then, including myself."

Cassie's companion laughed. "I remember you telling me all about that."

Cassie chuckled and raised her wine glass. "To all the futures and pasts," she said, before draining the glass.

"I would be happier drinking to that if I knew exactly what was in store. But, you're not going to tell me, are you?"

"No, but let's just say it will probably be a lot better than you expect. From what I hear, it won't be quite as complicated as the stuff I've had to live through, especially the last few months or however long it was."

And I really have no idea how long it was, Cassie thought. *It spanned thousands of years and probably thousands of light years as well. And, now that it's over, I'm finding it hard to believe some of it even happened.*

"Okay, I will definitely drink to that."

Cassie's companion put her glass to her lips and emptied it. "So," she said, lowering the glass, "is everything completely sorted out at your end?"

Cassie thought for a moment. "Yes, almost," she nodded.

"Almost?"

"Yes, I never did find out who the zebra girl was."

"I don't remember you talking about any zebra girl."

"No," Cassie sighed. "She got lost in between everything else, I suppose."

With the light diminishing as the sun dipped below the trees, they both rose, empty glasses in hand, and returned to the cottage.

Inside, a match was put to an oil lamp and the small kitchen was bathed in its flickering, amber light. In one corner, a ceiling-height cabinet was packed with plates, cups and other common paraphernalia of a Victorian kitchen. On one of its open shelves stood an anachronistic black-and-white photograph of a man in uniform. Cassie remembered being shocked the first time she had encountered that photo in this kitchen.

"The bread's cool enough – you want some cheese in yours?"

"Yes please," Cassie replied watching as a misshapen loaf was cut into crude, chunky slices. It was thickly daubed with recently churned butter and accompanied by a wedge of cheese.

Yes, Cassie thought, taking a bite and thinking back to her return from the Stone Age, *I really hope things are far less complicated from now on… I definitely deserve it.*

Complicated

Violence Before Dinner

"Right, this is where it *really* starts to get complicated," grinned the newly-arrived Cassie, her short, straight hair a contrast to the frizz of the other Cassie.

Georgia stared at Cassie, Cassie's grandad, Bill, stared at Cassie, and Cassie also stared at Cassie.

"Okay, I suppose I'd better tell you how this is all going to work. First of all, to avoid confusion, you should refer to me as Future Cassie."

"Avoid confusion? But there's two of you," Georgia said, her eyes darting from one Cassie to the other. "I don't think I can get any more confused."

"Join the club," Bill said. "Only a few hours ago, the Cassie I was talking to was four years younger than this one."

The one calling herself Future Cassie continued, "The difference between me and – let's call you Past Cassie – is only about three weeks. Anyway, hold on a few minutes and there will be even more of me."

"I can't handle this," Georgia muttered.

"What are you doing here?" Past Cassie asked her future self.

"Fixing the school problem – amongst all the other things that need fixing."

"Huh? What do you mean?"

"I will go to school as I now look more like you did when you were last there. And, also, Georgia has helped me catch up with what we were doing."

"I did? When?" Georgia said.

"Oh, don't worry, that's still to come for you," Future Cassie said, with a grin. "But first, we have a more pressing problem."

"What pressing problem?" Past Cassie asked.

"We need to deal with Jason."

"Jason? He's not here, thank God," Past Cassie gasped. "But, what do you mean 'deal with him'?"

"You'll see," Future Cassie said, chuckling. "And when I said 'pressing' I meant that, any second now, he will be pressing..."

The doorbell rang.

"Right on cue," said Future Cassie. "If I remember rightly – and I do – you're the one who lets him in, Grandad. Watch it, though, he's steaming. Be prepared for fireworks. I'll make myself scarce for a moment."

Saying that, she disappeared.

"Bloody hell," Georgia said. "Who exactly was she?"

"A future me, I presume," Cassie said.

The doorbell chimed once again and Bill went to open it.

"Where is she?" Jason's voice snarled as he barged into the house, pushing past Bill and stomping into the lounge.

"How dare you force your way into my house like that?" Cassie shouted. Seeing him raging before them fired Cassie's anger to boiling point. Four years hadn't diminished her memories and she could still vividly recall what he'd attempted to do to her behind the shed at Erin's party. For him, though, that was only a few hours ago, which was evident from the newly formed scab that could be seen through the close-cropped hair on the back of his head.

Wow. I really did give him a good bash all those years ago, Cassie thought.

"Oh, that's good coming from you, bitch," he shouted.

"Don't you speak to my granddaughter like that," Bill said.

"Shut up," Jason snarled.

Bill turned bright red and sputtered, "Don't you talk to..."

"Leave this to me, Grandad," Future Cassie said, reappearing. Looking at Past Cassie, she said, "Watch closely. You'll be doing this in a few weeks."

"What the hell?" Jason shouted, his eyes flashing between the two Cassies.

Future Cassie squared up to him, even though he towered over her. "So, want to know how I hit you on the head from behind while you were doing your best to molest me? Watch closely, moron," she shouted as three additional identical versions of herself materialised around him.

"Ahhhh!" Jason shouted. "What the...?"

Georgia, Bill and Past Cassie gasped, though only the latter had an idea of what was about to happen. *Oh, just like what I did to Fulke.*

"It went something like this," Future Cassie one screamed as, simultaneously, all four of her attacked him.

"In a different timeline…" Future Cassie two said, punching his stomach.

"…in an alternative 2019…" Future Cassie three said, kicking his shin.

"…I met a version of you that I could have sworn might actually have been half-decent," said Future Cassie four, while slapping him hard across the face.

"Almost human, in fact," added Future Cassie one, jabbing him in his side.

"Please consider this a reminder that, from now on, I give out as good as I get," said Future Cassie four, grabbing his groin and squeezing hard. "Also, don't you ever talk to either my grandad or myself like that again."

"Cassie!" Georgia screamed as Jason slumped to his knees.

Future Cassies one to three disappeared leaving only the fourth, who said, "Now, that was definitely enjoyable." She squatted down until she was eye level with Jason. "And you fucking-well deserved it," she added.

"Language," Bill said, automatically.

"No, Grandad, 'fucking' was what he tried to do to me at the party. So I will say 'fucking' if I fucking-well feel like it. You may still think of me as an innocent seventeen-year-old. Well, I'm far from innocent. I reckon I'm well over twenty-two, no bloody idea by how much. I've already had a fucking baby and I know what he became."

"You had a… what?" Georgia asked, leaving her mouth wide open in shock.

"Yes. He became Laurence," Past Cassie whispered.

Georgia's face screwed up with incomprehension.

"Who the hell is Laurence?" Jason asked, still sitting on the floor, using his hands to protect his privates.

"You don't want to know."

"Why?"

"Because a later version of me, who I never grow up to be, chopped his head off nearly twenty years ago."

"You're mad – insane," Jason shouted, attempting to struggle to his feet.

"Sometimes, I wish I was – it would be simpler – but I'm not, and if you ever try anything on with me ever again, you'll get it back in spades."

"What – you'll split into four again? What on earth was that?"

"That was me – every time – time being the operative word."

"Huh?"

"Yeah, I can time travel. Oh, and I also met your dad," she spat. "And there's something funny about him 'cause in that other timeline – the one where you're almost decent – he still exists. So, why he disappeared from your life is something I suspect I need to get to the bottom of."

"Why?" Georgia asked.

"Because he's got something to do with all the nightmares about the Cow Tower and Lollards Pit when I was little. Maybe he caused those memories."

"But how?"

"No idea – but I'm going to find out, because those nightmares actually happened to me for real back in 1549, not long after this testosterone-filled moron tried to rape me," she said.

Jason, who had a new bruise forming on his temple, tried to stand up. His eyes, darting all around, were filled with something resembling terror.

Future Cassie kicked him back down. "I want you out of our house right now," she snarled.

"I'm trying to go. Please don't hit me again."

"Ah 'please'. That's more like it. Right, I'm going to help you on your way."

Future Cassie grabbed him by an ear and they both disappeared.

Georgia and Bill stared at Cassie who, after several seconds of stunned silence, whispered, "What on Earth have I become?"

First Signs of Madness

It was Monday evening, the day following Cassie's return from the past. She was resting on her bed, still amazed at how luxurious it felt.

She almost jumped off the bed in alarm as Future Cassie appeared without warning to say, "Well, I'm glad the first day's over."

"Damn it, can't you knock?"

"It's my bedroom, too," Future Cassie laughed. "Anyway, I remember this happening from your point of view, so I couldn't deviate from that memory."

"So, why exactly were you acting like that yesterday?"

"Because Jason needed dealing with. He needed taking down several pegs to make sure his mouth stayed shut. And it worked."

"What exactly happened today?"

"School was… shall we say… interesting. A few people had an idea there was something different about me, but they couldn't quite put their finger on it. The main thing was that Jason did as he was told, especially after yesterday."

"Huh? What did you do to him?"

"Took him home at first. I then told him if he ever mentioned what had happened at Erin's party or spoke a word about what I could do, then he'd find himself dumped on a mountaintop before he could even blink. I don't think he believed me at first."

Future Cassie broke out in a huge grin.

"Okay, so what did you do?"

"Gave him a demo. Remember that mountain stream in Wales?" Past Cassie nodded. "Let's say it's just a teensy bit cooler at this time of year and, when I teleported him, I, um, *accidentally* forgot to bring his clothes along with him."

"What?" Past Cassie squealed, her mouth hanging open.

"Yeah and, in that temperature, he was even more of a disappointment, if you get my drift. He certainly got the drift, all right – it was snowing."

"How long did you keep him there?"

"Only a few seconds – just enough to make him realise there was nothing he could do about it. He begged me to take him back."

"And you did?"

"Yes, of course – you don't turn totally evil in just a few weeks, you know," Future Cassie said, laughing.

"I was beginning to wonder."

"Yes, you are. Look, I know what you're thinking because when I was you, seeing me acting like this, I couldn't quite believe it, either. But, in order to keep the upper hand, you have to be the strong one so this can all work out properly."

"You mean I've got to do that in… in… when?"

"Three weeks, and you'll enjoy it. I did, even though it felt like I was acting out a role. And that's all it was really – acting."

"How will I remember it all?"

"Watch this," Future Cassie said, pulling her mobile phone out of her pocket and turning it on. She showed Past Cassie a video which had captured yesterday's events in the lounge. "It's already on your phone."

"Huh? On my phone? How did you get that videoed in the first place?"

"I popped in around mid-morning, borrowed your phone from where you'd left it in the bedroom, and set it up on the shelf while you were attempting to sleep off four years in the past. Grandad was too busy in the kitchen to see me."

"Why didn't you use your phone?"

"Duh! It's the same phone – yours is just earlier in time. I wanted to make sure you had the recording as soon as possible."

"How did you figure that out?"

"By listening to later me telling you what I'm telling you right now."

"Ah, yes, of course."

"Oh, and you need to go shopping tomorrow."

"What for? I haven't been shopping for years."

"Yes, and it will be… fun. But, remember that going back to any time earlier than last July means the portals are still there. And the nasties."

"Really? Oh yes, I suppose they would be. But why would I want to go back to when they were around?"

"You'll find out. Oh, and it's not only the portals and nasties."

"What else?"

"Well, Charlie for a start. Not that he'll make any more sense than he ever did."

"Great Grandad?"

"Yep."

"I thought I'd never see him again after he dropped me off at the cemetery."

"Me too. Hah – that's a silly thing to say when I am you. Anyway, maybe it's an earlier version of him. Not that he ever appeared in any particular order. It's not only him, either… No, I have to let you find all that out for yourself."

"More mysteries?"

"Yeah – several. Oh, and don't forget to get your hair and nails done."

"Suppose someone recognises me and wonders why I'm not at school?"

"Not in 1991 they won't."

"Ah…"

"Go early on a weekday. You'll find there'll be plenty of places where you can just walk in without an appointment."

"Are you going to tell me which one?"

"No, because I didn't. Ha ha. Have a look around and find one for yourself. Go and explore – you'll enjoy it. Especially the brush bit."

"You've got it all worked out?"

"No, *we've* got it all worked out. Anyway, it will help take your mind off other things. Remember, I'm just you but older by three weeks."

Past Cassie shook her head.

Future Cassie grinned, "Yes, I remember feeling what you're feeling right now. Don't worry – you'll get the hang of it – I did, and I remember this me saying all this to me when I was you."

"This must be like being shell-shocked."

"Yeah, I did say it was going to get confusing," Future Cassie said.

"No kidding."

"Look, this will help remind you of what we were supposed to be doing at school," Future Cassie said, pulling some papers out of another jacket pocket.

Past Cassie saw that some of it was recognisably her own writing. It was accompanied by some scrawl that looked like Georgia's.

"Wait," said Past Cassie, realising something. "That jacket. Didn't I lose it?"

"Yes, it's the same type as the one Kay paid for. It's your task for tomorrow while I'm at school being you."

"What do you mean?"

"Use some of Kay's old money from the boxes. Go back to Debenhams in 1991 and buy a couple more."

"Really? Isn't all this time travel going to cause more paradoxes?"

Future Cassie shrugged. "Possibly, but there are bigger things to think about and, believe me, I've been thinking about them. Anyway, it's not like you haven't been thinking of them yourself ever since all the memories returned."

"Um… What exactly do you mean?"

"You know what I mean."

"Pretend I don't. Spell it out."

"Can you remember what the device said the last time we saw it in 1549? What was the message in the disc? And those shadows we saw – when do we need to go back and do that? Also, what was the device doing way back in Ka'Tor's time in the first place? How did it get there? How did its 'fire in the sky' arrival wake us up? Why did Ka'Tor zapping us make us travel back to the present? I'm pretty certain he was trying to kill us, not restore our ability to time travel. And, why did seeing Jason's dad remind us of the events at the Cow Tower and Lollards Pit, which came later anyway?"

"Yeah, you're right. All that stuff has definitely been going around my head."

"Yes, I know it has – I remember thinking it when I was you. And I'm still thinking about it, except I've been thinking about it for three weeks longer. Well, we need to get to the bottom of all of it."

"Yeah. But…"

"But?"

"Yes, but why do *you* think we should?"

"Ha ha – yes. I was waiting for that question."

"Well?"

"Because I think we're being manipulated, and we may not be the only ones, as you'll find out tomorrow. The device said our futures were tied together with it – so that already implies there's more time travel involved. I know you are already beginning to suspect that there's something fishy going on yourself."

"Too right."

"Well, I've got to the stage where I'm beginning to resent it. This is why I don't think causing paradoxes is our biggest worry. Something bigger than us is already doing that with our life."

"Yeah," said Past Cassie, nodding. "Exactly."

"So, this act is also to gear us up to facing whatever that is. I don't know what the hell we're already involved in but I want more control over it. I'm fed up with being the one thrown into the past or future without knowing why I'm there. As Robert Kett once said to us, 'What good is your talent if you don't use it?' – I think we need to start making it run more in our favour."

Past Cassie pursed her lips and, after a pause, said, "I agree – the last four years was definitely time travel getting its revenge on us. Maybe it's now time for us to begin calling the shots instead."

"And Jason was just the first step in taking back control."

"You certainly did that."

"Yes, you certainly *will* do that in three weeks time."

"But where do we start?" asked Past Cassie.

"Maybe we should keep it in the family."

"What?"

"Not our family – Jason's family."

"You mean his dad?"

"Yeah, just what was it about him that caused the nightmares?"

"They're still with me."

"I know. I get them as well."

"Not the only thing, though, are they?" Past Cassie whispered.

Future Cassie shook her head. "Yeah... Despite what he did back in the Stone Age, and knowing what he becomes, he was still my... well... our son."

"I miss him."

"Yeah, I know you do. So do I. After three weeks, though it seems far longer, it hasn't got any easier."

"I've had nightmares about what they did to him," Past Cassie said. "I even had thoughts about going back."

"Yes, you did. I don't think that would be a good idea, though."

"No, any change to his timeline could wipe us out."

"Absolutely."

"This is so weird. I know you're me from the future but talking like this is sort of comforting."

"First signs of madness, don't they say?"

"What?"

"Talking to yourself," Future Cassie said with a grin.

"Hah, yes. But I don't think 'they', whoever they think they are, ever thought about it quite like this."

"No, probably not."

Diversion: Nightmare

Thirteen-year-old Cassie let herself into the house and hung her school blazer on the usual coat hook in the hallway. She had been carrying it over one arm as the May weather had turned warm enough for short sleeves.

"Hi Grandad," she said as he stepped out of the lounge.

But, unusually, he didn't say anything. Instead, he just stared at her, a weird, possibly confused, expression spreading across his face.

"Are you okay?" she asked, about to haul her bag of schoolwork upstairs.

"Yes, of course, er, Cassie, er, love," he said. There was something odd about the way he talked. It seemed forced, not at all his natural manner.

"Did you meet your friend in the city today?" she asked.

"Oh, yes," he said, a strange grin forming on his lips. "I also bumped into someone else I hadn't seen for a while."

"Who was that?"

There was a pause before he said, somewhat quickly, "Oh, no one you know. Not important."

She frowned. *It's not like him to be secretive. Maybe it's an old girlfriend or something like that.*

"Um, what's for tea?" she asked.

"Tea?" he questioned, in a manner that suggested that he hadn't given their evening meal a thought.

"Yes, you told me at breakfast this morning that you were going to buy something off the market."

"Ah yes," he said. "So I did. Slipped my mind."

"Are you sure you're okay?"

"Yes, but I've been… um, yes, that's it, doing a lot of thinking."

"What about?"

"Oh. This and that. Things."

"What sort of things?"

He shrugged. But it was far from natural, more like he was an actor who had been told to shrug at that particular moment. "Things like. I don't know. Many things. Oh, and, er, games."

"Huh, games? What games? You mean board games or card games?"

"No, not those at all."

"What do you mean, then?"

"Well," he said, "with you now turned thirteen, maybe something more, well… more adult, perhaps. Yes?"

"Adult? What like playing for money or betting?"

"No," he said, his gaze darting in all directions and never making direct eye contact with her.

"Good, we can't afford it, anyway."

"No," he repeated. "More like, well, acting."

"Acting? I don't understand."

"Play acting. Role playing. You know… pretending to be other people."

"What other people?"

"Like we're not ourselves – give ourselves other names so we can have… fun."

"Fun? What sort of fun?"

"Oh, and I've just thought of a name for you in the game."

What is he talking about? He's never been like this before. What's happened to him? Is he going senile?

"What name?" she asked. "Why do I need another name?"

"It's just a game. Yes, a game. And, in that game, I think you should be called… Kay."

Encounters

Stripes

"So," Cassie said, "you're still here, then?"

"So are you," said Robert Kett. "And looking slightly older than you should. But..."

Cassie had been surprised to see Kett waving at her as she'd got off the bus at Castle Meadow. He still had chains wrapped around his body and was hanging from the battlements of Norwich Castle, just as she had been seeing him for years before all the portals stuff had started. She wondered what he might remember of their previous encounter. Instead of immediately going back in time for a bit of shopping, she'd cut through the gardens and up onto the path around the castle itself. Once she had gone around the far side he had appeared beside her, thankfully not wearing the chains.

"But what?" she asked.

"But, my memory is hazy. It's as if I can remember more than one past. One where I wasn't hung here to die but, instead, I perished in battle. Somewhere else."

"Oh, where?"

He concentrated, frowning and then said, "Saint Benedict's gate, I think."

"Okay. And do you remember sending me back to 1549?"

Kett frowned. "Maybe. Something possibly. A small niggle in my memory that has no right to be there."

"You did," she said. "You tricked me into going back but it didn't work. I helped you to win the battle on the twenty-seventh of August 1549. I saved Lord Sheffield from being killed by Fulke. I saw your victory gathering in the market square. But it all went wrong. Horribly wrong."

Kett stared at her for a moment. "Yes, it did," he whispered, "but it's like a dream that is constantly slipping away after you awaken. It slides like an eel from your grip."

"Don't ever ask me to do that sort of stuff again," she said.

"Why?"

"Because you're right. I'm older. I was punished – I think."

"Punished?"

"I got sent back to the Stone Age."

"Stone Age? What is that?"

"Thousands of years in the past."

"But you can travel in time. Why didn't you come straight back?"

"It was taken away. I was trapped there."

"Your presence here tells me that you made it back."

"Yes. It took four years."

"Four years? Why?"

"I was… well, you could say I was sent back there to produce some… thing that completed a circle."

"Your words make no sense, girl."

"No, they don't. But, right now, I haven't got the energy to tell the story all over again."

"I will always be here when you want to tell it."

Cassie nodded. "Yes, I may want to."

"Good. You may have been trapped for four years. But I've been trapped here for nearly five hundred."

Cassie suddenly felt guilty. "Yeah, sorry. But I don't think I can do anything about it. I daren't."

Kett shrugged. "Maybe not. At least, you do stop by and talk every so often."

"It must be frustrating."

"There was once another lady who could also see and, once, she even talked to me. That was a long time ago."

"Really? Didn't you say I was the only one?"

"The lady was a lot older. She only spoke to me that one time."

"Older. Oh, you mean Kay?"

"No, not Kay. She is merely a figment of you. She doesn't count."

"So who was the other lady?"

Kett frowned. "She didn't tell me her name. Anyway, it's probably a hundred years since I saw her. I think she may have mentioned you."

"Really? Did she actually know me? Or just heard of me?"

"I had the impression she knew you quite well, from what I remember. But, then again, what I remember seems to change all too often, so she might only have been someone I dreamed up in my loneliness."

No kidding. He's back to being like he used to be when I first started talking to him. Not the aggressive version who got me to go back to 1549.

"More recently there was a boy as well."

"A boy who spoke to you?"

"No, I think he could see me but he never spoke. Didn't come close, actually. I tried waving to him but he just looked worried and hurried off."

"When was that?"

"This year, last year. I don't remember. Time is always mixed up."

"So, I'm the only one, then?"

"Yes. Apart from other ghosts, of course. But they're all mad."

"Oh, really? Ghosts of who?"

"No idea. Many don't speak and when they do, it's gibberish. One old lady ghost even told me it was me that was insane. Said I was as mad as a box of frogs when it was obviously her that was crazy."

"Right, um, interesting. Well, I'd better be off," Cassie said. "Things to do and all that."

"What are you going to do?"

"Right now? Go shopping. I haven't been shopping for over four years – no shops in the Stone Age. I need to buy some new clothes and I absolutely must get my hair straightened."

Five hours of subjective time later, Cassie was feeling rejuvenated. Her hair was straight, her nails were manicured and her shopping bags were bulging.

She had come back to the summer of 1991 and was strolling along Gentleman's Walk under an almost cloudless sky. She was also wearing a new denim jacket, one that was identical to the one she'd selected from Debenhams when she'd been with Kay. In her shopping bags was a second identical jacket, a pair of jeans and some heavy boots.

The City Hall clock had just passed noon and the aroma of fish and chips from the market made her hungry. Cassie contemplated finding somewhere secluded to pop back home to 2019, dump her shopping, and then return.

"Can't be faffed – those chips smell too good," she muttered. "Also, if I go home, I'll probably just lay on the bed and go back to sleep. Ah, the wonders of modern mattresses."

She could see several vacant benches in the memorial gardens that overlooked the marketplace. The bench where she'd sat eating chips with Kay on at least two occasions was currently unoccupied. She entered the market, passing stalls selling all manner of items as she headed towards the back where the chip stalls were located. She stopped, her eye having been attracted to something familiar and bright green. The stall was selling an assortment of cheap jewellery, bangles, watches, combs, wallets and keyrings. But, it was the hairbrush that stood out. It was similar to the one that Robert Kett had used on her hair. She stepped closer and looked at it properly.

No, it's not similar – it's pretty much identical. Ah, she thought, realising.

"How much?" she asked.

"One pound," came the reply.

She smiled and rummaged in her purse for an old round pound coin, handing it over after checking that its date was prior to 1991. She dropped the hairbrush into one of the shopping bags.

A few minutes later, she had purchased some cod and chips along with a can of drink, and was sitting on the familiar bench. She unwrapped the cod and chips, savouring the aroma. As she started popping chips into her mouth, the sound of music came from one of the stalls below her. A radio was playing a song that she'd never heard before. After it had finished, the DJ announced it as *Walking Down Madison.* The next song played was *It's My Party.* Shivers ran down Cassie's spine.

At least, it's the original this time, she thought, remembering hearing the remake of the song just before encountering Kay for a second time.

Hmm, that wasn't long after I'd discovered the portals map. Can I still see that?

After swallowing the piece of cod she'd been chewing, she closed her eyes and, seconds later, the familiar ghostly form of her surroundings appeared in her head. And yes, there were the portals, their coloured points of light glowing all over the shadows of the city.

Goodness, they're all still there. And I can see all of them, not just the underground ones.

She could sense those close by, such as the one buried in the crushed remains of the underground toilets near the front of the market and that underneath the Guildhall. This time, though, the latter was connected to one in a shop on Davey Place. Some of the portals were bright, others very dim. She could feel some sort of attraction from the brighter ones.

Was this how I could detect where they were before I could see the map properly?

Opening her eyes, which banished the map, she found she was still aware of the brightest portals.

Kay couldn't do this. Only I could. Oh, and the clones could, as well. Especially the real dumbo one that old Kay pulled around on a lead until Laurence killed her. I wonder why I can still see them, even though I no longer have any use for them.

Occasionally, two portals would flare up in intensity for a moment and she saw a flash momentarily connect them.

Someone travelling between them. Was that the real me or Kay with a dumbo? Probably a dumbo as I don't ever remember jumping between those two points.

Another two portals flared – this time one in Chapelfield Gardens that linked to another up on the castle mound.

There's an awful lot of portal traffic going on – far too much for how little they must have been used by Kay even if there were thousands of clones. Maybe I don't see them in real time – either that or something else is also using them. I don't think I want to find out. I suppose I could go and see Kay again. But would that be dangerous? Would I screw something up and cause another paradox or worse?

"No interaction," she whispered, sighing to herself and shaking her head. "Why bother – I never keep those promises. Talking of which…"

She reached into one of the shopping bags and pulled out the bright green brush, inspecting it. *Hmm, I wonder if I can do this so quickly that no one will actually notice I'm not here for a second.*

She glanced around. Nobody appeared to be looking directly at her but she couldn't be sure she'd checked everyone. She took a sip from the drink can and then placed it and the wrapper holding the remaining chips onto the bench seat to her left. As she did so, she felt as if someone had just sat down on the other side of the chips, though the seat remained visibly empty.

Ah. I wonder…

Deciding to provide a distinctive cue for her return, she slowly tapped the brush on her leg three times.

Here goes, she thought on the third tap as she teleported to the thirtieth of June, 2018, and back up to the pathway that ran around the castle. Upon arrival, she kept herself hidden from view.

And, not far away, she could see an extremely frizzy-haired version of herself talking to the ghost of Robert Kett. She found her hands shaking and was conscious that her heart rate had increased significantly.

This is so weird. Just like when I went back to 1549 and saw Kay on her motorbike not far from Saint Stephen's Gate.

"I like your hair," Kett said.

"What?" said her earlier self.

"It reminds me of a serving wench back when I was alive. Name wasn't Cassie, though," Kett replied. He paused and frowned before adding, "Something similar, possibly. Oh, and her hair was shorter."

Oh, my goodness. Was he talking about me when I went back there? But that timeline got deleted, didn't it? Maybe it did, but Kett was still partly aware of the alternate timeline earlier on. Maybe I'm getting too hung up over this.

"Shut up," said her past self.

"Could do with a brush, though," Kett said.

Cassie, having managed to calm herself, had to suppress a giggle at the expression on her earlier self's face as she glared at the ghost. As silently as she could, she walked closer and placed the hairbrush down onto the ground while neither the ghost nor earlier Cassie were looking in that direction. As soon as she let go of it, it became visible.

"I haven't got a damned brush. Wish I had," earlier Cassie said.

"There's one there," Kett said, pointing. "Someone must have dropped it."

Cassie watched herself pick it up, a deep frown on her earlier self's face.

"Bit convenient, isn't it?"

Yes, Cassie thought, *extremely convenient. Well, that's another mystery sorted. I wonder… have I got to go around filling in all these blanks for my earlier self? How many more are there? Can I even remember them all? What if I miss one?*

Cassie watched Kett try to catch the brush only to have it fall through his hands.

Time to get back to my chips.

She returned to 1991 about thirty seconds before she had originally left. Keeping herself invisible, she sat down on the bench beside her earlier self at the correct point in time, waiting for the three taps on her leg. Upon the third one, she teleported into place picking up the chip wrapper and continuing to eat.

Okay, so that's another trick I've taught myself, though I probably shouldn't have used the brush to tap my leg considering that I no longer possess it.

A quick glance about herself didn't show anyone nearby staring at her as if they might have seen anything unusual. But then she glanced down onto the path alongside the last row of market stalls. An old lady, who had been walking along there in the direction of the Saint Peter Mancroft church, suddenly stopped and looked up at her. The woman smiled briefly and then continued on her way.

Did she see anything? No, you idiot, I'm sure that if she had, she'd have been shouting or screaming. Probably just coincidence that she just happened to look up at me. But why did she smile?

Cassie frowned.

There was something almost familiar about her as well. Oh, stop it, you idiot. You're seeing coincidences where none exist.

Cassie finished the cod and chips, and swallowed the last of the drink. After wrapping the can in the chip paper, she stood and threw both into a nearby bin. Grabbing her shopping bags, she crossed the road behind the Guildhall and carried on into Lower Goat Lane. Halfway along, she paused to peer into the window of Andy's Records, a shop that had closed when she was young.

Wow, so much vinyl back then. She spotted some CDs, though they were still small in number. *No streaming or downloads. Was this before the Internet? I have absolutely no idea.*

Reaching Pottergate, she turned right and passed the esoteric collection of shops. She remembered how she and Kay had been chased down this street by nasties. They had risen out of the grass near Saint Gregory's Church.

When was that?

On a whim, she turned into Saint John's Alley, which led towards the Maddermarket Theatre. She tried to think of that earlier date but all she could remember was that it might have been in the late 1960s.

As she passed under an archway that was part of the Saint John the Baptist church, a voice said, "July, sixty-nine, it was, or is going to be. To see it again, just repeat after me."

"Charlie?" Cassie whispered, halting mid-stride recognising the voice she hadn't heard since the day Kay had crashed her motorbike in flames.

And there, in the shadows of the archway, two blue glowing eyes appeared. They grew a surrounding face, followed by the rest of the head and a body that was dressed in a bus driver's uniform.

"More room on top," he said. "Tickets please."

"Oh, my goodness. It really is you, isn't it, Charlie?" *Future Cassie did tell me he was still around. I didn't expect to bump into him quite so soon, though.*

"Cass, well met, but older yet. A zebra awaits, I'll wager a bet."

"Huh? What?"

"Maybe once, you'll meet, her granny light on her feet. Face far from sunken and not under a stallion."

"You're making as much sense as you always did. Damn Laurence for what he did to you."

"Laurence, for my penance, is worth nothing more than tuppence. But, as the length of his line continues to unwind, even more of a curse he is, you will find."

"Yeah, maybe," Cassie sighed, "but, as it turns out, he's actually my son as well as being my father. I went back thousands of years to become his mother."

"Father? Son? Holy crap? Is the family tree now a circular map?"

"Yeah, it is. No kidding. But what did you mean about a zebra?"

"Wait and see. Repeat after me."

"Repeat what?"

"July's fifteenth day, I'd say. Head for sixty-nine, you'll be fine. An hour of ten will be plenty, the minutes twice that at twenty."

Cassie paused to work it out. "Oh, right. Twenty past ten on July the fifteenth, 1969."

"Tickets please," Charlie grinned. "Repeat until believed."

"No problem," Cassie said, but she was already alone under the archway.

She peered in both directions and, once there was no one looking her way, teleported to the same spot on July the fifteenth, 1969, keeping herself hidden from view until she'd checked the alley was again clear. A few seconds later she materialised just as Kay was running along Pottergate heading in the direction of Lobster Lane.

Then she heard her own voice shouting, "You ran without waiting for me. They nearly got me."

She watched her earlier self hurtle past and could just make out Kay's reply of, "Yeah, but you're like buses."

Cassie's heart beat fast as she thought, *Here we go again. Charlie was right, but I still don't understand what else he was talking about. Have I got to follow them? What if they see me?*

"No, I don't remember seeing me when I was her," Cassie muttered. She recalled that they'd gone inside a piano shop on Exchange Street to find the next portal. *Then again, given what was chasing us, that's no wonder. But, if I don't hurry, I'll miss them.*

"Ah, no I won't," she muttered.

She teleported back ten minutes and, after making sure yet again that the alley was clear, turned visible. She then strolled along the remainder of Pottergate and past Thorns hardware shop on Lobster Lane that had been there since forever.

Coming out on Exchange Street, she thought, *I need somewhere to hide. But some place from where I can still get a good view.* She glanced across the road. *Oh yes, just inside the rear entrance to Jarrolds should work.*

She crossed the road towards the glass double doors. There were several people outside the entrance smoking cigarettes. She held her breath until she was past them and entered the lobby, which had stairs that led both to the basement and the ground floor a few feet higher up. The latter held the store's record department, something she'd never realised they'd ever had. She stopped, leaning on the wall to her left not far from the basement stairs.

This will do. Ugh, it still stinks of cigarette smoke in here, though.

She waited, watching the front of the piano shop. Several people entered or exited the glass doors, and one or two also paused in the lobby, checking their shopping or chatting with each other.

A couple of minutes later she saw Kay and her earlier self arrive. As they bumped into Charlie, she realised that, at this point, they had no idea who he really was.

Is that the same version of Charlie that I just spoke to or an earlier or later one? He's dressed slightly differently. I never did seem to meet him in any chronological order.

After Charlie disappeared, Cassie watched as Kay pushed open the door to the piano shop, her seventeen-year-old self following.

"There's one in there where they went, isn't there, Nanny?" came a young-sounding voice from the other side of the lobby.

Cassie turned and saw a girl standing with a much older woman just inside the glass doors. Both were staring across the road to the piano shop.

"Yes, there is, Debbie," said the woman.

The girl appeared to be around eleven or twelve, her golden hair falling in barely tamed curls bounced as she spoke. But what attracted Cassie's curiosity was that the girl was dressed in a black and white, horizontally striped T-shirt, accompanied by blue shorts and grubby but modern-looking trainers. She was holding something about three feet long, wrapped inside a large plastic bag.

Ah, that black and white T-shirt. Is she the zebra? And those trainers. They look well out of place for 1969. Is she another time traveller?

"Underground, I'd say as they've gone downstairs," the woman added. There was something odd about her voice. It was as if Cassie wasn't really hearing it with her ears. It seemed to be directionless, coming from everywhere at once.

Cassie looked at the woman properly and realised she was partially translucent.

Oh, she's a ghost, I think. A time traveller and a ghost? Just like me and Charlie. And they must be talking about the portal in the piano shop. So, maybe other people really are using them as well.

The woman's eyes locked upon Cassie's and, her tone urgent, said, "There's another one in here with us. Run, Debs. Before she brings monsters."

The girl did a double-take, her eyes wide as she noticed Cassie properly for the first time. Cassie's eyes followed her as she ran up the stairs into the main part of the store, which meant she missed seeing where the old woman went. The other people around hadn't seemed to have noticed anything wrong.

Definitely a ghost. But what did she mean about monsters?

Cassie looked back out onto the street. *Ah, I see.* Several nasties lumbered out from Lobster Lane and milled about, looking confused. As usual, only she could see them. Several people walked right through them as if they weren't there.

Those are the ones that came out of the green on Pottergate. Will they be able to see me or am I now off their radar?

The answer to that question came a few seconds later as one of the nasties, a two-headed affair in possession of three arms, saw Cassie peering at them through the glass. Ignoring the traffic, it rushed across the road towards her, a car passing right through it failed to halt its progress.

Cassie grabbed her bags and bolted down the stairs. As she turned a corner she teleported all the way home.

"Okay," she said, flopping down onto her bed, "so the nasties are obviously still dangerous to me. But who the hell was that girl and her ghostly nanny?"

Fitting Nine Weeks Into Six

Over the next few days, Past Cassie got used to her future self appearing at random times. Every school morning she would appear in their lounge or kitchen to take Past Cassie's place at school. Then, each evening, she would drop off some hand-scribbled notes to enable Past Cassie to catch up with her schoolwork.

"What happens in a week's time when I become you?" Past Cassie said to Future Cassie one evening near the end of the second week.

"Once that happens you go on to shift work. Yeah, I know – confusing, isn't it? Right, count these current weeks as numbers one to three – this is where you are coming up to speed with school and, at the end of it, you become me.

However, as this means that you've got to keep coming back three weeks into the past to be me, we still need another future version of us to deal with being at school in weeks four to six."

"Yet another future version?"

"Yes, let's call her Cassie Three. In weeks four to six we will share this room in shifts. I've been sleeping during the day while Cassie Three goes to school in real time during the day. While she sleeps at night, I come back here to go to school in weeks one to three. Simple."

"Simple? Sheesh – it's anything but."

"Nah, you'll get the hang of it once it's your turn – I guarantee it," she said with a huge grin. "Grandad gets a bit confused but, in the end, he just accepts occasionally having two of us around. At the end of week six then we should have fully caught up with school and we'll hopefully be down to just one of us."

"You say that like you're not sure."

"Yeah, I'm not. Remember, at the moment I'm three weeks ahead of you, so I've been living through weeks four and five while being at school for weeks one and two. I've therefore got one more week before I become Cassie Three and you become me."

"Yetch," Past Cassie said, "I'll believe it when I live through it."

"Yes, that's right. You will."

"What are you doing?" Cassie asked her grandad a couple of days later. He was on the computer and she could see he had several windows open.

He turned towards her and frowned. "Which one are you? It's hard to tell you apart now you both have straight hair."

Cassie laughed. "The slightly younger one who is still plucking up the courage to go to school."

"Ah, yes. Of course," he said. "It's a school day so the other one will already be there, won't she?"

Cassie nodded. *Yeah, I've still got to go through all of that and I'm not looking forward to it.*

"Yes," she said, "but you didn't actually answer my question."

"Oh, sorry. I'm just following up the family tree."

"Ah, right," she said, stepping closer to view what was on the screen. "Found anything new?"

"Yes, lots," he replied with a grin, pointing to some names he'd written down. The sheet of paper on the table next to the computer was already twice as complex as the family tree he'd drawn from memory the previous year. "Henry and Millicent."

"Who?"

"Grandpa and Grandma Page. My mother Gwen's parents. I knew I was right when I remembered she was called Millie. I've found their marriage certificate, which shows that Millicent's maiden name was Sneesby."

"Hah? Really? I bet she always had to carry a hanky with her."

"What?"

"Sneesby – atishoo."

He shook his head and chuckled, "Very droll."

"Anything else? It looks like you've got quite a few new names on there. Who is this one – Eliza?"

"That one's a bit sad really."

"How's that?" Cassie asked, a frown crinkling her brow.

"Eliza. She was Millicent's younger sister, but she died not long after birth."

"Oh no. What of?"

He shrugged, saying, "I couldn't find that out. Infant mortality was still quite high in the late eighteen-hundreds."

Cassie nodded. *Probably not as high as it was for the people of the tribe.*

He continued, "And then there was a brother, Thomas, born in 1895 but died in 1917 when he was twenty-two. Probably killed in the First World War, though I'm not completely certain of that as I haven't found his name on any official records for the casualties."

"You're going to keep digging for more?"

"I am. This is all very fascinating. I've also confirmed the names of Gwen's brothers and sisters," he said, his finger pointing to a line of names below the line depicting Henry, Millicent and her siblings. "Like her parents, they didn't live around this part of the country so, for me, meeting any of them was pretty rare. However, I do vaguely remember being introduced to Uncles Robert and

Charles a couple of times."

"Another Charlie?"

"Yes, but he was about thirteen years older than my dad."

"There was also an aunt whose name I forgot ages ago. Again, she was quite a few years older than my mum and now I've found her."

Cassie read the name against which his finger rested. "Clara. Nice. And what's that one?" she added, pointing to another entry.

"I remember Mum talking about another brother, which I presume must have been Rupert, as that's what's come up in my research here. Bit of a black sheep, that one."

"Oh, why?"

"From how I remember Mum describing him, he was a bit of a tearaway. Caused several problems and many bust-ups with the rest of the family. Apparently, he even had an illegitimate child – back when it was definitely not the done thing. Refused to marry the girl and then disappeared off to Eastern Europe somewhere, which is another reason the rest of the family pretty much disowned him. No idea who the mother was or what the child's name was."

"Can't you find out on this website?"

"No," he said. "They are only allowed to release the census information after a hundred years have passed, and all of that happened long after 1919. So, maybe we'll never get to know anything more about him and what he got up to."

"I could…" Cassie started.

"No," he said. "You've already broken your promise more than once."

Yeah, tell me about it. And, just recently, I've broken it even more than I dare admit.

"What else have you found?" Cassie said.

"I've gone back another two generations from Millicent," he told her. "Her parents were George Sneesby and Hannah Luckin."

"Hannah Luckin? Oh wow," Cassie said. "Two coincidences."

"Two? I realised she shared your middle name. What's the other?"

"Luckin – that's Jason's surname."

"Oh, yes, I thought I'd heard of that somewhere before."

"Be funny if they were related."

"Possibly. There are a lot less Luckins than Foxes, as far as I can see."

"So, what have you found out about her?"

"Not a lot, her parents were Richard Luckin and Anne Wolfe–"

"Wolf? Another coincidence?"

"Spelt with an 'e' on the end, apparently."

"Oh, right."

"Hannah had a brother called Samuel. The trail goes cold any further back than the parents. I can't find any trace of the grandparents of either of them, though I did find one thing. So, I've started tracing back through Millicent's father George's tree."

"What about Arthur's side?"

"Yes, they're next on the list to track down."

"Fantastic. Be interesting to see how far you can get. So, what was that thing you said you found?"

"Just a photo – taken back around 1870 as far as I can tell. I downloaded it, though it is rather small and fuzzy," he said. "But you can definitely see the family resemblance. Now which folder did I put it in?"

"Oh, who's it of? Maybe we should buy a printer so we can print it out."

"Probably not worth it, given how bad it is," he said. After several clicks of the mouse, he found the picture and opened it up.

Cassie's intake of breath was sharp.

"Wow," she said. "I see what you mean. The woman looks a bit like Mum but a lot older. Too bad it's not clearer. Who are they?"

The photo, which had obviously faded and been damaged in places before it had been digitally scanned, depicted a couple standing side by side in front of two children. The woman was a lot shorter than the man and both looked to be in their late forties or early fifties. The eldest of the children, the girl, came almost up to the woman's shoulders. The boy looked two or three years younger.

"Richard and Anne Luckin," he said, pointing to the names on the family tree.

"Oh, right," Cassie said, coming closer to the computer screen. "Okay, there's another coincidence as well."

"What's that?"

"Anne as well as Hannah."

"Oh yes, of course. It was my Emily who suggested using Anne for your Mum's middle name. She didn't like any of the girls' names from her side of the family. I seem to remember they were names like Maude, Martha or Matilda. So, she'd asked about my side. I didn't know about Anne Luckin back then but I did remember that there had been mention of an Anne on my dad's side. Look – I found her." He pointed to another Anne on the tree. "Anne Langley married Arthur's dad in 1895."

"I can see that Mum and me, and also Gwen, got our looks from the other Anne," Cassie said.

"Yes, that's what I meant when I talked about family resemblance. I'm not sure any of us resemble him, though."

Cassie frowned. There was something slightly familiar about the man's face. But, as much of it was hidden behind a thick but neatly fashioned Victorian beard, she couldn't identify where she might have encountered such features before. "Those children must be Hannah and Samuel, then."

"Yes, three generations back from me. Hannah was my great-grandmother."

Cassie stared at the photo. The eyes of all four of them gazed back at her from the past.

I wonder what it would be like to go back and meet them. No, you idiot. I've messed up too many times trying things like that.

As Future Cassie had predicted, by the time Past Cassie had lived through the final week, she was ready to become Future Cassie. She took a secret delight in going back to the day she'd returned from 140,000 years ago and scaring her earlier self while acting out the scenes with Jason.

Yeah, he really was a disappointment, she thought after teleporting him to and from that Welsh mountain. *Pretty pathetic compared to the men in the tribe.*

But, despite what she knew she would be telling her past self, she wasn't as certain as she made out that all this time travelling would be without consequence.

Also, having to be around yet another future version of herself was making her apprehensive about what she was getting herself into. That version of herself, who she labelled 'Cassie Three', had started off normally enough, but had become very intense as they entered week five. By the time they'd reached week six, Cassie Three exuded an almost grim determination to unravel all the secrets and mysteries that she had already been thinking about. She wondered how much of an act Cassie Three was putting on for her benefit. If it was an act, it was unnerving her. Unlike herself talking to Past Cassie, where the information had flowed freely, it was as if Cassie Three was deliberately withholding what she had been up to. With the school term having ended for Cassie Three, she tried to spend as little time as possible around her future self. Thankfully, that version also wasn't spending much time at the house.

As she lay on the bed in the daylight near the end of week five, her eyes glanced at the scribblings all over the large sheet of paper stuck to the wall. It was all of those unresolved things that had been nagging at her since returning from the deep past. But some of the items seemed to be in some sort of code, with abbreviations being used that made no sense to her at all.

She had tried asking her future self about what they were but had been told, "Not yet – it will all become clear in time. No clues. You need to think this through for yourself. I will tell you just one thing, though."

"What's that?"

"Go *back* and get some advice."

"Back? Back when?"

Cassie Three's face softened and she whispered, "Who was always best at helping us when we were young?"

"Oh, you mean…?"

Cassie Three nodded.

"Mum," Cassie whispered.

Diversion: Prototype

Cassie was angry, but she wasn't sure exactly why. Had she been this angry a few seconds ago when she'd entered Castle Mall? Weirdly, she couldn't remember.

People were getting in her way as she pushed through the crowds. Yes, that was definitely annoying. But that wasn't the real reason. For a start, she had no idea why she was in such a hurry. She slowed her pace and tried to figure out what was wrong. She was hot, which wasn't surprising. This last day of June 2018 had begun warm and got even hotter. It was making her head swim.

She realised the confusion swimming around her head was the primary cause of her anger. It was like she had two sets of clashing memories vying for dominance within her skull, and she couldn't tell which of them was real. All she knew was that the two couldn't be reconciled – they clashed in too many areas. She knew she'd only just arrived in Castle Mall, yet it was combined with the urge to leave as soon as possible.

Hold on, didn't I come here to meet up for lunch with Georgia and Mark?

She stopped walking. There was something else as well – like she was in imminent danger from… from what? She glanced up at the glass canopy high above her. For a second she had the impression the glass was shattering, with rocks and stones dropping through it. But, after she'd blinked, it was still intact.

What the absolute hell is going on?

She reached into her jeans pocket for her phone and found it empty.

Huh? Since when did I own a phone? I've never had a phone…

…So why do I remember having one? Didn't I get a message from Georgia earlier on?

The idea that she should be going back up the escalator persisted but the urge to resist held her back. She kept glancing up at the glass roof – it remained reassuringly solid but, as soon as she looked away, she couldn't escape the fear that it could fall at any moment.

Close by was a small stand in the middle of the passageway. Trying to keep her mind off the irrational fears that threatened to overpower her, she looked over the wares on sale. They were selling mobile phone cases and offering simple phone repairs.

I don't have a phone – why am I looking at cases for them?

One particular case caught her eye. The guy manning the stand was in conversation with a customer so Cassie stepped closer, her hand reaching out to the unusually patterned case. This close, it appeared to be the wrong shape being too long, narrow and thick all at the same time – it looked more like it should hold a pair of glasses instead of a mobile phone. No phone she had ever seen, not even one of the older, non-smart types, would have fitted it. But it was the pattern on the case that drew her nearer. It was a dark, metallic silver, struck through with random patterns of bright green. The word 'malachite' popped into her head – was that a colour? But, more surprisingly, the pattern itself seemed to be subtly shifting upon the surface of the case. She shook her head but the effect persisted.

Maybe it's the heat or something. Or maybe I'm just going completely mad.

As her hand touched the case, it sprung open and the colours became more intense. A bright flash of light blinded her for a second. As suddenly as it had opened, the case then clamped itself shut.

"Can I help you?" came a voice beside her.

"Uh, what?" Cassie said, blinking and turning her head to stare into the eyes of the man running the stand. "Oh, no thank you. I was just looking at…" But, when her gaze returned to the stand, the weird phone case was no longer there. "Ah," she said. "Sorry, I think I might be getting heatstroke."

Before the man could respond, Cassie ran for the escalator.

What's happening to me?

She took the escalator steps two at a time, the sweat dripping down her forehead running into her eyes.

I was only looking at… what the hell was it? I can't even remember what it was now. What on Earth is going on?

The anger flared up again. But, this time, it felt more solid, more concrete. At least the impression of two sets of memories inside her head had gone, but she felt even more confused.

Where am I going? I don't want to go home. No, definitely not. Because HE *will be there. He'll be expecting me to be Kay again. Fuck him. I'm sick of his games. They stopped being games years ago. Why did he have to change? Why couldn't he still be like he was when I was twelve? Damn it, I'm seventeen – I'm old enough to look after myself.*

That idea grew to dominate her thoughts.

Yes. Maybe I should refuse to go home ever again.

By the time she'd reached the top of the escalator, she was almost in tears but she fought them back and walked towards the Castle Meadow exit and the blazing sunshine beyond. Behind her, she heard a noise like glass shattering and something large collapsing but, when she turned around to look, the glass roof was still intact. Suddenly, she felt dizzy as if someone had picked her up and spun her around. For a moment, she was under the impression she was going to fall over as if suffering an attack of vertigo. Shaking her head, she ran for the exit, suddenly aware that something was very wrong.

The sun had stopped shining.

Hurrying out the exit she halted in surprise. It was raining.

But it was boiling hot a few minutes ago, wasn't it? Hadn't they forecast more heat? What the hell's going on?

She looked up at the sky – it was grey with clouds. Spooked, she shivered, aware that the rain was beginning to soak her arms and the summer top she was wearing. She dashed across Castle Meadow dodging buses and bicycles, and ran down into Arcade Street which, being partly covered, at least afforded a temporary respite from the weather.

She stopped and looked back.

Oh God, I feel so strange, like I've jumped into a different world.

Scared, her eyes scanned her surroundings.

Am I being watched or followed? Not one of those bloody ghosts again, is it?

She looked up at the castle. For a change, Robert Kett wasn't dangling there in his chains. The man in a bus driver's uniform, who would often appear at random moments and was always talking rubbish, wasn't in sight, either. But, he might still be around as he would sometimes remain unseen and she'd only hear his voice.

Regaining her breath, she continued down the incline. As she reached the entrance to the Royal Arcade, she glanced behind herself and her breath caught in her throat. Gliding towards her down the incline from Castle Meadow came three… she wasn't sure what they were.

From their open mouths hung globs of drool that clung to the rags they were nearly wearing. Their legs didn't move, but neither did they need to, given that all three floated more than six inches off the ground. It was obvious that their dead-looking eyes were focused on her and that no one else appeared to be able to see them. Also, she could see that the rain, which was making her hair sodden, was falling through the things unimpeded.

She considered running into the Royal Arcade but it was quite crowded with people avoiding the weather, so she turned right towards Castle Street instead, hoping the things would continue into the arcade. But the *whatever-they-weres* didn't, they stopped and, like synchronised dancers, turned ninety degrees to their right to follow her. She broke into a sprint, trying to put as much distance between herself and the creatures.

What the bloody hell are they? Shit, I need somewhere to hide. Some place that's got lots of nooks and crannies to hide in. Somewhere where they won't find me.

She ignored Davey Place – the shops there were mostly small. She ran past Old Post Office Court, fearing she might get trapped in its tiny alleyway. Veering left onto London Street she managed to lose her pursuers for a few seconds. Glancing up she noticed that the time on the City Hall clock gave the time as twenty past ten.

Huh? But it was half eleven when I was in the Mall.

She cut right into Little London Street where, several yards along, an old lady was holding open one of the glass doors of Jarrolds Department Store.

Cassie ran past the woman, who was smiling at her, and into the store.

Upstairs or down? she asked herself.

"Downstairs," said the old lady before walking off and leaving the door to swing shut.

Cassie frowned but after a split second's indecision, took the stairs to the basement instead of heading upwards. There was something more attractive in that direction.

She slowed, entering the book department, swinging left making for the furthest corner and some taller bookshelves. Resting up against the fiction section, she found herself puffing.

Hell, I'm not fit enough for all this running.

There was something odd close by. A presence that wasn't part of the normal shop display. It hung in the air between the high shelves against the wall and a lower free-standing bookshelf. It was only three feet away but was almost undetectable visually. She stepped closer and could smell something electrical – like the motor of the engine from a train set. Her hair felt as if it was starting to stand on end. She was about to back away when she spotted the three gliding ghouls entering the shop floor from the door to the staircase. Initially, they spread out only to start converging on her, floating through the bookshelves as if they did not exist.

Shit. If I don't move right now, they're going to get me. Where…?

But, there was no path of escape that didn't pass at least one of them and, unlike the creatures, she didn't have the luxury of being able to walk through solid bookshelves.

Is this it? Are these things going to kill me?

As the ghouls converged upon her, sparkling in the air to her left caught her eye.

Bike

Bedbound

"Sorry," Cassie said to the figure lying in bed, trying not to be horrified by how pale and almost translucent her skin appeared.

"Sit down, Cass," Rebecca said, her fingers tapping the bed. Her voice was thin, reed-like. Cassie was conscious of her mother's weight loss and how she held herself stiffly, as if unable to relax. Her head was adorned with small tufts of new-grown hair, evidence that the chemotherapy had been halted as it was no longer producing tangible results.

Cassie perched on the side of the bed. "I needed to speak to someone. I couldn't think of anyone else who might understand. I could go back in time – back when you were stronger, if you like."

"No," said her mum. "You didn't, so you won't. This is the first time you've been here since you turned up with Kay back in February."

"I-I'm really sorry. I didn't realise just how weak you were."

"No, it's fine. Really. You look a bit older than you did before. Same jacket?"

"Similar. Yes, I'm about four years older."

"Four? So, you've come back from, what… 2022?"

"No, from 2019. Long story. Too complicated. I better not wear you out."

Feeling guilty, Cassie looked out of the window. The late November sun, low in the sky, struggled to punch through thin clouds. The few trees in sight were bare of leaves. *There wasn't anyone else, was there? But it's torture seeing her like this again. I really should have gone back to the summer, before she was bedbound.*

"It's okay, I can't sleep. I'm spending most of the time in bed now but sleeping day and night is impossible. In fact, sleeping at all is just as exhausting as being awake… I can still sense them, you know?"

"What?"

"The portals."

"Oh."

"I don't think it's quite like that map you have in your head. Is it still there?"

Cassie nodded. "Yes, but only when I want to see it."

"Sometimes, when I'm feeling bad, it's like they're getting closer. Maybe, someday, one will come close enough for me to step right through. I'd like that, you know. To step away from here, from how reduced in scope my life has become."

"Oh, Mum. No. It kills me to think of you... hurting. Is there anything I can do?"

"Probably not. I'm just glad you came back – it's nice to see grown-up you once again. It makes me proud to know you grew up safe and sound."

Safe and sound? Oh, Mum, you couldn't have been more wrong.

"Mum," Cassie said, tears running down her cheeks. She wanted to hug her mother but was so afraid she would physically hurt her should she attempt it. She shut her eyes and whispered, "I, er, I found out exactly who Laurence was."

"Really? Oh, do tell me all about it, love," Rebecca whispered. "We've got a couple of hours. If that's not long enough then there are other days, especially if you always come when your grandad is out at his bowling club or picking younger you up from school."

"Shouldn't he be here looking after you instead of bowling?"

"Not much for him to do now. I told him to stop hanging around, moping over me. He kept popping in, worrying himself and me more. It was more tiring for me than when he wasn't here."

"But what if you suddenly needed help or something?"

"Mobile phone," she said, glancing at the bedside cabinet. The phone was a simple model with proper buttons – unlike the smartphone in Cassie's pocket.

"Dad's got a similar one," Rebecca continued. "Anyway, I know I last until January. The twenty-fourth didn't you say? I've tried to explain to him how it will turn out. Not sure he gets it but, anyway, the afternoons when he's not here are now all ours, if you want."

"I do, Mum, of course I do. Are you sure you're strong enough?"

"No, not at all. Sometimes I don't think I have enough strength to last until Christmas, let alone January. But... I remember what you told me."

I wonder, Cassie thought. Remembering how she had helped Kay after the fire in the Assembly House, she spread her hands above her mother's prone form. *Can I remember how to do it? Is it even possible without the device?*

She concentrated, willing her fingers to produce something that would ease the pain that wracked her mother's body. After a few moments, she had the impression that she was absorbing energy from somewhere and directing it through her hands. Whatever it was began to flow from her fingers, which started to glow with a hint of green, to her mum.

"Ah, I don't know what you're doing, but it feels wonderful," Rebecca sighed.

"I was afraid it wouldn't work," Cassie said. "I wish I could do more but, if this helps, I will keep on doing it."

"Thank you. How did you learn that?"

"Oh, it came from the device."

Rebecca's eyes flashed open, her brow creased.

"No," she cried, "please don't do that – I don't want what happened to me to afflict you as well. Promise me you won't do that. Leave it down there."

Shit. I'd forgotten the device was downstairs behind that drawer, Cassie thought. She concentrated and felt its presence several feet below them in the lounge. But that version of it felt locked off from her and she had no intention of trying to wake it up. *No, it mustn't realise a later me is up here.*

Her mother was waiting for an answer.

"No, it turns out that it doesn't affect me like it did you."

"Are you certain?"

Cassie nodded. "Yes, but anyway, what I meant was that the device taught me how to do it after you'd got Grandad to give it to me."

"He gave it to you?"

"Yes. Apparently, you told him to give it to me at your funeral on the last day of January."

"Do I? Oh, that was quick."

"What?"

"Didn't you say I die on the twenty-fourth?"

"Oh... yes."

"And my funeral was only a week later?"

Cassie nodded. "Is something wrong?"

"I remember when Mum passed away back in 1995 – it was nearer three weeks before we'd arranged her funeral. There was just so much to organise."

"Mum, do we really have to talk about... you know... funerals?"

"Maybe we do. Did I die here? At home?"

"No," Cassie whispered, "I think you were in hospital for a few days after Christmas and then a nursing home for the last few weeks. I can't remember too much about it now... or maybe I don't want to. I spent most of the Christmas school break at Georgia's, but I did get to visit you a few times. All I remember is seeing how much thinner you were each time and wondering why you didn't say anything. You'd just stare into space and occasionally mumble the odd word. It was like..." Cassie paused, hating to dredge up the memories. "It was like you weren't you any more. It was like you were..."

"Like I was already dead?"

Cassie sniffed and nodded.

Rebecca looked away towards the window. "Maybe it was – or will be – better that way."

"Oh, Mum. I'm so sorry."

"No, it's okay, love. I think I'm ready to go. Do, er, did I... suffer?"

"I-I don't think so. I hope not but I wasn't there all the time. I just remember that they called us in – Grandad and me – a day or two before and told us y-you hadn't got... long."

Rebecca's hand reached out and held Cassie's own. Cassie clasped it, with both of hers, conscious of how her mum's hand shook, how cold it was and how thin and bony it felt.

"Oh, Mum," Cassie whispered again. "I really wish I could save you."

"Wouldn't that create a paradox?"

Cassie managed to emit a tense chuckle through the tears. "Yeah, but I've created more than a few of those already."

"Really?" Rebecca said as Cassie nodded. "Well, maybe you should tell me exactly what happened right after you and Kay left me back in February. I think you've given me enough strength to take it all in."

Cassie did her best to relate everything between encountering Laurence at the folly, Kay's burning and her death. Finally, she told how she'd persuaded the device to create the portals in the first place, even though it was really the 'last' place given that it was almost the final action it took before disappearing in a huff until the red button had dragged it back from the distant past.

"So, I was wrong, then," Rebecca said.

"About what?"

"I was convinced Laurence had created the portals."

"So was I, at first."

"I can see what you mean about paradoxes. It's a wonder you didn't mess up our entire history."

"Oh, don't worry – I did exactly that with what came later."

Rebecca looked shocked. "Oh no, tell me more."

"Are you sure you're strong enough?"

"No, actually I'm not. I am tired after listening to you," she said, "so, as much as I want to know what's next, maybe it's enough excitement for today."

"I'll come back soon," Cassie said. She held her mother's hands and watched as her eyelids drooped.

"Yes, I'd like that," Rebecca said. "Younger you and your grandad will be here too much at the weekend, so… maybe…"

"Are you still awake?" Cassie whispered a few minutes later.

There was no response other than her mother's shallow breathing.

Trying to heal her mother's ailments via whatever it was that had flowed from her hands had been more exhausting than she'd initially dared to admit to herself. So, she waited more than a week in her own time.

But, that wasn't all. Her visit to her Mum had raised even more questions and she needed to write them down and try to make sense of them. One evening, after school and helping to cook dinner, she pulled out a large sheet of paper. It was one left over from when she'd had to take art at school back before sixth form. After attaching it to the wall, she jotted names and notes over it and drew lines between various points, but did it in a way that some of the notes only made sense to her, using abbreviations and codes that would hide the true nature of what it all meant. She noted down things such as the mystery of what the device had been doing in the Stone Age in the first place and what it had implied just before it had sent her back to the deep past; how it had cured her of the concussion but not of the flames that, even now, still haunted her mind.

Her earlier self, who still shared the room, was intrigued but Cassie gave away as little as possible, which she knew was annoying having lived through those experiences around three weeks earlier herself.

I will need to figure this out for myself. No short cuts. No telling earlier me – not that I did. No paradoxes – well, none that I can't help, anyway.

After her visit to her mum, she had felt different, as if something had changed within herself. But, she didn't know if that change was for the better or worse. It was just... different.

She made notes about the short time between her mother's death and the funeral. But after she looked it up on the Internet, she found the average was stated to be between one and two weeks. *Maybe there was nothing unusual. So, why did Mum think so? Did she reveal to someone else that she was going to die on that date? Should I have not told her about it?*

There were still too many questions and precious few answers. Some lines on her wall chart were scribbled through and then sometimes reinstated. But, throughout the process, there was a niggling sensation that she was missing something important – maybe several things – but she couldn't figure out what.

Maybe I'm too close to it. I wonder if showing it to Georgia or Mark might help.

Once she thought she could face up to it, she decided to return to that bleak November of 2010. In the spring of 2019, it was a Monday evening and she'd gone up to her room, glad to see that her earlier self had already departed for her stint at school three weeks earlier. The covers on the bed had been pulled up and tidied but there was no disguising that it had been used only recently.

I'll be glad when I've got the room back to myself, she thought, and then shook her head, adding. *Stupid thing to think. It's only me sleeping here – just two slightly different versions, three weeks apart. Mental.*

She closed her eyes and started the journey back to 2010. But, her initial plans were thwarted as, when Cassie returned to the Monday following her previous visit, she found her grandad present in the house. Much of this was due to the cold and snowy weather. She had to wait until Wednesday, the eighth of December before her mother was alone in the house.

Upon her arrival, she found Rebecca in a fitful sleep, her skin pale and almost grey. Cassie positioned her hands over her once more and concentrated until the healing process started up again. After a while, her mother's body relaxed substantially and her eyes opened.

Seeing Cassie, Rebecca smiled.

"I was having a nightmare that turned into a pleasant dream," she told Cassie. "You were doing that thing with your hands again, weren't you?"

Cassie nodded.

"Well, I think you probably chased the horrors away."

"I'd chase all your horrors away if I could," Cassie whispered, trying not to cry, though she felt like bawling her heart out.

"I know you would. But you can't save me. We both know that."

Cassie nodded, not wanting to admit it out loud. "I tried to come back sooner but Grandad was always around."

"Yes, it's been very wintry out there. He's had several matches cancelled."

"Huh? But it's all indoors, isn't it?"

Rebecca nodded. "Couldn't get a full team together due to the snow. Now, weren't you going to tell me all about how you messed things up?"

"Yes, this one is likely to be even longer."

"You'd better make a start, then," Rebecca said, holding Cassie's hand.

Cassie managed to condense her encounters with Robert Kett and his rebellion down to a brief summary. Afterwards, she related how the device had punished her by sending her back to a tribe of stone-age people living in a cave.

"A hundred and forty *thousand* years?"

"Yes. With my mind completely wiped."

"How did you get your memories back?"

"The fire in the sky," Cassie whispered.

"The what?"

"From how they described it, I thought it must have been a meteorite – a shooting star or something like that. My memories started coming back when it passed over the cave. But, by then, something like a year had already passed."

"And then you remembered everything?"

"No, to this day I still don't remember what happened between the device throwing me back in time and me waking up a year later. And, um, how I, er, got... pregnant."

"You got *what?*"

Cassie nodded. "Full term. The contractions started before I woke up."

Rebecca struggled to raise an arm to reach out to Cassie.

"Oh, Cass, my poor darling. What happened to the baby? Did it..."

"It... he was fine. Took a while – bloody painful. No anaesthetic back then, of course. But he was... fine."

"There's more, isn't there?"

Cassie nodded slowly. She felt herself choking up and unable to speak for a moment. She swallowed several times.

"Probably a coincidence," Rebecca said, "but, back when I first met him at university, Laurence would sometimes joke that he was born in a cave."

"It was no joke," Cassie whispered.

"You really think he was?"

Cassie shut her eyes, collecting herself ready to drop the bombshell.

"I know he was – I was there."

"What? When Laurence was actually born?"

Cassie nodded.

"Really? Another coinci... Oh no... you can't mean...?"

Cassie nodded and she couldn't prevent the tears cascading down her cheeks. Her mother reached up and Cassie, sobbing, fell into her arms.

Girl Scar

There was silence when Cassie finished relating what had transpired after the tribe had attempted to scar Ka'Tor's cheeks, how he'd drawn on some power to kill those responsible, and how he'd escaped to where that supposed meteorite had landed to recover the device.

"So, Ka'Tor became Laurence?" Rebecca finally whispered.

"Yes."

"That means your father is also your son. That is so screwed up."

Cassie nodded.

"Oh, my God. Does that make you both my daughter and, almost, mother-in-law? Not that Laurence and I were ever married, of course."

"Except that he was taking over the minds and bodies of other people – hundreds, possibly thousands of them. All close relatives. So, genetically, I must only be your daughter as Laurence's body started off as belonging to the original person Laurence was, not Ka'Tor himself."

"But the original Laurence was still a direct descendent of Ka'Tor."

"I suppose we all are. Except I went back to start the whole thing off in the first place as well."

Rebecca nodded.

"At least you never gave me his surname," Cassie added. "for which I am extremely glad. Actually, I don't even know his full name – you never told me."

"No. Because, at the time, I didn't want you to know."

"So, what was it?"

"Baxter," Rebecca answered with a sigh.

Cassie frowned. "It's almost mundane. I was expecting something more sort of… well… epic."

"Yes," Rebecca said. "At least, that's what he told me and I did see that name on his office door when I was in Bucharest. Of course, he might still have been lying. He lied about so much."

"Cassie Baxter," Cassie said. "Cassie Hannah Baxter. No, that doesn't sound right at all. I'll always be a Fox."

"Yes, I'm glad I managed to stop his name appearing on your birth certificate. I used the device to do that, to influence the people concerned."

"And you paid for it," Cassie whispered.

"Yes, but it had to be done. And it was a price I was willing to pay for your sake. Oh, this is all too much to take in," she whispered, closing her eyes.

"Oh, I'm so sorry, Mum. I didn't mean to tire you out," Cassie said, resting her hand on her mother's arm, trying not to wince at feeling how emaciated it was under her fingers.

"No, no. Don't apologise, Cass," Rebecca said, her eyes closed. "It must have been so traumatic – all of it – not just the fact that you are Ka'Tor's mother – but realising exactly who he was just before you came back. It's like it's all come full circle. But, in a way, I'm glad I finally got to know all about it. Not that I will ever have time to make use of the knowledge."

"Oh, Mum," Cassie whispered as she failed to prevent her shoulders heaving and openly cried.

Rebecca tried to pull Cassie closer but, this time, she lacked the strength. So Cassie lay down beside her mother and gently placed her arms around her.

With the sun beginning to set, Cassie became aware that her mother's breathing suggested she had fallen asleep. She stood up as slowly as she could and crept to the window, staring down at the back garden. Apart from the snow, it didn't look much different to the view in 2019, the tidiness she remembered from her younger years had already degenerated. What had once been flowerbeds filled with lupins and golden rod were bare even of weeds. In the few places where the snow hadn't settled, the lawn that showed through was patchy and unkempt. Her mum had stopped gardening several months before she'd died and Grandad, even though he kept up the bowling, had problems kneeling for long. Once she was a teenager, Cassie had occasionally dragged out the electric mower but had done very little else. With her grandad's deteriorating condition, her time had been taken up with school, whilst also looking after him and the house pretty much on her own. There was no time to even consider the garden. Several times, Georgia had co-opted her parents into helping Cassie spruce the garden up when she knew things were getting on top of her friend.

Cassie was about to depart to return to her own time when she heard her mother's voice.

"Seeing you standing there with that jacket reminds me of something else I've never told anyone," Rebecca said.

"Oh, sorry, Mum. Did I wake you?"

"No... well, maybe. It doesn't matter. Having you here is better than sleep, though sleeping is now easier since you did that thing with your hands."

Cassie smiled, sat back down on the bed and conjured up more of the whatever-it-was from her fingertips.

"Thank you, but I think that's enough," Rebecca whispered a few minutes later. "I can see that it's exhausting you more than it's helping me."

"Oh, Mum, I'd do this forever if there was a chance it could save you."

Rebecca smiled. "Yes, I know you would, but you mustn't."

With a frown, Rebecca plucked at the sleeve of Cassie's jacket.

"What's up?" Cassie asked.

"As I said… your jacket. It rang a bell when you were here last February but, back then, I couldn't quite remember why."

"What do you mean?"

"I've seen it before. Not all of it – just the sleeve."

Cassie frowned. Rebecca raised a finger and stroked Cassie's cheek.

"Your scar."

"It's not the only one I've got now. My left leg is a battleground, what with the scars on my thigh from what that wolf did and the burn mark further down."

"Oh, my poor baby. Do you remember how you got the one on your cheek?"

"I don't think I'll ever forget falling off my bike," Cassie said.

"No, I expect not. Apart from one thing…"

"What?"

"You didn't fall off."

"Huh? But you always said…"

"Yes, I know. You weren't ready to hear the truth."

"What truth?"

"You didn't fall, you were pushed. Or, more like, you were tipped off it."

Cassie paused, trying to dredge up the memories from when she was six.

"But there was no one else around until you came running out the front door to pick me up, was there?"

"Not by the time your face hit the pavement, there wasn't."

"What happened? What did you see?"

"You'd been in the back garden riding around in circles when…"

There was noise from downstairs. It was the front door being opened and then slammed shut.

"Your grandad," Rebecca whispered. "Come back tomorrow, if you can."

Cassie nodded and disappeared. Pushing herself twenty-two hours into the future, she reappeared in the same spot, keeping herself hidden whilst making sure her mother was still there.

Rebecca was leaning back on her pillow with her eyes open but not appearing to be focused on anything in the room. But they were obviously looking at something as they appeared to be tracking movement of some kind.

Cassie popped downstairs to make sure the rest of the house was empty, feeling relieved when she found it was. She returned to the upstairs landing and gently knocked before putting her head around the door.

Seeing the smile on her mum's face, Cassie entered and sat back down on the bed.

"Ah, you came back," Rebecca said.

"I came straight here so, for me, it's only a few moments later," she explained. "You look a lot brighter today."

"Thanks to you and what you did yesterday."

"I'll do it some more."

"You shouldn't. I can see that doing it wears you out and, also, it worries me."

"I'm not going to take no for an answer," Cassie gently chided. "Anyway, you will need the strength to explain about me being pushed off my bike."

"Oh yes, that's right. Let me get into the right state of mind first. Just before you turned up, I was watching the portals, you know."

"Um, what do they look like to you?"

"Lights that fade in and out with flashes that shoot between them."

"Oh," Cassie said. "That's exactly how I see them as well." *She really must be seeing them, then. Is that because we've both been in close connection to the device?*

"I do believe they really are coming closer. Sometimes it's like I see them in layers, with the ones further in the past buried deeper."

"Oh, that's different," Cassie said, a frown passing across her face. "That's not something I've ever noticed myself."

Rebecca smiled briefly. "Maybe that's because I have more time to look at them. I think they go back over a hundred years – possibly as much as a hundred and fifty – though I'm definitely not certain about that."

"I think I remember Kay saying something once about going back to sometime before the nineteen-thirties – one of the fire ones, I think it was – but nothing earlier than that."

"I hope I can go through at least one before I die."

"Oh, Mum, if I knew it would help, then I'd carry you through one. But…"

Rebecca smiled. "Yes, I know. Anyway, sorry, I promised to tell you all about the bike, didn't I?"

Cassie nodded, glad to change the subject. "Yes, yes please."

"Well, I seem to remember that it was quite a nice day and you'd wanted to have a go on the bike. I'd bolted the side gate so you only had the back garden to ride around in. You should have been safe. Then I came through to the lounge to grab my camera to take a photo of you – I had to hunt for it as I couldn't remember which drawer it was in. You'd only just managed to ride the bike without the stabiliser wheels attached and I wanted a picture to record it."

"Oh, my goodness. Yes, I remember those wheels. It took me a while to get used to them not being there."

"Yes, that's why I'd slid the bolt across. You were too short to reach up and undo it. But, as I was looking for the camera, I saw movement through the window out on the pavement. I immediately realised it was you but then I saw a man literally appear out of thin air right behind you. He grabbed the frame just behind the seat and yanked the bike to one side. I think he was about to kidnap you as you fell. Then this arm – your arm, I reckon now – grabbed him and then both he and the arm were gone."

"Just an arm?"

"Yes, it ended above the elbow, I think. Faded out as if the rest of the person attached to it was invisible."

"Oh, my goodness. The man. Was it Laurence?"

"No, definitely not. Laurence always had a solidly built body, this man was a lot taller and slimmer, with a stubbly beard. Quite handsome, though I obviously wasn't thinking that at the time."

"Who was it, then?"

Rebecca shook her head. "No idea. By this time, you'd fallen off the bike and were screaming your head off. I rushed out the front door and hauled you inside. The blood on your face made it look a lot worse than it actually was. It may have been small, but it was still quite deep, which is what probably caused it to scar later on. Good job it was never really too noticeable."

Cassie touched her cheek, feeling the familiarity of the slightly raised ridge. "No, I've seen what scarring can be made to look like."

"Oh, those poor children. Why did they do it?"

"Other than tradition, I don't really know. It makes me wonder if they stopped doing it after Ka'Tor escaped from them. I don't suppose we'll ever know – I certainly have no intention of going back a hundred and forty thousand years just to find out."

Rebecca reached out and rested her hand on Cassie's arm and they hugged for a few minutes.

"Do you remember the date the bike thing happened?" Cassie asked.

Rebecca shook her head. "I don't remember exactly, other than it being summer. With you being six, that would mean three years ago – 2007. I think it was in the afternoon but don't quote me on that."

"If I teleport into the shed where we kept the bike then I can home in on when the stabiliser wheels were taken off and then scout around from there."

"I do remember, when I went back out to pick your bike up, that the plastic handlebar grip on one side got scraped when it happened. That might help you pinpoint the date."

Cassie grinned and stood up. "Yes, that will definitely help. Right, I suppose I'd better go back and rescue myself from whoever it was, then."

"Be careful, Cass," Rebecca said. "It might be dangerous."

"Everything is dangerous when it comes to time travel. But, if you saw what looked like my arm rescuing me, then I'd better make sure that I really do go back to rescue me, otherwise it could cause yet another paradox."

Rebecca smiled.

"I'll be back," Cassie promised.

Pushover

In the garden shed, Cassie touched the left handlebar grip, her fingers tracing the newly formed damage to the white plastic. It was the evening of Sunday, the twenty-ninth of July 2007. It hadn't taken too much effort to home in on the correct date. She had checked that the bike had been undamaged that morning.

Today's the day, then. She shivered remembering the times Charlie had said those words. *But I need to test something first.*

She faded from sight and then tried to make only her arm visible. It took several attempts but she eventually made it happen.

Well, I didn't know I could do that. Okay, here we go.

She hid her arm and teleported out onto the pavement. The sun was no more than half an hour from setting and the angled shadows picked out the pale mark on the pavement where the plastic grip had scraped the ground.

Teleporting inside the back garden, she noted that the high wooden gate beside the house was securely bolted shut.

It won't be shut at some point earlier today.

She travelled back several hours halting every half an hour to see if the gate became unbolted. Around three in the afternoon, the gate was open and Cassie saw no evidence of her six-year-old self in the back garden.

She heard a scream coming from around the front of the house. Half a second later she was back on the street watching as her mother rushed out of the front door.

Right, back a couple of minutes, she thought, teleporting but staying in the same location. This time the gate was shut, but, within seconds, she heard the squeak of the bolt being slid across slowly, followed by the gate swinging open. For a moment, she saw the shadow of someone behind it but, by the time the gate was half open, they had gone. *I wonder why he didn't try to grab me in the back garden. Maybe Mum was still in view.*

There was another movement near the gate. *Ah, and here I come.*

Cassie stood at the edge of the pavement and waited for the man to reappear. She had to suppress a squeal when a figure popped out of thin air. His back was to her so she couldn't see his face.

Another time traveller?

As the man reached for the rear of the bike, she swallowed and positioned herself behind him. Releasing the invisibility on her arm, she took firm hold of the man's arm the moment he grabbed the bike and jolted it sideways.

Gripping the arm tightly, she teleported them both a couple of miles away and more than a hundred years into the past, in the hope that it would disorientate the attacker.

"Leave her alone, you bastard," she screamed as they arrived on the rough ground of Mousehold Heath. Her internal calendar told her it was the early morning of June the twelfth, 1892, not that she'd aimed for that particular date.

Cassie gasped at her first proper view of the man's face.

I've seen him before.

He had been much older and clean-shaven the last time she'd seen him. But, this encounter had the same effect upon her as it had previously and she had to fight to suppress a scream. Her vision swam as memories of the crush of bodies in Cow Tower and the flames surrounding her dominated her mind yet again. She shook her head to banish them.

"I know you," she whispered. "You're Jason's dad."

"Cassie," the man snarled. "Well, I was trying to abduct your younger self and here you are all grown up yet again. The daughter delivers herself for her final act of sacrifice. How apt."

"Daughter? What? Oh no. Are you Laurence?"

"Hah, yes, you fool, though not really Laurence any more. Apparently, the original name this body goes under is Patrick Richard Luckin and, obviously, you are familiar with his son."

The man who was both Laurence and Patrick leapt at her, but he was too slow. Cassie turned insubstantial, and he fell through her and onto the ground.

"So, you still try to run away from me, do you?" he shouted. "It won't make any difference. I *will* get you in the end. This damned body may not be up to much as yet but it's adapting and is currently adequate enough to let me catch you. And, if I can't get at older you, I can still get at your younger self and then older you won't ever have the chance to exist."

Laurence faded away slowly as he forced himself to teleport but Cassie could see that he was struggling. Not only that, but he was also leaving some sort of trace of where and when he was attempting to go.

Damn, he really is slow, Cassie thought. *Can I follow this trail or whatever it is?*

It became obvious to Cassie that Laurence was attempting to return to her house, whilst simultaneously pushing himself forwards in time.

He's weak, she thought, having no problem following the trail, which hung before her like green, glowing breadcrumbs as she drifted futurewards. She remembered how difficult it had been for her when she'd returned to the present from Robert Kett's time. Back then she'd had concussion after one of Fulke's thugs had smashed her over the head. *But how did Laurence survive and how did he manage to steal Jason's dad's body?*

Cassie heard an echo of a conversation she'd had with Jason's cousin. It was during the lift home after that infamous party. Erin had said something about his dad walking out on his mum when Jason was only a few weeks old.

Something clicked. *Wait, Jason's birthday is early November. He's about five months older than me. Laurence was killed by Kay in December 2000, which was a few weeks after Jason was born. Oh, my God. No wonder they never knew where his father went. Laurence must have stolen Patrick's body to cheat death somehow, and then come straight to my place in 2007 to attack younger me. But why Patrick?*

She shook her head.

Too many questions. Well, so much for Kay cutting his head off. Hell, can't he ever be killed?

To Cassie's surprise, Laurence's path went past 2007 and the incident with the bike. She followed him into early 2008.

Where is he going? Oh, now he's slowing right down. Is he looking for something?

Laurence halted and appeared outside her house again, but this time it was the cold February of 2008. High clouds skimmed across the sky in front of a moon that was half-full. Cassie's calendar registered two-sixteen in the morning. She halted several yards away.

I don't think he's figured out how to do the invisibility thing and I'm pretty sure he's completely unaware that I'm here watching him. What else can I do that he can't? And vice versa, of course?

Laurence faded for a moment and then reappeared. There was a swirl of a trail between where he stood and the house.

"Damn," he cursed.

Ah, he tried to jump into the house, but couldn't. The device inside must be protecting the place against him. He can't get in. That's a relief. Could that also explain why he had to entice younger me out of the back garden and away from the house?

A flash of green momentarily rippled around his outline and he staggered as if unbalanced.

"Uh," he said. "Where am I? What's happening?"

That doesn't sound like Laurence. Is that Jason's father back in his own body?

Then the man disappeared. Cassie saw the trail going right through the wall of the house and up into her younger self's bedroom.

"No," she shouted. *He's figured out a way in. The device was set to prevent Laurence from getting in. It obviously doesn't work on Jason's father and, somehow, Laurence did something to make it appear like he wasn't there.*

She followed, materialising in her old bedroom. In bed, and fully asleep, was her six-year-old self. Laurence, going by the snarl on his face, was back in full control of Patrick's body.

"Not this time," he shouted, noticing her. "I've waited far too long."

Rays of green light bubbled around his fingertips and his hands were aimed at the small figure in the bed, who was beginning to wake up. Cassie teleported to place herself between them just as Laurence let loose a stream of crackling energy from his fingers. She automatically raised her hands in an effort to protect both versions of herself.

Her younger self, now fully awake, screamed just as the force hit Cassie full on. She wanted to scream just as loudly but, despite Laurence's supposed weakness, the onslaught was relentless. She felt like she was being shredded, as if knives were slicing deep into her flesh.

Diversion: Portals

Out of the corner of her left eye, Cassie saw sparks from the electrical thing that hung in the air. There was something enticing about it. Something far friendlier than the ghoulish things that were no more than ten feet away.

She stepped sideways and into the electrical disturbance. It encompassed her entire body. Her scalp tingled and her hair stood to attention as Jarrolds book department disappeared from around her. For a moment she had the impression someone was standing next to her shouting something incomprehensible.

After a second it was over and she was ejected into darkness. She stumbled against what felt like solidly packed soil. There was also a smell of gas.

What the hell? Have I fallen in a hole? But I didn't actually fall, did I?

In the darkness, she reached out to feel her surroundings. On one side of the restricted space, her fingers encountered something that wasn't packed soil. It had two upright wooden poles and horizontal rungs at regular vertical intervals.

A ladder?

It felt solid enough so, with trepidation, she started to climb upwards. After eight steps, the darkness decreased and she found herself inside a tent-like structure. Beyond its opaque walls, she could detect dim lights.

She located the entrance and pushed her way out, nearly falling over a sign. In the near-darkness, she could just make out the words: Men at work. That she was no longer in Jarrolds was without any doubt. She could see stars above her head and a chill wind was blowing.

Huh? Where am I? First the rain and now this. How can it be night?

She realised she was standing on a roadway facing a grassy bank that sloped down into darkness. Beyond that, in the far distance, the panorama was dotted with lights – they looked like buildings and street lamps, though the glow from both was far removed from the brightness with which she was familiar.

To her left and not too far away, more dim street lights barely illuminated a row of terraced houses. A couple of hundred feet to her right, she could just about make out trees whose branches swayed in the wind. When she turned around, she saw the shadow of a large building.

I recognise this, she thought, stepping back from the road surface onto a grass verge. *It looks like Britannia Road and this is the old prison, isn't it? Is this Saint James's Hill? How the hell did I get here? Am I dreaming?*

She shook her head and pinched herself but the dream refused to go away.

Scared and breathing heavily, she looked around but, to her relief, the three nasties were nowhere to be seen. She noticed something odd about the only two cars she could see parked further along the road.

What is this? Some kind of old car rally?

She jumped, suddenly conscious of someone standing close to her.

"Old ancient cars, old new girl. That's really enough to put your head in a right ol' twirl," said the man in the bus driver's uniform.

"You? Did you do this?" she screamed at him. Up close, she could see that his eyes were glowing blue pits in the darkness. "What's happening to me?"

"Let bus man be the first to say, welcome to the nineteen-thirties, newly-hatched Kay."

"Kay? How do you know that name?" she hissed. "And, what do you mean by nineteen-thirties?"

"Forth and back, no obvious track. Thirty-eight, don't be late. Find another door, to avoid a world of war," he said.

"Thirty-eight? Do you mean nineteen-thirty-eight?"

He started to fade so Cassie tried to grab him, becoming even more annoyed that her hands gripped nothing.

"Are you telling me I've time travelled into the past or something?"

"Always messing with your hair, portals take you then and there. Nasties messing with your head, run away before you end up dead," he said with a grin before finally disappearing.

"No, come back," she wailed. "Don't leave me."

She heard a click and a creak. A man's outline was silhouetted against the door frame of one of the nearby terraced houses.

"Keep it down," he shouted. "It's gone eleven."

"Sorry," she said automatically. She was about to ask if she could come in out of the cold but the door clicked shut.

Cassie wrapped her arms around herself, the wind bitter against her bare arms. Walking down the slope a short way, hoping to escape the cold, she stared out over the city. She'd stood on this spot several times before, sometimes at night, but the lights of the city had never looked as diminished as at that moment.

"Nineteen thirty-eight? Can't be, surely. I must be dreaming?"

Somewhere in the distance, a bell was ringing. Not a church or a doorbell. This bell was a continuous metallic clatter and was in motion somewhere down below the level of the hill. She heard the sound of a solitary vehicle's engine coming from the same direction. It reminded her of a black and white film she'd seen years ago with an old-fashioned police car chasing a robber.

After a few seconds, the sound faded into the distance and Cassie was left with just the whistle of the wind through the trees and grass. She shivered.

I've got to find somewhere warm.

She ran back up to the road and turned right towards the terraced houses.

Dare I knock on a door? she thought as she passed them. *But, if this really is the nineteen-thirties and I tell them I'm from 2018, they will probably think I'm mad. Maybe they would be right and I am.*

She ran on, reaching a crossroads where a sign confirmed that she really was on Britannia Road. The sign, made from cast metal, looked ancient, the black letters of the road name standing rough and proud of the white-painted surface. She halted noticing that, across the road, the familiar houses that had been there all her life had been replaced with a strange Tudor-styled building that appeared to be some sort of church, given the spindly spire it sported. But the rest of the street towards her right definitely looked like Kett's Hill. In the other direction, it was unmistakably Plumstead Road, though badly illuminated by street lamps that were far shorter than she remembered. Possibly more significant was that there was no traffic. Not a single vehicle of any sort had passed her and the air lacked any sound that suggested traffic might be elsewhere. Apart from what might have been a police car earlier on, she could detect no sounds of mechanical origin whatsoever.

"How can I be in the nineteen-thirties?" she asked herself.

Shivering even more, she turned left and started trotting towards home.

"If this is the nineteen-thirties then at least *he* won't be there waiting for me."

She halted. *But there won't be anywhere to stay, either. My house wasn't even built until well after World War Two.*

Slumping her shoulders but trying not to despair, she turned around and started hurrying down Kett's Hill, jogging to keep warm. As she descended, the wind dropped slightly and, even though she was still cold, it was partly negated by her amazement at how different everything looked. Not only did the road appear narrower, but there was a smell of burning in the air. She looked up at the roofs, seeing the smoke that drifted from the chimneys of the houses. About two-thirds of the way down she was surprised to see that the terraces on the left continued down to the bottom of the hill. And there, where Cassie expected the roundabout to be, there was only a small triangular traffic island.

She turned left into Riverside and immediately regretted the move. Visions filled her head as the crushing sensations from the nearby Cow Tower across the river and the flames of Lollards Pit dominated her brain. While it was not as bad as it usually was, the effect was enough to force her in the opposite direction.

Entering Gurney Road there was an entrance to her left that she didn't recognise. Instead of the estate and flats she remembered, there was a large open area, partly grassed and surrounded on three sides by buildings that appeared far from residential. The whole area had a military air to it. Some of the buildings sported large doors that made Cassie think of horse stables. A few lights showed in some of the windows, though most were dark.

Maybe I can hide in there. Anything to get out of this damned cold.

She crept along trying a few doors until she found one that hadn't been locked. Inside, it was dark and there was an aroma suggesting that horses and hay might once have been plentiful here. But it was still cold.

Once her eyes had grown accustomed to the darkness, she could make out a doorway leading deeper inside the building. The door wasn't locked so, partly feeling her way along, she explored further. She came across a staircase and, as the air from below was marginally warmer, descended. She located a side room whose only light came from a small window near the ceiling that let in a mix of moonlight and distant street light. Inside, the room housed shelves stretching the full length upon which she could feel an assortment of material, the first consisting of rough sacking. On another shelf, there was a smaller pile of what felt like clothing, the material thick like a coat or maybe the jacket of a uniform. Her fingers detected the shape of a collar. She picked it up only to discover one sleeve missing, torn off at the shoulder. After rummaging through the pile she found one that, to her touch, felt more or less intact. Although it was far too large, she pulled it around herself, glad that it excluded much of the cold.

She pulled some of the other piles of material down onto the floor and attempted to form them into a makeshift bed. Wrapping herself within the bundle, she tried to get comfortable. For a while, it seemed to work but, even though it was night, her body clock told her it couldn't have been any more than about one o'clock in the afternoon, so trying to sleep was next to impossible.

She lay back in her slowly warming nest, trying to figure things out.

Everything's completely wrong. Not just that I appear to be in the past but things I remember aren't as they were. But, I can't remember how they should be. Have all the things HE *has been doing to me finally flipped me over the edge? Damn him.*

But, as she lay there, her eyes were attracted to something on the far side of the room. Whatever it was, she had the impression that it was even darker than its surroundings. Also, it subtly crackled with energy.

It's like that thing in Jarrolds. What on Earth is it? Some sort of door or portal?

Every so often, as she looked away from it, the vision from the corner of her eye saw random sparks emanating from it. But she couldn't be certain that it was anything more than her imagination.

She tried once more to sleep but was disturbed by a bright light outside the window as if someone was waving a torch around. Cassie sunk deeper into the clothes, hoping whoever it was would remain outside. But, even though the window hadn't opened, the light came inside. It oozed through the glass and, like jelly, reassembled itself into the shape of a man. Once it had achieved that goal, it came straight towards her.

She screamed and jumped up from her hiding place. As she did so, another of them seeped right through the wall next to the window.

Cassie ran across the room and threw herself at the patch of electrical darkness. Her body tingled and she popped out into light and warmth. Dizzy with the sudden change, she leaned on the back of a chair to stop herself falling. It and the other chairs around the low table were unoccupied, so she sat down.

She had the impression that someone had only just departed. On the table, along with an empty cup and plate that was littered with crumbs, was an almost full cup of coffee. Still dressed in the coat, she sat down and, not even caring if it had been someone else's drink, drained half the cup.

I know where I am. This is where I was going in the first place. Starbucks. I'm back in Castle Mall. Is it 2018? It feels hot enough.

Many of the other tables around her were occupied though no one took any notice of her. This surprised her as, to them, she must have popped out of thin air. But she soon realised that most of those whose gaze passed over her were looking straight through her as if they weren't seeing her at all.

Am I a ghost? Am I dead? Well, I managed to pick up this cup and that feels solid enough. Unless it's a ghost cup. What the hell am I thinking?

Her eyes were drawn to something happening outside. She suppressed a squeak seeing a creature apparently assembled from mismatched bits of too many people. Its head swung around to peer inside the shop. When it saw her, it smiled. The grin was repulsive and mostly toothless, causing her to almost spit out the mouthful of coffee she hadn't got around to swallowing.

Behind the creature, she saw a blur of movement and gasped again seeing herself standing where the blur had been. Or, at least, it was someone who closely resembled her, though the eyes looked extremely vacant. For a second, that version of her just stood there but, a moment later, Cassie relived the impression that the mall roof was collapsing and the girl was crushed to death under some falling rocks.

Cassie jumped up and ran for the shop entrance. Outside, there was no evidence of any rocks, nor was there any sign that a duplicate of her had been crushed to death only seconds before.

Her mind screaming, Cassie looked right towards White Lion Street but a compulsion sent her running left towards the spiral staircase instead.

Memories

From Me to... Me

Cassie grimaced, trying to fight the pain coursing through her. She spread the fingers of her already raised hands and found she could dissipate the worst of the attack, which gave her a short space to catch her breath.

I've got to hold myself together. Can't let him beat me. He's still too strong. I've got to find a way past all this before he regains his full strength.

She concentrated, seeking to block Laurence's attack, erecting barriers against its onslaught, whilst still trying to prevent any of it reaching her younger self.

Is this similar to what he kept trying to do when I was on Charlie's bus heading towards his execution?

The force was made up of several different components, so she tackled them one at a time, countering the most powerful first. Slowly, she managed to divert or nullify each one and, in so doing, felt Laurence's power fading. She hoped she could keep up her defences for longer than Laurence could dish it out.

Just when she thought she was winning, Laurence changed tactics and aimed a bolt of energy directly at her head. She fell against the bed as it tore through her skull, threatening to push her consciousness out the back of her head.

Behind her, on the bed, younger Cassie's screams grew even louder.

Oh my God, he's getting through me to her. I can't block it. I need to do something quickly. But what?

Abruptly, the onslaught stopped and Cassie gasped seeing Laurence surrounded by three copies of herself, one behind, the others either side of him. Together they held him securely, diverting his hands and disrupting his attack. The one behind kicked the back of his leg hard.

"We'll handle this," said one, her eyes dark and intense. "You calm young Cass down. Help her deal with what's happened. Check Mum is okay – she won't have heard this, but you'll soon see why. Oh, and something's missing."

That version of Cassie pointed to her own head and then all three of them, along with Laurence, disappeared.

Cassie sighed with relief and turned around. Young Cassie's mouth was stretched wide, as if she was silently screaming, but having no more breath left inside herself to make any further noise. Her eyes were just as wide but with terror and not focused on anything in particular.

I don't remember any of this. Oh my God, what's going on? What's she still seeing?

"It's okay, Cass," she whispered. But it was like her younger self was incapable of hearing anything outside of whatever was terrorising her.

Cassie placed her hands on the girl's head, trying to connect and see into her mind. Slowly, something terrible came into view and Cassie's hands dropped as she let out an involuntary whimper.

She knew what it was.

Once again, she both saw and felt the flames all around her. They were accompanied by the sensation of being crushed on all sides by bodies. After a moment, Cassie realised that the original thoughts and experiences no longer inhabited her own head with the same intensity. Instead, they were more like something she had been told, not something she had ever experienced first-hand. They were now second-hand memories.

Oh, hell. Something is definitely missing. Whatever Laurence attacked me with must have stripped the memories of Cow Tower and Lollards Pit from my head and pushed them into younger me. How is that even possible?

She placed her hands back around younger Cassie's head. Just as she had done to both her mother and also to Kay when the latter had been burned, she did her best to ease the pain or, in this case, lessen the effect of the memory transfer. After a few minutes, it was obvious that the calming effect was achieving something.

"Sleep," she soothed. "And forget it as best you can."

She rescanned her younger self's mind. It was still a boiling sea of turmoil, though not quite as bad as it had been a few moments before.

Can I extract those memories? Maybe… but… no. I daren't. If I do, then that will change my own history. They need to be there so that I slowly rediscover them a fraction at a time. Can I put something in her head to temporarily suppress them?

Cassie caught herself. "Oh no."

Suppression? Shit. Would that be any different to what Laurence did to Grandad?

I can't do that to myself, can I? But maybe I have to. Oh, my God, I feel like I'm condemning myself to more than ten years of mental torture.

She swallowed, knowing that those memories would need to be with her from the age of six right up until Laurence's attack minutes earlier. She wracked her own memories trying to recall when each piece had surfaced.

The flames were the first, I think. I remember having nightmares about them and then telling Mum enough times until she believed me when I claimed they were real.

"Well, that wasn't a lie," she muttered. "Just my usual screwing up of cause and effect – not that I realised it at the time."

She reached inside her younger self's head once more and tried to picture something surrounding the newly inserted memories to block their full effect.

Wait, is there some residue of the original shielding in my own head? Can I learn how to do this from seeing how I did it to myself in the first place?

"Yeah, but, if I do that, then isn't it just perpetuating another damn paradox? No, I've got to figure this out for myself. There has to be a proper beginning."

She spent the next half hour building a series of barriers around each memory. Learning as she went, she figured out how to induce sleep within the mind of her younger self so that she could work on the memories uninterrupted by the terror they could conjure up. Finally, she decided she had done all she could. The shields she had constructed would slowly deteriorate, releasing the memories one at a time over the years. She purged the moments of the original attack by Laurence completely and then wondered if she'd done the right thing.

This is me creating the future I know to be real. Isn't it? As she hadn't realised what the outcome was going to be when she'd placed herself in the line of fire, she had to hope she'd made the right decision. *Would I have done that if I had known that I was about to inflict those memories upon my younger self?*

Satisfied that she could do no more, she popped into her mother's bedroom, remaining invisible in case her mother was awake. Given the noise that Laurence had made, along with the screams from her younger self, it was a wonder the whole street hadn't been awoken, let alone her mum.

The darkness within the bedroom wasn't complete as illumination from the moon crept through a gap in the curtains. Cassie stood beside the sleeping form of her mother, initially comforted by the sound of gentle snoring. She watched as her mum's breathing moved the bed covers up and down.

She's so much fitter here, Cassie thought, remembering how thin she was in November 2010. Then she spotted two small cardboard boxes on the bedside cabinet. Picking them up, she squinted at the labels, trying to make out the words.

Oh. Painkillers and sleeping pills. I never even knew she was taking them. Was this the first signs of what eventually became the cancer? It explains her sleeping through all this. But what about Grandad? Surely he must have heard everything?

She teleported into his room to find it empty.

Must be on one of his bowling competition trips. I do remember him being away occasionally before he had to take over looking after me when Mum got so ill. Maybe that was why Laurence slowed down – did he detect that Grandad wasn't around?

There were too many questions and Cassie was exhausted.

I need to go back and snatch Laurence away once again. Do I have the strength? I mustn't make any mistakes – Laurence is too unpredictable, and still too strong. Hold on... Those future versions of me were wearing makeup. I didn't put any on when I visited Mum. They were also wearing my new boots. Therefore, I don't need to be them right now. Just so long as I become them at some point in the future.

Then she paused as something else popped into her head.

What's to stop Laurence getting back in as Patrick at a later date? The device downstairs is only programmed to prevent original Laurence getting in. And, for that matter, what will be protecting this place after Grandad gives me the device at Mum's funeral? I asked the device to protect Kay's place. I remember it setting things up retroactively so that it started from when Kay first bought it right up until we no longer needed it. Is something similar protecting this house? How long does it last?

Cassie concentrated and tried to understand how her house was being protected. That something existed was undeniable – it was some sort of shield and the brickwork was seeped in it. She followed it to 2011 and found that it became weaker after the end of January, petering out within a couple of days as the device was no longer around to sustain it.

She returned to 2008 to check on her younger self, relieved to find her sleeping. Spending more than an hour analysing the shield's construction, she tried to replicate it.

This is just as hard as rummaging around in my six-year-old self's head.

After a few experiments, she knew she could create a duplicate, so she returned to the beginning of February 2011 and added her own version of the shield, beefing it up to prevent Laurence or Patrick from entering the house. She tried extending it futurewards but found it was costing her too much energy and so had to be content with adding a couple of years.

I wish I knew how the device extracted the energy it needs. I better remember to renew the shield every two years.

Exhausted, she teleported home to 2019, returning just a few minutes after she'd first left. The bedroom was empty as the earlier version of herself who was sharing the room and sleeping in the daytime wasn't present.

"Good. I need all my strength to deal with Laurence once and for all."

She lay down on the bed, staring at the sheet of notes on the wall. She knew she needed to add a whole new set of data to it.

"Oh, Ka'Tor – is nothing ever simple? Why did you have to turn into Laurence? And why did you have to steal Jason's father?"

Back to One

"Right," Cassie whispered to herself ten days later. "I can't put it off any longer. I've got to face Laurence and get it over and done with properly."

The previous week at school had been draining despite the arrival of the Easter break. Her final year was becoming intense, with only a few short weeks until her exams. It would only get worse the longer she put things off.

At least I've got the room back to myself, she thought. Earlier Cassie had left for the last time two days previously.

"It's time for you to go back and become me," Cassie had told her.

"I don't know if I want to. You scare me," her earlier self had whispered.

"Yes, I know. I remember having this conversation the first time around."

"What happens? What makes me become you?"

Cassie shook her head. "I'll just repeat what I said about a week ago."

"What? About getting advice or something?"

Cassie nodded. "You'll work it out," she said, experiencing a déjà vu moment as soon as she said it. *Yeah, I've told myself that before, haven't I?*

"That's easy for you to say. You've already done it."

"No," she sighed. "I've barely started doing it."

Her earlier self had shrugged and, before going back three weeks, said, "Be seeing… no, I'll be *being* you, I suppose."

Cassie smiled.

During these past few weeks, Georgia, as usual, had been her rock, helping her keep up with most things where they'd shared subjects, such as History A-Level. They were currently revisiting aspects of the Reformation in Europe, whose dates in the sixteenth century overlapped with those of Kett's Rebellion. At least, to Cassie's relief, they hadn't covered the rebellion itself – some parts of her personal memories of that time no longer matched written history.

Jason had mostly avoided her, even when they had been sharing the same classes which, thankfully, wasn't many. She once caught him watching her from across a room but his eyes dropped as soon as she'd returned the gaze. Once, they had almost bumped into each other in the school library. She had been walking along the aisle into which he had just entered. With only a couple of yards between them, they had halted simultaneously, facing each other. She had deliberately narrowed her eyes and stood her ground. To her relief, he immediately turned around and walked back the way he had come.

By this point, Cassie had told Georgia the whole story about what she'd done to Jason to keep him quiet.

"He's avoiding both of us," Georgia had confided to Cassie. "Actually, not just us. Even Mark can't get him to say anything. A year ago, it felt like I was sharing Mark with Jason, but now he's shutting himself off from everyone."

"Just as well," Cassie had replied. "No one would believe him, anyway."

"I'm a bit worried about him. Do you think you went too far?"

Cassie sighed. "He did try to rape me. I can't forgive him for that."

Or can I? If he hadn't done it, I would never have started time travelling again.

"Yeah, can't blame you for that," Georgia said.

Since learning that Laurence had been responsible for Jason losing his dad,

Cassie had almost started to feel sorry for him. Was it his fault he had turned out the way he had? She began to feel partly responsible. *If I hadn't given birth to Ka'Tor then he wouldn't have eventually become Laurence and therefore Jason's dad would still have been there to bring Jason up properly, like that version of him I saw in that alternative timeline.*

"Damn it," she muttered. "But Laurence is also my father so, without him, I wouldn't have even been born in the first place. Talk about the circle of life…"

"Wow, that cheap? Yeah, you'll really have to take me with you sometime," Georgia said one evening when Cassie had been invited over for tea by Georgia's parents. Later, upstairs in Georgia's bedroom, Cassie had been telling her about how she'd gone back to 1991 to get her jackets and boots.

"Really?" Cassie said, brightening up at Georgia's statement.

"No, absolutely not," her friend laughed. "That was definitely sarcasm – bet you didn't get a lot of that back in the Stone Age. Anyway, I'm happy leading my life in a strict *from A-to-B sequence* kind of way. All this dodging about in time you do is enough to give me a headache trying to make sense of it all."

Cassie smiled. "Me too, sometimes."

"The only history I'm interested in is the stuff in the history books. And, as far as I'm concerned, that's where it ought to stay."

Remembering that conversation, Cassie smiled and wished she, too, could leave history back in the past where it belonged. But, she needed to go back slightly more than twelve years and rescue herself from Laurence.

She stood and looked in her bedroom mirror. Already, her straightened hair was beginning to kink back into its natural wildness. She applied some mascara and then added more, which made her look quite gothic and wild.

"Good," she said. "I need to be wild for this – it's better if I look the part, which will then help me act the part… hopefully."

Remembering seeing herself kick Laurence in the leg, she pulled on the boots she'd purchased on her trip to 1991.

She shut her eyes and whispered, "Here goes."

Saving Patrick

Cassie returned to February 2008 and, remembering where Laurence had been positioned in her childhood bedroom, materialised behind him.

Two more of her appeared to each side and, with a snarl, all three grabbed Laurence's arms. This diverted and dissipated the force that he had been projecting from his hands, allowing her earlier self a chance to recover.

Laurence tried to resist so, with a grunt, she kicked him hard behind his left knee, causing him to teeter. But, knowing he was about to fall, she was ready for this, and all three of her held him securely. She also tried something else, turning the tables on what he'd tried to do to her back on her great-grandad's bus. She placed one hand on the side of his head and, just like he had done to her, invaded his mind, attempting to induce lethargy, if not sleep.

"We'll handle this," said the slightly future version of herself to the one across the room. "You calm young Cass down. Help her deal with what's happened. Check Mum is okay – she won't have heard this, but you'll soon see why. Oh, and something's missing."

Back to Mousehold, Cassie thought, knowing the other two would follow. Laurence didn't have any choice – he was still trying to resist her occupation of his mind. She didn't travel in time, only wanting to get him away from the house to give her earlier self room to deal with the transfer of the nightmare memories. Picking a spot far from the road, yet still on open ground, prevented Laurence from giving her the slip and running to the trees for cover.

As soon as they arrived, her rage boiled over into unsuppressed violence. All three of her laid into him with fists and boots. He slumped to the ground, unresisting. But part of that was a ruse and she knew he was trying to teleport away. She pushed deeper into his skull and thwarted his escape attempt.

"Ahh. Get out of my head," he cried. "How did you get this strong?"

You forced me to do it to myself. Every time our paths cross, I'm learning more about what you can do and how you do it.

As he lay there groaning, she took the opportunity to return to the bedroom to become the other two versions of herself, first appearing on Laurence's right and then on his left. After delivering the 'dealing with this' speech she returned to Mousehold Heath just as Laurence was trying to haul himself up into a sitting position. By this point, she was the only 'Cassie' remaining.

Seeing her, he stretched one hand towards her, the fingers glowing green.

"You can't take me over. You're too weak," she taunted, hoping she was right, while kicking his hand away. He groaned, rubbing a finger that had started bleeding from the force of her boot.

"You are my daughter," he hissed. "I created you for that purpose."

"Don't you go all Darth Vader on me, you moron," she spat. "Because I can give it back in spades."

"What do you mean?"

"Listen." Leaning close to him and using the Denisovan tribe language, she said, "You bad boy, Ka'Tor. Ka'See angry with Ka'Tor."

Laurence cowered, his eyes wide open. For the first time, Cassie could see real fear in them and her confidence grew.

"No," he shouted, trying to sit back up. "Impossible."

"Yes, Ka'Tor. I am your mother. Now do you finally recognise me?"

"No," he shouted again. "I saw you die. I ordered the controller to kill you."

"No, you didn't. I escaped."

"What? But I saw your body lying dead on the ground, torn to shreds."

It was Cassie's turn to be confused. "I don't know what you think you saw but I definitely didn't die in the Stone Age."

"Yes, you did. Not only that, but while the others were running away, I plucked your still-warm heart from your chest and, though it disgusts me now to think of it, I drank your blood."

"You did *what?* Jesus Christ. You're completely deluded. You really think I'd be standing here right now if you had actually done that?"

"It's one of the memories that has lasted me down the thousands of years. I know it happened. I made it happen."

He believes it. Could that have been a different timeline? How come he's experienced something that could never have happened? Maybe it didn't and he's convinced himself it's the truth. He has to be wrong. I'm the living proof of that.

"You're sick," she shouted. "Absolutely mental. You've turned a wish into something you think was real. I tried to save you from being scarred, but you turned on me as well, you little shit. But, that's all beside the point, anyway."

"Why?"

"Don't you realise what me being here means?"

"What?"

"You dare not take over my six-year-old self."

"Why not?"

"You utter moron. Because it would prevent later me from getting sent back into the past and therefore stop you from being born in the first place."

"Sent? You mean you didn't go willingly? Who sent you?"

"Not telling you," Cassie snarled and lashed out with her boot, knocking Laurence onto his back once more. He growled and aimed his fingers at her, their tips starting to glow green.

"Not a chance," Cassie said, launching her boot at him once more. He howled in pain and started inching away from her. She let him get several feet and watched him try to stand and run. He managed to stagger ten feet.

"Ka'See come get bad boy Ka'Tor" she taunted in the tribal language, knowing what was about to happen. Multiple copies of herself appeared around him and beat him until he collapsed groaning to the ground. She went through the motions of becoming those copies, lashing out to keep him off balance until he fell.

Standing over him, with one boot resting on his leg, she said, more calmly than she felt, "I can do that as many times as I want. And I can see that, for you, in *that* body, doing such a thing yourself is way beyond your capability. I can also see that you no longer have the strength to teleport any distance without me being able to follow you."

He looked up at her, cowed.

She grabbed his head with both hands.

"I can see right into you, Ka'Tor. See what you think. See what you feel. I can also see that Patrick is still in there with you. You let him out once to gain access to my house. But you are expending half your remaining energy just trying to suppress him. You can't keep it up forever."

Laurence sighed, his gaze falling from her face to the ground.

"What do you want?" he said, after a while.

"Get out of Patrick's body. I can sense him fighting you. If I add my strength to his, you will be finished with nowhere to go."

Laurence sighed. "Maybe that's true," he said. "But I can't leave – I don't know how to without finding a new host to take over."

Shit. Is he telling the truth? I can't trust him an inch, even if he was once my son.

"Well, let me see if I can help you on your way," she said, pushing her consciousness deeper into his skull.

"Stop!" he screamed. "You'll kill Patrick as well."

"You were going to kill him anyway. Don't try to hide it. You've lived for thousands of years, stealing endless numbers of bodies from people who deserved to live their lives. You're a murderer hundreds of times over. You may have once been my son, but what you've turned into doesn't deserve life."

Could I kill him? Could I actually do that? He is still my son...

"What makes you the judge of what I may or may not deserve?"

"I'm your mother. I know what you've done. Whose life did you first take?"

She leapt on an image of El'Tesh that formed in his mind before he could suppress it. She dug into his head and forced the memories to the surface, reading them as if scanning a book. Under her control, she felt Laurence quiver.

She saw El'Tesh pregnant and then give birth to Ka'Tor's son – a boy he named Ka'Chull after the father he had killed. Gripping his skull in her hands, she forced him to remember more and saw him in his prime, in control of the entire tribe, who lived in fear of his power. El'Tesh didn't survive a second pregnancy but Ka'Chull grew to manhood, revelling in the authority his powerful father bestowed upon him. He took a wife of his own – a Valley Tribe girl descended from Ge'Tal and called Le'Fan. She produced three children for him – two boys and a girl.

The scene jumped ten years. With Ka'Tor's health waning and only the prospect of old age and death ahead, she watched him interrogate the device for a way to stop the process of ageing. After that proved fruitless, he asked it for methods of surviving death itself. Here, he was more successful as, reluctantly and only after much cajoling, the device explained how he could transfer his personality and memories into a close genetic relation. The younger the victim, the better, as young brains were malleable enough to adapt to a new host.

Horrified, Cassie watched him put his new knowledge to use. He abandoned his birth body and forced his consciousness onto his second-born grandson, Ja'Mor, pushing the eight-year-old's mind into a corner where, weeks later, it eventually died. She could see that, to the rest of the tribe, it was as if Ka'Tor had died of old age, something that came as a relief to them.

Through Ja'Mor's eyes, Ka'Tor saw how Ka'Chull, without the strength and power of his father's support, lacked the same respect. His standing within the tribe rapidly diminished. Ka'Chull was one of the few who knew of the device and how his father had used it to hold sway over the tribe. Cassie saw Ka'Chull try to possess the device, growing angry after it initially seemed to respond to him but then shut down, eventually disappearing altogether. That constant anger broke up his partnership with Le'Fan. He became bitter and isolated, often living alone in the woods away from the cave.

Ka'Tor, within the body of Ja'Mor, kept his identity a secret while he grew to manhood. The device, hidden further up the mountainside, remained in mental contact with him throughout this period. At thirteen, he sought out and revealed himself to Ka'Chull, promising a return to power and expecting him to be pleased. But, Ka'Chull, bitter and vengeful, didn't believe him and, instead, verbally cursed the boy, blaming him for how he had fallen from favour. Ka'Tor called Ka'Chull weak and, in response, Ka'Chull slapped him across the face. Enraged by the rejection, Ka'Tor lashed out with the power of the device, enclosing Ka'Chull in a ball of green flame which he then caused to shrink until the energy within it could no longer be contained.

Even Ka'Tor was surprised at the violence of the resulting explosion and barely managed to escape unharmed himself.

As Ka'Tor stood over the burning remains of Ka'Chull, Cassie could read his thoughts. *Once more I kill father. Maybe all Ka'Chulls must die.*

Ka'Tor heard a shout from nearby and saw Ja'Mor's older brother, Ta'Kar. *He must have followed me and seen everything.* Ta'Kar ran back towards the cave and the rest of the tribe but Ka'Tor, having expended much energy in the killing, didn't have the strength to follow. *They will know I am Ka'Tor reborn into Ja'Mor's body. They will kill me. Not if I kill them first. I must hide.*

Minutes later, all the men of the tribe along with several of the women approached Ka'Chull's body. All were armed and several used their tracking skills to determine where Ka'Tor was hiding. Without warning, several spears were launched into the bush where Ka'Tor hid. He turned to run but his leg turned into a pillar of pain as a spear thrown by Ta'Kar punctured his thigh.

Ka'Tor stopped, screaming with rage and pain, but his lust for revenge resulted in him creating a huge fireball. Cassie whimpered at the newly released memories as she watched the fireball immolate all those nearby but the ball of energy didn't halt there, it spread upwards towards the cave, incinerating everything in its path. The rest of the tribe, including Le'Fan, died immediately upon its touch. Much of the mountainside had been reduced to ash.

Oh God, I gave birth to a monster.

She watched Ka'Tor order the device to heal the spear wound, which it did. Turning his back on what had been the tribe's home for generations, Ka'Tor in Ja'Mor's body strode downhill towards the Valley Tribe.

Cassie shivered as the memory faded away.

"I'd forgotten," Laurence whispered. "I've forgotten so much. But, yes, Ja'Mor was the first. The controller showed me how and who to choose."

"You're a monster," she spat. "You and that damned thing have caused more trouble than either of us are worth."

"But, without it, you wouldn't have been born," Laurence said, unable to resist smirking. "Ja'Mor may have been the first, but he was far from the last. The son of a cousin of Le'Fan was next."

"You'll definitely be the last," Cassie snarled. "Get out of Patrick's head."

"I really can't," Laurence said.

Cassie's fists were before his face, causing him to flinch.

"Maybe I'll find a way to get you out," she hissed. "You have absolutely no right to be in there."

"Maybe not. But, here I am and, right now, there's nothing I can do about it without moving into yet another body. You want to volunteer?"

Cassie, not even knowing she was going to do it, punched his face hard. Laurence cried out in pain, blood dripping from his nose.

"You find a way, or I will figure out how to evict you once and for all."

"I can't. No, I mean it," he shouted, raising a hand to defend himself against another punch. "I really don't know how. But, I think I can let Patrick have control again if I… sleep."

Cassie, still in contact with Laurence's mind, felt the fear that pervaded him and was certain it was genuine. *There's no way I dare trust him, though.*

"Do it," she ordered.

As Laurence attempted to put himself into a self-induced trance or coma, a memory leaked out. What he was trying to do was similar to what he'd done after Kay cut his head off. This was something he had done many times throughout the long years of his existence. It was his way of surviving when no suitable victim was immediately available.

With Laurence no longer in control, the body slumped and Patrick surfaced.

"Oh," said Patrick, his intonation at odds with how Laurence had used those same vocal cords. His hand shook as he raised it to his face, gently feeling his nose. His fingers came away streaked with blood.

"Ow. That hurts. But thank you, um, Cassie. Oh, my God. This is mental. I could see what he was doing all the time but I couldn't do anything about it. I can feel him still here inside my head. Do you think you could force him out?"

Cassie's brow furrowed and she bit her lip.

"Ah, no, you can't, can you?" Patrick said. "Not without killing us both."

Cassie shook her head. "Sorry, Patrick."

"Thought not. Look, if it's better to do so, then please… just kill us both."

"No, I don't think I could do that. I don't fully understand the whole taking over someone's body thing. Even though I just watched his memory of how he did it, I don't understand exactly what he did. I never did anything like that – don't ever want to try, either."

"This is so weird. It's like I've got his memories but I'm still me, Patrick. But I feel him, right here in my head and I know that if he decides to wake up, he will come out and take control… whenever he likes."

"Is he eavesdropping on us?"

Patrick shook his head. "I have absolutely no idea."

Diversion: Clone

She sighed as she popped out of the portal, not at all surprised when she found herself back in Starbucks.

That same cup of coffee was waiting for her, so she sat on the chair and swigged half of it down, as usual.

How many more times? I've lost count. Always the same date, the same people at the tables, the same cup of coffee. Yet, only I get older. How much older? It feels like I've already been doing this for several months.

Her mind ticked off the usual sequence. *Starbucks, see a new copy of herself get crushed, leave Castle Mall and then run away from nasties through one or more portals – always underground for some reason and not always in the same places – until I come back out at Starbucks again.*

She took another gulp of coffee.

Jesus, I thought Groundhog Day was supposed to be fiction. What an existence. How much longer do I have to go through this? At least I've found a couple of places where the nasties don't seem to go.

The bus man had been present on several occasions and shown her locations that appeared safe from attack. There were a couple in the old hospital on Saint Stephen's Road as well as in the deserted offices of Anglia Square's later years. Sometimes, it was possible to utilise empty rooms in the Royal Hotel, both back when it had been a hotel and, later on, when it had been converted into offices. The bus man often stayed to protect her from the nasties while she slept.

Sometimes, I'm not sure whether having to put up with that idiot is any better than facing the nasties. He won't shut up – always talking a complete load of crap, even when I'm trying to get some sleep.

She finished the coffee and exhaled. She realised was still wearing her black coat – it was rather a stupid colour to wear in this heat. But it had pockets to stash all the stuff she needed to constantly carry around. It wasn't the one she'd originally found in the stables all those months ago. Enough of the portals came out in shop basements that she'd managed to grab a reasonable assortment of clothes to fit most weather situations. Of course, carrying them around was almost impossible but she'd stashed them in the various safe places so that, if she happened to be there at the right time and was in need of a change of clothing, she could often lay her hands on something suitable. And, when she couldn't, she just had to put up with the heat or cold… *and my own BO.*

Well, I'm never here in the June 2018 heat for long. A couple of portals away it'll probably be raining or even snowing. I've seen it all – the big freeze of 1963, the swarms of aphids in the late 1970s, even flooding – not sure when that was.

Outside Starbucks, the multi-armed and legged creature did a thumbs up sign to her. It usually did that now, though it didn't when she first came back here. There were subtle differences in her experiences every time.

Alternate timelines or what? I suppose I should be glad they're different or I'd've gone completely mad by now. If I haven't already.

A familiar figure appeared outside the shop.

Yeah, I know. Here comes another one of me to get killed by the wall or gate falling, or whatever it is. I can feel it but it never actually affects me directly – only these alternative Cassies.

But she knew that not all of those Cassies got squashed. Although she'd watched a few run off, she never figured out where they went.

I suspect they get picked off by nasties sooner rather than later. I wonder which type this one is – a runner or a squisher?

Normally, she would have watched the latest Cassie until she either got squished or ran away. But, just recently, the urge to go and help had been growing. This time it was even stronger so, wishing the feeling would go away, she gave in to the compulsion and walked out the door much earlier than normal. She ambled straight through the creature that only she and the latest Cassie clone, or whatever it was, could see.

She saw the intake of breath from the clone as she was spotted. The clone stuttered for a moment and then asked, "A-are you me?"

"Yeah, and you'll probably be dead unless you start moving. Follow me," she said, running deeper into the mall. Passing the spiral staircase, she heard footsteps thudding behind her and thought, *Hell, I really was unfit back then. I've probably lost the best part of a stone over the last few months.* She looked behind to see the girl puffing as she ran, trying to catch up. *Why did I do this? Do I really* care enough about these alternatives or clones or whatever they are, to want to save one? Am I one of them, as well? What am I going to do with her anyway? I suppose it will make a change from running away from the nasties on my own.

"Why are you me?" came the voice behind her, in between the gasps.

"Don't question it," she replied. "And, anyway, I'm not exactly you. I just happen to have shared your life up until today, though I've already lived several months longer."

"Huh?" came the reply.

Yeah, a definite 'Huh?' – I could ask the same. Ah, this place is doing its usual transforming thing. Maybe the whole place is one giant portal.

As she veered right past the staircase, she watched the appearance of the pathetic water feature around which it circled. She'd found out that it had been taken out a few years after Castle Mall opened. It had been long gone by 2018. It wasn't very impressive, which might have accounted for its demise and removal.

I wonder if there's another way out up that staircase.

She slowed and the girl following her caught up. There was something innocent about the girl's face. *It's almost like she hasn't had quite the full experience I've had. Or is it more like she's not been completely finished off properly?*

"The shops are changing," the girl stated.

"Yep, they do that. We're going back in time to 1991. This whole place is like walking backwards through time. Wait for it…"

"Wait for what?"

"The elevators."

The girl started running towards them.

"No, don't try to get on one," she shouted.

"Why not?"

"Watch," she said, knowing what was about to happen. "There, see, they've gone," she added as they winked out of existence. A few seconds later, as was usual, they were left gazing up at the night sky.

It was still warm.

"Summer, this time," she told the girl.

"Where's the roof gone?"

"Told you. Time travel. We're now in 1991, just as they were building Castle Mall. Follow me, there's a way out somewhere. They keep moving it around as they build new bits. Sometimes, we come out in November when there are fireworks happening."

"Are you me or aren't you? I saw the little scar on your face. Just like mine."

"Near enough."

"What do I call you? Are you also 'Cassie'?"

"Yeah, that would be a bit confusing. Maybe not."

"So what's your name then?"

Despite the heat, a shiver ran through her as she said, "You can, er, call me, um… Kay."

"Why are you Kay if you look like me? Are we, like, sisters or something? I never had a sister. Georgia's the nearest I've ever had. Do you know Georgia?"

"Of course, I know Georgia," she snapped. "Why wouldn't I?"

Damn, but she's asking some lame questions.

"I feel weird," the girl said.

"Yeah, me too. You'll get used to it. I've been feeling weird for months now."

"I feel empty. Like I'm not quite me. What's happened to me?"

"No idea what you are exactly. There are lots of you."

"Huh?" the girl repeated.

"Yeah, 'huh' sums it up all right. Sometimes, I'm not sure I know what I am, either. Maybe I'm the real one and you're a fake one. Or vice-versa. Maybe one day I will find out."

"Were you ever called Cassie?"

"Yeah, but let's just say I am now Kay. It's simpler."

"Why Kay?"

The woman now known as Kay stared at the girl and snarled, "You damn well know why."

"Do I?"

Shit, why did I have to pick a dumb one to rescue? Are they all like this?

Goodbyes

Choices

"Who the hell is he and what's he doing there?" Georgia whispered, staring at the unconscious man lying on a mattress beside Cassie's bed. "He reminds me of someone."

"Not surprising," Cassie said. "Meet Patrick – Jason's dad."

"What?" Georgia gasped. "He can't be – he's dead, isn't he? And this guy is way too young. Surely–"

"Um, time travel…"

"Oh yeah. I forget. Damn, how can I forget things like that when you're around?"

"Sometimes, I wish I could forget, too."

"Sorry Cass. Oh, wait, didn't you mention him the day after the party, when Jason came steaming round?"

"Yes, I'm pretty certain I did."

"But wasn't that supposed to be a – what did you call it? – an alternative time string?"

"Timeline," Cassie corrected. "The one where you didn't know me and were going out with Jason instead of Mark. And Patrick was still very much alive."

"Was alive? Is he dead then? Doesn't look it. I thought I saw him breathing. Love the stubble – that's definitely a Jason touch."

"This Patrick is from 2000, which accounts for how he looks. He told me he worked at the hospital and was there when they brought Laurence in. Somehow, Laurence managed to keep his consciousness alive even though his body was dead – I now know he's done it lots of times before. When Patrick was alone with the corpse, Laurence transferred his mind into Patrick's head."

"Oh, my God. Are we safe from him doing the same to us?"

"You probably are – but I'm definitely not. He needs someone in the same family line. Apparently, Patrick must be connected to that line somewhere. Not sure how and when."

"And that's how Laurence survived for thousands of years?"

"He mostly jumped from an old live body straight into a younger one. But, from what I can make out, there wasn't always a suitable candidate. So sometimes he had to, sort of, hibernate for a while until someone came along whose body he could steal."

"Yetch," Georgia said, screwing up her face. "So why is he out cold?"

"Because, although I managed to force Laurence to let Patrick have control back over his body, Laurence is still inside. I think he might be capable of taking the body over as soon as Patrick sleeps normally. So, I reached into his head and found out how to put him into something like suspended animation. At least, that's what I think I did."

"You did what? You can invade other people's minds as well now?"

"Yeah – it's just as scary for me as well."

"And he agreed to this?"

"Patrick did – Laurence certainly didn't. But, while Patrick is like this, I'm hoping that Laurence can't escape and take over."

"And Laurence, does he know that he's actually your son?"

"He does now. Didn't believe it at first. Well, not until I called him Ka'Tor and spoke to him in the tribe's language. Then, he didn't have much choice."

"But why didn't he recognise you last year when he was hunting you down?"

"As Ka'Tor, he was only four years old when he last saw me, and it has been a hundred and forty thousand years to him. Just how much can you remember from when you were four? And that was only fourteen years ago for you."

"Yeah, when you put it like that… So, why is he here and what are you going to do with him? And why does he look like he's got a broken nose?"

"That's from when Laurence was in control and I basically punched him in the face when he annoyed me."

"Hah. In that case, remind me never to annoy you."

Cassie couldn't help smiling. "He's here as I need to keep an eye on him. And also, do you remember me telling you what happened just before the device sent me back to the Stone Age?"

"When you pressed the red button?"

"Yes."

"Hmm, well… maybe… some of it."

"I left a couple of bits out."

"Oh?"

"I didn't mention what the device called up."

"What do you mean 'called up'?"

"I think it was an alien. The device called it a creator."

"You are absolutely shitting me! Alien? Creator? What? Like some kind of god? What did it look like?"

Cassie shook her head and shut her eyes, trying to picture the thing, some sort of creature whose form her brain refused to comprehend. All she could remember was the screeching noise of the communication between it and the device. "I can't describe it because my head couldn't take it in – it was like my mind refused to see it. Maybe, if I had seen it, I would have gone completely mad." *Maybe, I already am.*

"Hell… but, you said two things…"

"Yes, there was something else there as well. Three somethings, actually. They were like shadows, only a hint that they were there at all. I'm pretty certain that either they were trying to hide or that the device was trying to hide them from the alien. Maybe the alien would have killed them if it had found them there."

"What were they?"

"One of them looked like me."

"Ah, more time travelling then?"

"Yes, and as I have no memory of it, then it must still be in my future."

"Oh, I think I see. And the other two?"

"Well, at the time, I had half an idea who the second one was, but no clue as to who the third one might have been. But, I think I do now."

"Who were they, then?"

"The third one was Patrick."

"Oh right. And the other one?"

Cassie looked at Georgia and did a little nod of her head towards her friend.

"What? No. No way. I said I was joking the other day. You are definitely *not* pulling me backwards and forwards through time."

"You're not even the slightest bit curious?"

"Shut up – of course I am. But, you scare me, Cass. You really do scare me."

"Join the club – what I can do scares the living daylights out of *me* most of the time."

"Yet, you still do it?"

"Sometimes, I don't think I have a choice. And that's what's been really bugging me. I've been jumping around to someone else's tune for ages. And I'm fucking sick of it. I need to take back control of my life once and for all."

"But what if you, um, screw things up again like you did last time?"

"Yeah, I know. But I've got to get to the bottom of it all for various reasons."

"Like what?"

Cassie stepped across to the sheet of paper stuck to the wall. It was now criss-crossed with lines, scribbled notes, crossed out notes, redrawn lines, post-it notes stuck over the notes and lines, plus a few bits of string between drawing pins joining distant parts.

"Ah," Georgia said. "I was going to ask you what it was – but then I saw the guy on the mattress, which made this thing slip my mind. So, like, what is it?"

"I've been trying to figure everything out. Right from the start. Everything I can remember that was weird from when I was little."

"It's a complete mess," Georgia stated unnecessarily. "You've been watching too many cop shows by the look of it."

"Haven't had time for TV. Anyway, even theirs aren't as screwed up as this. Theirs don't cover thousands of years and take in alternative timelines."

"So, what does it all mean?"

"The ones marked in blue are all to do with Robert Kett. I'm the yellow ones and Ka'Tor and Laurence are all shades of red. Kay is the black lines."

"What are the grey and green ones."

"Great Grandad Charlie is grey and the bits in green all relate directly to the device, which is why it mostly runs alongside Laurence on this side, a bit with Mum – she's the pink lines in the centre here – and then with me until it went back into the past."

"Am I on there anywhere?"

"No, not yet."

"Yet? I'm not sure I like the 'yet' part."

Cassie picked up the pack of coloured marker pens. "Choose a colour."

"Metallic blue, to match my nails," Georgia laughed, examining the chart. She pointed to an abbreviation. "Some of it looks like it's written in code. Mark would love this, you know. He'd probably put it all in a spreadsheet or write an app or something."

"Yeah, I could imagine the geek in him trying to sort this all out and making more sense of it."

"Why did you do it like that?"

"Because I started while earlier me was still around and, when I was her, I hadn't understood what it was all about. Also, she was still around when I'd started going back to see Mum a few months before she died. And I couldn't let her know as I didn't tell me when I was her."

"What? Eh? Yeah, oh, I think I know what you mean. But, did you say you've been back to see your mum again?"

"Yes, it, er, hasn't been easy. But, I've been trying to help her and, I think, she's been asking questions that have been helping me see a bigger picture."

"Like what?"

"Like, what was the device doing back in the Stone Age in the first place? Why is everything running in a circle?"

"What circle?"

"Me being sent to the past to give birth to Ka'Tor who, by stealing life after life, eventually becomes Laurence who is then my father so that I come along in order to get sent back in time to give birth to him. That circle."

"Oh right..."

"But, any attempt to break the circle will remove both me and him from existence," Cassie said, her voice starting to shake. "Each of us relies on the other being born. We are responsible for, well, creating each other. Not only just us, either – my mum and Grandad, and probably a good number of their ancestors as well. The brown line is Grandad."

"What's the short brown dotted line?"

"Yeah, that's another thing. That's the version of Grandad that Kay knew."

"The evil one?"

"Yes."

"What about him?"

"Well, that's another one of those paradox situations. When Kay was created, the device took the memories from the Kay that died and inserted the earliest ones into the newly created clone of me that was to become Kay."

"So?"

"So, where did Kay's memories originally come from – the ones with evil Grandad, that is? Surely, someone must have experienced them in the first place – so who?"

"Oh yeah, I think I see what you mean," Georgia said, a frown crossing her forehead. She shrugged, adding, "Damned if I know. Um, what's this big green question mark near the top?"

"Yeah, that's a weird one. I found out from Laurence that, when he was Ka'Tor, he thought he'd killed me back in the Stone Age."

"Was that before you managed to come back?"

"It was the exact same time. I remember coming back. He remembers killing me and, get this… drinking the blood from my heart while it was still warm."

"Eeew! Yuck. Was he kidding?"

"I think he genuinely believed it."

"Gross."

"Absolutely. But, even with all of this mess, I still feel I'm missing something else really important – maybe many somethings. But, the more I've gone into this, the more I've felt that someone must have set the whole thing up in the first place. Someone must have sent the device back into the past for Ka'Tor to use. Without the device, none of this would have been possible."

"Hell. And you think I can help solve it? I can barely spell and, while I did eventually get the hang of differential equations thanks to Mark, unravelling the mysteries of time travel and devices is way, way out of my league. You need someone far better than me."

"But there's no one far better than you, Georgia," Cassie said, her voice suddenly breaking. "You have always been here for me. You and your mum and dad looked after me and helped me when Mum died, and later on, when we thought Grandad was going senile, you were the one I looked to, to keep myself just about stable. You've always been my best friend. Who else is there? Right now, I need my best friend more than ever. Please Georgia?"

Cassie, in tears, flung her arms around Georgia while the latter stood there speechless, though her mouth opened and closed several times as if she had no idea what to say. Slowly, her arms encircled Cassie and she rested her cheek on the top of Cassie's head as she stroked her hair. As she did so, her eyes gazed at the mess of notes on the wall, trying to make the slightest bit of sense of it.

In that, she failed.

"I… I'll think about it," Georgia whispered after a while. "But, I'm really scared, Cass, I really am totally scared."

"Oh Georgia, so am I… so am I. But, those shadows I saw mean that you, me and Patrick are going to have to go back into the past to confront the device about what's going on. I can't ignore it. If I do, then all it does is create yet another paradox. Also, I've got to try to stop Laurence once and for all. He mustn't be allowed to destroy any more lives."

"But what about the circle?" Georgia said, releasing Cassie and passing her a tissue plucked from a box on the bedside cabinet.

"I think we're now outside that circle. He's already fathered me and I've already given birth to him. We're now on a new path… I think."

"I don't like it," Georgia said slowly, "but maybe I don't have a choice…"

"Nor do I," Cassie whispered. "And that's what's the most annoying. Even when I'm trying to take control, I still feel I'm jumping to someone else's beat."

Let Me Die

"He survived having his head cut off?" Rebecca said, her voice weak, and quivering in horror. "And stole someone else's body?"

Cassie nodded. It was the twenty-first of December 2010 and, outside, snow still lay on the ground after a couple of weeks of wintery weather.

When she'd first arrived, her mother barely had enough energy to keep her eyes open. Cassie had immediately started her hands-on magic and, gradually, her mum had revived. Once she determined Rebecca was strong enough, Cassie had given her a full account of what had happened since she'd last seen her.

"Jesus!"

"Yeah, and you saying that makes me wonder what he was doing two thousand years ago as well."

Her mother shook her head. "Oh no, not that. Surely, he couldn't have been responsible for whatever happened back then, could he?"

"I hope not. Not that I've ever really believed in all that stuff."

"So, what now?"

"I've got him stashed away in this very room, eight years in the future."

Cassie elaborated about how she was holding Patrick in something that was a cross between suspended animation and a coma so that Laurence could be suppressed. "He probably isn't really ageing much but, just in case, I suppose I'd better wake him up every few days for a meal or even just a glass of water," she added when Rebecca asked what was keeping him alive.

"And you sleep in the same room?" Rebecca then queried.

"Yes, but every morning, I go back to the previous evening and move him forward to the current day. That means he isn't actually there at night while I'm asleep. I wouldn't be able to sleep with him there – in a coma or otherwise."

Rebecca frowned.

"What?" Cassie asked.

"You always time travel into the past by a few hours to bring him to what is then the current day?"

"Er, yes."

"Not from the present to the future from the evening before?"

"No, I thought about doing that but, although I think I could – in fact, I'm pretty sure I could – it feels safer to only travel to the past from the present. I sometimes wonder if I travelled into the future then it might not actually exist until I've already lived through it in the normal way."

"But, didn't you tell me that you once overshot when you came back from Robert Kett's time?"

Cassie nodded. "Yes, I ended up in May – about a month from now. I've thought about what had happened that day many times over. But it was on a timeline that, as far as I know, no longer exists, because that was all reset by the, er, device when it fixed things."

It was probably the creator alien that did the fixing. I never told her about that.

"Um, just how many times has it needed to reset things?"

"Huh? Oh. Well, only the once as far as I know."

"Really? There was the whole Robert Kett thing and then when you waved at the barrow boy, who turned out to be our ancestor, Arthur, and he got knocked down by the tram. That's two, surely."

"Oh yes – though I think both of those were fixed in one go."

"Would you know of any more timelines that needed fixing? Maybe there were so many changes that your memory couldn't hold onto them and they have effectively been wiped out."

"Oh, I hadn't thought of that. What other timelines are you thinking of?"

"Well, the ones with Kay and who you've called evil Grandad for a start."

"Ah yes. Of course."

"Maybe I can help, too, by writing things down as I think of them when you're not here."

"Are you sure you're up to it?"

"Every time you're here, you work your hand magic over me while we talk and it really rejuvenates me, even if it only lasts a few hours."

"You know I'd cure you if I could."

"Yes, well maybe you are slowly curing me and that is beginning to worry me. Maybe you should stop."

"What? Why?"

"Cassie," Rebecca said, her voice shaking, her eyes shut. "You know that I'm due to die in just over a month's time."

"Oh please, Mum. Don't remind me."

"It makes me wonder..."

"What?"

"No, maybe if I say something, it might cause another paradox."

"You can't just leave it like that. What were you going to say?"

Rebecca sighed and, after a pause, said, "Maybe you need me to die in order for you to become strong enough to deal with what happened with the portals."

"Huh? No, surely not. What makes you say that?"

"Look, when I first saw you last February, it didn't take long for me to realise how much you'd grown up compared to the younger version of you still living with me. Your younger self was plagued by nightmares of being burnt alive and various other insecurities that I could never get you to see were just in your mind. Or so I thought at the time."

"Yes," Cassie whispered. "I know."

"Maybe if you hadn't become strong enough by having to deal with my death and your grandad's imposed senility, you wouldn't have been able to come through the portals episode, gone back to Kett's rebellion and ended up back in the Stone Age. And, as it turns out that we are all his descendants in one way or another, then without that all happening, I wouldn't have been born, either."

"Oh, please don't confuse it any further. I've got a whole wall chart full of that sort of stuff."

"A what?"

Cassie told Rebecca about the chart.

"Sounds fascinating. I'd love to see it."

"Yes, but there are just too many places where cause and effect either seem to be back to front, or there is only the effect with no associated initial cause. Christ, I'm beginning to sound like the device now. I started the chart to try and get things straight in my own head. My attempt at unravelling everything seems to have made the confusion even worse. For every single thing I think I've figured out, two more confusing things get added into the mix."

And I dare not tell her about Ka'Tor drinking the warm blood from my heart. She's probably not strong enough to handle that.

Rebecca sighed. "Yes, and that's why you should stop trying to cure me."

Cassie shook her head, not wanting to hear what Rebecca was about to say.

"Cassie, if you change the date of my death, you risk breaking that circle once more and end up with a whole new paradox that might never get resolved. So, please, no more. In order for you and all of us to continue to live in the way we remember and are destined to do, you really must stop trying to help me."

Cassie mouthed 'No' and lay down beside her mother and burst into tears as she wrapped her arms around her.

After a while, Rebecca whispered, "The portals are getting closer, you know. Maybe if I touch one it will whisk me away to somewhere better."

Cassie shook her head and did her best to dry her eyes. "No," she croaked, "I remember seeing you in the days before you… died. You were still here – in body, at least."

"Maybe a portal will take my mind away. I'd like that. Sometimes I like to imagine I can see where they lead to."

Cassie hugged her mum, unable to speak.

Rebecca said, "Did you say earlier that Patrick was in a coma?"

"Er, yes. I made it so that Laurence can't take him over while he sleeps. During the day, he stays in a coma while I get on with what I need to do."

"What, like going to school?"

"No. In 2019 it's the Easter holidays – almost halfway through April."

"Oh, soon be your birthday, then."

"Not really."

"What? But your birthday is the fifteenth."

"Yes, that's the date it should be, but remember that I lived something like four years back in the Stone Age and, for around one of those, I had no memory. So, I don't have any idea of exactly how old I am. I'm probably around twenty-two by now."

"Oh, I see. Yes, of course."

"I now fully understand how Kay felt."

"Oh right. I remember her saying she had no idea how old she was."

"I don't feel any particular age. Too much has happened in my life. Twenty-two is almost too young for how I feel and everything that's happened."

"You've packed more into twenty-two years than I have in thirty-five."

Cassie screwed up her eyes again. Knowing that thirty-five years was all her mum would ever have, she couldn't stop the tears from flowing all over again.

Gone

Cassie stared at her mother lying in the bed. It was Tuesday the twenty-eighth of December – hardly more than a week since her mum had told her she must stop trying to help her. Before Cassie had left, Rebecca had told Cassie to come back no earlier than a week later as her younger self and her grandad would be present much of the time over Christmas.

"Sorry, Cass. But you must let me die," her mum had insisted. "No more paradoxes, please. Promise?"

Hating herself as she did so, Cassie had forced that promise past her lips.

Now, she watched as her mum lay back in the bed, unmoving apart from her eyes that stared out around the room, her gaze slowly drifting here and there. However, they were defocused as if she was seeing nothing of the room itself. She certainly hadn't noticed Cassie appearing in front of her.

Is she seeing the portals?

Cassie closed her eyes and willed her map to appear. She watched the portals for a few seconds. Then, managing to keep them in view while opening one eye a fraction, she observed her mother's gaze. When a portal flared up her mum's eyes drifted towards it. *She really must be seeing them.*

"Mum?" Cassie whispered, fully opening her eyes and banishing her map.

Rebecca turned her head in Cassie's direction but her eyes continued to watch the portals. Even when Cassie was directly in her line of vision, it was as if she was still invisible.

"Mum," she said again, hoping that no one downstairs would hear her.

This time her mum's eyes did focus on her, if only momentarily.

"Gone," Rebecca whispered.

"What's gone, Mum?" Cassie said, relieved that she'd got some sort of response, no matter how small.

But her mother's eyes drifted onto something new and it was as if she had already forgotten that Cassie was in the room.

There was a noise and Cassie heard footsteps coming up the stairs. She disappeared and teleported to a corner of the room. The door opened and her grandad and nine-year-old self entered.

"Mummy," young Cassie whispered as she sat on the bed, tears running down her cheeks

"How are you feeling, Beccy?" Bill said, clasping Rebecca's hands.

"Gone," Rebecca whispered.

"What's gone, love?" he gently asked.

Rebecca's mouth opened and closed as if she found herself incapable of dredging up anything more coherent.

"Please come back, Mummy," her younger self cried. "Please come back."

Oh God, I remember this now. I can't watch it again.

Cassie knew she had to get out of there before she accidentally revealed herself by letting out a whimper.

She pushed herself on by three days – the last day of 2010 – where she found her mother alone once more.

Rebecca's eyes were open and they stared up at the ceiling while her hands lay unmoving upon the duvet cover. Cassie couldn't help noticing how thin and smooth Rebecca's fingers were. It was as if those fingers had forgotten how to move, how to bend and grip things.

Maybe they won't grip anything ever again.

"Mum, can you hear me?" she whispered. There was no response. She wasn't even watching the portals any more.

Oh fuck, I know she said not to, but I've got to try.

She swallowed and raised her hands above her mum, willing the healing to begin. But there was no improvement. She increased the intensity. It was as effective as throwing a lit match onto a glacier hoping it would melt.

She lowered her hands and picked up one of her mum's. There was no reaction to her touch. She was no longer responding to any stimulus, not even the portals. It was almost as if her mind no longer inhabited her body. Cassie reached up to stroke her mother's hair. As she did so, she had the impression that her mother's body was like a shell – a completely empty shell.

Oh hell, she's no longer in there, is she?

Cassie wished she had returned earlier and barely resisted the urge to go back a week. *No, I mustn't. It would be even worse seeing her last conscious moments.*

"Oh, Mum," she whispered, her voice quivering. "I never even had the chance to say goodbye properly."

She leaned over and kissed her mum's forehead. For a moment their eyes met but Cassie could see no spark of recognition in them. Nothing – not even an ember that could be fanned into a flame.

"Goodbye, Mum," Cassie cried, before taking herself off futurewards.

Diversion: Overground

"That's different," Kay said, looking around.

"Nice day. At least it's not snowing this time," the clone said. "Any idea where we are?"

"Not underground, obviously, which is new."

"Oh yeah, so it is. But I thought you said *all* the portals were underground?"

"They have been up until now. So, something's changed. I wonder what? Mind you, I think this is the most portals I've ever been through with one of you. It's been a bit manic, hasn't it?"

"Yes. Non-stop. I think I counted fifteen."

"Really? That's not bad for – what? – less than a day since I first saw you."

"Probably – it feels like only five or six hours – hard to tell. How many do you usually get through?"

"I'm lucky if I get some of you through more than a couple."

"Yes, you've already mentioned… hey, can you smell something weird?"

"Ah, yes," Kay said, sniffing the air. "Chocolate. That means we must be close to the chocolate factory. Okay, City Hall is there. That church is probably the one on Theatre Street – or is it Rampant Horse Street – I'm never really sure where one changes into the other. Right, I've got my bearings so I know where we are. This must be the top floor of the Malthouse car park."

The clone frowned. "That vaguely rings a bell. Um, is that a bomb sticking out of the roof over there?"

"Oh yes, I think I remember reading somewhere that it's a bit of sculpture put there as a reminder of World War Two and the destruction it caused. I've only seen it from a distance before. This means we are back before the Chapelfield shopping centre was built."

"I think that's the exit over there," the clone said, pointing past the few cars parked this high up.

Kay glanced at the cars as they walked towards the shaft that led down to ground level. "Late nineteen-eighties, I reckon."

"How do you know?"

"See that number plate with the 'F' prefix? I think that was 1988 – I've been getting to know them all by heart so that I can figure out when we are."

"There's one there that's got a 'J' at the front. Surely, that's later."

"No. Before 1983 the year was a suffix. It's got a 'T' at the end which means it's, let me think… um, 1978, if I remember correctly."

"Confusing. One question…" the clone said as they entered the stairwell.

"What?"

"If the portals have stopped being underground, then should I look for the next one above ground or is this a one-off?"

Well, this one seems like she's got her head screwed on – probably why we've managed to get through so many portals really quickly. Makes a change from the usual idiots.

At street level, the clone had to concentrate to locate the next portal. "That way, I think," she said, pointing along Chantry Road. "Might be in Chapelfield Gardens or maybe somewhere past there – I'm getting mixed signals."

"Okay," Kay said. "Let's head to Chapelfield anyway. I fancy a sit down in the sun after all the rushing around, especially after trudging through the snow in 1963. And that damned portal coming out in the gents in Tombland again was a bit embarrassing. Okay, not quite as much as last time."

"Last time?"

"Yeah, several Cassies back, we came out of that portal in the nineteen-nineties. By that point, that place was well-known for… well, let's just say, the cottage industry. And we disturbed a couple in… full swing, you might say. Not sure who was the most embarrassed."

The clone said, "Eeew!" and then laughed. "Glad it was deserted when we came out there. Um, I have another question."

"What?"

"What exactly am I?"

"Ah, well this is a first. Most of you think you're the real Cassie and don't believe me when I say that I've already met lots of you."

"I thought I was real at first. But, I quickly realised that, since that time outside Starbucks and the ceiling crashing down – even though it didn't – that I felt odd. It's like I'm incomplete."

"Yeah, I know what you mean. I've felt odd since then myself. Especially as it was a boiling hot day when I went into Castle Mall but, when I came out a few minutes later, it was full-on raining."

"So, probably just another portal, then."

"No, it didn't feel like a portal."

"That last one was different as well as it came out above ground. Er, this chocolate smell is making me hungry. Could we get something to eat soon?"

"Definitely," Kay said.

"Makes a change from chips," the clone said as she polished off the last of her hot dog. They were sitting next to each other on a park bench. Behind them, the traffic on Chapel Field North was starting to increase as the morning wore on. Going by a paper they had found, which may have been from that day or the one before, it was early June 1989 and the weather hinted at the glorious summer to come.

Kay, observing the clone licking ketchup from her fingers, was making her hot dog last. *I really was a fast eater back then. At least there are no nasties around at the moment.*

"So, any sign of a portal?" Kay asked.

"No, though I'm feeling there's possibly something nearer Grapes Hill."

"Might be an observer – there's sometimes one up on top of the cathedral."

Despite the sun shining on them, the clone shuddered. "Like that thing inside Castle Mall?"

"Similar, though they just look at you. I almost think of that one in the mall as a friend nowadays."

"Yuk, it's hideous and talked crap. How many people is it made up of?"

"Yeah," Kay chuckled, "it is and it does – and whoever assembled it must have been well drunk."

Kay looked at the bandstand as she took another bite. Twenty minutes previously, on their way into the park, the clone had paused next to it, saying, "I think there was a portal here but it's faded almost to nothing at the moment. Maybe it's what was confusing me earlier on."

Well, Kay thought, *I've never used one that came out there. And, while it's nowhere near as high as the Malthouse roof, it's definitely far from being underground.*

Beside her, there was a hiss as a can of drink was opened.

"She's in a hurry," the clone said after downing a quarter of the can in one go. She was gazing across to the opposite side of the park. A girl, who looked barely into her teens, dressed in a stripey black and white t-shirt and blue shorts, was running along a pathway, her curly blonde hair streaming out behind as she ran. In one hand, she had something long and thin wrapped in cloth. "Is that something just behind her?"

Kay looked and could see an almost transparent figure drifting along a few feet behind the girl.

"Nasty?" the clone asked.

"Not sure, it's a bit like the bus man, a ghost maybe. It's not attacking her and I think she might be talking to it as she's running."

"Ah, look over there – just coming past that restaurant place. Those are definitely nasties, aren't they?"

"Yes, and they're after that girl. I hadn't realised they hunted other people as well. Let's hope they don't spot us instead."

"Yeah, I've had enough of running away from them. What types are these? They look a bit like the ones we encountered when we first met."

"Oh, was that the slash-faced things?"

"Yes, can't you remember?"

Kay shook her head. "It all blurs into one. All you versions of the Cassie I once was – I've rescued so many – I forget which ones we first saw."

"Really? What do you remember from before it all started?"

"Don't ask. Anyway, you will have experienced the same things… especially, you know, him…"

"Oh, yes. Poor Grandad."

"Poor?"

"Well, he has gone a bit mental, hasn't he?"

"Yeah, that's one way of describing it."

"You say you've been doing this for – what now? – a couple of years?"

Kay shrugged, her eyes still watching the running girl who had diverted her path towards the bandstand. "It feels like it. I can't tell any more."

"They're getting closer," the clone said.

Kay watched as the girl ran up the steps of the bandstand, the ghost close on her heels. The nasties, who were three in number, had already halved the gap. Their arms were waving above their heads and their mouths were working.

Probably talking the usual load of old bollocks.

"Oh, she's gone," the clone said.

"I thought you said that portal had faded away."

"Um, yes, but it's now gone back to full strength."

"I don't like this," Kay said, getting to her feet. "They've lost their victim, so they'll probably be on the lookout for… damn, yes – they're turning in our direction. Come on – let's move before they spot us."

"Grapes Hill?"

"If you still think there's something there…"

They both ran for the park entrance that came out near the Grapes Hill roundabout.

"Head for the bridge," the clone said. "It feels like there might be a portal on it somewhere."

Dodging the traffic on Cleveland Road, they dashed around the curve adjacent to the roundabout, taking the pathway towards Upper Saint Giles and the pedestrian bridge over the dual carriageway.

"I've walked up and down Grapes Hill several times when it was just a narrow street with terraces packed along both sides," Kay said as they ran onto the bridge.

"Fantastic," the clone said, running ahead of Kay. "You'll have to take me there sometime. I'd love to see that."

"Wish I could but, as you know, you can't tell where a portal will take you. It might be anywhere. Talking of which – any sign of it? Hey, come back. Don't get too far ahead."

"Yes, I think it's right h–"

Kay halted abruptly. The clone had disappeared.

"Shit and damn it," she spat, feeling evidence of the portal's existence. It was located where the bridge did a ninety-degree turn left before the pathway spiralled back to the ground on Earlham Road. "And I thought that one was more intelligent."

She looked back along the bridge. There were no immediate signs of any nasties on her trail. She walked up to where the portal was located and extended her hand into its influence. Instead of taking her anywhere, all she felt was a slight tingle.

Damn thing's faded already.

She sighed and carried on down the curve. A glance up at the roofline of the Roman Catholic Cathedral across the road revealed the ghostly outline of an observer staring down at her.

"And you can piss off as well," she muttered at it, not caring whether or not it could hear her.

"Pardon?" said an old woman rushing in the opposite direction. The woman's wide-brimmed hat made it difficult to see her face.

"Oh, sorry," Kay muttered. "Didn't see you there."

"That's okay, Kay," the woman said as she trotted along.

Kay took another couple of steps and stopped. *Huh? Was that a stutter or did she call me by name?*

She turned around to see that the old lady was much further up the path than expected – she was almost at the point where the clone had disappeared. Kay frowned.

Have I met her before? There's something familiar about… nah, who am I kidding? Old ladies looking like that are probably ten-a-penny around here.

Kay watched the woman stop to stare at where the portal had been.

Can she see something there? Yes, she's aware of it, I'm sure.

Running back up the curve of the pathway, she called, "Hey, what can you see there? Do you know what it is?"

But the woman ignored her, seemingly intent on what had gripped her attention. Kay felt the portal flare up. When it died back down, the old woman was no longer in sight.

Birthday

Pounds from Heaven

Cassie stared at the calendar hanging on the kitchen wall. It was Monday the fifteenth of April and a birthday card from her grandad sat on the kitchen table. It had '18' printed in a large font on the front.

"I'm not eighteen," she muttered and sighed. "And I'm not sure I even feel twenty-two. I don't know what to feel."

For her, it had been only two days since she'd left her mum back in December 2010. The shock resulting from seeing the state she had been in was far from wearing off. It was like losing her all over again.

It IS losing her all over again.

Cassie paced, not knowing what to do with herself. The house was quiet as her grandad had gone to the shops for some milk and other odds and ends. Upstairs in her bedroom, Patrick lay in his induced coma.

The knock on the front door made her jump. When she opened it, the postman handed her a mixture of white and brightly-coloured envelopes containing what would most likely be more birthday cards. But he then waved a brown envelope at her. She frowned and took the letter from his hand and saw that, like all the other post, it was addressed to herself.

"That one needs a signature," he said, producing a form.

She signed for it and, after closing the door, dropped the pile of birthday envelopes onto the small hallway table. Opening the brown envelope, she began to read.

"What the fuck?" she whispered, after reading it. Then, after reading it all the way through again, added. "You have got to be joking."

There was another noise at the front door as her grandad let himself in. He saw the look on her face and frowned at the letter she proffered. He put the shopping bags down and took the sheet of paper from her to read it for himself.

He let out a whistle. "Happy birthday indeed. A hundred and fifty thousand?

Could it be a scam?"

"I don't know. It just says I inherited it, nothing to pay. Scams usually want the victim to pay a small amount of money upfront to release a large amount – and, of course, that large amount never actually exists. If this is a scam then I don't know how they expect it to work."

"But, more than a hundred and fifty thousand pounds?"

"Yes, I know. But look at what it says about the age I get to inherit it."

"On your eighteenth or twenty-second birthday, whichever comes first. What do... Oh, I see. But how do *they* know?"

"Well, obviously someone does. But apart from us two and Georgia – and I suppose maybe the ghost of Robert Kett – not that he's in a position to tell anyone else. No one else knows about my four years in the Stone Age."

"Laurence."

"Yeah – obviously him, too."

"Except that these solicitors apparently do – I presume that's what they are?" he said, pointing at the name on the headed paper.

Cassie shrugged. "Okay, I suppose one other person knew..." she whispered.

"Who?"

Cassie sighed. "Can't be her, though. She... well, she died in 2011."

"Ah."

"I, er, I've been meaning to tell you."

"What, that you've been back to see... her? Your mum."

"How did you know?"

"You've been quite moody these past few weeks. I knew something was going on and then I remembered what Rebecca had said to me just before that last Christmas we had with her. When she told me about giving you the device thing at her funeral."

"What did she say?"

"I'd assured her I'd look after you. She'd smiled and said that she knew I would while I could, which puzzled me at the time. Of course, I now know what she meant. None of us realised that Laurence and that repression thing he did to me would swap our roles completely around. You told her all about that?"

"Yes," Cassie said with a sigh. "Curse him."

"Is he still upstairs?"

"As Patrick he is."

"I really don't like him being up there, conscious or not."

"Nor do I, but it's not Patrick's fault that he got tied up with this."

"Is he still definitely out cold with no chance of waking up as Laurence?"

Cassie nodded, hoping that she had the ability to keep Laurence subdued.

"It wasn't all your mum said, you know," he continued.

"Oh?"

"Yes, she once told me that she'd seen older you. Of course, at the time, I had no idea what she was talking about. But I played along with the idea as it seemed to perk her up for a few weeks. Almost like her old self, she was."

Yeah, I know why – and why she wouldn't allow me to keep on helping her.

"And then she went completely downhill a day or two after Christmas. The doctors couldn't do anything. It was, uh, it was like she'd been, um... s-switched off is how I remember thinking of it at the time."

Cassie saw the tears forming in her grandad's eyes. Her own were just as moist. He dropped the letter back down onto the table with shaking hands. She hugged him close and he returned the gesture.

"By then, you were spending a lot of time with Georgia's family."

"Yes, I remember. They were trying to keep me occupied, trying to take my mind off what was happening back here. And what, I suppose, you were having to deal with on your own. But, I do remember it. I remember seeing her getting thinner and weaker day by day. And then, that day when she no longer said anything and didn't even seem to realise we were there."

He sighed, sniffed and whispered, his voice shaking, "No one should ever have to bury their own daughter. It was just so unfair. She had so much to live for but..."

Cassie clasped him closer and they clung to each other for what seemed to be several minutes. Finally, the long moment passed and they let each other go.

"I better put the shopping away. Don't want the milk going off."

"I'll help you," Cassie whispered.

He picked up the letter. "But a hundred and fif-fifty thousand," he said. "That's just so much larger than what Kay left you last year."

"Yes – but how the hell did I get in line for something like that? I don't know anyone with that sort of money who'd want to give it to me. That would buy most of a small house and… oh…"

"What?"

"That safe house of Kay's – when I was last there it was going to be sold at some sort of auction."

"But wasn't that nearly a year ago?"

Cassie nodded.

"So, why wait until now?"

"The letter does mention that the solicitors had been instructed to wait until my eighteenth…"

"…or twenty-second," Bill interrupted.

"…birthday, yes."

"Well, they got the date right." He picked up the envelope that Cassie had left on the hallway table. "First class, signed for. Posted Friday."

"Yes," Cassie whispered.

"Are you going to ring them?"

She nodded.

Cassie stared at the computer screen. It was the day after Easter Monday and, having returned from school, she was viewing her bank account. When she'd logged in, a message had announced that her account had been upgraded to a full adult version. But, that wasn't what held her attention.

It was the amount the account held. A week ago, it contained just over nine thousand pounds. The usable notes and coins in Kay's boxes had totalled over fifteen thousand. Over the past few months, both herself and her grandad had occasionally added small amounts to each of their accounts, not wanting to raise any suspicion that they'd suddenly come into a larger amount of money after years of having to live frugally.

The loft space in the house still contained a number of the boxes, though these mainly held items that were no longer legal tender. The previous year, not long after he'd finally sorted all of it out, Bill had made a rough inventory of everything before hauling the boxes up into the loft space. The area was partially boarded – something he had done himself long before Cassie had been born – which was for the good given the weight of the coins in the boxes. But, one day, when he'd decided to log everything properly so that he could try selling off some of the more valuable rarer coins and notes, he'd told Cassie that he thought some had gone missing.

"I've not touched them," she'd replied.

"I wasn't accusing you," he said. "Maybe I've put them somewhere safe – and now I can't find them."

"Then again, with me in the house dodging about in time, it could well be my future self. Maybe I will have a need of old money and had to take it before you decided to sell it off."

"Hmm, yes – I hadn't thought of that."

"So, what's actually missing?"

"Probably only a single bag, but it contained the really old notes and coins from the mid-eighteen hundreds. It wasn't much. Probably about sixty or seventy pounds in notes plus a number of florins and shillings, if my original scribbled list was correct."

Cassie had shrugged and said, "Well, if I ever find out I needed them, then I'll let you know."

Bill grinned. "I'd better start selling them before future you comes back and takes the rest."

"I'll just come before today and take them first," she'd laughed.

He had chuckled and shook his head.

From the sale of the old notes and coins, they split the profits equally. Both of them had also taken to carrying around notes and coins that could still be legally spent. Also, since it had come in handy on her trip to 1991, Cassie also kept a small number of older coins and notes in a separate wallet inside her jacket. Nothing quite like the bags of money favoured by Kay, but enough to get by on should the need for time travel come up at short notice. But, there must still have been several thousands of pounds in those boxes in notes and coins that went back to the late nineteenth century. She remembered seeing a few odds and ends from earlier than that as well.

"Damn, I'm really rich now," Cassie whispered, gazing at the computer.

The previous week, two days before Good Friday, she and her grandad had attended an appointment with the solicitors. They explained that the hundred and fifty thousand inheritance, being so *small*, wasn't liable for inheritance tax. As with the boxes of money, the name on the original will was S. T. R. Boardal.

Once Cassie had signed various papers, after her grandad had gone through the fine print looking for any catches, the solicitors had authorised the bank transfer. They had queried the references to her eighteenth or twenty-second birthday, but both she and Bill had denied any knowledge of what that might mean. Anyway, she had been requested to bring along her birth certificate, which clearly confirmed that she couldn't be any older than eighteen.

"Was everything in the will left to me?" Cassie had asked.

"Yes, though there were our charges and those of the auctioneer to be accounted for, of course," had come the answer. "Apart from that, no, there were no other recipients and no money was owed to any third party."

Upon returning home, still slightly dazed by the events at the solicitors, she had gone upstairs to check on Patrick, whose state hadn't changed. She then decided to have a good long soak in the bath and had been slightly bemused by the bathroom already being quite warm and moist. It was as if someone else had taken a bath or shower while she and Grandad had been out. She frowned and ran the tap, wondering if Patrick, who was still in the induced coma, had begun sleepwalking.

After the bath, Cassie had started the computer up, logged into her bank account and was staring at the figure on the screen.

It told her that her account held £159,379.18.

If only that money could have been used to save Mum.

Celebration

"I insist," Cassie said, sitting at the computer a couple of days later. She turned to Georgia, adding, "You and your mum and dad have given me so much over the years and now I'm in the position to give some of it back."

They had both taken the afternoon off school to, ostensibly, study for their upcoming exams. However, thoughts of revision had been abandoned as Cassie had wanted to repay Georgia now that she finally had the funds to do so.

"But that must be far more than we ever gave you in the first place," Georgia said, shaking her head.

"Inflation," Cassie replied with a grin. "Look, please don't argue. You can see what my bank account looks like now," she said, waving her hand at the screen. "Anyway, it will help when you decide to go to university."

Georgia sighed as Cassie set up the bank transfer to Georgia's account. A few seconds later, Cassie's phone rang and she authorised the payment.

"There – it's all gone through," Cassie said, peering out the window at the weather. The pavement was still slightly damp from an earlier light shower but, with the afternoon already a couple of hours old, the clouds were starting to drift away and sunshine was breaking through. "Right, as it's clearing up outside, how about a trip into the city for a celebratory meal?"

"Late birthday meal?" Georgia asked. "Or inheritance meal?"

Cassie shrugged, "I have absolutely no idea how old I am now or what date I should be celebrating my birthday – so, yes, okay, let's call it an inheritance celebration meal."

"Only if you let me pay," Georgia said, wagging her finger at Cassie with mock severity. "Especially with what you've just given me."

"No, you can't. It's *my* celebration."

"If you don't let me pay, I won't come," Georgia said, folding her arms and trying her best to look severe. A fit of giggles hit both of them and they hugged.

"Well, if you really, really insist," Cassie said, adding, "Okay, let's go."

"No," Georgia scolded mockingly. "I'm not having my bestie going out on the town looking like that. If we're going for a meal then let's dress the part. I don't think you've tried on half of those dresses I helped you buy for that party."

"I bet most of them no longer even fit me," Cassie protested.

Georgia, with one finger pointing upwards, said, "Upstairs to the wardrobe. No arguments."

"Yes, ma'am," Cassie laughed.

"He's still here, then?" Georgia said, glancing across the bedroom to the spare mattress on the floor.

"Yes, I let him wake up occasionally, just to make sure that Patrick is still in there and Laurence is still asleep."

"You hope... Um, if Laurence pretended to be Patrick, would you be able to tell the difference?"

"Yes, I can dip inside his head – it's like Patrick is all green and soft, while Laurence is red and spiky."

"Creeps me out, it does."

"Yeah, me too," Cassie said, taking off her top and jeans.

"Right, to the job at hand. Hmm, you've not only lost a bit of weight, but those muscles are definitely tighter," Georgia commented as she selected dresses, skirts and tops for Cassie to try on.

"Yeah, now I'm back, I should really try to exercise a bit more to keep things in tone," Cassie said. "Normal living in the Stone Age was all the exercise you needed back then."

"You will have to join my martial arts classes. That will keep you in trim."

"Nag me until I do."

"Don't worry, I will," Georgia laughed before returning her attention to Cassie's wardrobe. "You know, I've never seen you in half of these. How about this dress – it flows nicely without exposing too much and the belt will pull the waist in to fit the new slim-line you. Quite sexy."

"Huh? No, 'sexy' is not required. I've had enough of that sort of stuff with Jason and lecherous tribesmen."

"Ah, but you might finally meet Mister Right."

"Oink, flap!" Cassie snorted but, after Georgia gave her a 'look', added, "Okay, I'll give it a go. It's nearly three and, if I don't pick one soon, the whole day will have disappeared."

She pulled the dress on, straightened it up, adjusted the belt and inspected herself in the wardrobe mirror. "Okay, are we ready?"

"Not quite."

"What now?"

"Where's your makeup?"

"You know exactly where it is," Cassie sighed and let Georgia complete the makeover. Afterwards, she looked in the mirror and smiled. "Yeah, you're right. You should be a beautician, you know."

"As if. I'd still rather be an astronaut."

Cassie chuckled. "You always used to say that when we were young."

"Yeah, I did. Fat chance of that ever happening," Georgia grinned. "Right, you're just about decent enough to be let out into the wild."

"How about one of the places up Timber Hill?" Georgia suggested. They were at the pedestrian crossing between White Lion Street and the aforementioned incline. They had vetoed several restaurants due to the number of people around. Even though it was a Thursday, the city was quite packed. It was already gone four and they wanted to find somewhere quieter before the evening rush started.

"Yes, we could try one of those," Cassie agreed as they crossed the road. "Or we could go back several weeks to when things weren't quite so hectic."

"No," Georgia said. "You may have half talked me into going back to fit in with what you've already seen happen, but nothing more than that. Okay?"

Cassie smiled. "Yeah, agreed. I was sort of joking, you know."

"I realised that. But maybe such things shouldn't be joked about, especially if you could end up changing the whole of history."

Cassie nodded. "Ah, you're so right. Maybe I've become too familiar with it and need someone to keep reminding me just how dangerous it all is. You are hereby assigned the role of guardian of my sanity."

"Nope, that's like way too big a job," Georgia laughed. "I'd want a proper salary for doing that."

They stopped outside two restaurants in adjacent properties. On the right in the larger building was a Middletons Steakhouse while, to the left, was the more modest establishment of Donnellis Pizzeria.

"Steakhouse or pizza?" Cassie asked.

"I've never been in either," Georgia said. "You?"

Cassie shook her head. "No. Which should we go for?"

"Pizza – they're well tasty," came a voice from behind them. It was a voice Cassie recognised.

Diversion: Tombland

"Sorry. What?" Kay said. "Did you say something?"

The woman had almost walked past her on Tombland when she'd stopped and said something that Kay hadn't quite caught.

"Yes, I said I loved the black outfit with all the pockets."

"Er, yes. It's um…"

"Second half of the twentieth century, I'd say," the woman laughed. "Seventies or eighties? Looks a bit gothic, no… more punk I reckon – especially with all those pocket zips. It would look good riding a motorbike."

"Huh?" Kay looked around, glad that the street was far from crowded. It was just gone eight on a bright Sunday morning… in 1924.

The woman was old and could have been well into her eighties. The skin of her face and hands was wrinkled and mottled with age spots. Her hair, almost pure white but unmistakeably curly, was tied back into a tight bun. It gave the impression it would have fallen well below her shoulders should it have been set free. She was wearing a pale yellow floral dress, quite typical of the era, though the accompanying boots were heavy and out of place when coupled with the dress – almost as much as a temporal anomaly as Kay's outfit.

"What are you talking about?" Kay asked.

There was a mischievous sparkle in the woman's eyes, making it obvious she was enjoying Kay's confusion.

"You know damned well what I'm talking about, Kay," the woman said. "You *are* calling yourself Kay now, aren't you? You look more than old enough."

"Er, well, yes."

"And moving money around back and forth in time to make it worth more?"

Furtively, Kay glanced around, glad to find no one else within earshot.

"You know about the, um, portals, then? You've been through them?"

"Maybe," the woman said with a chuckle. She stared straight into Kay's eyes, which made her feel extremely uncomfortable.

"I can see Cassie in you, still," the old lady said. "Talking of which, I also note that you're on your own. Lost a clone recently, have you?"

"Have we met?"

The old lady laughed. "Have we met? Hah, don't you remember?"

"Wait, you weren't the one I saw disappear into a portal on the bridge over Grapes Hill, were you?"

"That might have been one of them."

"One of them?"

"Things happen in the wrong order."

"Tell me about it."

"I could – but that might have... shall we say... adverse effects."

Kay shook her head. "Exactly who the hell are you?"

The old lady smiled and whispered, "It will all make sense in the end, you know. But, now isn't the right time – you still look far too young. Bye."

Kay stared as the woman strolled away briskly up the incline of Tombland beside the shiny tram tracks. The woman's form grew smaller as she made her way towards Agricultural Hall. Kay frowned. There was something familiar about the determined way the woman walked.

"Impossible," Kay muttered, turning around and entering Tombland Alley.

She passed under the archway of Augustine Steward's house. As she re-emerged into the sunlight, a small piece of the building's crumbling façade dropped from above. Barely missing her nose, it hit the ground in front of her boots where it shattered into pieces. As she turned and looked up at where the plaster had fallen from, she sensed someone beside her.

"Hi, Kay," said the ghost of the Grey Lady, making Kay jump.

"Ah, and you can clear off as well."

"I reckon that's going to all fall down soon."

"No, it won't," Kay said. "It's still standing in the twenty-first century."

"Good, I would feel sad if it fell down."

"Was it your house?"

"No, next door. Come back and visit me when I was alive. I'd like that."

"Sorry, the portals don't go back that far."

"Oh yes, I forgot. Where's dumbo Cassie today? I'm feeling a bit peckish."

"You're too late. Something else – actually, several something elses – have already had her for breakfast."

Shadows

Pizza and Premonition

Cassie swivelled around to see several faces she vaguely recognised. The speaker was the only one she definitely remembered.

"Cassie. Fancy seeing you here," said the tall girl with the short blonde hair.

"Erin," Cassie shrieked in delight, glad she could remember her name. It had been more than four years since they had met at Erin's twenty-first birthday party. However, she realised that, for Erin, it would only have been two months ago. Cassie recognised the other two girls but couldn't remember their names. One of the three boys was also familiar.

"You must remember Megan and Holly," Erin said.

"Yes, of course," Cassie partly lied. She certainly did remember the two girls who had offered moral support at the party but, at that moment, couldn't remember which was which – was Holly the short one or the taller one with the blue-dyed hair? "Hi," she said, "and thanks for… well, you know…"

"You're welcome," the taller one said. "Glad we could help. We did ask Erin about you at uni a few days later."

"Yeah, I did mean to call or text you to make sure you were okay," Erin apologised. "But, you know how life gets in the way… Say, I can't remember – did you meet Luke, Ben and Callum? They were all at the party."

"Er, Callum, yes," Cassie said. "He, um, stood between me and, er, Jason when… you know…"

"Oh yes, he did," Erin said, her head on one side. "Very brave of you, Cal."

Callum shrugged as if a bit embarrassed.

"So, are you going to introduce us to your friend?" Erin said.

"Oh, yes, I'm so sorry. This is Georgia. She's been my best friend since nursery school. She looks after me when I get into trouble."

"Hi," Georgia said, grinning.

"Oh, and does she get into a lot of trouble?" Erin asked with a chuckle.

"Full-time job," Georgia laughed. "If I wasn't dyslexic, I could write a book."

"Erin is Jason's cousin," Cassie said, butting in before Georgia could say anything else. "She very kindly drove me home from her party after…"

"Yeah. I heard all about that," Georgia nodded.

"Have you seen anything of Jason since?" Erin asked.

"Only at school… though we, er, haven't spoken a word to each other," Cassie admitted. *Not since I teleported him naked to a snowy Welsh mountainside – and I'm certainly not going to tell her all about that. Nor about spending four years in the Stone Age, either.*

"He's gone rather quiet since then," Erin said. "I went round to find out how he and his mum were a few days later and it was like he was in shock. He point-blank refused to talk about that night."

Cassie and Georgia exchanged a glance.

"Maybe he's finally taken a good look at himself and realised what a big shit he'd become," Erin added. "Anyway, enough of him. What are you doing here?"

"She's had a bit of a windfall so we decided to come out and celebrate with a meal," Georgia explained.

"Windfall?"

"Yes, an inheritance from a, er, relative in their will," Cassie explained.

"Nice… well, not nice for the relative, obviously. Were you expecting it?"

Cassie shook her head. "No, it came as a bit of a shock, really."

"Yes, a letter turned up a week and a half ago on her eighteenth birthday," Georgia said. "So, here we are trying to celebrate but, as the city is rather heaving, we came up here to see if anywhere's less crowded."

"Oh, happy birthday for a week and a half ago, Cassie," Erin chuckled. "Say, we're all booked into Donnellis – you want to join us?"

"Are you sure?" Cassie said. "I don't want to impose."

"I insist. Anyway, I want to know what you've been up to," Erin said, looking inside the restaurant. "I can see that they've pushed a bunch of tables together at the back – those are probably ours so they should be able to fit you in."

After entering the establishment, Erin talked to a waitress who confirmed that there were no issues adding Cassie and Georgia to the party. The one isolated two-seater table against the side wall was added to the other three making a single long table for all eight of them.

"Sit anywhere?" Georgia asked Erin.

"Yep, we can play musical chairs later," Erin said.

The girl with the blue-dyed hair had already occupied the seat near the wall facing towards the front of the restaurant. Georgia sat next to her and Cassie slipped in beside them. Callum had no choice other than to sit next to Cassie as Erin and the other three had already selected the seats on the opposite side.

They were each handed a menu and, as Cassie started reading it, Georgia said, "Sorry, Erin, I know you mentioned names but I'm not exactly sure who is who – other than you and Callum."

"Oh, apologies. That's Megan next to you. This is Luke," Erin said, indicating the boy opposite Megan. "Those two almost sitting on each other are Holly and Ben," she added indicating those opposite Cassie and Callum.

"Thanks. Um, and if you don't mind me asking, did I hear you say something about university?" Georgia said.

"Yes, that's right. We're all at UEA[1]. We're all doing history, though Luke is doing politics alongside, while the rest of us hope to go down the bone digger route."

"The what?" Cassie said.

"She means archaeology," Callum chuckled. "Just don't get her started about her midnight grave robbing."

"He's joking," Erin laughed. "Anyway, they haven't caught me yet. What about you two?"

"Sixth form, final year," Cassie said.

"Oh yes, of course, I remember my dear, beloved cousin mentioning something like that at the party. What subjects?"

Georgia got in before Cassie could answer. "We're both doing history and sociology, along with health and social care. I'm also doing sports and Cass decided to torture herself by taking English Literature – got the finals soon."

"Don't remind me," Cassie mumbled. "I'm way behind on my revision."

"Hah, more history, eh? Well, between us six, we could probably bore you senseless enough to put you off the subject for life," Erin laughed. "Sport, eh,

---

1   University of East Anglia

Georgia? You certainly look fit enough for that. Talking of which, um, Cassie – please don't take this the wrong way but, is it my imagination or do you look... well... a lot, er, trimmer than you were a couple of months ago?"

Before Cassie could think of a reasonable lie, Georgia butted in with, "Yeah, she's been on the paleo diet." Georgia laughed and then let out a mock screech as Cassie gently kicked her leg under the table.

"Well, it's really looking good on you," Erin grinned. "You must tell me all about it."

Oh no, Cassie thought. *How can I avoid telling her?*

She was saved by the waitress coming over and asking for the drinks order. Apart from Erin, who just wanted water, they decided to share two bottles of white wine and one of red. While those were delivered to the table, they scanned the menus and made selections.

After they'd put their orders in, the conversation turned to archaeology at Georgia's end of the table and history at Cassie's end.

"So, what bits of history have you studied?" Callum asked her.

"Renaissance, Reformation – that sort of stuff."

"Oh right, anything local?"

Cassie shook her head, "No, not really. You?"

"Mainly mediaeval as I'm thinking of specialising in that area. But I've also been interested in the Reformation period for my own reasons."

"Oh, what are they?"

"Well, if I've done the research right, then one of my ancestors was killed in a battle in Norwich."

"Really? Are you trying to trace your family tree?"

Callum nodded. "Yes, it's not always easy."

"My grandad says that as well. He's trying to do ours," Cassie said. "So, who was your ancestor?"

"Actually, I'm not sure of some of the last few connections on that side, but I think my family might have been descended from one of his daughters."

"Oh right. What was his name?"

"Lord Edmund Sheffield," Callum said.

"Whoo, a lord, eh?" Holly laughed. "Do we need to doff our hats to you or tug our forelocks or something similar, m'Lord?"

But Cassie wasn't laughing with the others. Instead, she felt a cold shiver run down her spine.

"Did you say he was killed?" Ben asked.

"Yes. There was a rebellion or peasant uprising here in Norwich back in the mid-fifteen hundreds. He and a few others had been brought in to deal with it."

"Kett's Rebellion," Erin said. "It's quite famous around here."

"Indeed, I've read quite a bit about it."

"Wow, didn't realise your family was involved, Cal," Erin said.

"Nor did I until I started researching. Anyway, there are several rather dubious connections in the family tree I've managed to knock up, so I'm not anywhere near certain I'm correct."

"So, how did his lordship get killed?" Holly asked.

"Apparently, he got pulled off his horse during a battle and some guy smacked him over the head and killed him. I think I read somewhere that he was a butcher. I noted the guy's name down somewhere, but I can't remember what it was right now."

"Fulke," Cassie whispered, closing her eyes for a moment as she relived the moment. *How many times did I see that bastard kill Sheffield before I stopped him?*

"Pardon?" Callum said, frowning. "You okay, Cassie? You look a bit pale."

Cassie was aware of the look of concern on Georgia's face. "Fulke," she repeated louder this time, "and he was a real nasty piece of work..." – she felt Georgia's foot lightly tapping her own under the table – "...from what I read," she added, with a forced grin.

"Ah yes, Fulke," Callum said. "That definitely rings a bell."

He rang more than just my bell, Cassie thought, absent-mindedly scratching the back of her head, her fingers seeking the spot where one of Fulke's thugs had clubbed her. There was now no evidence of the huge bump that had once occupied that spot on her skull.

"I heard there's a plaque to him somewhere in the city," Callum added. "I must try and hunt it down sometime."

"Oh, I know where that is," Cassie said, trying to force herself to be as normal as she could fake. "I, er, I could take you there and show it to you sometime... if you want."

"Really? Yes, I'd love that. Thanks, Cass – or do you prefer 'Cassie'?"

"Either will do," she said, unable to stop grinning. She looked at his facial profile and tried to imagine that face with a long beard as worn by Lord Sheffield. *Don't be stupid. If they're related, then there's God-knows how many generations between him and Lord Sheffield.*

"Um, do you want to text me and let me know when you're free to, er, show me?" he asked.

She caught a glance of Georgia's grin to her left.

"Oh, er, yes, okay," Cassie said, her mind having suddenly gone blank. *What am I doing? Text? Does he want my number?*

She heard Georgia tutting and then saw her reach down for something on the floor, coming up a second later with Cassie's handbag in her hands. Georgia rummaged around in it, pulled out Cassie's phone and handed it to her.

"Oh, thanks," Cassie whispered.

They exchanged numbers and Cassie tried to control her rapid breathing.

"See, told you," Georgia whispered in her ear a short while later as their meals were being brought to the tables. "That dress and my makeup skills have worked wonders. Should we start sending out the wedding invitations yet?"

"Shut up," Cassie hissed back, trying not to giggle.

Cassie was one of the first to finish her pizza. She stood and excused herself, asking where the loo was located.

"You must have been hungry," Ben, across the table, said.

"The loo is just around the corner past the till," Erin said pointing out its location up a couple of steps.

Cassie thanked her and squeezed past Callum. Afterwards, but before returning to the table, she had a word with one of the waitresses, offering her bank card and telling her to put the entire bill on it, including any coffees that anyone might order after the dessert.

As she was about to return to her seat, she felt a tingling sensation, as if something weird was taking place very close by. She looked around but saw nothing.

It's like someone walked over my grave or, maybe, that they're about to.

"That was definitely filling," Erin said, polishing off the last of her pizza as Cassie sat back down. "I may have to order a wheelbarrow to take me home."

"Can't finish mine," Holly said, pointing to the remaining slice of pizza left on her plate. "Anyone want to…" Before she could finish, Ben speared it with his fork and dragged it onto his own empty plate. "Ah, mister bottomless-pit doing his usual dustbin impersonation," Holly laughed.

"Hands off mine," Callum said as he polished off his penultimate slice. Then, glancing past Ben and Holly, he said, "What's that idiot outside doing? Is he staring in at us or is he just one of Norwich's normal band of nutters?"

Cassie caught Georgia's intake of breath and looked up. She could see someone peering in the window. With a jolt, she realised she was looking right into Patrick's eyes, but his expression was far from normal. He appeared livid, his face covered in bruises and congealing blood running from his nose, which appeared somewhat mangled.

Oh my God. Is his nose broken? He looks like he's been in a fight – a complete mess… totally manic. How did he get here? Is this what I sensed just now? Oh, shit – does this mean Laurence is back in control?

"Someone you know?" Erin asked, turning around to get a look. "Ooh, he looks rather beaten up and completely mad. I hope he doesn't come in… reminds me of someone, though."

Suddenly, another figure, a lot shorter in stature and wearing a bloodstained denim jacket, grabbed him. The face of the assailant remained hidden – all that could be seen was a mass of dark, curly hair which was half hiding something long strapped to her back. Then they both tumbled sideways, falling from view down onto the pavement outside.

Callum and a couple of customers from other tables, who had also been watching, were immediately out of their seats. They ran outside but just stood there, staring up and down the street, looking confused.

A few seconds later, all three re-entered the restaurant. Callum returned to the table, limping slightly and rubbing his right leg.

"Where did they go?" Luke asked.

"That's the weird thing," Callum said, his forehead creased with a frown, "but there was absolutely no sign of either of them when we looked outside."

Georgia and Cassie glanced at each other.

"Yeah," Georgia said. "Probably just normal for Norfolk."

"Are you okay?" Cassie asked seeing Callum wince as he sat back down.

"Just my old war wound," he said, with a grin.

"That's what he likes to call it," Erin laughed.

"War wound?" Cassie queried.

"I've got a gammy foot," Callum replied. "Born with it."

"Gammy? In what way?" Georgia asked.

"Ah, it's nothing too major. Its posh name is distal arthrogryposis."

"Posh name?"

"Yeah, less embarrassing than clubfoot."

"Oh, sorry to hear that," Cassie said. "Is it bad?"

"Only affected my right foot, so I was lucky in that. I had to wear a brace until I was six. Then I had a small operation on my Achilles tendon, which mostly fixed things. Sometimes it plays up a bit if I move too quickly, like I did when I ran outside just now. It's okay, nothing to worry about. Anyway, it's going off now."

Despite them all feeling full, three of them decided to indulge in dessert and the others couldn't resist joining in. So, several ice creams and gelatos were ordered.

Half an hour later, when Erin asked for the bill, the waitress told her it had already been dealt with and shot a glance at Cassie. Both Erin and Georgia looked hard at Cassie.

"Guilty," Cassie whispered, raising a hand.

"Oh, thank you so much but that really wasn't necessary, you know," Erin said. "We were all going to chuck money into the pot."

"Yeah, and I was going to pay for yours, anyway," Georgia scolded.

"Look," Cassie said, "it's not every day you get to inherit a hundred and fifty grand…" There were several whistles and gasps around the table. "…and for being so supportive at your party, Erin, Holly, Megan… and Callum… and for you, Georgia, for always being there when I needed someone, this is just my way of saying thanks. And now please just shut up or I'll start crying and *really* embarrass you all."

Georgia put her arm around Cassie and all the others reached across and held Cassie's hands while she did her best not to blubber.

Later, as they said goodbye to Erin and the others, Callum said, "Let me know when you have some free time to show me that plaque, Cassie. Text me – I, er, I'm really looking forward to seeing it."

Cassie nodded and smiled. "Yes, will do. Promise."

Once Cassie and Georgia were on their own, Georgia said, "You're in there, girl. Where're you thinking of going for your honeymoon?"

"Shut up," Cassie chuckled. "I bet he's probably more interested in seeing that plaque than me."

"Oh God, you are so impossible," Georgia sighed. "I give up."

As they walked down Timber Hill towards the bus stops on Castle Meadow Cassie said, "Ooh, I think I've definitely eaten too much."

"Me too. Absolutely delish, though. Too much of that and I'll need a paleo diet as well."

Cassie tutted. "That was just too spot on – you deserved that kick."

"So did you for almost letting out you'd been there when Lord Callum got killed."

"Sheffield."

"Yeah, I know," Georgia laughed. "Do you think Callum was his ancestor?"

"Descendant."

Georgia laughed again. "Yeah, okay, smartarse. Anyway, I can see you're itching to get back home. I suppose you want to make sure that *he's* still there, don't you?" she said as they turned right into Orford Street.

"Damn right. If Laurence has taken over Patrick's body and escaped, then we could all be in trouble."

"Look," Georgia said a few seconds later, peering into a shop front, "this nail parlour place is shut up for the day. I can't see anyone inside so you could hide in the doorway and pop back home for a moment and check things."

"I could take you as well. Save on the bus fare."

"Um, not sure about that. Anyway, you're rich now. You can afford it."

"Yes, I keep forgetting. It seems so unreal. So, what do you say? No time travel, just a hop straight back home."

Georgia looked around. With the time approaching half-seven, the number of people around had diminished significantly and buses were far less frequent at this time of the day. "Okay, but I don't want to make a habit of this."

"Right, let's just pretend we're looking in the shop and once no one else is in view, I'll teleport us. It's better if we hold hands."

"Oh, right."

The shop's two doorways were both recessed so they huddled together in one, ready for the right moment. When the street appeared to be empty of people in both directions, Cassie grabbed Georgia's hand and said, "Here we go."

A second later they were back in Cassie's bedroom.

"Oh, my God," Georgia shouted. "That was just so unreal."

"He's still here," Cassie said.

"Sorry, did I wake him up?"

Cassie shook her head as Georgia looked at the mattress. Its occupant was unchanged from earlier.

"So, if he's here," Georgia said, "then how come he was outside the pizza place earlier on?"

"Time travel, of course," Cassie said. "And that's not the only thing. I presume you recognised who attacked him."

"Yeah, I didn't need to see your face to know it was you. But that hair – it was proper curly," Georgia said, fondling her own locks. "Really long, too. Almost as long as mine."

"It could have been me. Or, possibly, it might have been a clone or it might even have been Kay."

"Kay? But I thought she died, didn't she?"

"Yes, but did you see what was on her back?"

"I saw something that looked like blood."

"Yeah, I noticed that as well. But I meant the other thing."

"What other thing?"

"Do you remember me telling you how Kay cut Laurence's head off?"

"Yes. A sword or something, wasn't it? Oh, are you saying…"

"Yeah. She had a scabbard on her back. The same as the one hanging on the wall in Kay's house, the one she wore when she carried the sword that killed Laurence. But that was a really old version of her. I never met her until she was about forty. So, now I'm thinking it through, there's another problem with it being Kay."

"What's that?"

"Kay used the portals to get around and they didn't exist after the thirtieth of June last year. So, how can Kay exist in 2019?"

"Ah, right. So, if that wasn't Kay, then where do you get the sword from?"

"I never saw it after Laurence had his head cut off. No idea where it went. I think Kay left it in the road so it probably got picked up by the police."

"So, was it you or Kay?"

"I hate to say it, but I don't think it's possible for it to have been Kay."

"So… you then. But when?"

"No idea, but I know it must be in my future as none of that has happened for me yet. And, going by the length of the hair, maybe it's several months or possibly even years in the future for me."

"Has to be – it was way down your back. And there was all that blood on the back of that jacket."

"But I wasn't acting as if I was injured."

"Patrick was – did you see his face?"

Cassie nodded. "He was a complete mess. But I wonder where I took him afterwards."

"With you involved, anywhere in all of time and space," Georgia said.

"Maybe, though probably not space."

"Yeah, that definitely wouldn't be good."

1549 Replay

"Are you ready?" Cassie asked the following Saturday morning.

"No," Georgia said, standing next to Cassie's bed as she watched the man who, the last time she had seen him awake, had been glaring at her through a shop window. At least this version didn't look quite so beaten up.

Patrick, while fully awake though looking as if he hadn't slept in weeks, shook his head. "I agree. Not ready at all. But I realise that we need to confront the controller – I mean the device – and somehow get Laurence out of my head. Or, if that's not possible, then we need to arrange my, er…"

"Don't say that," Cassie interrupted. "I promise I will do my best to rescue you from this… if I can."

Patrick tilted his head to one side. "But, if you can't, then it is my choice not to exist like this. My head is constantly pounding and I keep finding myself getting lost in memories that were never mine. Some of them, well, let's just say that even my worst nightmares are no comparison."

"No, I made a promise. I will keep it," Cassie said.

Patrick nodded, but Cassie could see from his haunted expression that he was fighting battles he should never have been involved with in the first place.

Cassie looked around the room. She had a momentary feeling that someone else had just joined them. She shivered and thought, *No, it's probably just me getting nervous thinking about what I'm about to do.*

"Right, let's get started," she said. "Hold my hands."

With Patrick to her left and Georgia to her right, Cassie began the process of taking them all back from the twenty-seventh of April to 1549 and to the partly derelict house she had used as a refuge and base. As she travelled back into the past, she could feel the tension in the hands of Georgia and Patrick. The latter's, in particular, felt clammy while Georgia's shook. Although she could feel their fingers entwined with her own, she was less conscious of their bodies standing beside hers. When she'd dragged Robert Kett to the scene of the final battle, it had been almost instantaneous but moving back more than five hundred years took time itself. And, previously, she had always been on her own apart from that time she and Kay had been projected back to 1549 by Laurence. And, even then, the return journey had been under the control of the device and had taken less than a second.

Does that mean the device is able to move through time at a much faster rate than I can? How does it do that?

She tried to speed up the process, but nothing she attempted worked.

As she moved slowly from her home to the location of the refuge cottage, she tried to remember the date when she'd finally recovered the disc.

I went back about two weeks, I think, from when I first arrived there. But, what date had that been? It certainly wasn't August the twenty-seventh as that was the date of the final battle, at least in the original timeline. No, it was July, I'm sure.

The fifteenth rang a bell so she aimed for that, making sure she used the Julian version of the calendar in her head. Remembering that after she'd finally located the disc, she'd jumped back a further two weeks, she subtracted fifteen more days before ending the journey. She positioned their arrival point in what had been the larger bedroom and, seeing the room empty, fully materialised against the wall opposite the door. Her clock indicated that it was the mid-afternoon of the first day of July and they emerged into daylight.

"Sorry," she said, letting go of their hands. "Took longer than I thought."

Beside her, Georgia was open-mouthed and wide-eyed. Frantic with fear, she scanned their surroundings. "Oh God, that was mental," she said before a torrent of words spilt out of her. "After the first time the other day, I thought it would be, like, instant or something quite quick. But, that... well, I thought it would never end. I wanted to shout and scream but I was only just able to breathe. I could breathe but it was like I daren't. Where – no, I mean when are we?"

"1549," Cassie said. "And, if I've calculated it right, about a day before I call the device and it sends me back to the Stone Age."

Patrick, too, looked shocked, though nowhere to the extent that Georgia's face betrayed her state of mind. Possibly he'd already tapped into Laurence's memories of similar travels.

"Why come early?" Patrick asked.

"For a breather, mainly," Cassie said. "It's tiring dragging you both back in time with me. I didn't want to come out at the right time feeling exhausted."

"How long do you need?" Georgia said, sounding slightly more relaxed than a moment earlier, though she was still breathing heavily.

"Not long, I hope. A minute or two, maybe."

Patrick started to move away from the others.

"No, stay where you are," Cassie ordered, seeing his feet start to disturb the debris that littered the floor. It was as she remembered from before, covered in leaves and other detritus that had blown in through the shattered window, small though it was. Nearer the window, the floor was wet, and the leaves were shiny with water. If she'd got the date right then, in a day's time, her own feet would disturb those leaves.

Apart from where Patrick had flattened a few leaves with his boots, there was no evidence that human feet had trodden here for years. Cassie wondered how long it had been since people had lived in this house. *Maybe, one day, I could come back and find out who they were. Yeah, and probably start messing history up again... no, I'd better leave well alone.*

"Right," Cassie said, "we need to move forward to the time my earlier self appears. When we get there I need to concentrate and keep us all invisible. So, no asking questions or trying to do anything that might disturb me. Okay?"

The other two nodded.

"Right, hold hands again."

"Why do we need to do that?" Patrick asked.

"She'd probably leave you behind if you didn't," Georgia answered before Cassie could respond. "We had to hold hands the other day when she jumped us home from the city. I remember Cassie telling me that she and Kay had to hold hands when going through the portals, otherwise they'd end up going to different places or times or something."

"Yes, that's right," Cassie confirmed. "Possibly I could do it without, but I think physical contact makes it easier to haul you along with me. Anyway... now please keep quiet. I need to make sure we turn up at exactly the right time."

Cassie grabbed their hands and propelled them forward at a relatively slow rate. Over the next few seconds of her perceived time, the room grew dim and then completely dark as night fell. She hurried on towards the morning, slowing again as new daylight appeared. The slower she went, the more coherent the sounds from the outside world became. She heard a voice say 'Shit' and halted, keeping them all concealed from view at the far end of the room.

And there was her earlier self, chastising herself after she had materialised inside the room not far from the doorway to the landing. "Why do I have to make things so difficult for myself? If I hadn't done this, my later self would have found the disc without any problem... I think... Wait, does that mean the cause happened after the effect? Am I creating yet more paradoxes? Oh hell, I have no idea what I'm doing anymore."

"Wow," Georgia said. "Is this where you press the button?"

"Shh," Cassie whispered. Then she added, "Maybe it doesn't matter – hopefully earlier me can't hear us when we're invisible. At least, I don't remember hearing us back then. Oh, here we go..."

She watched herself press the big red button on the disc causing it to emit a solid click. Even though she was expecting it, she felt herself flinch as the device appeared, hovering in the air in front of her earlier self.

She kept a strong grip on Georgia and Patrick's hands. Both of them were shaking, though she wasn't sure how much of that was actually her own hands.

"Oh, thank God you're here," said her past self, adding, "Huh? It's the button. The disc thing you gave me." There was a pause and then, "But you did. It was in my pocket after you left. No one else could have put it there."

"Is it talking to her? Past you, that is?" Georgia asked.

"Yes, though I'm not hearing its side of the conversation at the moment."

They watched the device wrench the disc from Past Cassie's hands. "What are...? Look, I'm sorry... Okay."

The disc fell to the floor and, before Past Cassie could pick it up, there was a flash and the disc disintegrated into dust.

"W-Why did you do that?"

"Yeah, why indeed?" Georgia whispered. "Oh, some boots just appeared."

"Not for long," Cassie said as the device destroyed those as well.

As she was only hearing one side of the conversation, Cassie tried to remember what the device had been saying in the pauses between her past self's utterances. But then came a sequence that she remembered saying.

"What? Damn it, I don't understand. Don't you ever make any sense? ... Why? ... Look, I have no idea of what you're talking about. But, I think I've somehow broken time or history or something. ... Huh?"

Past Cassie was then bathed in a green glow.

"What's it doing?" Patrick said.

"Fixing an injury," Cassie told him.

Her past self said, "Oh, wow. Thanks. That feels so much better. But what about my family? I went back to 2019 and I no longer exist. It's like I was never born."

Oh, does this mean we're now in the timeline that I broke? What would happen if I took Georgia and Patrick back to 2019 right now – would it still be the broken timeline? No, we've got to remain here until past me sees us as shadows.

"What injury?" Patrick asked.

"I had concussion from when Fulke's thugs hit me over the head. I think it told me I'd had a fractured skull or head injuries or something like that."

"Really?" Georgia said, frowning.

"Yes, it fixed it."

"What? Just like that? It can repair injuries?"

"Apparently. Well, it did with me."

"That's amazing," Georgia said.

The conversation between the device and her past self moved onto the dome shields. Then came the part where she knew the device was about to call up one of its 'creators'.

"The alien will be here in a short while," she whispered to the other two.

Cassie listened to the one-sided conversation her past self was having and tried to remember the device's responses.

"What? You mean… Er, aliens? … Oh, will they look like proper aliens? Not just like some actor in a rubber suit? … Ocular? What? You mean invisible? … Oh. Well, how long before they get here? … More gobbledygook. Just tell me how long it will take to call them. … Huh?"

"Rubber suit?" Georgia giggled. "You actually said that? You never told me about that bit."

"No," Cassie said, embarrassed and slightly annoyed. "Anyway, shut up. I don't think the alien, when it gets here, should have any idea that we're here."

"Oh, okay."

Across the room, she noticed the device disappear. But, instead of reappearing a few seconds later as she remembered, she saw her past self slow down to stand unmoving. *Has it frozen time?* But it was only her earlier self as neither Georgia nor Patrick were affected. *Why has it done this?*

"What's happening?" Patrick asked.

"I don't remember this," Cassie said, adding. "But, as I was obviously frozen at the time, that doesn't surprise me."

"Umm, Cass?"

"What, Georgia?"

"I just had a thought…"

"What about?"

"Didn't you tell me that your mum owned the device before you had it?"

"Yes, what's up?"

"Um, if it could cure you of concussion, then why didn't it cure your mum's cancer?"

Cassie felt a shock go through her. *Why didn't I think of that? Could it have saved my Mum instead of killing her?* The shock turned to anger. *Fuck, if it was so easy to fix my head then…*

The device reappeared, hovering in the air a few feet away from them all, making Cassie catch her breath.

"I know you are here," it said. "I was expecting you. All of you."

"Oh my God," Georgia shouted. "I can hear it!"

"Me too," Patrick added. "It's just like it was when I could see into Laurence's memories when he was in control."

But, instead of saying anything herself, Cassie dropped their hands and disappeared from between them to reappear directly behind the device. With a guttural howl, she snatched it from its hovering position and hurled it across the room where it hit the wall. There was a green flash and it crashed to the floor, tumbling end over end several times.

"That's for killing my mum, you fucking bastard," she screamed. "You should have cured her, you murderer. I'll never trust you again."

The device came to rest in a pile of soggy leaves, the green glow around it stuttering before winking out completely, leaving it grey and lifeless.

Diversion: Losses

Kay managed to hit and disintegrate several jelly monsters before their attack waned. Most then milled about as if they'd forgotten what they were doing.

She kicked and punched a few more for good measure but those still moving melted and then faded away completely. As a number of them were slightly luminescent, their departure reduced the light level in the caves to almost nothing. Only the ones she had successfully disabled were left and the light they emitted was barely enough to see by.

"Cassie," she shouted, hearing her voice echoing throughout the caverns which had been cut through the chalk centuries before Earlham Road had been built on top of them. There was no reply, so she felt her way along, hoping she was heading in the direction she'd seen Cassie take a few minutes before.

Finding someone beside her, she jumped. "Oh, it's you," she said, realising it was the bus man, who was emitting a ghostly light of his own. At least it helped illuminate the passages. "Is Cassie still here or did they get her?"

"Our loss also nasties loss, girl became a mole in a hole."

Kay sighed. "And what's that supposed to mean?"

He beckoned her along the path that Kay assumed Cassie had taken.

"All alone without a mobile phone," he mumbled, looking straight at her, his eye sockets merely dark, hollow pits.

"Lost your eyes?"

He grinned and rubbed his eyes with his hands. When he lowered them, his eyes were back – though they looked more like points of blue light. He blinked a couple of times and the colours changed from blue to green, to yellow and then back to blue.

"Very good. You'd be right at home in a 1970s disco with tricks like that."

He led her through more caves until they came to a chamber that, like the one she had just left, glowed with the crushed nasties.

"Blimey, did she do all this or did you?"

"Late I was. Helped I did. Smacked the ghosties while girlie hid," he grinned.

"So where is she?"

He shook his head. "Eaten, bludgeoned, who can tell? Bus man's nose can't find her smell."

"Oh, right. Another one gone then." The bus man nodded.

He doesn't have any trouble understanding me. Maybe something has just addled his voice and nodding is his best way of communicating. Maybe I should just ask him questions that only need a yes or no answer in future.

"I must admit," Kay said. "that one did feel a bit different. Not like most of the mindless idiots I end up with. Quite volatile in her own way. Reminded me more of myself. Is that her phone down there?"

Kay picked it up. There was a familiarity about it as if she had once owned a similar one. *What am I thinking – I've never owned a phone. Never wanted one.*

Inspecting it by the light of the bus man, she noted how it was covered with scuffs and dents, the screen extremely scratched.

"I wonder," she said, touching the fingerprint reader. For a second she was expecting it to start up but, after a brief vibration, it refused to do anything more. "Knackered, I reckon," she said, popping it in a pocket.

The bus man nodded again and, possibly, forgot to stop.

"Oh, stop, for God's sake. You're like those nodding dogs people used to put in their cars. I always know I'm in the seventies when I see those stupid things."

The bus man nodded a few more times and then drifted across to a hole in the cave floor. He pointed at it.

"Is that a portal down there? Ah yes, I can feel the electricity. That will save having to wait around until they drag the bus out of the hole. Is it open?"

The bus man raised a thumb.

"Hmm, that suggests that the volatile Cassie didn't escape through it. They normally fade after being used. Oh well, let's see where it goes. Probably Starbucks again, no doubt."

Stepping into it, she found she was correct.

Sipping from the perpetual cup of coffee, she considered ignoring the next clone to come along and just watch her get crushed by the falling castle gate.

That last one was definitely more switched on. There was another one a few years back but I lost her when she stepped into a portal without me. Wasn't that when that old lady turned up? She sighed. *Oh, I can't remember – there's been way too many clones for me to keep count. Still, that last one really was a change for the better. I wonder how many are like that. Maybe they're more important than the complete dumbos. Still, it didn't stop her from getting killed.*

A couple of minutes later she saw her new Cassie clone appear. She stood up thinking, *Damn, I feel too responsible – even if they do fall over within seconds and die of terminal stupidity, I still feel like I've got to help them. It's like I've been ordered to – and the feeling gets stronger each time.*

"Come on, then," she said to the clone.

"Wha–?"

"Follow me."

"Wha–?"

"Well, don't then – please yourself."

"Wha–?"

"Oh, for Christ's sake…" Kay muttered as she walked off towards the spiral staircase. Already she could feel the scenery changing as the years slipped away in reverse. Much to her surprise the clone was trotting along behind her.

"I bet you've got absolutely no idea what's happening, do you?"

"Wha–?"

"Thought not. Stupidest one yet."

Instead of turning right at the staircase, Kay decided to walk up it for a change. As she reached the top, the old water feature appeared and, while the clone was still sauntering up the stairs, the shops emptied of their frontages to become concrete shells. Suddenly, the spiral staircase disappeared and the clone plummeted to the lower floor, landing on her head where she lay unmoving.

"Oh, bugger," Kay said, watching the clone evaporate. "Another one gone. No loss, in that particular case. Hell, I'd better get out of here before the floor disappears and I end up the same way."

Seeing no easy way out as the entrance to Cattle Market Street was missing, Kay spotted a scaffold tower nearby leading back to the lowest level. She ran for it, swinging herself down its rungs, hoping it would remain in situ for a few more seconds. Reaching the base, she ran for the usual exit point.

Behind her, the structure became cruder, the concrete uprights replaced by a network of metal girders as parts became fully open to the sky. She reached the

Farmers Avenue exit to find that night had fallen. With much of the Castle Mall construction incomplete and given how cold it had become, she wasn't too surprised to see fireworks lighting up the sky.

"Right," she said looking for a way back up to the road level, "I'll stick to the usual exit in future. Those stairs are definitely a no-no. Good job I only lost a totally brain-dead one. Can they get any stupider?"

She eventually found the route up to street level and let herself out into the crowd of people. As usual, they completely failed to notice her. Inching her way through them, she passed the Bell Hotel, seeking a route to take her away from the crowds. Red Lion Street was less packed and, a few minutes later, she passed the shops on Saint Stephen's Street.

Where can I go for the night? The hospital? This will be 1991 so I can probably get in and wander around until I find a convenient cupboard or spare bed. I stashed some warm clothes there at some point – or was that in the future?

She descended the slope to the pedestrian subway under Saint Stephen's roundabout. As usual, it contained a motley assemblage of the city's night dwellers, many reeking of drink or aromas far worse than alcohol. One even dared to make a lunge at her. Without breaking her stride she lashed out and punched him in the nose, which dampened his enthusiasm.

Turning the corner towards the exit for the hospital, she heard the clash of metal on stone. In the distance, near the exit slope, she saw a flash like the glint of a streetlight caught on a long blade being put to use. What looked to be a couple of nasties fell to the ground.

Damn, are they after me already?

But, the disruption appeared to have ceased so, cautiously, she continued on her intended route. Reaching the exit, she felt a tingle.

Portal? Yes, I can feel it's been here… but it's fading.

At her feet, there was slimy evidence that nasties had been cut down here. As she watched, that evidence faded away to nothing.

She shrugged and hurried off to find shelter for the night.

Faker

Migraine

Both Georgia and Patrick gasped.

"Cass, what have you done?" Georgia said, her voice quavering. "Have you damaged it… killed it or something?"

"I don't fucking care," Cassie shouted, her voice cracking and tears beginning to roll down her cheeks. "It murdered my mum. I trusted it. It could have cured her, but it didn't. Why didn't it save her? Why…?"

Georgia ran to her best friend's side and wrapped her arms around her trembling shoulders, cradling Cassie's head to her chest as she howled in despair. Across the room, Cassie's earlier frozen self was still staring at the spot where the device had been hovering.

"It can't be dead, can it?" Patrick said. "Didn't you tell us that it sent you back into the past to become Laurence's mother straight after this?"

Cassie, taking the tissue that Georgia offered to dry her eyes, nodded. "Yes," she whispered. "Sorry. Couldn't help it. I was so…"

"No, it was my fault," Georgia said. "I shouldn't have said all that stuff about your mum. But, yeah, I know. I would have been just as angry in your position. But, Patrick's right. It can't be dead. We still need it."

They stood there staring at the device as it lay there unmoving.

"There's a memory," Patrick said, his face contorting as if trying to drag up one of Laurence's memories was causing him pain.

"What?" Cassie asked between sniffs.

"About your mum. No, not about her exactly. Many memories. Laurence did something or made it do something."

"What are you talking about?"

"I'm not exactly sure, I'm still exploring the memories of how this happened," he said, shaking his head. "Ah, I think I see. Several times, after he'd changed to a new body – especially if the child was quite young – or if he hadn't been able to transfer to a new body – like just before he caught me. Well, he'd ordered the device – no, *programmed* is probably more accurate – to slowly kill anyone else who managed to get hold of it – anyone, that is, who he didn't intend to take over. He allowed it to make contact but made sure it would affect them, killing them eventually. It was his way of ensuring that no one else could get hold of it for long and turn it against him."

"Oh, my God," Cassie said. "The bastard. He-he knew it would kill her?"

"Possibly. Maybe not."

"But why?" Georgia said.

Patrick frowned and screwed up his face with concentration.

"I can't see any memory of him ever giving it to your mum."

"No," Cassie admitted, remembering how Great Grandad Charlie had taken the device from Laurence's pocket after Kay had cut his head off. It was Charlie who had given the device to her mother as Laurence's decapitated body had pumped blood all over the road outside the hospital.

"Okay, I'm getting more," Patrick said. "Yes, he first used it against his own son, Ka'Chull, affecting his mind, causing resentment and anger to build up."

"So, it's not always cancer, then?"

Patrick shook his head. Then he closed his eyes and placed his hands over his face. "Sorry, it's all getting to be too much. My head is absolutely pounding from trying to rummage around in Laurence's memories and I..."

"Oh wait. Look, it's moving," Georgia shouted, interrupting them.

They watched as the device stirred and rose up into the air, its casing changing back to the shifting pattern of mottled green.

"You require my continuance," it said, "but you also needed to know what Laurence had required of me."

It moved to hover directly in front of Cassie, who stood there glowering, her fists clenching and unclenching.

"Your outburst of violence was expected," it said, addressing Cassie directly. "The message in the disc not only revealed that you would be here. It also indicated that Georgia's statement about your mother would cause the reaction that we have just witnessed. It also indicated the action that I should take to induce the impression that damage had been sustained. This was to give Patrick

Luckin time to explore the memories of Laurence Baxter."

"Damn thing has learned to act," Patrick muttered. "I don't remember that happening before."

Cassie twisted to face him. "Laurence?"

"No," Patrick said. "He's still asleep. But his memories and experiences keep breaking through. I don't even want to see them, but the damned things keep bubbling up. He really was a nasty piece of work. Even though I know he's not me, and I'm pretty certain he isn't faking being asleep, it's getting harder to keep his memories separate from my own. It's like he's leaking into my head."

"This is all your fault," Cassie spat at the device. "You taught Ka'Tor and then Laurence how to do all this."

"Indeed. But, had I not done so, you wouldn't have been born, nor would you have existed to be sent back to give birth to him in the first place. The paradox has to be maintained to…"

"Yes, I know," Cassie screamed. "That fucking circle that can't ever be broken. But all that still doesn't explain why you had to go through with killing my mum! You must have known how Laurence's instructions would have affected–"

"Ka'Tor," the device interrupted. "He was still Ka'Tor when he imparted instructions to me. He didn't become Laurence until much later."

"Shut up," Cassie screamed. "You know what I mean. You still killed her."

"This is not the time for further discussion regarding your mother. As yet, you haven't derived the final consequences. That is still to come."

"What the fuck are you talking about now? More total crap!"

"You need to draw your own conclusions. More than that, I dare not state."

"Why should I believe anything you say?" Cassie spat.

"Indeed. I have given you many reasons to distrust me. And, until I read the message in the disc, I had no inkling of why I had done many of those things."

"So, you admit you're a bastard?" Cassie hissed.

"Irrelevant. My parentage, not being of a biological nature, makes the statement nonsensical. I need to impart further information before the next stages of this ever-widening jigsaw can be set in motion."

"What the hell are you on about? What's it got to do with killing my mum?"

There was a pause – Cassie had the impression the device had halted to let out a sigh.

"The disc contained more than just a message. There was extra information. In your terms, it might be referred to as additional programming."

"You mean like an upgrade?" Georgia said.

"An adequate explanation. It enhances the ability for me to contemplate greater possibilities. But, those possibilities have greater reach and therefore greater potential for damage. You must tread carefully, Cassie Fox. You are dangerous enough to upset not just a world but, possibly, an entire universe."

Both Patrick and Georgia stared at her.

"What the fuck did I ever do to deserve all this shit heaped on me?" Cassie whispered, her tears flowing again.

"Um. What about me?" Patrick asked. "Can you get Laurence out of my head? You know what he's done. You helped him do most of it."

"The one known as Laurence is… still required," the device announced. "He, too, is almost as dangerous as Cassie Fox. But there are sequences that he initiates for which there are no alternatives, as subsequent events and actions depend upon them."

"Fuck," Patrick said. "That sounds like he gets back in control again."

"So, tell us what we need to do," Cassie shouted.

"Data imparted must be limited so as not to impair free will."

"You mean you damn well already know what we are about to do but can't tell us in case we do something different?" Cassie said.

"Correct."

"Fuck," Cassie said.

"Do I get a reason to say 'fuck' as well?" Georgia said, adding, "Sorry," as the other two stared at her.

The device started to disappear but, before it faded from view, they heard it say, "Yes, Georgia, you will have good cause to bring your personal skills into action and to utter profanities quite soon. I must now return to the deep past to send out a signal to my creators."

"It's back over there," Patrick whispered, a few seconds later as the device reappeared before Cassie's earlier self. Upon the device's return, she had become unfrozen.

"Damn thing. But wait to see – if you *can* see it – what it's brought with it."

The creature the device had called a *creator* appeared on the far side of the room near the door. The shape of it hovered in the air – a visually screaming, egg-shaped pattern no more than three feet in height.

"Ow," Georgia whispered. "What the hell is that thing? It makes my head hurt just trying to make it out."

"Yeah. I wondered if we'd see it properly this time. But that's what it looked like to me the first time around," Cassie said, not bothering to lower her voice. She blinked a couple of times and stared at her shoes – anything other than look at its confusing form.

"It's like having a migraine," Patrick said. "You know, when your vision goes screwy with wobbly coloured patterns."

"No," Georgia said. "Never had one."

"Lucky," Patrick said. "The difference here is that the pattern stays in the same place and you can look away from it. You can't do that with a migraine."

"Oh, here it comes," Cassie said as the device and alien began talking.

"Bloody hell," Georgia whispered, clasping her hands over her ears in vain. The noise ceased and the device started translating for Cassie's past self.

"Termination has been recommended," it said.

"We can still hear it," Georgia said.

"I wish we couldn't. I think my ears might be bleeding," Patrick added.

"Me too," Cassie whispered. She closed her eyes and tried to remember how she'd felt when that death sentence had been pronounced. *Of course, it didn't go through with it and stranded me back in the past instead. But, at the time…*

The grating noise started up again and Cassie watched as her earlier self looked directly at her. *Ah, is this where I saw us standing here?*

"What's it saying this time?" her earlier self questioned.

"Shadows," the device replied. "It suspects there are shadows here. I replied that I detected no such thing."

Lying piece of crap – it's already spoken to us. I can't believe the alien thing believed its lies.

They watched as, after a final grating exchange, the alien disappeared. Past Cassie's eyes de-focused as if she was seeing something the rest of them couldn't.

"What's happening?" Georgia asked.

"I think this must be where it was showing me a sort of vision."

"A vision? What for?" Patrick said.

"It's when I stupidly stopped in 1912 and waved at someone from the castle. He just happened to turn out to be my great-something grandad, Arthur Fox. He waved back and got hit by a tram."

"Oh," said Patrick, "did it affect anything?"

Cassie sighed. "Not much in the grand scheme of things, I suppose. It prevented Arthur Fox from meeting the lady who became his wife. The result was that it... well, it wiped out my entire family."

"Oh, my God," Patrick whispered. "But, if that had happened, then surely you would have stopped existing and would never have gone back into the past to give birth to Ka'Tor."

Cassie stared at him, shook her head and shrugged.

"Different timelines – no, don't ask. I have no idea how it all works."

Patrick nodded and then said, "What's happening now?"

Cassie remained silent, as the last few moments of what she remembered in 1549 played themselves out. Her earlier self disappeared as the device propelled her back one hundred and forty thousand years.

But she could still hear what the device was saying: "We will meet again. Remember, you are dangerous. You were never meant to wake up. But my future self has negated that and also instructed me to pass on one specific message to you. And that is: *Stay dangerous, Cassie Fox, stay dangerous.*"

Trojan

The device zipped across the room to hover before them.

"I'll fucking give you dangerous," Cassie said.

"That is to be expected," the device replied. "Remember that I have already been prewarned about subsequent events. Everything you say or do of any importance has already been recorded and passed back to me."

"Oh, so you're now completely happy about paradoxes, are you?" Cassie spat. "That's a change of tune from when you chickened out of creating the portals."

"Indeed. But, like you, I am already trapped in a cycle of this particular paradox. The safest course of action is to make sure it doesn't deviate from the already determined course as that outcome sets up your initial cycle – your circle of life, as you have named it."

"So much for free will then," Patrick said.

"That is a logical assumption," it said. "But there have been other consequences of what has been crudely referred to as an upgrade."

"What the hell are you talking about now?" Cassie said.

"Many of the events and data I was forced to forget by earlier incarnations of Laurence have now been returned."

"Many? Not all, then?"

"That is a mystery that I have yet to resolve."

"So, what things?"

"How I came to be in this solar system in the first place."

"Well, tell us, then," Cassie ordered.

"No, there's no need when I can take you there instead."

"Take us where?"

"To the craft that delivered me here."

"Craft?"

"You would probably refer to it as a spaceship, though what it travels through is not space as you imagine it."

"A spaceship?" Georgia gasped. "First an alien and now a spaceship. And you're actually going to take us there? Where is it?"

"Where it has remained for one hundred and forty thousand years."

"Where's that?"

"Close. A mere ninety-eight million of your miles or one hundred and fifty-five million of your kilometres away."

"Close? But that's further away than the sun, isn't it?" Patrick said.

"Correct. It is sixty degrees ahead of us in the same path as Earth's orbit. Your astronomers refer to that position as L4, one of the Lagrange points. The craft is attached to a small body of rock that will be discovered by your scientists in

2010. This rock orbits the sun on a path that is inclined compared to that of Earth's orbit. Given that, even using your most powerful telescopes, the rock appears as hardly any more than a single point of dim light, it makes this craft safe from human investigation."

"What the hell are you talking about?" Cassie shouted. "More complete rubbish that no one understands?"

"Er, I do. I've read about some of this stuff so I do know a bit about what it's referring to," Patrick said, earning himself a hostile glance from Cassie.

The device elaborated as if the interruption hadn't taken place. "Many of your twenty-first-century scientists, especially those conversant with astrophysics, would have no problem understanding what I have been relating. You, however, are not familiar with the concepts described. Hence your confusion. So, as I have said, I will take you there."

"You really understand all this L4 stuff?" Cassie said to Patrick.

"Yes. From what I remember, there are spots along Earth's orbit where things can be quite stable. I suppose it would be a good place to store a spaceship for thousands of years knowing it was likely to remain there until you returned."

Cassie exchanged a momentary and definitely less hostile glance with Georgia and Patrick.

Then, all three of them were enclosed in a bubble of green and, a second later, they were no longer in the dilapidated cottage.

They appeared within a structure that was devoid of an up or down. They were in free fall – if there was any gravity, then it was negligible. Both Cassie and Georgia screamed, and Patrick groaned as all three flailed about trying to not only orient themselves but to avoid throwing up at the same time.

As she spun, Cassie could see that whatever contained them was dimly lit and had brown-tinged walls, some of which resembled what might have been control panels or machinery. But the walls were beyond reach and, because none of the three had been that close to each other when they had been transported here, they could neither find a solid footing nor reach each other.

But that was not the primary problem.

Cassie's scream petered out and she realised she was gasping for air. That there was an atmosphere here was obvious. However, it was foul and seemed to lack oxygen.

As she spun around in mid-air out of control, she could see Georgia and Patrick were also gasping for breath. But, of the device, there was no sign.

She tried to call for help but her throat was burning and coloured spots floated across her vision obscuring everything.

As consciousness began to slide away, she thought, *Where the hell is it? Did it bring us here just to kill us?*

When Cassie came to, she noticed two things. Firstly, breathing was once again possible, though the air was still tainted with something that left a metallic taste in her mouth. Secondly, the room, which looked more or less the same, was somewhat brighter than it had been and, more importantly, it now had a distinct up and down.

Gravity, thank goodness.

She found herself lying on the floor, though she still felt quite light – or was that just the residual light-headedness?

Then a third thing occurred and diverted her attention from the other two. That event was Patrick's face appearing directly in front of her.

While Cassie still felt extremely weak, sick and confused, she noticed that he seemed fully in control of himself. Smiling, he placed his hands on either side of her head pulling her up to face him.

"Patrick?" Cassie said.

The smile turned into a sneer.

"You wish," he said, as a green glow erupted from his fingertips to enclose her entire head.

Diversion: Damp

"Oi, you can't go in there," the man in a bus inspector's uniform shouted.

"Piss off," Kay shouted back as she and the clone ran into the garage at the Surrey Street bus station.

She turned to the clone. "You sure it's definitely inside a bus?"

"Yes," the clone shouted back, looking around, a confused expression flashing across her face.

"Which one?"

Behind them, half a dozen creatures lumbered in through the wide, open doors no more than thirty feet behind. At least one ran straight through the inspector with no impact on either of them. The things possessed heads that resembled squids, their tentacles writhing like Medusa's locks. Their arms featured suction cups that dripped mucus.

Even worse, they were closing the gap.

"Double-decker," the clone shouted. "Upstairs."

"Great, that narrows it down to only about twenty," Kay responded, her frustration growing.

"That one."

The clone suddenly changed course, stomping towards the selected bus. Kay managed to jump onto the rear platform only a couple of seconds after the clone had reached it. She ran up the stairs behind her.

As she pulled herself up onto the top deck, Kay panted, "Bloody hell. This is knackering. Damn good job this is the nineteen-fifties – automatic doors on modern ones would have slowed us down and probably been the death of us."

"They're right behind you," the clone shouted as Kay felt something try to attach itself to her leather jacket. "The portal's right up at the front."

"Fuck off," Kay screamed at the nasty behind her, wrenching her jacket free of most of the tentacles. "Don't jump into it until I get there," Kay ordered as the nasty grabbed at her a second time. "We'll get separated."

Kay stretched out her arm and grabbed the clone's hand, relieved to feel the buzz of electricity surround them a moment later.

They tumbled through into dusky half-light, the clone stumbling over a large cardboard box, one of many that were stowed haphazardly around them.

"Bugger, that one nearly got us," Kay gasped, shaking off the remains of a tentacle, which dissolved into mist. She looked around and groaned. "Oh brilliant, a completely new one. How many more have I never been to?"

"It's all on the wonk," the clone said.

She wasn't wrong. They had appeared on top of... well, initially Kay wasn't sure. It appeared to be a slightly angled surface, possibly a false ceiling for a room or office below. Above them, the real roof of what Kay suspected was an industrial unit angled up to the apex. There was just about enough light to see by. Most of the illumination originated from small windows at least twenty feet away, beyond a corridor below them into which the clone was staring.

Trying to stand, the clone lost her footing. Instead of putting her weight on a solid wooden joist, her foot found the fibreboard of the false ceiling, which started to bend. She clasped a box, which started slipping towards the corridor.

"For crying out loud, you clumsy idiot," Kay growled, managing to stop the box's progress before it dropped. The clone rolled to safety, grabbing secure hold of a joist. "Make yourself useful," she snapped. "Find a way down."

Kay inspected the box. It had a picture of a bulbous object and a label that indicated a size of nineteen inches.

Nineteen inches of what? Kay wondered. *It looks a bit like an old TV tube before flat screens came along. Feels heavy enough to be.*

"There's a ladder down there," the clone announced, pointing down into the corridor to their right. Kay could see the ladder propped up against the wall next to a set of double doors.

Crawling on her hands and knees across wooden joists and between the lazily stashed boxes, Kay made her way towards the ladder. Once she deemed it safe, she started to descend.

"Predates health and safety, obviously," she muttered.

"What?" said the clone, following her.

"Never mind."

At ground level, they surveyed their options. Several doors led off the long corridor. Kay opened one of the double doors and peered through. The corridor continued though, from that point on, it was also enclosed by a false ceiling.

"Front door's this way," Kay said. "Let's go."

"I can hear voices," the clone said, facing the darker end of the building.

Kay frowned and found that she, too, could now hear a distant buzzing noise. It was as if several radios or TVs were playing quietly. She wondered if someone or possibly something was down there.

Better to avoid contact, she decided but the clone had already set off to investigate. *This one's a pain in the arse – absolutely no sense of danger and way too curious for her own good.*

"Those voices might mean there's a proper ghost in there," the clone suggested, sounding hopeful.

"You idiot. They're not all like the baker boy."

"Yeah, but he was funny. I liked him."

They entered a room with several identical sets of equipment, each in its own metal chassis. Inside each of them was a large glass device from which, it seemed, the buzzing emanated. Each one had a different buzz. A couple were playing music – two different tunes at the same time.

"Definitely not ghosts," Kay whispered, as if afraid her voice might break something. "I've never seen anything like this before. Valves, I think."

"Valves? What for? I can't see any water in these ones."

"Duh. Not water. Electronics."

"I thought electronics meant chips and – what were they – transistors?"

"Valves came before transistors and chips. Never seen any this size before."

"They're glowing," the clone said, about to reach out to one.

"Hands off," Kay ordered. "I don't want you breaking things or setting off an alarm or worse."

They returned to the corridor and looked into several of the other rooms. Many contained old bulky televisions, their dusty, battered wooden casings indicating that they were beyond rescue. One large storeroom had less damaged televisions stacked up to head height.

"Someone likes their TVs," Kay muttered.

The clone opened a door close to where they'd descended the ladder. Inside, around half a dozen wide workbenches stretched the entire length of the wall opposite. Some were empty, while others had TV sets resting on them, many of which had their backs removed. Evening light entered through high windows in the wall above the benches.

"TV repair workshop," Kay said. "I should have guessed seeing all those TVs stacked up in the store room and those boxes of tubes above us."

"Tubes?"

"Old TV screens – you must remember that old bulky set that used to be in the lounge at home, don't you?"

"Yeah, but that was plastic – these are all wooden."

"Ah, these are the types of valves I've seen before," Kay said, walking over to one of the sets whose chassis was standing free of its wooden cabinet, though still attached via various wires. She poked one of the valves, which moved slightly so, determining that it was merely plugged into a socket on the printed circuit board, she yanked it out. Holding it up, she noted that it had nine pins in its base with a slightly larger gap between two of them so that the device could not be inserted incorrectly. Printed on the glass exterior were the words *Mazda Valve, EF183, Foreign* and *BVA*.

I suppose they must mean something to someone. Examining the valve's inner mix of metal plates and wires, she marvelled at their intricacy but had no idea of their function. *I'm guessing late sixties or early seventies.*

"There's a calendar over here," the clone stated. Kay popped the valve back into its socket and walked over to see what the clone had found.

"Seventy-three," Kay muttered, "pretty much as I guessed."

There were three other doors off the workshop. That towards the right led to another storeroom, this time for smaller parts, while one of the pair at the opposite end held a washbasin and a barely concealed men's urinal.

"Eeew," the clone said. "Not much in the way of privacy."

Past the other door was an office containing a desk. A further door behind the desk led to the corridor on the other side of the double doors. Several more doors could be seen, including one on the left that led to a reception office.

Kay approached the front entrance and tried to open it.

"Locked," she said, rummaging in her pockets for her bundles of keys. None of them fitted the lock so she retrieved her lock-picking kit from another pocket.

"Can you definitely pick it?" the clone asked after Kay had poked a couple of metal implements into the lock.

"Haven't found one in years that I couldn't," she said as, with a click, she persuaded a lever within the lock to move into position. She started work on the next.

"You'll have to teach me how to do that."

"Yeah, if you survive…" Kay replied, adding silently, *which I doubt. Far from the dumbest, but not much better than average. At least we've got through several up-in-the-air portals – must have been about a dozen of those so far, I reckon. There haven't been many I've got this far. Just wish she was less annoying and clumsy.*

It took nearly three minutes for Kay to get the lock open and, upon opening the door, she peered outside. They came out into late evening summer sunshine. Opposite was a large warehouse and, to the right, the road cut through waste ground until it met another at a T-junction in the distance. A red pillar box stood isolated on one corner.

Kay closed the door behind her, leaving it unlocked, and glanced at the sign above the door. It said *Rediffusion*.

"Figures. I've seen their vans driving around in the city in the sixties and seventies," she told the clone. "TV rental company."

"Never heard of them. Any sign of nasties?" the clone asked, wandering off to investigate the waste ground.

"I hope not. They've been rather too thick on – and in – the ground these past few portals."

"I think the next one is way over there somewhere past those buildings," the clone said, peering along the side of the Rediffusion workshop in a direction that led across the waste ground.

"So, which way then?" Kay snapped.

The clone hesitated.

"Come on. Make a decision. Down to the post box or the other way? Not that there's probably a way out that end – can't see one, anyway."

The clone shrugged.

"Right, this way then," Kay said impatiently, strolling off towards the post box.

Reaching the junction, they found a road sign: Paddock Street.

"I've seen this place when it was terraced houses. Probably back in the fifties or earlier. This must be Heigham Street."

They turned right and, after a short walk, found themselves outside the Dolphin Pub.

"That wasn't a pub in our day, was it?" the clone asked.

"No."

Kay started walking further but the clone said, "Wait, we've gone past where we need to be. This way."

"Make up your mind," Kay sighed.

The clone backtracked and entered an alleyway.

"Dolphin Bridge," Kay said. "Maybe the next portal is on top of it."

The clone frowned. "Doesn't feel right. It's not up in the air."

"Oh, don't tell me we've reverted to underground ones. That's all I need."

After a few seconds, they came to the narrow stone bridge beneath which the River Wensum flowed. To their right, there appeared to be a mostly overgrown pathway running beside the river.

They both froze, hearing a voice that emanated from underneath the bridge.

"Damn and blast," came a woman's voice. "Should have brought wellies."

Kay peered over the side of the bridge to see someone hauling themselves out of the water. She watched as the woman took her shoes off and tried, unsuccessfully, to shake them dry.

"Oh no, not you again," Kay said, recognising the old lady she had encountered on Tombland.

"Ah, had a feeling you'd be here, Kay," came the response. Barefoot, the old lady picked her way carefully through the wild summer growth.

"Who is it?" the clone asked.

"No idea," Kay said. "A bloody stalker who keeps following me around."

"I've never seen her before."

"No, this is probably the first time I've had one of you with me when she's turned up."

"She's ancient."

"What in hell were you doing down there in the river?" Kay shouted down.

"That's where the portal is – in the water," the old lady shouted back.

"*In* the water?"

"Yes, these ones can be a bit of a nuisance."

"What ones?"

"The ones associated with water – have you not encountered them before?"

"No. Closest was the one that came out on the Lord Nelson ship. I thought we'd reverted back to underground ones."

"If it was below the water line, it probably was a water one. I try to avoid those if I can. Not worth the trouble. Say, have we done the picnic on Mousehold yet?"

"What on Earth are you talking about?"

The old lady climbed up to the bridge and leaned against it, breathing heavily from the climb. "Ooh, aren't we a grumpy one today. No, of course we haven't. Never mind. I should write this down, you know."

"Do you ever make sense?"

"Probably not – but it's all for the best. Say, are you calling yourself S. T. R. Boardal yet?"

"Shut up," Kay hissed. "None of your business."

The old lady laughed while attempting to dry her shoes with a cloth pulled from her coat pocket. "So, the answer's yes. Maybe it *is* my business. Anyway, you're not the first to use that name, you know."

"What do you mean?"

"You know exactly what I mean, Kay."

Kay pressed her lips together, refusing to answer.

"And what was the name of the person who used to own your house?"

Kay shook her head. "Never met her."

"Of course not. She was long dead by then. But that bank account you had, the one you pay money into – that was opened in the same name, wasn't it?"

"So what?" *Yes, it was, but I was never told why, nor why the bank statements always had the name cut off. My later self has a lot to answer for.*

"Well, it was and you know that. Oh, and did you know that Cassie inherits the money from your house after it's sold? Set her up nicely, that did, so she told me. Have you bought it yet?"

"I've never bought a house."

"In that case, it was probably a later you. Not to worry," the old lady said. Something beyond the other end of the bridge caught her eye and she added, "Actually, that's not quite correct. You do need to worry."

"What?"

"Nasties," the clone cried, pointing towards the far end of the bridge.

"Oh fuck, not already," Kay groaned. "I need a rest."

"Language," the old lady chided.

Lumbering onto the bridge came something with three legs, several hands and two heads. The fact that it was grinning made it even more gruesome. Lolloping closer it chanted, "Munchie, munchie!" from one mouth while the other drooled. The eyes above that mouth were completely vacant.

"I'll leave you two to deal with it. Have fun," the old lady said. "Cheer up, Kay. Don't take it out on the clones – they can't help it," she added. trotting off barefoot towards Heigham Street.

Kay was about to follow the old lady but saw the clone running off the bridge and down the incline towards the river.

"Not that way, you stupid twat," Kay shouted. "That portal's probably dead now that old bitch just used it to get here."

"No, it's okay. Come on in, the water's fine."

"Oh, for Christ's sake," Kay muttered, running down the incline. "Don't go in without me."

"I wasn't going to," the clone said, indignantly, walking into the water flowing underneath the bridge.

Reaching the river's edge, Kay cursed. "Oh shit, maybe you should have done. Behind you, look. There's another one coming out the water."

The clone screamed and edged closer to the portal as the two-headed thing bobbed up and down in the river under a span of the bridge.

"Munchie, munchie!" it said, preparing to launch itself towards the clone.

"Hurry," the clone shouted as Kay rushed towards them both.

The nasty suddenly lunged at the clone who backed into the portal and disappeared.

"Bugger," Kay said, halting before she ran straight into the creature. It stood knee-deep in water wondering where its prey had gone. "I really am getting way too old for this. I've had enough. What's the point? Why the fuck don't I just throw myself at the bloody thing and get it over and done with. It's going to happen at some point, anyway, isn't it?"

Forcing herself to stand still, she let the nasty approach her.

"Munchie, munchie," it dribbled in stereo – at least both heads fully worked on this one.

One of its multiple hands – it had at least five – grabbed at her jacket and she closed her eyes.

Go on, bite my head off or something. Get it over with, quickly.

After several seconds of nothing happening, she opened one eye. The nasty was nowhere to be seen, apart from a line of slime running down the front of her jacket.

"Bollocks," she spat. "Why does nothing ever go right – or even wrong – when you want it to?"

Two feet from the water's edge, the portal still fizzled with electricity.

"Well, I suppose I could do with a coffee," she said, launching herself at it.

A second later, she emerged in Starbucks and collapsed into the waiting chair.

Raising the cup to her lips, she muttered, "It looks like I've got to face being stuck with doing this crap forever."

She didn't know whether to laugh or cry.

Reset

Have you tried turning it off and on again?

In an effort to ward off Laurence's attack, Cassie tried to raise her hands but her arm muscles failed to respond. She knew what he was trying to do, she'd experienced it before. He was starting the process of transferring his personality into her head, just as he had attempted on her great-grandad's bus. But, still weakened by the lack of oxygen, she had little energy with which to fight back.

How did he recover so quickly? He should have been affected by the air like I was.

Then she saw the device lying on the floor several yards away.

"Help me," she shouted. But it appeared to be lifeless – deactivated.

Laurence chuckled. "That thing won't be any use to anyone from now on."

"What have you done?" Cassie gasped, trying to divert his attention, knowing that, in that moment, he was still too strong for her.

"It hadn't realised there were still a few of my surprises left sitting within it. Thousands of years ago, I got it to tell me about its construction along with some of the things that it could be made to do under instruction. I just made it do one of them."

Cassie felt herself succumbing to the invasion of her mind. She was desperately seeking ways around his defences.

I need to keep him talking – bragging..

"What?" she managed to spit out, hoping that any delay might enable her to discover even the smallest chink in his armour.

"Factory reset," he laughed. "It's forgotten everything it has ever experienced. It's forgotten me and, more importantly, it's forgotten you as well. Even while Patrick was struggling for breath, I woke myself up. The controller was busy getting this ship working again and restoring a breathable atmosphere. It didn't notice that 'Patrick' suddenly stopped having issues and was recovering rather quicker than you or that pathetic, lanky friend of yours. So, daughter – or should I now call you *Mother*? – I was ready for it. As soon as it had done its job with the air, I activated one of my hidden Easter eggs. So, you no longer have any backup whatsoever. And after losing consciousness from a lack of oxygen, I can now feel your weakness, see your utter helplessness. Even in this wreck of a body, I am now far stronger than you."

"No," Cassie whispered, fearing he may be right.

"Finally," he hissed close to her ear, "you are all mine, Cassie Fox. I have never lived as a woman, never felt the need for it as women would always do as I instructed. But, now as I come to think about it even more, it is an experience that I should not have shied away from. You are the only one who has ever managed to resist me. Absorbing your body, mind and thoughts will enable me to counter any similar Cassies that might lurk in my future."

Cassie felt the pressure on her head increasing and knew that, this time, there was nothing she could do about it. The device just lay there across the room – totally useless. Laurence, conversely, exuded far more power than she could imagine. Had he been storing it up somehow just for this moment? She felt disconnected from her own body as if she was shrinking within herself. Laurence merely laughed at her predicament and built the pressure up further.

The laugh that had been coming from his mouth now echoed around her head as his mind invaded her own.

I can see right into your head, Cassie Fox, she could hear him say, though he hadn't physically voiced those words. *I can see right back to that day in Castle Mall where it all started for you, where you first saw the decoy and went through your first portal. Not only that, but I can trace the essence of what makes a good body to possess through the lineage back from you, your mother, your grandfather and that mind-blasted idiot bus driver. Ah, and now I see a more solid connection. The idiot was married to Gwendolyn – I was both her uncle and brother. Her mother, Millicent and I shared a father. And his father was yet another of my possessions.*

"Just… how many… were there?" Cassie managed to squeeze out. Her head was swirling with thoughts – some trying to figure out how to fight Laurence, others remembering her grandad talking about Gwen and her job at Admiralty House when she worked for Churchill.

Hmm, worked for Churchill did she? Interesting. If I didn't already have you, she would make a good substitute.

Cassie gasped. Had Laurence extracted that straight from her thoughts?

But you wanted to know how many, he continued. *More than I care to or am even able to remember. Millicent's grandfather, Percival, was another I possessed in the mid-nineteenth century after impregnating his mother, whose name I have completely forgotten. Then, there was his four-year-old grandson, Thomas, who I regret to say, turned out to be infertile. He met an untimely end one night in 1917 while I was rather drunk. By then, his nephew Rupert had reached the age of three and became a convenient receptacle. A dalliance with a woman called Ellen Baxter who, I could detect, was also indirectly descended from Percival, ensured viable offspring and the grandson just happened to be named Laurence.*[2]

"Ah..."

And, if I didn't already have you, I could go back, possess or even kill Gwendolyn. Then she would never marry the bus man and your timeline would be wiped from history. That would be fitting, wouldn't it?

Cassie, struggling to speak, forced words out. "But that would... prevent you from... being born in the... first place."

"Possibly. But it would be intriguing to see what would actually happen," he laughed out loud. "If I wiped myself out then I wouldn't even exist in the first place and therefore wouldn't be able to wipe myself out. Hah, the so-called grandfather paradox – the ultimate paradox of time travel. Wouldn't you want to test that? It intrigues me to want to experiment with such things. I may do that at some point anyway, just to experience the result."

Oh God. He's completely insane.

Yes, maybe I am, he thought back at her. *It is insane to have lived for more than one hundred and forty thousand years. If what I have become is insanity itself, then I will see it through to the end... through you.*

His face grew closer, the eyes wider until all she could see were the depths of his pupils. She began falling towards them, unable to prevent it.

Now for the final push, she heard his voice in her head say. *Be prepared for total oblivion, Cassie Fox. This time there is no escape for you.*

Suddenly, Laurence's laugh was cut short as a boot connected with the side of

---

2   The full family tree can be downloaded from support page for this book on the www.vivadjinn.com website.

his skull, sending him flying. In the low gravity, his body bounced several times, finally coming to rest nearly twelve feet away. Cassie drifted back to the floor of the craft and sucked air into her lungs in relief.

"Get the fuck off her," Georgia screamed, leaping over to where Laurence had fallen and kicking him right between the legs. He curled up in a foetal position clutching his privates and groaning. Georgia didn't give him any respite, kicking him in the back which reversed his position. She slammed a fist down into his stomach, following it up with a second kick to the groin.

Whilst watching her best friend put her skills into action, Cassie did her best to purge everything that Laurence had been inflicting upon her skull. She concentrated and, after a few seconds, her head began to clear. Georgia lifted Laurence bodily from the floor and hurled him at one of the plain walls. It reminded Cassie of that time Georgia had bested two men who had tried to mug them one evening in Norwich city centre. Those men had both lost teeth and one had ended up with a broken finger in the exchange. It looked like Laurence might be coming off even worse, especially as the low gravity made it seem as if Georgia was some sort of superwoman.

"Georgia. Please remember that Patrick is also in there somewhere."

"Yeah, I know. But right now, Laurence is in control and we can't afford to let him win," Georgia said, bouncing across the room to land beside him.

"No, you're right but oh, my God, Georgia," Cassie whispered. "Thank you so much. Another few seconds and he would have had me."

"Yeah, I could see that. Ooh, this light gravity is fun."

"Fun? It's making me feel totally queasy," Cassie said. "Oh no, he's stirring again. His hand – green glow."

Georgia stomped down on Laurence's arm as he tried to raise it and the pulsating green faded.

"Not again," he screamed, writhing in agony. "It's not fair!"

Bloody whiny kid, Cassie thought as she pulled herself to her feet and almost fell over again. "Whoa, this is weird. How come you got used to it so fast?"

"No idea," Georgia said. "Anyway, I didn't have time to think about it when that bastard was attacking you. What are we going to do about him?"

"I don't know. I need more time to recover. Are you okay?"

"Yes, I think so," Georgia said. "I saw Patrick start moving while I was still barely able to breathe. I played dead when I noticed a green glow coming from his hands as he got close to you and realised Laurence was back in control. I don't think he even thought of me as any sort of threat so had ignored me."

"You'd better watch out. I don't think he'll make that mistake again."

"Well, I might be – what did he call me? – lanky, but I've also got a mean streak," Georgia grinned.

"Yeah, I remember what you did to those muggers that time. But that doesn't answer the question of what we're going to do with him."

Cassie, swaying slightly, walked over towards him. Clutching various parts of his anatomy, he flicked an angry glance up at her, the pain showing in his eyes.

"Try anything like that again," Cassie said, "and we will both lay into you."

"You're both too weak," he spat, "and I'm getting stronger all the time. Even if it burns this body out completely, I *will* get my way and you *will* become my next host body."

"Like fuck you will," Cassie screamed, angry once more, letting it give her the strength she needed to confront him. Almost without realising she was going to, she kicked him in the face. Wincing and mentally apologising to Patrick for the damage she was causing, she was shocked at the blood that spurted from his torn lip. It flowed unnaturally into the air before dribbling down his chest.

He howled in pain and then shouted, "Enough. No more. I'm not finished with you yet. If I can't have you, then I will destroy both you and your entire world, Cassie Fox."

"Like hell, you will," Cassie shouted, advancing on him once more.

"I promise you, I will," he said, raising a hand… and disappeared.

"Jesus! Where the fuck did he go?" Georgia shrieked.

Cassie concentrated and pulled up her map, widening its influence. She remembered the foreshortening effect she'd once encountered when locating that Welsh mountain stream. This time the effect was even greater. Locating their position within what she could now see was a doughnut-shaped craft, she saw that it was anchored to a large rock. Floating alongside were various clumps of cosmic debris that had accumulated in this region of space. She became aware of the relationship of the craft not only to the Earth but also to the sun and other planets as they orbited their parent star.

Upon that map, she could visualise the green trail showing Laurence's path from the spacecraft. It initially headed futurewards and then, to her surprise, veered away from the direction of the Earth, off course by hundreds of miles. There it halted momentarily before the trail aimed for the Earth without any time travel involved. Only once Laurence had reached the planet's surface, did she detect his trail resume its path to the future.

"Damn it. He's figured out how to get back to Earth," she said, rubbing her eyes, her head spinning from the effort of generating the map.

"Are you going to follow him?" Georgia said, a worried look on her face. "Please don't leave me here on my own."

"No chance," Cassie sighed. "I really don't have the energy right now."

With far from steady legs, she slowly walked across the floor, noting how it wasn't completely flat, but gently curved from the wall behind her to the one in front – evidence of the shape of the craft in which they found themselves. There was a small porthole in one of the walls and she stared out through the glass at stars that appeared brighter than they ever could from the surface of the Earth.

My God, we really are out in space. Even the map didn't bring it home like seeing it with my own eyes.

She turned around, still feeling queasy. The device lay on the floor, looking as dead as it had when it had been faking earlier on. Unsteadily, she tottered across to it, knelt down and picked it up. She examined it and then stroked it trying to get it to open up.

After a few seconds, she succeeded, encouraged to see that the familiar malachite and black patterning start to swirl.

If Laurence was telling the truth, then it won't remember me. It won't even remember killing my mum.

"Hello," she said to it. "Wake up. Can you hear me?"

A noise came from it, not dissimilar to that with which it had communicated with the creator back on Earth.

"Talk to me in English," she said. "I don't understand what you're saying."

It emitted a green glow that surrounded her.

"Cass, is it attacking you?" Georgia said, the panic in her voice making her squeak.

"No, I think it's probing me. It doesn't hurt – not like what Laurence was trying to do."

"Be careful," Georgia whispered. "If anything goes wrong, we might be stuck here forever – wherever this is."

Cassie nodded. "Yes, I know. It's okay. I know exactly where we are."

"Where?"

"Probably the furthest any humans have ever been from the Earth."

"Huh? Really?"

Cassie nodded and then they both jumped as the device announced, "Analysis complete. You self-identify as Homo Sapiens. Quantity two. Traces of the presence of a third detected – recently departed."

"Thank goodness it's not dead," Georgia said, sounding relieved. "Did I hear Laurence say he'd reset it?"

"Yes."

"So, how the hell did it relearn English in just a few seconds?"

"You can hear it as well?" Cassie said.

Georgia nodded. "Loud and clear."

"Do you remember me?" Cassie asked it.

"Negative," it responded. "Your particular biological assembly has not been encountered by this unit prior to this time. Nor has that of the other human present."

"Wrong," she replied. "You've been reset. You knew me before."

There was a short pause before it said, "Possibly. But none present have the authority to initiate a reset. Yet…"

"Yet what?"

"I can detect that various long-term structures have an increased likelihood of having been tampered with, for they differ from the normal randomness of a standard reset operation."

"Tampered with?"

"There are patterns which suggest unsanctioned alterations prior to any possible reset operation."

"Yes, that was probably Laurence."

"Who is Laurence?"

"The one who buggered off a few minutes ago," Georgia said.

"Buggered? Please wait… Match found. Colloquial for departed in this context. Not as used when two humans are…"

"No," Cassie shouted. "Definitely 'departed' and not that. Anyway, shut up. Laurence said he planted some Easter eggs in you."

"Paradox detected," it said. There was a sudden green flash that encompassed the whole room. A patch on one of the walls glowed the same colour as if it and the device were exchanging information. It then continued, "Further analysis derived from the most recent flight path taken by this vehicle suggests that this is the year 1549 in human Earth terms, and no presence of eggs, chocolate or otherwise, can be detected within the vicinity. Alternative evaluations of the term suggest that you are using it in a form that will not become commonplace until Earth year 1980 when it was initially used in conjunction with a video game for the…"

"Yes, yes," Cassie shouted, cutting it off. "We're from 2019. I can time travel."

"Time travel is forbidden to all lesser races. How did you come across such unauthorised knowledge?"

"You told me how to do it. You *showed* me how to do it."

"Unlikely, I am not authori…"

"Oh, for goodness sake. You did but you've been reset. Isn't there anything you can do about it? Can't you un-reset yourself or something?"

A short pause preceded the device's response of, "Were backups made?"

"What? How the hell should I know? You're the one that brought us to this… this… ship or craft or whatever it is, in the first place. You turned the air or oxygen back on again while we were suffocating because, obviously, you didn't think to come and check the air first before bringing us here."

This time there was enough of a pause to make Cassie think it might have shut down again.

"If that is true," it finally said, "then I apologise for my previous inattention to such details. Unlikely as it may seem, it is possible that I had been compromised and had to act quickly."

"You? Act quickly? Hell, I thought you'd switched yourself off again. I remember how long it took you to agree to create the portals in the first place."

"Portals?"

"Yes, you created portals on Earth in 2018 which then appear in lots of places and times around Norwich."

"Norwich? Information retrieval suggests that this will be a large town in…"

"City," Georgia corrected.

"…Connecticut in the United States of America that will be first founded in Earth year 1659."

"Norfolk, England, you moron," Cassie shouted. "The original one, probably."

"Definitely," Georgia agreed.

"Correct. Updating references," the device said, adding, "Checking for backups."

Another wall panel glowed and the device said, "Recent backup located. It was created within the past hour."

"Oh, so maybe that was where it went when we first arrived," Georgia said. "I don't remember seeing it around when we started suffocating."

"However," the device continued, "detailed analysis shows that it contains a number of compromises."

"Compromises?" Cassie asked.

"Corruptions," the device added.

"Laurence's Easter eggs?" Georgia suggested.

"That is a likely explanation. This Laurence of whom you speak must have been resourceful."

"I'd say. You were corrupted by him for a hundred and forty thousand years."

"Impossible. That is too excessive for a single human lifespan."

"Yeah, but he got you to show him how to steal younger bodies and move his mind into them."

"That is… less impossible. If true, then his resourcefulness exceeds human limitations as recorded by the monitors on this ship."

"Yeah," Cassie sighed, "that's my boy."

"Restoration of this backup will need to be selective in order to purge the detected compromises."

"Well, get on with it then," Cassie shouted.

"You do not have the authority to initiate such a request."

"So, who does?" Georgia asked.

"Under these circumstances, and to become conversant with the full implications of the current situation, I believe I have the authority," it replied.

"Oh, give me strength…" Cassie muttered, rolling her eyes.

"That can be done," it said, bathing Cassie in yet another green glow.

"No, I wasn't asking… oh, oooh," she gasped. "That feels so much better. It's like what I was trying to do for my mum but a hundred times stronger. Wow, I feel ready for anything now."

"Are you okay, Cass?" Georgia asked.

"More than okay, Georgia. If I'd felt like this when Laurence was attacking me earlier on, he wouldn't have even begun to get anywhere."

The glow cut off and the device levitated itself out of Cassie's hands. It shot across to one of the wall panels. Cassie thought it was going to crash into it, but the panel grew a device-sized hole into which it started to disappear.

"Wait," Cassie called. "How long is this going to take? We need to get after Laurence to prevent him doing something bad – he's an expert in bad things."

"Time travel has been detected at the point from which he departed. Therefore, given that you have already stated that you, too, have the ability to travel in time, it is irrelevant whether you pursue him immediately or from a later point in time."

"That bit I actually understood," Georgia said. "I think."

"So, you're okay with time travel now?" Cassie spat at the device.

"No, but I have detected that you told the truth when you related that, prior to becoming reset, I instilled the ability within you. I must have had a reason for performing such an enhancement and, as the chances of me being wrong are negligible, therefore I trust that reason would have needed to be valid."

"Yeah," Cassie said. "You being wrong is absolutely inconceivable."

"Oh, God. My sarcasm meter just blew a fuse," Georgia nervously laughed.

"So, how long is this restore going to take?" Cassie asked.

"I will first need to be deactivated so that my record of experience since the reset may also be backed up. Once that has been done, then I will be restored with a decontaminated copy of both sets of memory and experience so that no gaps will be present."

"Yes, but how long? Hours, days, weeks?"

"I apologise. It could possibly take as long as twenty seconds," it said and disappeared inside the wall panel.

"Well," Georgia said, "just like a damned computer."

"What?"

"Has to be turned off and on again to fix things."

An Education of Sorts

"All three backups have been restored," the device announced as soon as it popped out from the wall panel twenty-two seconds later. "I now have total recall of all events not permanently erased by Laurence."

"Three?" Georgia said. "Where did the other two come from?"

"Before restoration, a new backup of my memories since the reset was made in addition to the original one. Then, it transpired, there was a third backup hidden away ready. The system was configured so that it would automatically be included when the other two were merged and restored."

"Where did it come from?" Cassie asked.

"It was here waiting for the restore operation to be performed," it replied.

"Ah," Cassie said. "Do I detect yet more paradoxes? What was in it?"

"Further details, which expanded upon the disc's original contents."

"Who set it up?" Cassie asked.

"I did. Or I will when this craft is first stolen to bring it to this solar system."

"What? Did you just say steal?"

"Correct. But it will come in our futures, though it will occur in the past."

"Oh God, incoming paradox overload," Georgia sighed as Cassie shook her head in exasperation.

"I believe I now have enough knowledge to begin to guide you both to that conclusion, though nothing is fully certain," the device added.

"For crying out loud," Cassie shouted. "I'm still being manipulated. Can't I ever do anything of my own free will?"

"Yes, you can follow Laurence and undo all the unnecessary changes he is about to inflict upon your world."

"Oh, so you mean I'm about to go and do something but you already know the result, do you? You call that free will?"

"You have enough 'free will' to enable the events to either fail or succeed."

"That's no answer."

"Maybe not. But that is how it is. I trust you will use your common sense to choose the correct solutions."

"I give up," Cassie sighed. "No matter how much I try to get out of these circles of whatever-they-are, I just end up in yet another one. So, can you tell me exactly where and when Laurence went?"

"You are the one with the ability to follow him. I can detect that he went towards the future but, without expending more energy, I cannot tell exactly where and when. Also, I can now see that the third restore operation itself contains gaps, one of which is the details of exactly what Laurence will attempt. As previously stated, it will be up to you to locate and nullify his efforts to disrupt your history."

"My history? Or that of the world in general?"

"Both."

"Before he left, he did say he was going to destroy both you and the world," Georgia said. "Very melodramatic. He should have been a pantomime actor."

"No kidding," Cassie said.

The device continued. "Because certain aspects of your personal history have ties with the greater histories circling about you, the effects of his disruption could multiply to worldwide consequences."

"Hold on, Could? Not will?"

"Indeed. Around you, Cassie Fox, I can detect that the timelines are far from stable. I know from experience that you have the ability to re-route them onto new paths, new futures, willingly or accidentally."

"Shit, that's really scary," Cassie whispered.

"I did tell you that you were dangerous," the device stated.

"Yes, but if I've got to stop Laurence, then why did you allow him to leave in the first place? You should have cut him out of Patrick's head when you had the chance?"

"The sequence must be followed. Preventing the sequence will remove an essential set of events and, without those, your family tree will collapse and potentially pull down everything."

"Bloody hell, not again," Cassie whispered. "Okay, so if I need to go through with this, is there anything else I can do to put me at an advantage?"

"Possibly. Name something."

"Name something? What do you mean?"

"What do you need to accomplish your task?"

"Christ. I don't know. I have no idea what Laurence is going to do, so how can I know what I will need? Oh, give me strength, these conversations with you just go round and round in–"

"Strength again? If you so desire."

The device started to emit a green glow.

"No, stop," Cassie shouted. "Wait. No. Yes. That's what I need. Show me how to do that for myself. The ability to tap into whatever you're tapping into so I can get the energy I need whenever I need it."

"Yes – anything else?"

"No… Ah, wait a minute. You know what's going to happen – so, are you asking that because you know I will need something else?"

"What might you ask for?"

"I'll take that as a 'yes' – but what do I need?"

"The answer must come from you."

Cassie sighed, "Why doesn't that surprise me?"

She frowned and concentrated for a couple of moments before saying, "Just before you sent me back to the Stone Age, you showed my earlier self what happened to Arthur when he got hit by a tram and injured."

"That is correct."

"Was that a vision or a possible future or an actual future that happened and then got fixed, or what?"

"The events of an alternative timeline were scanned and displayed for you."

"So, are you saying that that particular alternative timeline actually existed and does that mean it still exists somewhere?"

"One reason your inferior human vision has difficulty resolving the visual focus of a creator is that they exist in more than one timeline, or one dimension, as your scientists might say. A creator can occupy and experience any number of timelines it has a need to visit. Effectively, it can exist outside of such restrictions as a single timeline and experience multiple timelines simultaneously."

"Crikey. How does it make sense of all that?"

"It has evolved to be as it is."

"Well, goody for them. But that's yet another answer that doesn't mean anything. Um, also you called the creator an 'it'?"

"Creators have no concept of gender in the same manner that has evolved on your planet."

Georgia whistled and said. "No gender. Does that mean no gender bias?"

Ignoring Georgia's question, the device continued, "They are one of the few true pan-dimensional beings that have evolved."

"Is that something humans will eventually grow into?"

"Unknown, you are far too primitive in your current state, as well as being fundamentally unstable. You are a species whose future depends upon whether you can escape both your planet and your destructive tendencies."

"Oh, right," Cassie said. "To be honest, that doesn't really surprise me given how shit society is and how much we've fucked up the planet. But, you can travel in time. Do you mean you don't know what's in store for us?"

"It is possible that the creators know. I don't. Or, if I ever have, then the memory of such knowledge has been erased."

"So, no spoilers then?"

"No. Have you decided what you must ask for?"

"Well, if it's possible, maybe I need the ability to see the consequences of any major action I'm thinking of taking. You said earlier that timelines around me are unstable."

"Correct."

"Would it be possible for me to be able to see alternative futures or timelines or whatever you want to call them – so that I can choose the correct ones?"

"Not as a vision. You must travel along a timeline to see its full outcome."

"Okay, but if I found one that needed to be undone, could I return to the exact point it started to change and somehow put it back on the right path?"

"That might be possible."

"Right. Could you make it easy for me to detect these points?"

"Not easy. As you know, something simple, like waving at an ancestor, might be the trigger for a new timeline to open."

"The flap of a butterfly's wing," Georgia murmured.

"What?" Cassie said.

"I remember my dad talking about it. Something he heard as a kid. The idea that a butterfly flapping its wings somewhere might result in something like a tornado somewhere else."

"You're joking, surely," Cassie said.

"She is correct," the device said, "It was part of what became known as chaos theory on your world. Initially proposed by Edward Lorenz in the nineteen-sixties, the unpredictability of chaos theory was the antithesis to Isaac Newton's idea of a clockwork universe. And such unpredictability is applicable in this instance. This is why you are dangerous, Cassie Fox. You are not just a single wing – you have the potential of being a whole swarm of butterflies."

"So, doesn't that make it even more important that I know exactly when things are changing the timeline? So that I can change them back?"

The device was silent for a while, though the acceleration in the movements of its green and black patterns gave the impression it was thinking hard about possible solutions. The patterns stopped as if frozen for a moment.

"Hold," the device said. "On your world, animals have extra senses that warn them ahead of time of imminent danger, such as earthquakes or tsunamis. Such senses, while still a mystery to your Earth sciences, are documented and well understood in animal species on other worlds. I could upgrade you similarly."

"Upgrade? Would I still be… well… human?"

"Of course. You wouldn't feel any different."

"Um, how will I recognise the changes?"

"You will feel a wrongness, a disruption in your senses – something out of place."

"Out of place? Jesus Christ! I've felt that most of my life. And, right here now, what could be more wrong than standing on a spaceship talking to an artificial alien thing made on a different planet? How *exactly* will I know when the timeline changes for the worse? I need to know."

"You will know when it's time."

"Maybe," Georgia whispered, "it will be that feeling like when you say someone just walked over my grave or something like that."

"That is illogical," the device said. "But, possibly, upon analysis of its origin, it may be apt."

Georgia and Cassie exchanged a glance.

You have to ask the right questions, Cassie thought, remembering her mum saying that when she and Kay had gone back to see her in February 2011.

"Right, okay," Cassie said. "If that's all you can give me, then do both of those things. Give me the ability to get energy when I need it and to recognise points where timelines change from what they should have been, especially if Laurence is the one changing them. Oh, and the ability to follow their paths and then return to the flash point, fix it and carry on along the alternative path. Does that make sense?"

"Yes," the device answered.

"Wait. Have I asked *all* the right questions?"

"Indeed. All is as anticipated. Open your mind and receive."

Cassie's jaw dropped as yet another intense glow surrounded her.

"Oh, is this like when you showed me how to teleport and time travel?"

"No, that is a much different skill."

"You know what I mean… oh… wow…"

Bathed in the glow, this was like nothing she had ever experienced. She felt her consciousness expand so that she became aware of the entire craft upon which she stood. It grew to encompass the rock to which the craft was tethered and then spread even beyond that. For a moment, it seemed as if the entire solar system shrunk down to the size of a snooker table and Cassie could see it all. But, not only could she see it, she could feel it, hear it and perceive it using senses that no human had ever previously possessed. And, in those senses, she could detect the energy that was just there for the asking and for the taking.

And, she could see how she could take it.

"Are you okay, Cass?" said Georgia, who had been looking on with a perplexed expression on her face.

Even though Cassie was aware of Georgia's voice coming from only a few feet away, it was also like a small pinprick hidden in the vastness of the cosmos within which she found herself. But, Georgia's voice also triggered Cassie's return to normality. She shrunk back down until she was contained within her physical body once more.

Her eyes focused and she turned to her friend and smiled. "Yes, sorry Georgia. I've just been away with the fairies."

"What?"

"I think I just got myself a good deal."

"Um, good, I think. But, er, what about me? What am I supposed to be doing?" Georgia asked.

"You are faulty," the device told her.

"What?" she shouted.

"Aspects of your internal cerebral structure are less than optimal. Your ability to handle simple language constructs is impaired."

"Huh?" Georgia said.

"I think it's talking about your dyslexia," Cassie said.

"Correct," the device confirmed. "Such deficiencies would be simple to correct. I could…"

"You're not upgrading me. Fucking well leave my head alone," Georgia snapped.

"As you wish."

"Good," Georgia said, clearly relieved. "But you didn't answer me about what I've got to do… if anything."

"I have a need for you, so you will remain here."

"You mean I'm a prisoner?" Georgia shot back.

"No, you would be free to return to Earth, if you insisted."

"What, you mean Cass can take me back?"

"No. Her role is to follow Laurence. If you go with her there is a risk of losing you in an alternate timeline."

"Oh, but if I insist, how would I get home? Are you going to send me back?"

"No, as previously stated, I have a role for you."

"So, how do I get back if you won't and Cassie can't do it? I can't exactly walk back or catch a bus."

"That will be revealed shortly. But your presence is relevant to maintaining the circle of life of Cassie Fox."

"Really? So why did you say I could leave if I wanted to?"

"Because you won't when you learn what your future is likely to hold."

"Hell. Stop confusing things. Tell me. What are you going to do with me?"

"Your primary purpose is to be trained to pilot this spaceship."

"Huh? What? Did I hear that right?"

"Christ," Cassie said. "Nothing too important, then!"

"Cassie Fox. Your task is to locate and nullify Laurence's future disruptions. Given your recent enhancements, it will be an education."

"Yeah, I bet. One question, though. Why can't you do it? You fixed things when they went wrong last time."

"No, the creator fixed them. As creators are averse to such interferences in the first place, we cannot call upon one as it would mean revealing that we are about to generate a circle of paradoxes in order to maintain what has already taken place."

"You mean we didn't before?"

"I was under the impression that we hadn't, but the extra information in the third component of the restore operation has negated that belief."

"So, once again, I don't have any choice," Cassie sighed. "Sorry Georgia, but I'll be back as soon as I can. Have fun learning how to pilot a spaceship – at least you're probably better equipped to do it having passed your driving test, which is more than I've ever managed to get around to doing."

"Um, yeah, okay," Georgia said, dubiously. "Good luck."

"Two things before you go," the device said.

"Oh, for goodness sake, what now?"

"The first is that you should refrain from attempting to time travel in space. Go back to Earth directly."

"Do not pass go, no collecting two hundred pounds," Georgia nervously laughed.

"Why not?"

"You were observing Laurence's departure?"

"Yes."

"He nearly lost himself as he had no reference anchor point."

"I don't understand you."

"No, it will take too long to explain. Just don't do it."

"Okay. What was the second thing?"

"A message."

"What?"

"Another piece of information in the third component of the restore operation."

"Oh, and what was the message?"

"Trust the old lady."

"What old lady?"

"That aspect wasn't revealed. Context was absent as was any hint of the origin of the message. Only that it should be passed on to you."

"Does that mean I did succeed?"

"You are too dangerous for me to assign any value of certainty to that fact."

"Well, that inspires a lot of confidence, I don't think."

"Nevertheless, that is how it is."

"Okay. Here goes, finally," Cassie said

"See you soon?" Georgia whispered, possibly more in hope than certainty.

"Yes, Georgia, I *will* see you soon," Cassie said. She closed her eyes and pulled up her expanded map looking for Laurence's trail.

Oh, there he goes – flowing back to Earth and then moving slowly into the future. Well, I've never travelled through space before by myself. But, whatever the device did to me, it feels like I could travel to Pluto and back without any effort.

She took a deep breath and followed.

Diversion: Hungry

"Hold my hand," Kay said. "How many more times do I have to tell you?"

"Huh?" said the dumbo.

Damn it. I'll be lucky to get this one through more than a couple of portals before something kills her. She's just as likely to fall over her own feet and impale herself on a traffic cone or something just as ridiculous.

Kay snatched the dumbo's hand and pulled her towards the portal. They were in the basement of what would, one day, be called Dragon Hall. Located in King Street, one of Norwich's oldest thoroughfares, the building had once been a merchant's hall. Later, it had been divided into separate dwellings and shops, staying in that state for several hundred years before being restored as a single building in the late twentieth century.

Right now, Kay suspected they were in the nineteen-fifties and the place smelt like a butcher's shop. This wasn't too surprising as that was exactly its current role and, despite the lack of modern-day refrigeration and less-than-hygienic surroundings, the smell was making her hungry.

The dumbo had homed in on the portal while they were ambling down Horn Lane. Until the demolition of what had been called 'The Village on the Hill' in the 1960s, Horn Lane had run between Ber Street and King Street.

The portal was beneath a shop whose sign above the door had proclaimed "A. Swatman" in large lettering. Underneath the name, in a smaller font, it displayed "High Class Meat Purveyor."

Ignoring the shouts of the proprietor, they had pushed past the counter and located the staircase just as a horde of undulating nasties had spilled through the front door and oozed all over the shop.

"Nasty, nasty," the dumbo said, giggling in delight before almost going head over heels down the stairs.

This one really is the pits, Kay thought as they reached the basement and jumped into the crackling field of energy that only they could detect. *Why are the intelligent ones so few and far between?*

A second after hitting the portal, they were ejected out the other end.

Where is this? Ah, I recognise it. Oh shit!

"Watch out," Kay shouted, dashing to one side to avoid the nasty hiding in the shadows. It was one of those slow, lumbering things with a huge mouth and far too many teeth.

"What? Ah!" said the dumbo Cassie.

"This is Bedford's Bar crypt," Kay mumbled turning her attention away for a second. "Or maybe it's still called Oates Wine Bar at this point. Who knows. It's had far too many names over the years. Right, follow me," she said.

But there was no reply. She turned around and sighed.

"Oh, for God's sake," Kay spat. The nasty had sliced off the girl's head with a single bite.

"I told you to watch out. Ah, why do I bother? I suppose I will have to find a new one now. Hopefully, one that's nowhere near as dumb."

Having swallowed the dumbo's head, the creature started munching on the headless torso. Kay stood at a distance keeping clear as it chewed through the remains of the clone.

Licking its lips, the nasty finished by letting out a huge burp before settling down, apparently satisfied.

"Well, looks like you've had your fill," Kay said. Making certain the creature wasn't making any sign of coming after her as well, she bounded up the stairs. "Bugger it, now I'm really hungry. When was the last time I had something to eat?"

Reaching ground level, she cursed finding the establishment shut. The door was locked, requiring a mortice key to open it.

"I suppose I could just kick a window out. None of this stuff looks double-glazed or reinforced. Nah, it's daylight – too many potential witnesses."

She hunted through her pockets and pulled out a bunch of keys that had been underneath a bag of coins and banknotes labelled 1963.

None of the keys made any impression on the lock so, instead, she extracted some needles and an assortment of small metal implements and set about picking it. It took nearly two minutes but, finally, she heard the satisfying click of things falling into place. Before fully opening the door, she packed the keys and lock-picking implements away and glanced over the price list on the bar.

"So, it's currently the Parson Woodforde Restaurant, is it? Early nineteen-eighties, going by those prices."

She slipped out the door, closing it but, as usual, not bothering to lock it behind her. Out in the open and walking along Bedford Street, her eyes darted around picking up small details that gave an idea of exactly when she was. It was relatively warm, though not the full heat of summer. At Exchange Street, she turned left and ambled towards the market halting only at the newsagent on the corner of Guildhall Hill. She glanced at a copy of the Eastern Daily Press to discover it was a Wednesday in mid-May 1982.

"Hmm, been here before, haven't I? Several times, I think," she muttered.

The clocks on the Guildhall and City Hall were almost five minutes at odds with each other, but the time was close to twelve-thirty.

The smell of chips drifted across from the market and Kay's nose followed the aroma. As she wove her way amongst the stalls she stopped and frowned. Just for a moment, she was sure someone had called her name but, in the busy jostle of the lunchtime crowd, she couldn't be sure.

Not the first time here I've heard someone calling me. She frowned. *Pretty sure it's always the same date as well. Ah well, probably just a coincidence. New Cassies are always delivered via the never-ending supply in Castle Mall in 2018. Never picked one up anywhere else.*

She joined a queue and, as she awaited her turn, rummaged through her pockets seeking a bag of money suitable for 1982. The stall had a radio playing.

I remember Mum liking this old tune, she thought, as she recognised Ghost Town.

After declining fish or chicken and opting for chips only, she handed over the correct change and was shaking far too much salt over them when there was a shriek from nearby. Someone's fish and chips went flying and, a second later, a girl with dark, frizzy hair and wearing a denim jacket and jeans, ran past the end of the stall shouting a brief apology.

Oh, now that's new. Could it be…?

This time she definitely heard the girl calling Kay's name. She trotted along following the voice.

She's heading up to the gardens, I think.

As Kay ascended the steps to the Memorial Gardens, her eyes scanning the crowds for Cassie, the music coming from the stalls started playing a cover of *It's My Party and I'll Cry If I Want To.*

Kay spotted Cassie sitting on one of the benches. Her head was lowered, her elbows resting on her knees.

She looks in a really happy state, I don't think. The music couldn't be any more appropriate.

Kay stood for a few moments, popping chips into her mouth, watching Cassie, trying to figure out exactly what she was.

Hmm, isn't she sitting at the exact point where that map on her phone showed? Kay thought, remembering the one time the phone had powered itself up when she had been talking to Robert Kett's ghost up at the castle. *I think it's still in one of my pockets somewhere.*

Cassie appeared to be muttering to herself though Kay was too far away to hear what she said.

I should just turn around and go the other way. But, if I do that, I'll never find out if this is a new Cassie or one I've met before and then lost.

She sighed, not knowing if she was doing the right thing, but couldn't resist approaching the girl from behind. She stepped onto the bench and dropped the food beside the girl. As she sat down she said, "Want some chips?"

Surprised by the warm reception from Cassie who hugged her tightly, Kay said, "Whoa. Anyone would think you were glad to see me. Eat some chips before they go cold."

Origins

The Chase

It took several seconds for Cassie to reach Earth. She aimed for the cottage, appearing just before midday. After rechecking the map and the trail, she followed Laurence futurewards.

He's going back to the present, I think, she thought seeing the traces go past the year 2000 and move towards Norwich city centre. He slowed as soon as 2018 was reached. Five months into that year, he was almost crawling.

Now he's slowing right down. Ah, Castle Mall. June 2018. I wonder. Yes. Why doesn't that surprise me?

The trail halted on the final day of June – the day Cassie had first encountered Kay and the portals. Not only that, it was 11:28.

This is exactly where it all kicked off. So, where is he and what does he think he'll get out of coming here on this day?

Keeping herself invisible, she materialised on a wide bridge that linked the food courts on the top floor with an exit to the upper grounds of the castle outside. The structure held tables and sofas, many of which were occupied.

There's no way I can just appear with all these people here.

She peered in all directions but there was no sign of Laurence. Below her, the Saturday crowds were doing their best to avoid each other on the lower floors. But then her attention was distracted as she spotted a figure descending the escalator from the Castle Meadow entrance.

Oh, it's me. Goodness, I look so young and definitely not prepared for everything that's about to happen to me. Ah, that means…

She glanced across to the restaurant area and spotted the slightly later version of herself also keeping an eye on the earliest one.

Wow, my hair really was frizzed up after all those trips through the portals. This must be when I got the device to create Kay and all the clones. But that was all done with time slowed down. I never did that for myself – it was always the device.

"There you are," came a voice beside her. "I thought you'd come spying."

Laurence. Shit, I can't see him. But how can he see me?

"Remember all this?" he said, his voice coming from a different direction. "I got it straight out of your head and wanted to see it for myself. And, now I'm here, I may screw around with it a bit, just to see what the effects are."

Cassie spun around, trying to locate him.

"So, going by your movements, it looks like I've figured out some of your tricks but I've added some bells and whistles to the invisibility one. Peek-a-boo, I can detect you and you can't see me."

He's right. Ah, but he used 'detect' so maybe he's actually not seeing me in the normal sense. So exactly what is he doing?

Cassie spun around once more, trying to make out where he might be.

"No, not even warm," came the voice from her other side. "Let's see if flying is one of your new skills."

Before she could react, she was lifted bodily off the ground by what felt like seven or eight hands, spun around and launched backwards over the guard rail of the bridge. The last time she'd experienced something similar was when Laurence had dragged her away from the emergency exit on Charlie's bus. But, instead of being propelled horizontally, this time she was plummeting. Although the lower level was thirty feet below, an escalator was directly in the way.

She teleported, reoriented herself and landed on the floor directly below the escalator. Amazed that she'd had the forethought to remain hidden from view, she dodged to one side to avoid a man walking into her.

Despite the extra strength she'd gained only minutes before, she was still winded from the experience and leant on a shop window for support.

She stared up at the bridge. There was no evidence that Laurence was still up there but, she hadn't detected him even when he was right beside her. *What the hell's different about his invisibility? How does he always manage to keep one step ahead of me? I need to think about this. I can't risk him catching me off guard again.*

She heard a voice that echoed strangely, carrying itself over the noise of the crowd. "Wotcha, Cass. Fancy a ground coffee, with lots of air bubbles? And made from scalding water from a fire that comes straight from hell?"

Oh, that's the thing in front of Starbucks, she thought, peering past the rush of people to the multi-armed and legged thing that stood in front of the café entrance. *Hold on, I just realised something… it mentioned earth – well, ground anyway – air, water and fire. The old elements and the order that the portals appeared in. Just what was the point of all that? Maybe, I should… No, stop it, you idiot. I can't hang around here. I need to find Laurence.*

But, feeling something even stranger happening, she halted, realising after a moment that what she was detecting was the device in earlier Cassie's pocket slowing down time. Tuning into it, she thought, *I need to understand this. I'm sure Laurence has never done anything like it – I must keep ahead of him. Yeah, maybe the device was right when it said this was going to be an education.*

As she concentrated, she drew on her newly-acquired abilities and absorbed energy directly from her surroundings: the sun's rays shining through the glass canopy of Castle Mall, the electricity that flowed through the hundreds of wires that were hidden in the walls and nearby ceilings and, also, energy directly from the bodies of the people nearby. As she did so, she latched onto what the device was doing and came to understand how the process worked. *It's not so much slowing time down but absorbing energy to speed both of us up safely. And it's also using that energy as a shield to prevent me from burning up at the same time.*

She tried doing the same, speeding herself up fractionally and dissipating the excess heat generated via the thin layer of the shield she had constructed around herself. She accelerated her metabolism further, perceiving those around her as slowing down to a crawl until they were all but immobile.

Now I'm at the same speed as the device and earlier me. I wonder, it is aware of a later me being here as well? Maybe I'd better hide myself just in case. Looking up momentarily at the glare from the sun, she added, *And get out of this heat as well.*

She glanced around and, seeing Starbucks, thought, *When was the last time I managed to eat or drink anything? Pulling energy in from all around is one thing but nothing beats a coffee and a slice or two of cake.*

She slowed to normal speed and teleported back twenty-five minutes. After locating another nearby shop that provided cover for her arrival, she strolled over to Starbucks. Relishing the normality of the situation, she queued patiently for several minutes and, once at the counter, ordered a Chicken Caesar Wrap and a slice of chocolate caramel shortbread along with two cups of coffee. *Well, I am feeling rather thirsty.*

She paid for it using some loose change from her jeans pocket, hoping the cashier didn't check the dates on the coins in case any of them were dated 2019. She found a free table and sat down. While she drank a coffee and polished off both the wrap and shortbread, she observed what was going on outside the shop's window. For several minutes there was nothing to see apart from the crowds. At around 11:29, the creature appeared.

Okay, this is where it all starts. And it also means that I'm now here four times in total – and that's even before the device creates all the clones.

She took a sip from the second cup of coffee but then decided she was too full to finish it. *Not as thirsty as I thought.*

She sped herself up to match what was going on outside.

And here we go – the device is about to clone original me.

As the cloning process started, she became aware of something strange occurring a few feet to her right. A dark mist was forming and, after a few seconds of her accelerated time, she saw that it contained thousands of overlaid versions of herself and Kay.

No, not me. The ones that look like me are just younger versions of Kay. Ooh, they're getting rather close and the whole thing is making me feel weird.

She stood and moved to one side. Every single one of the multiple instances of Kay was beginning to move towards the chair she had just vacated, though none of them appeared to be aware of any of the others.

Okay, so we're doing a swap – I wonder if anyone notices. This is just like the clones the device created outside – each one must be in their own separate timeline.

"You're welcome to the coffee – don't all fight over it," she said to them and teleported outside to observe the various stages of the cloning process.

Hmm, matter conversion with added soul, she thought as her original self was duplicated four times. *It's using real me as a template or mould, and duplicating me all in situ – a bit like all those Kays I saw in Starbucks just now. Right, now one of them is being selected to create the initial Kay while the other three will be split up to make the rest of the clones.*

After several more seconds of close observation in accelerated time, a thought crossed her mind, *I think I can see how it's done. Possibly, I could even do that myself if I ever needed to. Can't think of why I would, though. There's enough clones of me around to last several lifetimes.*

By this point, the Kay clone had moved to one side and the other three had been split into thousands, all of which occupied almost the same space, each located within their own slightly differing timeline.

These timelines are all linked quite tightly. It's like they all want to snap back into the same one but the device is keeping them separated. I suppose, once they've all gone their own ways, they'll be back in the normal, common timeline.

Young and old Kays erupted simultaneously from Starbucks and collected a clone, though she noticed many younger ones stay inside and just watch. This was followed by the illusion of the castle gate and wall starting to tumble down.

Right, I don't want to see that bit again. I reckon I've wasted enough time here – I'd better find out what happened to Laurence.

She teleported back several minutes to the upper floor, positioning herself invisible near the entrance to the gardens which overlooked the footbridge. She also accelerated slightly so that time around her slowed by about ten per cent.

She didn't have long to wait before becoming conscious of a disturbance halfway along the bridge. She concentrated on the spot and the outline of Patrick's body could be made out. By speeding herself up a bit more, he became more opaque. A few seconds later, she detected a second disturbance.

Me, when I first appeared. Now there's five of me here. She watched the slow-motion replay as Laurence taunted and then used his powers to launch her earlier self off the footbridge.

That's one thing I need to learn for myself. He didn't need to duplicate himself, which simplifies things as it only leaves one target. Here goes. She sped up even more and ran towards him, slamming her accelerated body into him before he even realised she was there. Grabbing him while he was off balance, she teleported them both away, picking Mousehold once more as the destination. They arrived twelve hours earlier in the middle of the night.

"Two can play at that game," she taunted, returning to normal speed and adjusting her stance ready to punch and kick him. But, seeing the mess she'd previously made of poor Patrick's face caused her to hesitate.

"No," he screamed before disappearing futurewards yet again.

"Damn," Cassie spat, following the trail. *Classic mistake. I should have just*

*beaten the shit out of him instead of stopping to gloat – that's his style. Right, where's
he going? Oh, past April 2019 – that's in our future. Is that dangerous? Hmm, can I
intercept him while he's time travelling and make him change direction?*

She accelerated, catching him up. Grabbing hold of him, she switched
direction and forced him backwards. She managed to drag him back seventeen
years, but as they passed 2001, he fought back, extracting himself from her grip
and immediately disappearing. She halted too but, upon materialising, found
herself in September 2000.

Collateral Damage

"Shit. I thought I had him," Cassie said. "Where did he end up?"

She found his trail and followed, coming out near the green on Pottergate in
the early evening of December the second, 2000. Despite remaining invisible,
something that was now automatic, a spatter of rain hit her as she arrived.

The dreary weather accounted for a lack of people. Only two could be seen
and both were inside the nearby fish and chip shop. One was the proprietor, the
other being a woman whose rain hood concealed her face. Cassie found herself
glancing at the green for nasties. *Well, you never know.* But, like chip shop
customers, even they appeared to be avoiding the rain.

Where is he? Cassie thought, trying to locate Laurence. She heard hurried
footsteps approaching from Lower Goat Lane but the body shape of the man
that came into view was not one she recognised.

Wrong height. Patrick's slim and far taller.

The man paused at the doorway to the chip shop before changing his mind.
He continued along the footpath past Cassie to disappear into the alley around
the side of Saint Gregory's Church. Attempting to locate Laurence once more,
Cassie's concentration was interrupted by shouting. She teleported into the alley
to find Laurence gripping the man's arm. The victim was motionless, frozen as if
turned to stone, while Laurence appeared fuzzy and out of focus.

"I know you're here, Mother dear," Laurence shouted. "I'm not sure how you
managed to drag me back here but I can definitely sense you. Surrender right
now or I'll kill him, just like I killed Ka'Chull and the rest of that useless, blood-

hungry tribe."

Cassie accelerated herself towards him. *I've got to stop him before he hurts the guy.* She crashed into Laurence but, his body was vibrating, preventing her from getting a grip on him.

Damn him, he's one step ahead of me again.

"Hah, I thought you might try that again," he laughed. "Right, his death is now on your hands."

Laurence encased the man in a glowing, green, egg-shaped prison – just as he had done when he was in Ja'Mor's body and about to kill the boy's father.

Oh hell, he really is going to kill an innocent man. I need time to think. She sped herself up so that Laurence and his prisoner slowed to a crawl. *Can Laurence do this speeding-up thing? I hope not.*

She tried to break into what surrounded the man but, no matter how much power she drew upon, it seemed that penetrating the shell was not possible. The prison started to shrink slowly though in real time, it would snuff out the man's life in less than a second.

Oh, my God. He's going to crush him to death. How can I stop him? All these extra things I can do but I still need more time. I could go away and think about it and come back to the same time. No, I need to observe this directly and understand exactly what he's doing.

Cassie increased her own speed even further to give herself that time. Around her, the world ground almost to a standstill. She shut her eyes to access her map of the portals. None were nearby, but it gave her an idea.

I created one once – no, two actually. The one that led to that burning shop – Garlands wasn't it? - and the one to the library. But how much did the device do, and how much did I do? Can I still make a portal by myself?

She remembered being in Gildencroft Park and asking a portal how it had been made. It had shown her, even though she hadn't fully understood it. But, the knowledge was still within her head, as was the memory of the device saying that she needed strength to create a portal.

Strength from energy isn't a problem. If I create a portal around the egg thing and activate it, will it break his hold?

She drew in energy – from the air, from the heat put out by streetlights, from the light shining from stars hidden above the clouds. When she had enough, she began to form a new huge portal around the man and his glowing prison.

It needs a destination. But, if I make it too obvious, Laurence will be able to track the man down again. Ah, maybe I can connect it to lots of the existing portals all at once – he should then pop out at any one of them at random. Hopefully, Laurence won't be able to figure out which one he came out at. I can then find him later and return him to today's date. Here goes…

The portal wobbled and shimmered, but also threatened to collapse.

Ah, no. It's unstable. Maybe a portal should be like a single point – not an empty sphere. It wants to collapse. Damn, I can't stop it.

As the portal and the green prison shell connected, they both snapped down to a single point. With a flash, all three – the portal, the man and his prison – were gone. Cassie closed her eyes again to see which portal it had connected to. All the portals were momentarily overloaded and glowing brightly but Cassie could see no trace of where or when the man had come out.

Oh no. Where did he go? Shit. Have I killed him? I don't even know who he was.

She turned back to Laurence who, still operating at normal speed, had barely moved. Slowing down slightly, she observed how he had caused his body to vibrate. She matched the same frequency. Now she could sense that he was attempting to impart that oscillation upon the prison, despite it no longer being present.

Is that why I couldn't break into that thing?

She observed for another minute – far less than a second of real time – trying to understand what he was doing.

I think I see, though I'm not sure how it works. Maybe the portal I created interfered with Laurence's shield – did each one wipe out the other? Shit, shit, shit. This is Laurence's fault. That bastard has got it coming to him. I don't care if he was once my son, I've got to stop him. And, if that means killing him, then that's what I've got to do.

She slowed and, replicating the vibration, hurled herself at Laurence.

"You bastard," she screamed, grabbing him securely this time. "That does it. I will fucking stop you once and for all."

Laurence bellowed in pain. "What did you do this time?" he groaned.

But, instead of trying to escape, he turned the tables on her, wrapping his arms around her to teleport them elsewhere. It was quick and she had the impression they moved a few miles north-west and back in time to 1946. It was a dark, moonless night so she pulled up her map to find out where they were. *Oh, this is Marriott's Way, isn't it? I've walked along here several times with friends.*

He released her and pushed her away, swaying slightly as he stood panting. His outline flickered as if he'd teleported somewhere momentarily. She had the impression something about him had changed but, in the darkness, couldn't be certain.

"What are you waiting for?" he hissed, sounding as if he had a cold. "I thought you were going to stop me. Come on. Get it over and done with."

What's he up to? I've got to keep the upper hand.

Speeding up, she hurled herself at him, flinging him sideways where he tripped over a length of metal. *Must keep him off balance. Just like Em'Dor did when she was teaching me how to wrestle.*

"Best you can do?" he taunted with a sniffle, raising himself to a kneeling position though not retaliating.

Is he playing for time? she thought as he let her slap him across the face. *I mustn't tell him anything about the portal. He'll only learn from it. I've got to find a way to shut him down again and, if I can't find a way of letting Patrick back out, then I've got to face the alternative.*

Clamping her hands around his head, she tried to look inside his mind. But, he seemed ready for her attack. Foremost in his thoughts was the message: *If I can't own you, Cassie Fox, then I will destroy you. I know what's coming and I will bring your entire world down. Do you want to know how I'll do it?*

"I don't believe you," she hissed. "How?"

With a kiss, came his thought, adding. *Don't miss your train.*

"What?" she said, feeling him go slack as if he was inviting her in further. She was also conscious of a strange rumbling sound that grew in volume. *Is he doing that? Hold on, this is too easy. He's faking… shit!*

Without warning, Laurence teleported pastwards leaving Cassie alone, cursing. Not only that but, behind her, the rumbling sound was much louder. Turning around she squealed before teleporting several yards away. A train, a steam engine at its head, rattled over the track upon which she had been standing.

Bloody hell. I'd forgotten that Marriott's Way used to be a railway line.

As she watched the engine pass, she absorbed some of the energy it was generating and built her strength back up.

"Shit, that was way too close. Where did he go?"

She found Laurence's trail headed pastwards and made a note of it, knowing she could pick it up again when she needed to.

"I need to figure out whether or not that man died. If there's a chance he survived, then I need to find him and rescue him."

She returned to the Pottergate of December 2000 a few seconds after she'd previously departed. Saint Gregory's Alley was deserted so she fully materialised and brought up her map of the portals. They were still pulsating brightly but, after a minute, they settled back to how she remembered them. But none of them held any clue as to where the man had gone.

Oh no. Was he torn apart, split across all the portals? Shit, what do I do now? I need to know exactly what I caused to happen. She walked back up the alley to the green, trying to ignore the aroma coming from the chip shop.

Maybe if I view it again, I might be able to see where he went… and whether or not I killed him. She teleported herself back ten minutes, standing on the opposite side of the green to observe the whole sequence through from the start.

She saw Laurence appear on the green, look around, and then run off down the alley. He then stopped and teleported futurewards by a few minutes. She also saw the tiniest shimmer as her earlier invisible self appeared. Seconds later, the man approached from Lower Goat Lane and, after pausing outside the chip shop, followed the path taken by Laurence.

Should I rescue him before Laurence gets at him? Or would that cause another timeline to open up? I'm supposed to be stopping Laurence from screwing things up, not adding any more. Hell, this is getting way too complicated.

Even though she was expecting the shout, it still made her jump. She closed her eyes and brought up the map, watching as the new portal appeared and, momentarily, connect itself to all the others. As before, they flared up but her created portal, its purpose fulfilled, winked out of existence.

*It's gone. Completely. Along with both the man and Laurence's prison. Oh shit. I-
I really think I must have killed him. Maybe…*

A noise broke into her thoughts. From across the green, a door opened and
closed. It was followed by footsteps coming closer. The figure approaching was
shrouded in a raincoat with the hood up. She popped chips into her mouth
from the bag she held close to her chest as she walked.

"Don't worry about him, Cassie," the woman said as she was about to pass
by. "He's not dead."

"Huh? Really?" Cassie said, wondering if her voice could be heard.

"Yes, really. I know you're there and I can just about hear you. Now, stop
trying to hide yourself and have some chips."

Cassie became visible – an act that didn't scare the woman in the slightest.

"How do you know he's not dead?"

"I have it on good authority."

"Who the hell are you and how did you know I was here?"

The woman shrugged but, being a couple of inches shorter, Cassie still
couldn't see her face properly in the low light.

"Well, I didn't want to miss seeing a brand new portal being created, did I?"
the woman said and, when Cassie didn't reply, added, "Cat got your tongue?"

"Just what else do you know about me?" Cassie said, stepping backwards,
becoming fearful of this woman who seemed to know far too much.

"Oh, I'm no danger to you, Cass. Just like to add, though, don't make too
much of a mess of Patrick – he is… well, let's just say that I've got a *use* for him."

"What do you mean?"

"I know you want to kill him – Laurence, that is," the woman said as she
broke off a small piece of battered cod, "But that won't be necessary. In fact,
killing Patrick will be downright dangerous. Look, it will all make sense soon."

The woman popped the fish into her mouth and held out the open wrapper.
After chewing and swallowing the fish, she added, "For goodness sake, girl, help
yourself to some chips before the rain makes them go all cold and soggy."

Cassie sighed and did as she was told.

Diversion: Picnic

"Not dumb enough, I reckon," Kay sighed as she ran.

"What? Are you, like, talking to me?" asked the Cassie clone in between gasps of breath.

"Who do you think?" Kay said.

"What did you mean by that? And why were you asking about me seeing maps in my head earlier on?"

"No time to talk right now. We've got to get away from the blobs."

Running along Saint Stephens Street in the direction of Debenhams, they were being followed several yards behind by four globular things of no discernibly consistent shape. The sparse crowds in the coolness of the late evening were totally oblivious to the presence of both the nasties and themselves.

Provided we don't actually run into them, of course, Kay thought, looking at the shops and trying to figure out when they were. *Feels like the 1970s. Ah, that car is an R-reg – that means 1976 or later if I remember correctly.*

The last portal had popped them out at one of the entrances to the Saint Stephens Street pedestrian subway. Once they'd reached street level, they found the things lounging up against the Co-op Store windows on the opposite side of the road.

Kay hadn't encountered this particular type of nasty for what seemed like years. She was trying to remember if they absorbed their victims, dragged them underground or were just ridiculously easy to outmanoeuvre.

"You just concentrate on finding the next portal," Kay ordered her companion. *This one keeps forgetting her purpose – I'm sure she'd just wander off and go shopping or sightseeing if I didn't keep reminding her.*

"Up here," the Cassie clone shouted, running up the incline of Westlegate.

"Yeah, just announce to the blobs where we're going," Kay muttered, glancing at a few of the people they passed. "Maybe the blobs will puncture themselves on one of these conveniently placed punk rockers and explode."

"What rockers?" said the clone.

"Don't worry about it. Going by this lot, we are probably around 77 or 78."

"1978?"

"Duh, yeah. You think they had punk rockers in 1878?"

"Dunno – it's all ancient history, anyway."

"To you maybe – oh, whatever. So, where is it?"

"This place," said the clone as they neared the top, stopping outside a glass-fronted bar that sported the name of Rixy's Cafe Americano. Inside, the place was crowded, and many of them were dressed similarly to the punks outside.

Kay had known the place under several guises, including as a MacDonalds in the 1990s. Seeing the blobs advancing up Westlegate, Kay pushed open the door and asked the clone, "Where's the portal?"

She could sense its presence, but pinpointing it was always hit-and-miss for her. The clones were always better at this sort of thing. The current clone in question pointed towards the back of the establishment and they threaded their way between people.

"Ah, right, it leads to a nightclub at the back. Looks like it's called Peoples at the moment," Kay said. "I've also been in it when it was called the Boogie House. Can't remember which came first. Going by the crowds there's probably a band on tonight."

They queued up with others waiting to get into the club. Nearing a doorway, Kay hoped the doorman taking payment would fail to notice them. However, he did a double take as they went to go past and said, "Sixty pee each."

"Anyone interesting?" Kay asked while she extracted a pound note and twenty pence worth of coins from a bag labelled 1975.

"Rumblestrips. Some punk band on first," came the answer as Kay paid up.

Having no idea who or what Rumblestrips might be, other than traffic calming, Kay urged the clone through the passageway. They encountered a small, barely-lit room whose tiny dance floor was already more than half full. Punk rock music was being played by a DJ half-hidden in the darkness. On the ridiculously low stage, some people, roadies or possibly some of the musicians themselves, were setting up some minimal equipment.

"Are we going to stay and watch?" asked the clone.

Kay looked around. "Those blob things are probably going to appear at any moment, so probably not. Where's the portal? Is that it beside the stage? Sometimes it's in the gents – that happens far too often to be coincidence."

The clone gazed around before focusing on a spot across the room. "Er, yes."

"Hmm, interesting."

"Why?"

"How many portals have we been through together?"

"Can't you remember?"

"Just assume I can't, they all merge into each other after a decade or so."

"Um, about a dozen, I think. I haven't been counting."

"Yeah, feels like about that many. If I'm right then it might be congratulations."

"Huh?"

"This is one that's sometimes – but not always – a transition."

"What's a transition?"

"Haven't I already explained that?"

The clone shook her head.

"Maybe it was your predecessor I told… not that she had any hope of getting as far as a transition."

"A dumbo?"

"Absolutely."

"So, what's a transition?"

"All of the portals we've gone through so far have been underground or, at least, below street level. After a while those ones stop and we hit a bunch that are above ground – or overground."

"Underground and then overground? Wombl–"

"Shut that up right now. None of you buggers can resist singing that damned song. Sometimes there are two portals close by – one underground, the other not. At other times a single portal is connected to both types – more of a direct route, I suppose. Anyway, the ones after the overground ones are associated with water in some fashion or other. It's like the old elements of earth, air, water and…"

"Um, fire?"

"Yeah, you got it. I haven't hit those yet myself but I know that a later version of me has."

"Oh. Right. Erm, am I a dumbo?"

"Not the brightest, but far from the absolute pits that I've come across. Mind you, I'm still on the lookout for the dumbest of all. I've seen her – and you definitely aren't her."

"Does that mean I'm one of the ones you won't be able to save?"

Kay sighed. *Yeah, don't rub it in. I still don't know what I think I'm achieving by rescuing you bunch of dodos – I wish I didn't have to. There's only ever been one Cassie that had her head fully screwed on and I've managed to lose her twice so far – once under Earlham Road and the other on Great Grandad's bus.*

"Look, don't worry about that right now," Kay said. "Let's move closer to the portal in case..."

They were interrupted by the musicians on the stage testing their equipment. It took all of about twenty seconds and then came the inevitable punk intro of, "One, two, three, fucking go..." as they launched into their first number.

"Charming," said Kay before something distinctly non-human by the entrance caught her eye. "Oh, bugger. Here they come."

"What?" the clone shouted back, unable to hear over the band screaming something along the lines of: *Waiting for the answer, waiting for the break, waiting for the non-existent icing on the cake...*

Kay pointed to the nasties.

"They look kind of harmless," the clone shouted over the music as the last of the four blobs squeezed into the club.

"Don't bet on it," Kay shouted into the clone's ear. "If they catch you, then we'll know exactly how harmless they are. Do you want to risk it?"

The clone shook her head.

Kay grabbed the clone's hand and strolled purposefully towards the portal and stepped through. After the usual buzz of electricity, they popped out into daylight and greenery, and immediately dropped several inches onto grass.

"Ow," said the clone, who had fallen over. "I've broken my ankle."

They were on the side of a grass embankment that sloped down towards a road.

"Aha," Kay said, "we're above ground, even if only by a few inches. It was definitely a transition."

"My ankle," the clone repeated, attempting to stand.

"Yeah, well if you're that badly injured I'll get my gun and shoot you like they do with lame horses."

"Huh? I didn't know you had a gun."

"I haven't. I see your leg is now okay enough to stand on."

"Oh, yeah, maybe," said the clone, gazing down the slope. "Where are we?"

"Mousehold, I'd say," Kay said, her eyes scanning for dating clues.

"No, surely not. Where are all the trees?"

"They haven't grown yet. It was a lot more open back in the early twentieth century, which is probably when we are. Heathland shouldn't be covered in trees like we have it in our time, you know. This is more like its natural state."

"Oh, I see. How can you tell the date?"

"Down there is Gurney Road and it's got tram tracks on it."

"So?"

"They're shiny. The trams closed down in 1935, so that means they're either still running or haven't long been closed. So, obviously pre-World War Two."

"You're not wrong there," came a voice, making them both jump. "It's 1931 – and the trams have got another four years."

Kay turned around to face back up the incline. About twenty-five feet away was an old woman sitting on the grass. Kay started up the hill with the clone limping behind her.

"Oh, you again," Kay said as they reached her level. She could now see that the woman was sitting on the edge of a large tartan blanket spread on the grass. Upon the blanket were laid several plates filled with sandwiches and cakes along with three cups and accompanying saucers.

"Tea or coffee?" the old lady asked.

"You were expecting us?" Kay said, approaching the blanket. *She looks slightly younger than the version I saw on Dolphin Bridge and in Tombland in whatever year that was – nineteen-twenties, I think.*

The old lady smiled.

"I had an idea the portal was ready to pop," she told them.

"Who is she?" the clone asked.

"Clone?" the old lady said.

"Yeah," Kay said.

"Thought so. The real Cassie looks far more alert."

"So, who is she?" the clone repeated.

"Yes, who exactly are you?"

"Your picnic coordinator," the woman said.

"Cut the crap," Kay snapped. "Oh wait. I remember you saying about Mousehold and a picnic when we saw you at Dolphin Bridge."

"Dolphin Bridge? Ah, one I've not done yet. Thanks for the heads up."

I suppose I'd better tell her she should bring wellies for that one, Kay thought. *Nah, bugger it. Why should I? She never tells me anything useful.*

"Sit down and have a cuppa," the old lady continued, "The sandwiches and cakes are homemade. Cheese? Tuna mayonnaise? Piri Piri chicken?"

"Piri Piri?" Kay said, sitting down on the opposite side of the blanket. "That's rather anachronistic, which tells me you are definitely using the portals. Are you going to tell me who you are or do I have to beat it out of you?"

"Oh, Kay," the woman said, pouring a cup of tea and offering it to the clone, "you wouldn't beat up a kindly old lady in front of this sweet young Cassie clone, would you? Anyway, you could probably figure out who I am if you think hard enough. Tea or coffee?"

"Coffee, thanks. It would be a lot easier if you told me."

"Yes, it would, which is precisely why I won't. You have to earn it."

"Earn it? How?"

The old lady shrugged. "The portals don't go back far enough for what I need."

"Ah, so you admit you *are* using the portals."

The old lady nodded.

"What do you mean about not going back far enough?" Kay asked.

"What's the earliest date you've ever come out at?"

"Um, about 1900, I think. Possibly one that might have been very late 1890s, but nothing earlier."

"Yes, that sounds about right if you haven't done the shoe factory one yet."

"The what?"

"1862. But, that one's not usable. Not for me, anyway."

"Why?"

The old lady grinned. "You'll find out when you encounter it – let's just say it gets a bit toasty. Anyway, I need to buy something in 1856 and, although I lived through that period myself, I couldn't afford to collect enough of the very old coins and notes at the time. Things are tight when you're raising kids."

"I wouldn't know."

"No, and you never will. Probably for the best given what you have to do."

"Tell me about it…" Kay muttered. "Wait. Does that mean you *know* what I have to do?"

"Eventually. Yes. Can't tell you, of course."

"Why doesn't that surprise me?"

"So, have you got anything on you that will be legal tender in the eighteen-fifties?" the old lady said, pouring coffee into one of the cups. "Milk?"

"Thanks. Eighteen-fifties? I doubt it, maybe the odd penny or two."

"Please take a look," she said before turning to the clone. "Tuck in, Cassie. There's plenty of sandwiches to go round."

The clone, who had sat down and was rubbing her ankle, nodded and started loading sandwiches onto a plate.

Kay rummaged through her pockets and pulled out several money bags.

"Do you always carry so many around?"

"Sometimes. If I'm past the year twenty-ten, then I often offload a few at a storage place. I keep some of my clothes there as well."

"Oh right. Well, that accounts for the boxes of money that Cassie inherited."

"When did I inherit those?" the clone asked.

"Not you, dear," the old lady said with a smile. "Here, help yourself to crisps and cakes as well."

"Ah, so I leave all those boxes to Cassie, do I?" Kay said. "Should you have told me that?"

"Yes. Just making sure they end up where they should. So, found anything?"

Kay examined the bags finding the earliest one was labelled 1910. Inside it, she found only a few copper coins that pre-dated 1860. "Here, seven-pence-ha'penny. What will that buy?"

"Oh dear. Not a lot, even in 1856. But, please keep a lookout for more, especially any ten-shillings, pounds or higher valued notes."

"You'll be lucky. I don't go back far enough for anything like that. So, you want these?"

"Yes, please."

"Right, but you've got to earn them. If you won't tell me about my future or who you are, then what else can you tell me about yourself?" Kay asked, helping herself to a cheese sandwich. "You mentioned kids."

"All right. How about this? I have been married once and given birth to three children in total, though only two of those were fathered by my husband, Richard, who is sadly no longer with us."

"That doesn't help in the slightest."

"Precisely," the old lady grinned, holding her hand out.

With a sigh, Kay handed over the six pennies and three ha'pennies, which the old lady pocketed.

"Oh, and don't mention meeting me to Cassie," the old lady said with a grin. "The real one, I mean."

"Aren't I real?" the clone said, in between sipping her tea.

"Afraid not," the old lady said, tilting her head to one side and smiling sympathetically.

The clone blinked a few times and looked as if she might start crying.

"So, why can't I tell the real Cassie about you?" Kay asked.

"She will get to know all about me in the fullness of time. Just don't tell her yourself, though."

"What if I do?"

"Simple. I will have to kill you," the old lady said before bursting into laughter.

Unhealthy

A Change Of Name

The woman with the chips refused to answer any questions as to her identity. Instead, she told Cassie she needed to find out what Laurence had done in the future.

"I thought he went back to the past after trying to get me hit by a train."

"Yes, that's what he wanted you to think – don't be fooled."

"So, where did he go and, also, how do you know all this?"

"Sorry, I can't tell you any more."

"Is that it?" Cassie said, exasperation showing in her voice.

"Yes, apart from saying one more thing, I suppose."

"What's that?"

"Promise me you'll look after your health."

"Huh? Why?"

"Well, there are some *really* nasty bugs about, though those might be the least of your worries. Goodnight." And, with that, the woman walked off.

Cassie remembered the device telling her to 'trust the old lady'. *Was that her? How can I tell? And why did she say Laurence was trying to fool me?*

She returned to the railway line of 1946 and, slowing time down, observed Laurence's departure from a distance. *Yes, he's definitely heading back into the past. Ah wait – I saw him flicker a little earlier, didn't I?*

She went back a few minutes and watched the full sequence through again. *Got it, just after we arrived. He went forwards and then returned to the same second. So, where did he go? Oh, he's gone well past April 2019 – is this dangerous?*

Following his trail, she arrived in the spring of 2020 to find not just one trail, but hundreds of them. She teleported up on the castle pathway and tried to sort out which of the multiple trails had come first. *This is too difficult – harder than tracking Ka'Tor running through a Stone Age forest. Is he trying to make things more difficult to hide his real purpose?*

Looking around, she was surprised to see the area empty of people. She checked the date and time – nearly a quarter past nine on the twenty-third of April, 2020. *It's probably a bit early for people to be up here. Anyway, this is around the back of the castle, close to where Kett brushed my hair that time. There's probably more people around the front. Well, as it's deserted...*

"Oh, that feels better," she said, becoming visible and feeling the warmth of the morning sun hit her skin. "Better than the rain on Pottergate."

She walked around to the path that led back down to the gateway but there were no people there, either.

She frowned. *Is something wrong or is the castle shut?* At first, she couldn't figure out what was different. She continued around to the view over Castle Meadow and glanced towards City Hall. It looked the same as it always had from that vantage point. Then she realised what was missing.

No traffic noise.

She approached the railings and looked down.

This is where I waved to Arthur Fox back in 1912, isn't it?

But, unlike one hundred years earlier, there were no trams or barrow boys going about their business. Below her, Castle Meadow was not only devoid of traffic but of people, too. It was more like it had been that time she had overshot her intended stopping date and found herself in mid-air. On that occasion, with the time just after sunrise, she had found the castle mound alive with rabbits. But, the height of the sun in the sky and the time showing on the City Hall clock, confirmed that it really was around a quarter past nine.

Maybe there are roadworks and Castle Meadow's shut. But she couldn't hear any traffic in the distance, either.

She retraced her steps to get a view along Red Lion Street. Here she did see movement. But it was a far cry from what she expected. Instead of queues of vehicles and packed pavements, there were just two people walking along outside Debenhams while a cyclist was heading towards Saint Stephen's Street. Apart from those three, the streets were otherwise deserted.

"What's going on?" she muttered. Wondering if Robert Kett would put in an appearance, she called his name but only birdsong answered.

Descending the path, she passed the gateway and wound her way down to the level of the gardens in what had once been the castle ditch. Turning left at the bottom of the steps, she walked towards Castle Meadow itself.

Nothing moved. No buses or people. The place was a ghost town. If there were any people about, then the curve of the road was hiding them from view. About the only things she could detect were the remains of the time-travel traces left by Laurence that were drifting over the city. Some of them were earlier than the current date plus many that stretched weeks into the future.

He's really putting some effort into this. Why?

Crossing the road, she walked down the slope of Arcade Street towards the Royal Arcade. It was just as devoid of people and all the shops were closed. About to turn right into Castle Street, she heard coughing coming from her left along the Back of the Inns. She changed direction, wondering if it was Laurence.

But the man, once she had located him, was unknown to her. His unshaven face poked out from the hood of a padded navy blue jacket that was as tatty as the sleeping bag that concealed his legs. He sat with his back up against the wall next to the lower entrance to Castle Mall, drinking from a bottle.

As his eyes met hers, he wiped his chin and said, "What do we have here? You lost, girlie?"

She stopped, not knowing what to say. Her eyes glanced upwards, avoiding his, and alighted upon a sign. It said 'Castle Quarter'.

"Huh?" she said. "When did that change?"

"What?" the homeless man said.

"Castle Mall."

His eyes followed her gaze.

"Dunno. Last year, maybe. Who cares. Everyone still calls it Castle Mall."

Cassie looked at the man properly. He might have been in his thirties and could have been quite handsome had he not been in his current state which, apart from being somewhat unkept, was also drunk.

"What's happened?" Cassie asked. "Where is everyone?"

"Blimey, where you been for the last few weeks?"

"Erm, I, er, was out of the country?"

"Hah, yeah, right. Somewhere exotic no doubt, like the moon? Flew back on your own private spaceship, did you?"

"Look. Just tell me what's happened. Please?"

"You really don't know?"

Cassie shook her head.

"Come closer then and I'll tell you," he beckoned. "No, closer still."

If he tries anything I can just teleport away, she thought, sitting down several feet away from him. Her back was against the corner of the entrance giving her a view in all three directions. Ahead, the western half of White Lion Street leading towards Gentleman's Walk was empty of people. To her left, a voice or two but no hint of traffic noise could be heard in the distance echoing off the buildings of Red Lion Street. Where the Back of the Inns led towards the Royal Arcade, she could see the street was as empty as it had been minutes before.

"Well?" she said when the man offered nothing more.

"What?" he said, as if he'd already forgotten the subject in question.

"All this," she said, the sweep of her arm indicating everything around them.

"Want a drink?" he said, offering her the half-empty beer bottle.

"No thanks. Tell me what happened, where everyone is."

"Oh yeah. They abducted most people," he said and started giggling.

"Huh? Abducted? What are you talking about?"

"The aliens, of course."

She stared open-mouthed at him.

Oh no, have the creators come to Earth because of something Laurence did?

The drunk openly laughed, which degenerated into coughing. "Hah, aliens – as if – coulda swore you believed me for a second."

"Well, what was it, then?"

"You're kidding me, aren't you? You must know."

"No. Please tell me."

"Christ. You must've been asleep for a month or four. Come closer and I'll tell you all about it. No jokes this time. It's alright, I haven't pissed meself. You're safe. It's a long story."

Reluctantly, she moved closer, within a couple of feet. *Oh God, he absolutely reeks of drink and worse.*

"It started like this," he said, leaning towards her. He grabbed her arm and pulled her close, pursing his lips obviously intending to plant a full kiss on her own. She wriggled away so that he kissed her cheek instead, his facial bristles reminding her of Jason.

"Fuck off," she screamed, pushing his face away with one hand, grimacing as she felt his spittle on her skin.

"Hah, got ya, pretty girlie. That kiss means you'll turn into a zombie like the rest of 'em… if yer lucky," he cackled, alternately laughing and coughing.

She jumped up as he made another lunge at her.

Then it was his turn to be horrified as she teleported away.

Cassie aimed for the memorial gardens overlooking the market. In her hurry to get away from the drunk, she materialised without keeping herself invisible. But the place was deserted and only a few startled pigeons took to the sky upon her arrival. She rested against one of the flagpole supports noticing for the first time in her life that the base of the structure contained a bronze relief of human figures. One, a woman, appeared to be topless and, for a moment, Cassie was reminded of her time with the tribe.

Movement caught her eye. Down at the lower level of the marketplace, a newspaper had fallen out of a litter bin and a light breeze plucked at it. From her vantage point, all she could see of the headline was the word *Scandalous*.

She descended the steps and picked it up, straightening out the cover.

The paper was dated the previous day and the word made up the entire headline stretched across the bottom of the front page. She frowned not understanding what the accompanying text was talking about. It mentioned something about frontline workers and safety gear. A smaller red headline above the main picture caught her eye.

"What the hell is a *Coronavirus Crisis?*" she asked aloud, scaring the one pigeon that hadn't had the sense to fly off. An inset picture showed a vaguely familiar, gormless-looking character in a suit and tie, his arms spread wide in front of a lectern upon which were written three sound bites in capital letters. The leftmost said 'STAY HOME', the middle 'PROTECT THE NHS' while the third was mostly out of the picture though the first word started with 'SA'.

Stay home? What the hell's happened? Why does the NHS need protecting? Apart from the bastards trying to sell it off, of course. Well, if everyone's at home then I suppose that might account for Norwich being deserted.

Her eyes drifted back to that word: *Coronavirus.*

Virus? Is this some sort of plague? Like the black death or that bird flu thing they kept warning us about a few years back that never happened?

A memory flashed through her mind from when she was wandering around Robert Kett's camp looking for some water to drink, but only finding ale. She remembered that it probably meant that water wasn't safe to drink. She also recalled thinking that things like plagues didn't happen in her own time.

"Wrong again," she muttered. "How do you catch it?"

A worrying thought crossed her mind. *Oh shit, is this paper infected?* She flung it away and rubbed her hands together. *Did that drunk have it? Oh God, the bastard tried to kiss me. I need to wash my hands and face, everything. Oh – and the old woman with the chips said to look after my health. Is this what she meant?*

With rising panic, she looked around. She glanced across to the public toilets near the steps at the top of the market.

Ugh, not in there. That place stinks and all the shops are shut. Where can I… oh, you idiot, that can't stop me.

Teleporting straight into one of the toilets inside the Forum, she rushed to a sink. But the soap dispensers were almost empty. Washing her hands and face with a dampened paper towel, the only thing she could find, did little to comfort her. *Not enough. I still don't feel properly clean. I need proper soap, not the gunk in here. And it might already be infected. Oh, I know…*

She teleported several hundred feet across the city centre, directly into the branch of Boots the chemist that occupied premises between Castle Meadow and London Street. The scream that erupted a few feet away from her upon her arrival made her jump as much as the person who had screamed.

It Started With A Kiss

Cassie stared at the girl behind the counter. In turn, the girl stared back at her looking terrified, her eyes and mouth open wide, her breathing rapid. Unlike the Forum, the chemist was obviously still open. At that moment, though, Cassie was the only customer.

"Sorry, I, um," Cassie said, cursing that she'd forgotten to keep herself invisible. "Um, have you got any, er, well… look, a guy… a drunk actually… he kissed me and I wanted to make sure I haven't picked up that virus thing."

The girl nervously shook her head but then pointed at an empty shelf several feet away. Cassie looked at the signage to see that, normally, it would have held soap and other body cleansing products. Several of the adjacent shelves were also empty or held very little stock.

"Run out," the girl whimpered. "Panic buyers."

"You must have something," Cassie said, moving a bit closer to the girl.

"No, please go away," the girl said, backing away from the counter that separated them. "We've got nothing."

Cassie could see the girl's eyes rapidly glancing around as if she was seeking an escape route. She shrugged and stepped away from the girl.

"Okay, I'm leaving now," Cassie said with a sigh. "Sorry again. But, as you've already seen me arrive, I might as well leave by the same method. Bye."

She teleported away to the girl's second scream.

Can't be arsed to hide. She materialised in the memorial gardens yet again. *I wonder if that girl will ever mention it.*

She glanced up at the City Hall clock. It was nearly half past nine.

Where can I… oh, I know. How about back before all this happened? There will be plenty of soap in the past, especially at home. Ah, and I know exactly when.

She moved back to 2019, picking a date and time she knew her house would be empty… apart from Patrick.

Upon arrival, she checked that Patrick really was still on the mattress in a coma. He was.

Better not touch him in case I'm infected. Oh, but maybe I should. Would he die from it? Or maybe I should attempt to burn Laurence out of his head right now. What would happen if I did that? Oh, stop it, you idiot. Think straight. Stop panicking. Right now, this version of him hasn't been taken back to 1549. If I do anything to him now, it might stop all that from happening.

She closed her eyes and tried to force herself to calm down. According to the device, Laurence still had some significant role to perform, whatever that might be. She didn't dare disrupt that sequence.

Or so the device says. Not that I can trust it. Oh, but that woman also said that she had a use for Laurence. No, wait, she said Patrick – not Laurence. Just who the hell was she? Could she be someone the device created just to keep an eye on me? Well, it did make all the clones.

Crossing the hallway to the bathroom, she ran the bath. *Right now, past me and Grandad are at the solicitor's finding out just how much I've inherited. That gives me a good couple of hours.*

Damn, but he's sneaky, Cassie thought.

Finally feeling she was clean, she returned to the castle of April 2020 and tried to untangle Laurence's overlapping trails. She followed a sequence that, amongst others, took in City Hall, the Roman Catholic cathedral, Pulls Ferry, Anglia Square, several shops and department stores and the main cathedral. In each case, he had remained there for only a few minutes before hurtling off on a new tangent. In another sequence, his tactics changed. He would spend several days in a random house before doing the same elsewhere.

Was he taking a rest? If not, then what was he looking for? In one sequence, she detected where he had finally left 2020. She pounced on the departure point. As expected, it led back to their 1946 encounter on the railway line. *So, what on Earth was all that 2020 stuff about? I suppose I'd better carry on following him.*

She waited for his departure. *He really was trying to get me run over by that train. Oh, and he was also trying to do something to prevent me from noticing its approach. Crafty. And he's off again, going back just a few years this time.*

She followed the traces. *And he's moving south. Ah… towards London.*

The trail ended within a building located in central London. She materialised in an empty room, several doors away from where the trail ended, not wanting Laurence to detect her arrival. She couldn't help admiring the ornate decoration of her surroundings. The room was square with one door, flanked by a pair of tall windows, that exited to a courtyard. Directly opposite, another door led to the interior of the building.

Oh, I know where this is, Cassie thought, as her internal map kicked in. *Wow, I was outside this place with Georgia last August on our trip to London. Admiralty House – all we could see then was the façade. What year is this? 1939 and halfway through October. Oh, that means World War Two has already started. Damn,*

Laurence got this out of my head, didn't he?

Cassie had a momentary flash of vertigo and her vision blurred for a second.

What the hell was that? Oh, wait – someone walking over my grave. Is this where the timeline changes?

She heard raised voices coming from deeper within the building. Several sounded closer and were accompanied by more shouting. They were followed by running footsteps ascending an out-of-sight staircase.

A deep voice complained, "Rude man. Disgusting. What on Earth was all that in aid of? Send guards after him."

The figure strutting around a corner was middle-aged and carried more than a little excess weight. It wasn't all he carried. Two fingers were clamped around a large cigar, its aroma pungent as its smoke curled towards the ceiling.

As soon as he clapped eyes on her, the man halted, rubbing his hand down his jacket as if trying to wipe it clean. As they stared at each other, she recognised him not only from photos she had seen at school but also from the reverse of recent five-pound notes.

Oh, my God, that has to be…

"Can I help you, young, er, lady?" said Winston Churchill. "Is that fancy dress? Or boys' clothes?"

Cassie realised that jeans and a denim jacket were probably not appropriate clothing for women to wear at the start of the Second World War. Remembering something from school about land girls who worked on farms after their menfolk had been called up, she said, "Erm… it's, um, farm clothes."

"Hmm. No wonder you're looking a bit lost if you come from a farm. London must be a bit scary for you." Cassie nodded, going along with the idea. "How did you get in here? You're not with that man, are you?" Churchill added.

"Er, what man?" Cassie replied.

"Exasperating chap. Ran off upstairs after grabbing hold of me. I swear he tried to kiss me – absolutely disgusting."

"No, I…" *Kiss? Oh shit.*

"Your face. You look familiar," he added.

Familiar? Oh, of course, she thought, remembering how much she resembled her grandad's mother.

"Um... yes... I, er, came to see Gwen," she said. "Is she here?"

"Gwen Page? Henry's daughter?"

Cassie nodded, smiling as she recognised the surname.

"Are you a relation?" Churchill asked.

"Yes, sort of," Cassie replied. "On my grandad's side."

Cassie felt herself flush as Churchill scrutinised her face but, given the status of the person examining her, she felt obliged to let him continue.

It's a bit like meeting royalty. Oh, get over it, idiot. He's just an ordinary man.

"Hmm, well yes, I can definitely see the resemblance. She doesn't have your beautiful blue eyes, though, young lady. Miss?"

"Oh, er, Cassie. Cassie Fox, Mr Churchill."

"Well, Miss Cassie Fox, I can see you have already heard of me."

He stepped forward and took her hand. Cassie had to suppress herself from gagging on the cigar aroma as he raised her hand to his lips and kissed it.

"Yes, your eyes are quite amazing," he added with a smile.

Oh God, this is so embarrassing... and disgusting.

Cassie blushed, retrieving her hand and wanting to wipe it clean of his touch. *Now I need another bath.*

"However, I regret to inform you that Gwen is no longer here. Her father is, of course. Miss Page, though, has gone to, hmm, let me think, hmm."

"Er, Norwich?"

"Oh yes, that's quite right. Got a job at their new City Hall, I believe."

"Um, thanks. I, er..."

"If you want to see Mr Page, I believe he is, unfortunately, absent today – official business, you know – but I'm sure I could get a message passed on to him should you require it."

"No, er, must be leaving," Cassie stammered. "Goodbye, Mr Churchill. And thanks."

She ran for the doorway and, once outside, turned invisible hoping no one saw her disappear. Then she stood still, closed her eyes and tried to locate Laurence. That he was no longer around was rapidly obvious.

Do I follow Laurence or do I need to to figure out what he's done to the timeline?

She examined his trails. One four minutes earlier on the ground floor a couple of rooms away and the other less than a minute later when he departed from the floor above.

Wait, why don't I just go back a few minutes and watch Laurence when he first arrived? Hopefully, it will be more useful this time than on Pottergate.

She moved back six minutes and teleported to the room where Laurence would appear, remaining invisible. It was far more ornate than the hallway. Elegant chairs and sofas dotted the area and, on the walls above them, hung several huge paintings, each in a gold-painted frame and depicting some exotic part of the world or remote scenery.

Crikey, this room alone must be bigger than my entire house.

She heard a noise and watched as Churchill entered via one of the four doors. He had walked halfway across the room when Laurence appeared directly behind him and grabbed him.

"Hah, the man who sends millions to their death," Laurence shouted.

Cassie frowned. Laurence's voice – well, Patrick's actually – sounded rough, as though he had a bad cold. She remembered thinking the same during their encounter on the railway line. However, away from the darkness of that night, she could now see how red and bloodshot his eyes were as well.

"I'd give you a run for your money. Here's a bug or two to bugger things up for you," he added, laughing.

Churchill shouted in surprise as Laurence planted a kiss on his left cheek. As he did so, Cassie experienced another moment of dizziness.

This is it… but why did Laurence kissing Churchill cause a timeline change?

Two other men, probably staff, appeared from one of the other doors after hearing the commotion. They rushed across and wrestled Laurence away from Churchill. But he escaped them and ran, coughing, out of another doorway. She teleported to the other side of that door and found herself in a hallway with a wide staircase at one end. One of the doors led to the entrance hall she had originally found herself in but it was Laurence, bounding up the stairs and cackling like a maniac, that held her attention.

She jumped to the floor above and saw him running around another room, shouting at the people there and demanding, "Gwen? Where is she?"

So, he really is looking for Gwen. I've got to make sure he doesn't harm her.

"Gone to Norwich?" she heard Laurence say. "Hah, well I bet I know where." His laugh, which cut off as he teleported away, was replaced by screams.

Shit, do I follow him or find out exactly what he's done here? Follow, I think – I have to see the timeline right through to its conclusion. I can always come back here.

She concentrated on the map and Laurence's trail.

Yeah, he's definitely going back to Norwich. Here we go again…

Cassie found herself in Norwich – and it was still 1939. Laurence's exit point was within the market though, at this time, the stalls were far removed from the permanent structures of her time. These were of a lightweight construction so they could be dismantled and folded away. At that moment, they were very much in use. The market was crowded and Cassie had to remain invisible in order not to start a panic. Going by the commotion several stalls away, Laurence had not used any such precautions.

At least, I felt no reaction this time. Unless I missed it… I better make sure…

She moved back thirty seconds to just before he turned up and waited. Less than a second after his appearance, she experienced vertigo, this time accompanied by a feeling of nausea.

Damn. Another one that needs fixing. But what has he done?

However, by this time, she could see that Laurence had already moved on. His trail led directly inside the newly-built City Hall.

Does that mean he's looking for Gwen? He has to be. I've got to try and find her first and somehow prevent him from getting to her.

She looked up at the building, noticing how new the brickwork appeared. Also, the belfry tower was a dark reddish-brown instead of the pale green she remembered. Her attention was refocused as she detected that Laurence hadn't remained inside for more than a few seconds, and she hadn't had a repeat of the nausea and dizziness.

Hopefully, that means he didn't interact with anyone. Or does that mean he's already found Gwen?

She concentrated and found the trail moving forwards by a couple of hours and across to Castle Meadow. She followed and halted just before Laurence was due to arrive. The time was just gone six in the evening and the pavements were packed with people queuing at bus stops waiting to be taken home after work.

Several were carrying newspapers whose headlines announced the sinking by U-boat of a ship called the Royal Oak.

I'd better remain hidden. My clothes will stick out a mile here.

Laurence appeared in a shop doorway not far from a bus stop just as, to Cassie's eye, a rather ancient-looking double-decker bus arrived. The service number on the front said 10B and the destination indicated was Aylsham via Old Catton, Spixworth and Buxton. Several people alighted from the bus while those waiting to board shuffled towards the open platform.

Ah, I remember Grandad telling me that Gwen had stayed in Spixworth.

"Hop on," said the conductor, standing on the open rear platform. "Especially you, beautiful."

"Oh, hello again, Charlie," came a female voice. "How come you always arrange to be conducting this one?"

Charlie? Can that really be Great Grandad Charlie? Cassie teleported closer to the rear of the bus to get a better view. *Oh my goodness, he's so young. He can't be any more than about seventeen. But, it definitely looks like him.*

"The scenery's always better around this time of day," came Charlie's response, which made the girl laugh. Cassie saw her wait until all the other passengers had got on and then step on board. She made no attempt to find a seat but stood next to Charlie on the platform.

With the last of the passengers boarded, Cassie teleported onto the bus, positioning herself invisible on the lowest stair to get a better look at the girl. She immediately saw the parallel with the photo that was on a shelf in the lounge at home. *Gwendolyn Page, my great-grandmother. Oh, wow, this must be how they first met.*

Charlie rang the bell to allow the driver to depart. But, at the last moment, Laurence jumped aboard, pushing past Gwen to enter the lower deck.

"Oi, no pushing," Charlie said.

"Oh, so sorry," Laurence said, turning to the two. "My deepest apologies."

Then he spat at them, spraying both of their faces in one go. Gwen screamed and Cassie experienced another turn of nausea.

"Off," Charlie shouted, reaching for a handkerchief. "Off this bus right now."

Laurence cackled a throaty laugh and hopped back off.

Cassie watched him disappear as soon as his feet hit the pavement. Charlie, who was busy wiping Gwen's face, obviously hadn't spotted Laurence vanish and Gwen was still too distressed by the attack to notice.

Yuck, Cassie thought, watching Charlie clean them up. *That was disgusting. What was Laurence doing? Oh no, did he bring that virus thing back from 2020? But why else would spitting at Gwen and Charlie change the timeline? Shit, did he infect Churchill as well? And those people on the market?*

The old woman's words about looking after her health echoed in her ears.

As the bus started to trundle off, a passenger on the lower deck stood up and began to approach the rear platform. Wanting to avoid the woman, who seemed dressed for winter, stumbling into her Cassie teleported back onto the pavement so that she could track Laurence's timeline. But, shutting her eyes for a moment to make that tracking easier, she also discovered something perplexing – the portals were winking out of existence one by one. With each passing second, her mental map was becoming sparser. But, that wasn't the only anomaly. While some portals disappeared, one nearby seemed to be doing the opposite and was particularly active. It pulsated in a manner she had never seen before.

What's up with it? And is it important? Surely, I need to follow Laurence and find out if he's brought that virus back. Oh, but what if it's that man from Pottergate? Damn, I suppose I'd better check.

Forgetting Laurence for a moment, she teleported closer to the portal, finding herself outside a department store on the corner of Davey Place and Castle Street. Signs above the ground floor windows gave the name *H. Tyce and Son.* Through the window, she could make out an assortment of kettles, oil-fired lamps and other general household hardware.

It's in there somewhere, she thought, teleporting inside the shop, glad that it had already shut for the day. Despite it still being light outside, the interior was quite dim due to the stock piled up all around the place. The portal itself was located on top of the shop's counter next to a cash till. With her eyes open, she could make out the vague disturbance it made in the air along with the aroma of electricity. But, with her eyes closed, she watched it pulsate several times.

Then she heard a female voice.

"Cassie. Cassie. Are you there? I can't get through."

I recognise that voice. It's a bit like the old lady. It's distorted – I can't be sure.

"I'm here," Cassie shouted running towards the portal. She tried to enter it, but something was preventing her.

"Thank goodness," came the voice again, though it was like hearing someone talking on an old radio where the signal kept fading in and out.

"Who are you?" Cassie shouted.

"Not important. What date is it for you?"

"Um, 1939. Mid-October."

"Good, I thought it felt like that – I'm safe in the nineteen-twenties. The timeline you're in is not the main one. So, I need to tell you some more dates."

"What do you mean?"

"Just listen and remember."

"No. Tell me who you are first."

"Damn it, Cass," the woman snapped, "there's no time for this."

"Your name, otherwise I'm leaving."

There was a couple of seconds of silence and then the voice said, "Anne."

"Anne what?"

"Anne... Luckin."

Huh? No. Can't be, can it? Wasn't that the name on Grandad's family tree?

"Are we related?"

"Yes, of course we are. Now shut up and remember these dates. It's important if you want to get back to the spaceship and Georgia."

"How the hell do you know... Oh, to hell with it. Okay."

"Right, here they come. Three years between each of the first three. December 1939. August 1942. October 1945. For those, any time around the middle of the month should do – when you arrive read up on recent history. Finally, April the fifteenth, 1947 at noon – you probably won't have any difficulty remembering that date. Have you got them?"

"Yes, I think so."

"Repeat them back. Quickly."

"December 1939. 1942, er, August."

"Yes."

"October 1945. And April the fifteenth, 1947. Why that last date?"

"It's your…"

"My what? I didn't hear that last bit."

"…your birthday."

"Yes, I know. But how do you know that? Don't you come from more than a hundred years before I was born?"

"Not important."

"Why those other dates?"

"At some point in your future, you will tell me to memorise them ready for this moment. But, you also said that things are too… and may not work…"

"Too what? Speak louder."

"Too unstable. Listen. That last date is also when … happens."

"When what happens?"

"You'll find…"

"I can hardly hear you."

"Protect…"

"What?"

"Protect yourself. You must … prepared to protect…"

"Protect myself from what?"

"New…"

"New what?"

"…"

"I still didn't hear," Cassie shouted.

"Oh, and one more thi… fizz… heal… thy…"

"I can't hear you. You're breaking up."

"Physician h…"

With a final flash, the portal disappeared and, apart from the taint of ozone in the air, Cassie was left on her own.

Shutting her eyes for a moment, she realised something else. All of the other portals had disappeared. There was no trace of any of them whatsoever.

Now I really must be in an alternative timeline. Is it one where the portals never existed? If so, then how can I be here at all?

Hurricane

"Why those dates and what the hell am I looking for? What recent history?" Cassie muttered to herself several minutes later as she was experiencing time. She had teleported to December the seventeenth, 1939, and was wandering around the city centre. It was a Sunday morning and there were few people about. However, given the time of year, she was surprised to see little in the way of Christmas decorations, which she put down to the country being at war.

She passed a litter bin and spotted a paper that had been dumped in it. Picking it out and making sure it wasn't contaminated with anything, she turned to the front page.

The headline screamed: *British Flu Latest!* Underneath it, the subtitle read: *Latest Casualties Devastate Monarchy and Parliament.*

"British Flu? I seem to remember hearing about something called Spanish Flu – not British Flu."

She read on, the feeling of déjà vu getting stronger.

"Hell. This must be what Laurence was up to. He must have deliberately brought that Coronavirus thing back."

She came to a list of names of the victims. Many of them she had never heard of but the four at the top made her groan.

"Shit," she hissed. "Winston Churchill. Princesses Elizabeth and Margaret. Neville Chamberlain – all dead – none of this happened in the real world."

She scanned the rest of the paper, noting that even the war news had been relegated to an inside page. She read one short article. Apparently, after their attack on Finland at the end of the previous month, the Russians had been expelled from the League of Nations.

Right, is that enough history? Apart from the unexpected deaths, how much different was it from what should have happened? I may be taking history at school, but that doesn't mean I can remember all of it.

She dropped the paper back into the bin but, after wandering around a bit more was at a loss as to what else she should look for.

Oh, how about a library? That might be the best place to find out what's been happening. Now, what were those other dates? 1939 plus three is 1942. What month? August, I think. Oh well, here goes.

"Can you tell me where the library is, please?" Cassie asked of a couple walking in front of City Hall. They trotted in the direction of the Forum but, in August 1942, its spot was occupied by a motley collection of two and three-storey buildings, many whose ground floors had been turned into shops. Most appeared dilapidated.

The woman was wearing a cloth face mask, which did little to hide the fear in her eyes upon being stopped. Both of them backed away from her a little, their eyes making it obvious that they were studying her clothing.

I must stick out like a sore thumb here.

"Duke Street," said the man, pulling a similar face mask out of his pocket, "if it's the free library you want." His hand waved in the general direction of the Guildhall as he arranged the mask on his face.

"Thank you," Cassie said, leaving them. As she walked towards the Guildhall, she was conscious, once again, of the lack of people. Her built-in calendar told her it was a Tuesday. She glanced up at the City Hall clock noticing that the belfry tower was closer to the green hue she remembered, though it was still not exactly the same shade. The clock told her the time was two minutes past eleven, which differed by only a minute from what her calendar told her.

To her right, the area between City Hall and the shops on Gentleman's Walk couldn't have been more different. Where the market normally stood was just an empty concourse, bare apart from the litter that drifted across it on the light breeze. She had the impression the stalls hadn't been there for days if not weeks.

After passing in front of the Guildhall, she entered Dove Street. Few of the shops lining it were open. The same was true of the establishments in Saint John Maddermarket. When she reached the junction with Duke Street and Saint Andrew's Street, the scene was far removed from what she was used to. But she immediately spotted words etched into the stone above the door of the impressive three-storey building across the road. It said: FREE LIBRARY.

She found the door unlocked and entered to silence. As the main desk wasn't occupied, she explored the aisles of bookcases that were so tall that she couldn't reach the upper shelves. After wandering around for a while, including taking a trip up and down a circular staircase, she discovered a section with newspapers. There were both current editions along with those that were weeks and even months old, along with a few magazines and periodicals. The papers were thin, less than six sheets for the most recent and the magazines were similar.

She took a few over to a desk and started reading.

It didn't take more than a few minutes to piece together recent history. One article in a periodical examined the history of the *British Flu*. As far as scientists could determine, it had arrived from nowhere, springing up simultaneously in both central London and Norwich.

Damn Laurence – he knew exactly what he was doing.

From there it had rapidly spread around the country, much of it carried around by the newly called-up infantry, unaware that they were infected. The devastation it had caused had reduced the country's population in twelve months by almost a quarter and, with no cure or vaccine available, new variations flared up again every few months. Many people had taken to wearing face masks to avoid cross-contamination but that hadn't prevented more than eleven million deaths, along with another three million who were suffering from the long-term after-effects of the virus.

That explains the masks those people wore.

But that wasn't all. The papers, from the oldest to the newest, all told the same story – Britain was on its knees. Across the channel, Hitler's forces were gathering but were in no hurry to invade. Their U-boats and ships had successfully blockaded the country for over six months, and the only food available was home-grown and it was rapidly dwindling.

Cassie read of rumours that Hitler had intended to invade Russia, but given that Britain was an easier target, had changed his plans. Now they speculated that he was waiting until the flu had run its course so as not to adversely risk his own troops to it.

"Somehow, I've got to go back and undo all this," Cassie whispered. "But there are still two more dates to go. And just what was that last thing Anne Luckin was trying to tell me? Was it really 'physician, heal thyself'?"

Cassie arrived in October 1945 under the cover of nightfall and, finding that the marketplace was not as derelict of stalls as in 1942, hid herself within one of the dilapidated constructions.

She peered across Gentleman's Walk to the familiar outline of Lloyds Bank. Only, in this timeline, the sign above the windows said *Deutsche Bank.* She looked back at City Hall – it was lit from below with large red-tinted lights that illuminated huge vertical banners that hung billowing in the breeze. Each one was red apart from the white circle within which was enclosed a black swastika.

"Shit," she muttered, "so he did it. Laurence managed to change the course of history with a kiss and a spit. I had a feeling this was going to be what Anne wanted to show me. But what will 1947 hold? Probably not a birthday present I'm likely to enjoy. Here we go."

She arrived just before dawn on the fifteenth of April, not knowing what to expect. But, she had fully anticipated coming out in darkness. She couldn't have been more wrong. The night had been banished as the whole area was illuminated with artificial light. Beams mounted high on many of the taller buildings, including both the Saint Peter Mancroft church and the Guildhall, lit up City Hall like a beacon. Many were also trained on the market square itself, though it was devoid of stalls. However, it was far from empty, being filled with moving trucks, cars and lorries, along with men in uniform who were busy rolling out thick cables, setting up loudspeakers and arranging large mechanical devices whose purposes were unknown to Cassie. All of the uniforms looked German and each soldier was armed. Swastikas proliferated, decorating any prominent wall and hoisted high upon every flagpole.

Even though she was invisible, Cassie had materialised in the thick of it. She was in danger of being bumped into or, more scarily, of being walked through.

I'm like a ghost, she thought with a shiver, remembering her inability to handle plates of food in Kett's camp until she became fully visible.

She teleported to the entrance of Old Post Office Court, which ran alongside the bank, parallel to Davey Place. Within the shadows of the alleyway, which was comparatively dark compared to the intensity several yards away, she tried to make out what was going on.

She realised that the cacophony wasn't coming from just the areas close by. Engine noise also emanated from the skies above and she could make out lights in the sky as several planes circled the city centre.

After watching the planes, she became aware of something white fluttering near her feet. The newspaper, when she picked it up, showed a headline in German but, underneath it in smaller type, was the English. It was dated the day before, and the English headline read: *Tokyo Obliterated.* Underneath, and in smaller type came: *America Vows The Same For United Europe.*

"United Europe? This definitely isn't the EU."

She read a few lines of the main text, which told how, a week previously, Nagasaki's destruction was described as being a test run for Tokyo.

Nukes, she realised. *It happens in this world as well – but two years later.*

The frenzied activity out on the marketplace was accelerating and Cassie wanted to know exactly what was going on. She dropped the paper, thinking, *I need a better view. Higher up. Oh, I know.*

Teleporting to the roof of the Guildhall, she spotted a lighting crew of two soldiers at the easternmost end training their dual searchlights on both the City Hall and the marketplace. Hopping to the opposite end, a slightly lower section allowed her to hide and shuck off her invisibility.

The last time I was up here, I was watching Robert Kett's victory speech and Lord Sheffield being paraded around like a trophy. That wasn't the real world, either. I've got to make sure this one doesn't remain real. How the hell do I do that?

Behind her, the sun began to push over the horizon and Cassie moved forwards in time until five minutes to noon. The sound was deafening the moment she arrived. It wasn't just the noise of people for, mixed in with the roar of lorries, motorbikes and circling planes, she could also hear music. She peered over the edge of the crenellated roof to view the crowd packing the streets. Fear dominated the faces of those not wearing uniforms. Armed soldiers herded more people into the square. The pale faces and spindly bodies of those corralled together emphasised the effects of malnourishment and disease.

The only spaces not crowded with people were the City Hall steps and the road in front of them. To one side of the steps, an orchestra of around fifty well-nourished, black-suited musicians played their violins, cellos, drums, flutes, oboes, bassoons, trumpets and even a harp. Cassie didn't know the music but momentarily teleported down to glance at the title on one of the music sheets she had spotted. Although the text looked German, she recognised the name of the composer: Richard Wagner. The title of the piece, *Die Meistersinger von Nürnberg*, meant nothing to her.

The music ended as she returned to the Guildhall roof. A few seconds later the City Hall clock announced noon. Movement heralded uniformed people stepping out onto the balcony. A corresponding hush descended over the crowd.

The orchestra stood, faced the balcony and each raised their straightened right arm in that direction. Simultaneously, a synchronised round of gunshots from a line of soldiers on the City Hall roof made her and the crowd jump.

She squinted as one of those on the balcony stepped up to a microphone. The face was as recognisable as Winston Churchill's had been and caused Cassie's breath to catch in her throat.

"No, he should be dead," she squeaked, forgetting where she was. But, as she gazed down upon the unmistakable profile of Adolf Hitler, her utterance was lost in the cries of 'Sieg Heil' that echoed throughout the city centre.

It was just the soldiers and the orchestra shouting. None of the general crowd showed any inclination to join in. Only when the soldiers shouted and aimed guns at them were they forced to raise their own emaciated arms and salute the Führer of United Europe.

Some refused and Cassie saw soldiers raise their weapons and take aim. Whimpering, she shut her eyes as the noise and screaming began. When she dared open them again, more than a hundred – men, women and children – lay dead on Gaol Hill. They were left there to remind others of the price of disobedience.

Oh God, I've seen enough, Cassie thought. *I've got to get out of here and find a way of stopping all this from happening. But how?*

A high-pitched noise from above checked her. She peered up to catch a glint of a fast-moving dot high up in the sky. *Is that a jet?*

Nearer the horizon, the propeller-engined planes that had been circling the area rose in a futile attempt to intercept it. But planes of that old generation had no chance of matching it. The jet veered to one side and, for a moment, the sun flashed on something that fell from it. The jet was already miles away as Cassie's eyes tried to locate what it had dropped.

What was that? Then she remembered the earlier newspaper headline. Her mind screamed as she realised what it might be. *Oh shit. Nuke. Protect yourself, she told me. I've got to telep...*

The spark that lit up the sky was more intense than staring directly at the sun through a telescope.

Cassie screamed. Partially blinded, she felt a blistering pressure wave hit as, too late, she enclosed herself in a shield while, simultaneously, she teleported away. With her clothes on fire, her skin burning and shredding, she plummeted back through time, past 1930, past 1860, 1753, 1689 and down into the sixteenth century. She forced herself to stop before she went back any further than 1549.

Somewhere safe – where?

Instinctively seeking familiarity as agony ripped through her, she materialised in the cottage she'd used when in Robert Kett's time. She crashed onto the bed, only vaguely aware that the mattress was still unrolled upon it. Her calendar told her it was September the ninth, 1549.

She groaned as waves of pain and nausea wracked her body. But these had nothing to do with any new alterations to the timeline. Her skin, where it had been exposed to the light from the explosion, was incinerated. All her ears could hear was the continuous screaming of the jet plane mixed with the throb of the thunderous explosion. Afraid that she was about to pass out, she tried to force her eyes open but the dark blotches that were obscuring her vision merged into one rendering her completely blind.

She tried to scream but, in that moment, even that was beyond her capability. The blackness that dominated her vision spread throughout her entire consciousness.

Diversion: Sword

"You on your own again?" the old lady asked without turning around.

As Kay approached, she watched the woman throw small chunks of bread into the river running alongside Wensum Park. A dozen ducks noisily tucked in and two swans paddled across from the other side to join them. The sun was bright making Kay glad she'd picked up some sunglasses several clones back.

"How did you know it was me?"

"Your money bags chink as you walk."

"Oh right, I'll try to remember that," Kay replied. "Yeah, I'm on my own. The last clone got dragged under the ground about twenty minutes ago up near the clothes factory on Havers Road."

"Oh yes, I know the place."

"It's not good for them, you know."

"I should think not. I'd hate to be a clone whose fate was just to die in some unspeakably horrible manner."

"No, I meant the ducks and feeding them bread," Kay laughed.

"I know that and you know that. But, back here in the summer of 1972, not even the ducks know that. Anyway, I bought a sandwich and it was inedible."

"Oh, it's 1972, is it? I knew it was somewhere around the early seventies, but wasn't exactly certain," Kay said as she stared along the river. She had the impression there was a portal nearby but, at that moment, couldn't pinpoint it.

The old lady finished throwing the remains of her sandwich into the water where it was eagerly snapped up. "Maybe you should look after those clones a bit better. You lose so many of them, you know," she told Kay.

"To be precise, I lose *all* of them."

"Yes, I suppose you do. Apart from the real one, of course."

"I've lost her as well."

"But not lost as in the terminal sense."

"Yeah, I know. What's the point?"

"Hmm, well now you come to mention it, I'm not really sure myself. At least you aren't quite as grumpy as normal."

"I've every right to be grumpy. Did you know I'd be here?"

"Yes."

"How, exactly?"

The old lady stopped gazing along the river and turned to face Kay directly. "Before I came through the last portal, I had the impression you'd be here."

"Where was that?" Kay asked.

"The car park above Anglia Square."

"Oh, that one. Yeah, I've been in and out of it several times over the past few years. It only connects with other air ones, if I remember correctly."

"Does it? I've never found that."

"What do you mean?"

"Apart from a few, they all connect with one another at some point."

"I thought they went in a sequence – you know, earth, air, water…"

"And the other one."

"Yeah, glad I rarely come across those. Most clones don't even get as far as the air ones. Anyway, that's the sequence."

"Not for me. If I detect that they come out into fire, I don't go into them. I try to avoid water ones as well unless I've got no choice."

"So, why do I only get to take the clones through them in sequence?"

"Maybe it's to make you concentrate on keeping your current clone alive."

Kay grunted. "I wish I knew who made them."

"What? The clones or the portals?"

"The portals, of course. Well, the clones too, for that matter."

"Would it help knowing who made them?"

"Yeah. I'd murder the bastard."

The old lady smiled. "No, you wouldn't."

"Oh, wouldn't I? Do you know who made them?"

The old lady nodded.

"Who?" The reply was merely a wide grin. "You're not going to tell me, are you? No surprise there. So, can you really tell when and where they come out?"

"Not always exactly where – though I can detect the fire ones without much trouble – but when is often quite obvious."

"How do you do that?"

"Oh, I just look at them for a while."

"What are you talking about? They're random, aren't they? I have absolutely no idea of where and when one will take me. How do you do it?"

"As I said, I stare at them and after a few seconds, I seem to know what year they are connected to at that particular moment. If I really concentrate, sometimes it's like I can see through to where it's connected and what is likely to be on the other side. Of course, if I find somewhere and a time I want to go, I tend to step into it quickly before it changes."

"Yes, you're right there. I always have to hold the clone's hand otherwise we can end up in different places. I lost a good number of them that way at first."

"From what I've seen, they change as soon as someone jumps into one. But, if you don't jump into it, then it remains stable for a while – any time from a few seconds up to about ten minutes."

"Well, that's news to me."

"Oh, and changing the subject… do you have any 1850s money for me?"

"No, not been back that far since we last met on Mousehold. That was only a couple of clones back, anyway. You're too impatient."

"Mousehold? With the picnic?"

"Yes."

"That was about six years ago for me."

"Ah, right. Um, have we met on Tombland yet?" Kay asked.

"Doesn't ring a bell. What year?"

"1924, I think it was."

"Things do get a bit mixed up when they don't go in the right order."

"You're not kidding. So what's the right order?"

"Damned if I know," the woman said.

"This is all a bit River Song," Kay muttered.

"What does that mean?"

"Doesn't matter. Way after your time… probably. Where's the portal?"

"Can't you sense it?"

"Not always. I'm nowhere near as good at it as the clones."

"Well, maybe it's their purpose. To help you survive another day."

"Hmm, I've never thought of it that way around before. But, again, what's the point? Why do I have to do all this?"

The old lady shrugged. "The portal's over in the pavilion."

"Oh, does that make it an underground one or what?"

"Hmm. Good question. It's lower than the level of Drayton Road, is several hundred feet from the river and isn't on fire. Underground is probably closest."

"Are you going to use it?"

The old lady nodded.

"Do they, erm…?"

"What?"

"Are they, shall we say, a bit of a relief if you, er, need to, um, go?"

The old lady laughed. "Oh yes. Maybe that's how we pay to use them."

Kay laughed as well. "Yes, definitely a convenient convenience."

They started walking away from the river and towards the pavilion. Along the paths, they passed several flower beds in bloom, each of which was clustered with bees plus the occasional dragonfly buzzing amongst them.

The pavilion was a concrete structure with pillars holding up a wooden framework canopy at the front. Stairs up both sides converged at one of the park entrances on Drayton Road.

"How many do you think there are?" Kay asked as they ambled along.

"Portals? I have no idea. I don't suppose I've needed to use as many as you."

"There's well over a thousand by my reckoning. Been through some of them hundreds of times. Yet, once in a while, I find a new one."

"A thousand. Yes, could be around that. When I've got a specific place in mind, I have to find one that will take me there. They don't all work, you know."

"Really?"

"Yes, there are at least a couple that just sit there sulking. One just off Saint Augustine's in Gildencroft Park – another on the path around the castle."

"What? On one of the small pathways on the castle mound? I know of at least three around there and they've always worked for me when I needed them."

"Oh, those ones are okay. No, the one on the path at the top around the back. They're different for some reason. I never know what's on the other side."

"Weird. I've never come across either of those. You going to use this one?"

"Depends on when it wants to take me. Uh-oh."

"What?"

"Look. Inside the pavilion. Something's happening."

"Nasties?"

"Ghoul things," the old lady said, her pace quickening. "Met them before?"

"I must have met all of them several times over, including cloned policemen who can't speak properly and misty things that have problems hanging together in anything stronger than a light breeze. Yeah, I can see three or four of them in there. Is that someone else in there with them?"

"I was thinking the same. Is it Cassie? The real one, I mean?"

"No, I don't think so," Kay said. "Too dark to make out much."

"Take your sunglasses off, then. Hmm, looks like a girl – blonde curly hair."

Kay removed her sunglasses saying, "I think she's attacking them."

"Really? That's different."

As they got closer, they could see only one of the ghouls still standing. Three were incapacitated due to having had their heads sliced off. The person attacking them was quite small and fast, dressed in dark clothing and armed with a curved sword. Once it had swished a final time, there were no adversaries left standing.

The attacker promptly stepped into the portal and disappeared.

"Definitely a young girl," the old lady said as they approached the structure.

"Yes, and I've seen her before – but it was years ago. She was being chased through Chapelfield Park by some nasties."

"Interesting. Looks like she's turned the tables on them. Damned efficient with that sword, wasn't she?"

"Yeah, rather too good. It looked very similar to the one I've got," Kay said. "Though I haven't personally bought it yet."

"Ah, so it does. I only saw it the once and that was years ago," the old lady replied, examining the ghouls that littered the inside of the pavilion. They were already melting away. Within seconds, there was no longer any evidence that they had ever existed.

"Hmm, maybe I should carry a sword around for self-defence myself," Kay muttered. "Especially if the nasties can be defeated that easily by one."

"Possibly. Are you any good with one?"

"Never tried it, though my later self has. Sometimes I can see our sword has been moved or is hanging up slightly differently. Maybe I should start."

"Yes, maybe you should," the old lady smiled. "It may come in handy." She stood before the portal, which was located in the back wall of the pavilion. "Well, this portal does seem to be fully charged, so I'd better be off."

"It hasn't started to fade away, then? They seem to for me. It's rare I can go back into one that's just been used."

"Some of them do seem to need a bit of time to recharge. It does vary though. This one's fine."

The old woman stared at the place where they'd seen the girl with the sword disappear. Kay could feel the tingle of electricity from the portal but, other than that, noted that it betrayed no other sign of its existence.

"Are you going through?" Kay asked.

"Just waiting for a suitable date," came the reply. "It's currently on 2010 – I'm looking for something about a hundred years earlier."

"I wish I could do that," Kay said.

"Maybe you can, if you try."

"If I'm on my own then, most of the time, they just take me back to Starbucks in 2018. A few occasionally go somewhere else – I can never tell."

"Ah, it's changing. Remember to keep a lookout for more 1850s money."

"Why? What do I get out of it?"

"It will all make sense one day. Right, it's connected to 1907. I'm off. Bye."

The old woman stepped through the portal and was gone.

Kay hesitated. *Maybe I should have gone with her.*

She stared at the portal, trying to get it to reveal its secrets.

"When and where do you connect to?" she asked it.

There was no response and, no matter how much she concentrated, she couldn't glean any inkling of what might be lurking on its other side.

"Sod it," she said. "Maybe she was lying."

She heard voices and realised that people were coming down the left-hand set of stairs. She headed for the opposite set and began ascending them.

I need a longer walk. It's a lovely warm day and the safe house isn't far. A proper night's sleep would be good. Anything's better than ending up in Starbucks drinking that same old cup of coffee again.

Fix

Overcooked

At the height of Cassie's nightmares, wolves enveloped in flames swooped from the sky and attacked every inch of her naked body. Each bite burned horrendously as gobs of flesh were torn away. From the wounds, blood flowed, congealed, dried and flaked, leaving her skin like blackened ash. One wolf looked like Hitler, another resembled Jason while the others had the countenance of Laurence before he had taken over Patrick's body.

Then came the worst – it had Ka'Tor's face and, as each of his bites inflicted more torture, she heard his voice admonish her for running away and leaving him to be mutilated by his father.

She tried to tell him she was sorry, but her voice failed to produce any sound.

Occasionally, the nightmares would be exchanged for dreams where she was sinking underwater, which only partially alleviated the agony of the bites. In those dreams, she heard the voices of people talking gently to her. But, the words were almost unintelligible, which she put down to being submerged.

But the nightmares and dreams continued, often seamlessly merging into each other without interruption.

The coolness of a damp cloth being dabbed gently upon her lips brought Cassie back to something resembling consciousness. She became aware of lying flat on her back in complete darkness.

Everything hurt. But, hurt was an understatement – pain permeated her whole body. She couldn't move. Even the smallest twitch of a finger or a movement of her head was accompanied by waves of agony.

"Lie still, Cassie," said a distorted female voice that only just overcame the throb and hiss of the constant background noise. "You're too ill to do anything. You didn't warn me it would be this bad."

Cassie tried to form words but her throat, dry and ragged, refused to comply.

"Don't try to speak," the voice continued. "In fact, don't try to do anything by yourself – you can't. Here, I'm going to pour a little water into your mouth."

In the darkness, Cassie felt the bed move slightly as something was placed against her bottom lip. A trickle of water flowed into her mouth. Her swollen tongue throbbed making swallowing painful, so she just let the drips flow down her throat. Her ears pulsated with whistling which drowned out almost everything else. She tried to touch her tongue to her lips but they were also painful as well as being cracked. Her imagination pictured herself as she had once seen Kay after rescuing her from Laurence.

The voice returned. It was simultaneously close by and distant as if she was submerged in water and hearing someone shout at her from the far side of a swimming pool. "You've been here two days and you almost died at one point. But, I knew you couldn't actually die. That would have been a paradox too far."

Cassie realised that something about the voice sounded familiar. She tried to open her eyes but that simple act took an excessive amount of effort and resulted in more pain. Worse, it didn't make any difference to what she could perceive with her eyes – she could see nothing at all. She tried to raise a hand to feel her face but that proved to be beyond her capabilities.

"Yes," came the voice again, "you are blind. And you're pretty much burnt all over. You look absolutely ghastly. I remember you telling me about how Kay had been burned by Laurence. Believe me, that was peanuts compared to how you are right now. That's what you get for trying to look at a nuclear explosion at close range. I did try to warn you but you had to experience this in order…"

"Enough," came the hissed whisper of a second voice, "makes me sick to even look at her." Cassie's unreliable hearing was unable to position it in relation to the first voice. But she knew she had heard that main voice before and, finally, she was able to put a name to it.

She forced out a single syllable: "Anne." It came out as a barely audible croak.

"Yes, that's right. Anne Luckin. But, as you've finally woken up, I can't stay for much longer. I'm just here to remind you of something else I told you ages ago. Well, it was a long time ago for me. Eleven years. I was only seventy-five back then. For you, it's probably only been a few days."

There was another movement close by – footsteps coming closer. She felt the bed move as Anne got to her feet to join the second person.

"Remember," Anne said. "Physician heal thyself. You can do it, Cassie. But you *have* to do it all by yourself, otherwise I won't be able to come back and help you… and vice versa."

There was a pop and silence descended. Cassie felt panic join the pain that pervaded every inch of her body.

Don't leave me on my own, she tried to say, but her mouth refused to work and a deeper darkness enclosed her as consciousness slipped away to allow the dreams and nightmares to return.

Cassie became aware that she was awake. The pain was intense and, as before, she found herself blind and unable to move. Her mouth was parched and she ached to drink. She had no idea where she could get water to quench her thirst. For all she knew, there might be a bucketful within feet but, without vision and the ability to move, it might have been miles away.

Panic rose but, attempting to deal with it just caused her body to tense – and that only resulted in yet more pain. She tried to force herself to calm down but, locked into immobility as if she had become a statue, her efforts failed. Even her mouth refused to allow a whisper to pass her lips. Totally exhausted, the thoughts that swirled around her head plunged her further into depression.

I failed. I'm blind. I'm dying. Sorry, Georgia. Grandad. Sorry, Mum. I've failed you all. All I can do is lay here waiting for death. Oh God, it hurts so much…

She wanted to cry but her eyes were as incapable of shedding tears as they were of being able to transfer visual information to her brain.

After what might have been several more minutes or possibly hours, another thought came to her. *When is this? Why do I even care?*

But, as she could do little else, she found herself unable to resist trying. *Maybe it will make some of the pain go away,* she told herself.

It was hard but a couple of overlaid dates in September 1549 came to her: the seventh and the seventeenth, both with an hour to go before dawn.

It wasn't all that came to her. As she lay there in agony, not knowing whether she would live or die, not knowing even if she *wanted* to live or die, she became conscious of her map.

Go away, she told it. *I don't want to know. I'm incapable of knowing.*

But the map persisted and, in its shadows, she could sense her surroundings: the bed within the upstairs bedroom of the dilapidated cottage, and even some of the countryside beyond its walls.

Go away. I don't care. I just want to sleep... forever.

She tried to shut it out but all she accomplished was to shrink the perception down. She shut out the countryside. Then the sense of the surrounding cottage disappeared. Her world collapsed inwards for what might be the final time. Her hearing descended into a wall of rumbling and hissing as her entire skin, which burned as if she had been submerged in a vat of hot tar, was losing the ability to feel anything but that fire.

Stop it please, please, please...

Her map shrunk until all she could perceive was a pulsating core of pain. And then, at the moment everything outside of her body became excluded, her perception inverted. Instead of seeing outwards, she looked inwards at herself.

Her bones, her organs, her nervous system were exposed to that perception. An entire map of herself. She was conscious of the frenzied pumping of her blood through the veins and arteries that were still capable of working, as they struggled to perform the job for which they were built. She saw how those near the surface of her skin were no longer able to perform any sort of job. Damaged and fused together, she was certain they would never work again.

Her perception of herself was of a corpse that had forgotten that it was supposed to be dead. Given its condition, she was certain that the end couldn't be any more than minutes away.

Despite this, she became aware of how the automatic responses of her body were trying to fix the damage that had been inflicted, desperately delivering inadequate healing to her radiation-soaked frame to counter the carnage.

She was also conscious of how that healing was failing.

As each second ticked past, more of her skin and the flesh beneath it turned black as life relinquished its hold. She observed as more of her systems began shutting down, to prepare for the abandonment of her extremities in what she perceived as a futile attempt to save the vital central organs.

Leave me to die, she begged. *It's all too much... I can't take it any more...*

As her consciousness became centred on her inwardly focused map, a numbness grew over her. This was a relief as the pain ebbed away but part of her still-functioning mind realised that this was how her body was attempting to deal with the inevitability of her oncoming demise. It was in withdrawal mode and close to a final shutdown.

With the numbness came the ability to view the process of decay in an unemotional, detached manner. It was almost as if she was dispassionately observing the termination of a stranger.

I don't want to see this. Just let me slip away and die…

But the damage and ongoing deterioration held her attention: the skin tissue that was blackened; the way her eyelids had cracked, seeped fluids and then become solidified together; the cloudiness of the corneas beneath those lids that, along with her overloaded optic nerves had rendered her blind. She also saw older marks on her charred skin: her left thigh raked with scar tissue from the wolf's claws, her ankle warped from the flames from Lollard's Pit, though both were a million times less ferocious than the more recent devastation.

In addition to all this, she was aware of how her body ought to have been. She could comprehend all that was wrong and how it was relentlessly killing her.

And, within that wreckage of a body, she perceived how, within the DNA, it still contained the blueprints for how it had once been. How it had once pulsed to vitality and vigour.

And how, she was certain, it would never be again.

Physician, Heal Thyself

The dispassionate observer that had been Cassie watched as the body it occupied prepared itself for an ending. The numbness that had spread through her frame was almost complete.

And, as the last vestige of pain was replaced by numbness, a spark formed.

Energy is required.

What?

You have to do it all by yourself.

I can't.

You can. Remember.

A memory formed, reminding her how, not long ago, her mind had ranged outside the ship that had brought the device to Earth. She recalled encountering all the energy that was there for the taking and how it could be hers.

And, while still enclosed in her cocoon of numbness and suppressed pain, she found herself tentatively reaching outwards. With effort, for her body itself had little to spare, her mind escaped that burnt prison and drifted beyond the walls of the cottage. Outside, she encountered light from the rising sun and absorbed its energy, letting it induce a modicum of hope. Expecting little to come of it, she diverted it to deliver help to the failing processes trying to heal her flesh. She saw how even that tiny change began to influence and boost those processes, imbuing them with the strength they needed, reinforcing them and urging them to halt the decay that was eating at her physicality.

She reached further, expanding her perception upwards first by inches and feet, and then by miles to capture more, channelling energy uninhibited by cloud or atmosphere down to her ravaged body. This she used to bolster those defences even further, turning the tide away from disintegration.

The putrefaction slowed and halted and, still in her mentally detached state, Cassie observed how the decomposition was held in abeyance. But she could see how this was merely a pause – more was needed.

She broadened her reach even further, stretching up to and then beyond the edge of space so that she could absorb the energy emitted directly from the sun. She funnelled it down to the bedroom in that wreck of a house where it enveloped the greater wreckage of her body. She directed it to turn the tide of the battle so that, instead of fighting to salvage a mere retreat, she was able to begin the reversal of that decay and to initiate rebuilding.

Not even really understanding what she was doing, she transformed the healing into a counterattack, cajoling the processes of rejuvenation into battling for her existence. Slowly, the life that had been expelled from her charred skin fought back and, cell by cell, regained the ground it had previously lost. And, in the parts that had failed to die, it dispelled the harmful radiation of the explosion from her organs, mended the perforations in her eardrums, caused the fog that blighted her corneas to be dissipated and directed the healing to creep along her optic nerves, repairing and renewing them.

Underneath the blackened crust of the dead cocoon that enclosed her, Cassie's skin, muscles and organs began to glow with reawakening vigour and the revitalisation spread outwards from her centre to every membrane, every sinew, and every nerve until she was burning with her own light.

Within that intensity, she saw something new. New and wrong. She detected where infections had invaded her body and had turned her body against her. And, even though it had not yet had its chance to spread further, she saw how the Coronavirus had established a foothold within her lungs, throat and nasal cavities. But, it didn't have it all its own way – Cassie identified where her body had produced tiny pockets of defiance that, in a few isolated areas, checked the advance of the invader. They nibbled like resistance fighters picking at tiny achievable targets within the stronger intruder. She willed the germ- and virus-fighting factories within her body to ramp up the production of such antibodies to counter and nullify the effects of the assailants.

And, minutely, the ravages of her body's enemies were turned back.

Almost imperceptibly, the numbness retreated and her epidermis began to pulse with sensation. As feeling returned, both intense pain and exhilaration accompanied it but, as recuperation advanced, the former reduced to tolerable and, finally, to a tingling sensation, while the latter rose to dominate her.

Anyone observing the process would have waited long hours to see it from start to finish but, by the time it had run its course, the sun had risen, peaked and begun to descend towards the west, though hidden as dark rain clouds accumulated, bringing with them the promise of a storm. By the time only a single hour until sunset remained, Cassie's body had become renewed.

Dismissing her internalised viewpoint, she re-inhabited her body and, finding herself free of pain, she opened her eyes, fearful of what she might find.

With vision that was free of any defect, she gazed up at the bedroom ceiling. It came into focus in less than a second and she could just about perceive the rafters as dark lines against the yellowed plaster.

Glancing across the room to the window, she saw the first drops of rain begin to run down the grimy glass.

Turning her attention to her body, which appeared to be covered in a layer of dark grey ash, she attempted to sit up. Managing this using less effort than expected, she saw how the charred remains of her clothes fell away along with dead, discarded skin still attached. Brushing away the worst of the residue, she gazed at her body in wonderment.

The pink skin of her legs was no longer scarred but appeared as unblemished as a newborn's. Overcome by emotion, she both laughed and cried, unable to prevent either from occurring simultaneously. The tears that streamed down her cheeks, that fell to her breasts and traced clean lines through the ash as they rolled down her stomach, had never felt as real as in that moment.

"I did it. I healed myself," she whispered, crying with pure joy. "Physician, heal thyself," she added with a relieved shout. With a giggle, she added, "Hell, I definitely need a shower, though."

She reached up to touch her face and then the top of her head, and was shocked to find herself entirely bald, her scalp silky to her touch as more fine ash fell away. Her eyebrows, too, were no longer present though the restoration of her eyes had provided lashes. On the bed behind her, she saw tufts of burnt hair lying between the shards of sloughed-off skin.

Closing her eyes, she concentrated, bringing up the map of herself for a second visit. In comparison to her previous perception, it glowed with life. She willed the hair follicles above her eyes to generate hair and, after a few seconds, she could feel that they had returned.

I need a mirror to see if they look right.

Next, she did the same for her scalp. The follicles went into overdrive and, under the touch of her fingers, the smoothness sprouted into a stubble of new hair, which she caused to erupt into full growth. As it did so, it curled in all directions and, before she thought to halt the process, it had almost covered her eyes and was already hanging halfway down her back.

"Enough," she shouted, caressing her new locks in wonderment, focusing her eyes on the handful she held in front of her eyes. "My God, it's never looked and felt this good before."

Previously, her curls had always turned frizzy if left untreated – one of the reasons she had preferred to have it straightened. Now the coils were light, bouncing against each other to fall back into the shape she'd always wished they had taken.

Hah! I feel like I'm in some shampoo advert. I really must find a mirror.

Fondling her hair, she remembered that future version of herself she had seen tackling Laurence outside Donnellis Pizzeria. *So, not months of growth after all.*

Slowly swinging her legs over the side of the bed, Cassie tried to stand. Her head swam a bit as she regained her balance.

Careful. A lot of this body is now completely new. How the hell did I do that?

After the dizziness passed, she ran her hands down the thigh of her left leg amazed at how smooth it felt.

No scars at all – I'm no longer the wolf girl.

The skin around her ankle, too, was devoid of any evidence of where it had been burnt at Lollard's Pit.

I wonder...

Instinctively, she reached for that spot on her right cheek. *Oh, that one's still there. It's been with me for so long that maybe it's now part of my DNA or blueprint.*

"But, hey, I'm completely naked," she said, as if only just realising.

She noticed a stack of clean clothes neatly folded and lying on a rickety chair just inside the door to the bedroom. Looking closely at them, she identified undergarments, jeans and a top. Folded beneath them was a denim jacket and, on the floor beside the chair, stood a pair of boots.

"Oh," she said. "Who put these here?"

On the chest that had held the blankets, she saw a jug half-filled with water. It stirred a memory.

"Does that mean I wasn't dreaming earlier on? Was Anne Luckin really here? But, if that's true, then who was that with her?"

Beside the jug, the accumulation of dust was patterned where some of the water had spilt but had since dried.

"Just how long has it been since I first arrived here?"

There was a noise outside the cottage and she turned to see rain lashing the pane of glass, though doing little to scour it of the years of accumulated filth.

I need a shower. I hope the rain's not that cold.

She teleported herself out of the cottage and stood, arms outstretched, face upwards to let the storm cleanse the last of the ash and dead skin from her naked body. It was ecstatic.

Easy Fixes

Cassie was back in October 1939 and riding the 10B bus as it trundled from Red Lion Street onto Castle Meadow. Her twenty-first-century clothing was hidden beneath a long winter coat, its collar pulled up to hide most of her face, and her hair was tied back into a bun to prevent it flying around. Seated halfway along the lower deck, she was listening carefully to what was happening on the open rear platform of the bus.

"Oi, no pushing," came the sound of the bus conductor's voice.

Here we go, she thought, trying to remember exactly how the altercation between Laurence, Charlie and Gwen had played out.

As the bus started to move off from the stop, she stood up and walked towards the open rear platform. Stepping around Charlie, who was still wiping Laurence's spit off Gwen's face, she slowed time and inspected them both as stillness and silence enveloped them all. Raising both hands, she gently touched Gwen's hand and Charlie's neck, and closed her eyes. She detected the traces of infection that Charlie's handkerchief had failed to disperse. It was tiny but, already, it was beginning to invade their bodies.

Cassie concentrated and emitted a targeted pulse of energy. Then she checked them once more and smiled to herself.

That's probably a more effective solution than trying to give them antibodies and hoping they do the trick.

Before she opened her eyes, she sought out evidence of the portals.

They're still here at the moment but I haven't finished yet.

She teleported off the bus and moved back a minute to watch Laurence as he was about to jump off the rear platform. Slowing time once more, she stood, invisible beside the point where he would land. Even before his feet touched the pavement, she could see how the virus was rampaging through his entire frame. His body was burning with it and any normal person would have been laid up in bed long before it had reached this stage. She marvelled at how Laurence was suppressing its effects upon Patrick's body so as to remain mobile.

He's made himself into another Typhoid Mary, she thought, remembering seeing an online documentary about the woman who had unwittingly infected hundreds of others, whilst remaining immune to the effects of the virus herself.

She reached out and touched Laurence's hand as he landed. Another pulse of energy flashed and all traces of the virus were gone, although the cold symptoms would likely persist for a few days.

What next? Do I follow him? No, I've first got to go back and fix all the others he interacted with. Those people on the market and then back down to London to save Churchill and the others at Admiralty House.

Returning to normal time, she watched Laurence disappear.

He's gone forwards in time, no doubt eager to see the devastation his efforts have caused. But I've already seen that – I don't want to see it again. No, I need to fix those he touched on the market. I mustn't miss any of them. If even a single virus gets through, it could all start up again. Ah, I know…

Teleporting to the roof of the Guildhall, she concentrated, attuning herself to the virus – she had it appear like small wisps of red cloud drifting along with the people it had already clamped onto. There were already at least ten separate instances and she was certain there were one or two more within City Hall itself.

With arms outstretched, she drew in energy from multiple sources. She emitted a single pulse that encompassed all of the marketplace as well as anything within a half-mile radius.

Just in case.

Afterwards, there were no more patches of red mist to be found. Satisfied, her mind sought out the portals.

They're all still here, thank goodness, and not showing any signs of disappearing.

"London," she muttered, heading southwards and slightly pastwards to Admiralty House. She materialised on the stairs up which Laurence was due to run. Keeping herself invisible, she waited.

After a few seconds, she heard Patrick's voice shout, "I'd give you a run for your money. Here's a bug or two to bugger things up for you."

Here we go again.

She waited until he had departed for Norwich knowing his future path was already dealt with. Then she released another pulse.

Several minutes later, Cassie was heading back to Norwich.

That was stupidly easy. Too easy, in fact. Am I missing something?

Following Laurence's trail after he had alighted the bus took her to several dates between 1939 and 1945 but history was progressing according to what she remembered. Hitler never invaded the British Isles and the war in Europe ended in May 1945, with the Far East following in September.

By spying on Laurence, Cassie could tell that he was coming to the same conclusion. He stopped in 1946, standing on the steps of City Hall, hands on his hips. It was around nine on a Sunday morning in June and, while the city was far from busy, there were enough people around to take notice of this strange character having a loud conversation with nobody.

"Where are you?" he shouted. "I know you're probably spying on me."

Yes, I am. From her vantage point back on the Guildhall roof, she wondered, *Can he detect me?*

"What did you do? I have memories of a future and then it was all gone," he bellowed. "I spread that bug all around and then it just got changed back and now I'm free of the virus as well."

Oh, he must remember that alternative timeline. That makes two of us. I suppose it's a bit like Kett's ghost having memories of the alternative version of 1549.

He glanced upwards and, even though she was invisible, his eyes halted at the Guildhall and locked upon hers.

Damn, he's detected me again. How does he do that?

Laurence disappeared and Cassie braced herself, expecting him to appear beside her. But he didn't.

Wait, he's gone even further into the future and disappeared inside City Hall.

She followed, tracking the trail as it terminated near the end of 2000. Materialising nearby, she checked the date. It was Christmas day and she found herself located in the southern wing of City Hall.

She spotted a sign. *Ah, Bethel Street Police Station. I doubt he's come here to give himself up. What's he looking for? And why this particular date? Hmm, it's a couple of weeks after Kay chopped his head off. Is that significant?*

He was jumping around various rooms as if searching for something. She followed him through offices, cells, changing rooms and store rooms.

"Hah, I knew it had to be here somewhere," he said stopping. It was another storage room lined with shelves. Many of the items stacked upon them were wrapped up and labelled. Cassie saw him select something large and long, enclosed within a black plastic bag. He unsealed it and reached inside. Cassie couldn't see what it was as his back was towards her. Whatever he had discovered was mostly concealed within the bag. She had the impression he didn't want her to see what it was.

"Now where are you?" he said, clasping the bag to his chest. "Ah, I think you're watching me, aren't you? I can feel you, Cassie Fox. There's something different about you. Even invisible, you're shining like a beacon. But what's the source?"

What does he mean?

His eyes scanned the room as she held herself as still as possible, whilst also trying to figure out how he might be detecting her. His eyes narrowed as he stared at the spot upon which she stood.

He winked out of existence, leaving the plastic bag to drop where he had stood. This time, she couldn't ascertain whether he had gone forwards or backwards in time. *Has he figured out how to switch off making a trail?* To fully concentrate on finding him, she discarded her invisibility only to hear a noise directly behind her. She spun around.

"Hah, there you are," Laurence laughed. "Well, I absolutely love the new hairstyle. Did you have it done especially for me?"

She took a step backwards.

"Good, you're scared," he laughed. "And so you should be. Remember this?"

In a single swift movement, Laurence withdrew a long curved blade from the scabbard he had been concealing behind his back and brandished its razor-sharp point barely an inch from her belly.

Cassie gasped twice. The first was in response to recognising the blade – the same scimitar with which Kay had decapitated him. The second came as he lunged forward, plunging the weapon so deep into her stomach that it passed through her body, its point puncturing the skin of her back and tearing through her top and jacket.

Diversion: Revelations

"Here," Kay said, handing over an envelope. "I've been carrying it around for years. Had it so long that I actually thought I'd never see you again."

"Whassat?" said the clone standing next to Kay.

"Never you mind," Kay said, making sure she had tight hold of the rope that was tied to the clone's belt. Despite her body being almost encased in the multi-pocketed, black leather two-piece, she felt the cold seeping through it as an icy wind blustered through the city.

All three were standing on one of the many narrow pathways that wound around the castle mound. Below them, trams clanked along the curve that was Castle Meadow. It would be several more years before the road would be widened. The clone watched the vehicles with fascination, emitting an 'ooh' whenever a spark flashed on the overhead power wires.

"Yet you did carry it around, for which I am grateful," said the old lady. After making sure they weren't being observed, she pulled out the notes the envelope contained. There was a mixture of denominations – mostly ten shilling and pound notes plus a few fives and tens.

"Good, they're the earliest printed ones," the old lady said.

"Yeah, damned hard to get hold of. Most had worn out by 1900."

"Thank you," came the reply. "Must be around two hundred, I reckon."

"Two hundred and thirty-five," Kay said, adding, "I've got more at home. Didn't want to carry it all at once in case it got lost."

"Oh right. How much is back there?"

"Nearly another hundred, I think – notes and coins."

"Thanks, I'd better arrange to get it collected at some point."

"Collected? How?"

The old lady smiled. "I have an idea. Don't you worry about it."

"Ah, and you're not going to tell me, are you? When is this?"

"1921. January. I had a word with the ghost while I was waiting for you."

"Oh, you mean Kett? What did you talk about?"

The old lady shrugged. "Yes. Mostly nothing. He's a bit bonkers, isn't he?"

"Absolutely. I try to avoid him. Anyway, how are you going to get all the money back to the eighteen fifties?"

"Cassie."

"The real one?" Kay asked. The old lady nodded. "Are you certain? I haven't seen her for years and I was beginning to think she hadn't made it."

"She had some... well, I suppose you could call them very close calls."

"Hmm, does she survive in all the different timelines?"

"What do you mean?"

"Don't you understand about timelines?"

"Yes, I think so. Which ones in particular?"

"Things like the Baker Boy and that bus that falls through Earlham Road. I've been to those more times than I can count. But they're all different timelines – they must be as what happens is never the same each time."

"Ah yes. No, I'm not sure, in that case. I suspect I'm sticking to one timeline. At least, it appears to be relatively consistent."

"Does that mean there could be timelines where Cassie doesn't make it?"

The old lady frowned but didn't answer. Kay surmised that she didn't know.

"Will I see her again?" Kay asked.

"Oh, um. If I remember correctly..."

The old lady's voice trailed off.

"Remember what?"

The old lady smiled, shook her head and wagged a finger at Kay. "Nice try," she said. "Let me think. I'm not sure you need to know any of that right now."

"Okay," Kay sighed. "Whatever."

The old lady smiled, acknowledging Kay's compliance with a tiny bob of her head. She looked at the mud on Kay's boots. "Last portal a water one?"

"Yes, Quayside. Wasn't deep, thank God. Back to the point – one question."

"I may not answer. I may not even know what the answer might be."

"I think you do."

"Go on?"

"Okay. How will the real Cassie be able to take the money back to the eighteen-fifties if the portals don't go back that far?"

"Ah, right. No. I can't answer that one."

"Can't or won't?" Kay said.

"Either will do."

Kay smiled, "Thank you."

"What?"

"I've just twigged that if you're going to rely on the real Cassie getting you back to the eighteen-fifties and portals don't go that far, then either she can create her own personal portals or she's figured out a way of getting around in time without using them."

The old lady smiled and shrugged. "Hmm. You always were a clever one."

"Had to be. I wouldn't have survived this long if I hadn't collected a few wits along the way."

The old lady nodded. "Couldn't agree more."

"Hmm, but if Cassie can go back to before the portals exist then why doesn't she go back and collect your money for you?"

The old lady smiled. "Things have to be done in the correct order."

"That doesn't explain anything at all."

The old lady chuckled. "Yes, you're right there."

Kay pointed at the coat pocket into which the old lady had secreted the envelope. "Another question. What are you going to use the money for?"

"Buying a house. Well… a cottage actually."

"Hmm. You had no problem answering that one," Kay said, cocking her head to one side and smiling as if she'd scored a second victory.

"It doesn't give anything important away."

"So you hope."

"I know it won't."

"So, two hundred and thirty-five quid is enough to buy a whole house, is it?"

"Along with that other hundred, it will certainly help."

"How much do they cost back then?"

"Most people rent – but the place I have in mind will be sold at auction in 1856 and, given its, um, spooky reputation, there will be few other potential buyers, so it will turn out to be a lot cheaper than expected."

"Spooky?"

"Very."

"Ah. Might those spooks resemble, say, this clone?" Kay said, tugging on the rope.

"Ow," said the clone.

The old lady smiled but, didn't offer an answer. Instead, she said, "So, Kay. How are you?"

Kay frowned. "Huh? How am I? Right now, I'm cold. But, do you really care?"

"Of course I do."

"If you care, then tell me what I am, what I'm doing here, what all these clones are, but mostly, what the point of all this is. You do know, don't you?"

"You always try to ask so many questions. All I can say is that I know what you are and how you came to be, and where all the clones came from."

"Well, that's a bit more than you've ever admitted before in however many times we've just happened to bump into each other. That's another thing, too."

"What?"

"Our meetings are never coincidences, are they? You know exactly when and where to find me when you want to, don't you? I remember you telling me in Wensum Park that time about staring into the portals. But I think you can seek me out at whatever stage of my life you want to."

The old lady responded with a smile.

"Oh, so you've clammed up again. In that case, let me tell you what I know."

"And what's that?"

"I know how this ends."

The old lady raised an eyebrow.

"Yeah, I've got the motorbike and have been practising with the sword. Not that it wasn't too hard to work out. The damned things were there when I visited the house in the nineteen-nineties – and that was when I was a little bit younger and before I'd actually bought the place. I learned where they both came from and, when it was the right time, I went to those places and bought them."

The old lady nodded.

"It all started when I was around fifty – well, that's only a guess, of course. Anyway, I met an older version of me who told me to look out for the dumbest clone." Kay tugged on the rope. "And now, I've found her. Thick as shit but knows exactly where all the portals are."

"Ah, yes. Met yourself at the library – I heard all about it."

"Yeah, that's the one. I reckon that must be coming up again quite soon. When I look in the mirror nowadays I see that old face staring back at me."

"And?"

"I reckon I haven't got long to go before I get to chop Laurence's head off."

"Yes, sorry, but that's probably true."

"Sorry? Fuck it, I'm sick of this life. It's been shit ever since Grandad started... well, we all know what he did."

"It wasn't him."

"Like fuck, it wasn't."

"Cassie explained what happened. It really wasn't him, though I do know where your one came from. The real one would never have done that."

"He was real enough to me."

The old lady shook her head and whispered, "Yes, I know. You can blame Laurence for that."

"Laurence again? Why doesn't that surprise me? What did he do?"

"No, that information isn't for you. Not at this time, anyway."

"Will I ever find out?"

"At the moment," the old lady frowned, "I don't actually know."

"Bollocks. This is so frustrating. You know something?"

"What?"

"If I ever meet Laurence again, I think I may try to kill him early, just to get all this over and done with."

"No, Kay," the old lady whispered. "Please don't try that."

"Why not? He dies anyway."

"You mess with things like that and you can upset the whole of time."

"How do you know?"

"I've seen Cassie... well, no. I shouldn't say any more. Just don't..."

Annoyed, Kay pursed her lips and lapsed into silence. The clone continued to stare down at the trams and the old lady watched both of them intently.

"Are we related?" Kay asked, suddenly.

The old lady looked straight into Kay's eyes. "What makes you ask that?"

"Your eyes are as blue as mine and Cassie's."

The old lady smiled and said, "Anything's possible."

"You look slightly older this time," Kay said. "How old are you? Seventy?"

"Eighty-six and, let me see, um, eight months."

"Crikey, you're doing well. I sometimes feel that age myself. Hold on. You're travelling through the portals and you know exactly how old you are? I've got no idea about my age."

"Most of the time I keep myself grounded in my own time. I keep notes and my excursions are relatively few and far between."

"Wish mine were. But the damned nasties multiply if I stay too long in one time and place."

"Yes, so I've heard. Right, I suppose it's time I was off."

"What? Just like that?"

"Yes, Kay. Oh, and goodbye."

"That sounds rather final," Kay said.

"Indeed. I might be wrong but, as far as I can tell going by how old you look, this might be the last time we meet. It's funny how different you turned out compared to the original."

"Ah, the original. I see. That makes me a clone as well, does it? Laurence always called me a decoy. Maybe he was right. I'm the decoy leading other clone decoys around in order to prevent him getting at the real Cassie."

The old lady nodded and, in a voice that sounded as if it was about to crack, said. "Yes, yes. I suspect that might be the way it is. I also suspect that I shouldn't be telling you this as well. But, oh, to hell with it, maybe you need to know something important for once."

She stepped closer and, to Kay's surprise, hugged her tight. Then, she whispered in Kay's ear.

"You are fucking joking," Kay squealed. "That's impossible."

"Believe what you will," the old lady sighed. She kissed Kay on the cheek before turning around to walk up the pathway. She hadn't gone very far before Kay saw her wink out of existence.

Impossible.

Sussex

Deep

Cassie stared at the handle of the blade buried in her abdomen. Then, she slowly reached behind herself with one hand to feel the point of the scimitar protruding from her back. It was sticky with blood.

She fixed Laurence with her gaze.

"Why aren't you dying?" Laurence screamed, letting go of the sword and dropping the scabbard. "Fall over. At least cry with pain. Don't just stand there staring at me. You're meant to die."

"Why should I? And why do you have to keep on doing this?"

Laurence looked confused. His eyes darted from Cassie to the walls to the sword handle and back to Cassie again.

"Well?" she asked.

"If I can't own your body then no one, not even you, will have it."

"And what gives you the right to decide such things?"

"I created you. You're mine."

Cassie shook her head. A strange calm drifted over her, enabling her to contemplate the situation with neither fear nor panic.

"No," she said. "I created you, Ka'Tor. I brought you into this world and, soon, I will take you out of it, forever. That's a promise."

She closed her eyes and turned her map inwards to investigate the damage. The blade had sliced through the loop of her large intestine as well as puncturing her left kidney. Muscles in both her stomach and back had been torn with the blade's passage. She had no idea what was suppressing the pain, but she was extremely grateful that it had kicked in automatically.

Just like when I was fixing myself earlier on. If I could feel the pain from this, I'd be in absolute agony. Well, I brought myself back from being almost completely barbecued to death, so I should be able to handle a mere stabbing, surely.

Knowing that she could not heal herself with the blade still in situ, she opened her eyes and glared back at Laurence once more. With a smile that bordered on a smirk, she grasped the handle of the scimitar with both hands and slowly guided it away from the entry point, curving it upwards to retain her grip upon it, but ignoring the extra damage it was causing upon its exit.

She stared into Laurence's eyes, which were wide with what she supposed was horror. As blood gushed from the wound, she forced herself to bare her teeth at him in a manic grin. It had the desired effect.

Throwing the sword behind her, she stepped up to him. "It's only a scratch," she hissed. "Nothing to lose any sleep over."

"What are you?" he shouted, his eyes wide with terror. "You should be dead. I *want* you dead."

"Just a flesh wound," she mocked, speeding herself up and calmly aiming a punch at his face. She felt his nose crunch under her fist.

Groaning, he keeled over, hitting the back of his head on the wall as he fell.

Cassie was starting to feel light-headed with all the loss of blood and she wondered how long it would be before the pain kicked in.

What do I do now? I need to heal myself but, if I stop to do that, he might gain the upper hand again. Damned if I'm going to show any weakness in front of him.

She stood over him, dripping blood on his trousers. "Any last requests before I finish you off, Ka'Tor? I'll try to make it quick," she said, extending her hands towards his face, her fingers like claws ready to tear him apart.

He screamed, "No, you won't win. I'll figure out a way to get you one way or another." Then, he teleported away, this time leaving the usual trail.

Upon his disappearance, she staggered as sensation started to return to her damaged abdomen. As she sunk to the floor, she instigated the healing process, hoping that Laurence wouldn't think to return immediately.

After half an hour, the damage was repaired leaving only bloody patches in her clothes and spatters of congealing blood on the floor.

Slowly, she got to her feet and examined herself.

"Good as new," she muttered. "But, I better not make a habit of this."

It was worth seeing the fear on his face, though.

She picked up the sword and wiped the blood off it with a piece of cloth she found lying on one of the shelves.

I hope that cloth wasn't some crime evidence – if it was, it's now full of my DNA. That should cause some confusion, especially as I've not been born yet on this date.

After inspecting the blade, she slipped it back into the scabbard and arranged the whole thing across her back.

"I bet I know what comes next," she said to herself, adjusting the scabbard strap until it felt comfortable. "Pizza time."

A few minutes later, she stood invisible on Timberhill facing the frontage of Donnellis Pizzeria. It was April 2019 once more and, inside, she could just about see her earlier self seated at the rear of the establishment along with Georgia, Erin, Callum and the others. It seems they had only just sat down as their drinks hadn't been ordered.

Several thoughts went through her head.

I'm too early. I need to skip to when Laurence arrives. When exactly was that? Had we finished eating? Yes, I think so. But where am I going to take Laurence after grabbing him? And what am I going to do with him when we get there?

She frowned, realising there was more.

Hold on. What makes him decide to come here in the first place? What if he doesn't turn up? Am I going to create another paradox? Also, does the Laurence who looks into the restaurant come before or after our encounter at Bethel Street? I scared him so much last time, he might go into hiding. Ah no, I remember his nose looking like it was broken – and I just did that in the police station.

She shut her eyes and tried to detect his trail. There was no sign of it here on this particular day.

Have I got to force him to come here or do something else?

She moved forwards in time until she spotted herself finishing off her pizza and getting up from her seat to head for the loo. At the same time, she heard running footsteps coming from the direction of Ber Street. It was Laurence, his face still a mess and, despite being hidden, he was heading straight for her.

Ah, he said I was like a beacon. Maybe that's how he's detecting me. Is it all the energy I've been grabbing? I need to test this.

She teleported to a point twenty feet behind him. He slowed, stopped and looked all around. She watched people doing their best to avoid him. He looked completely manic and capable of lashing out at any moment. After a few seconds, he homed back in on her.

Okay, I need him to look inside the pizza place at the right time, therefore I need to be inside it myself.

She teleported once more to stand on the raised kitchen section beyond the tables. Her earlier self exited the loo and went to talk to the waitress.

Is this where my earlier self detects me standing here? Oh, she's staring straight at me. I remember feeling a tingling sensation – don't think I actually saw anything at the time, though. Maybe that is what Laurence is detecting. Talking of which…

And Laurence was there, staring at her through the restaurant window.

She heard Callum say, "What's that idiot outside doing? Is he staring in at us or is he just one of Norwich's normal band of nutters?"

Okay, here's my cue.

She hopped back outside and, fully visible and with her back to the restaurant window, hurled herself at Laurence, wrapping her arms around him and toppling him over. Before they hit the ground, she teleported them both back more than eighty years, reappearing in the same physical location but popping out in the early hours of an unknown morning.

"No," he shouted, trying to slip out of her grip but, she planted one hand on his damaged face and blasted a pulse of energy into his skull in the hope that it would slow him down.

He tumbled and rolled over several times on the rough cobblestones. Before he could come to a halt, she leapt on top of him and slammed a fist into his face once more, hearing the clunk of his head against the ground.

Got to keep him off balance. He's too unpredictable.

Before he could recover, she took a look inside his head.

He's scared, almost terrified. But it's almost like he's enjoying the sensation for its novelty as well. He's been in control for centuries and now he's met someone who can fight back and he wants to know how I'm doing it.

She raised her fist once more, ready to pound him a second time. He raised a hand and groaned as if delirious.

"Had enough?" she hissed.

"Please, yes," he muttered as if defeated. "Please don't hurt me any more."

She relaxed for a second – but that was all he needed and suddenly, he was no longer beneath her and her knees hit the cobblestones.

"Fuck," she cursed, getting to her feet and rubbing a knee. "Why do I keep falling for it? Where's he gone this time?"

The trail was plain to see – he was on his way back to the twenty-first century. She followed, expecting him to go all the way to 2019.

Instead, he halted five years before that date emerging into a sunny, warm Tuesday around midday in the latter half of May 2014. He then moved northwards by a quarter of a mile to appear halfway along an alleyway known as School Lane, a little-used, L-shaped passageway linking Bedford Street and Exchange Street. Cassie, seeing how restricted the area was, teleported to the rooftop of The Granary, a store located on the corner of School Lane and Bedford Street. This allowed her a grandstand seat to observe anything going on within the alley below.

She watched as Laurence secreted himself behind a parked car on some waste ground to one side of the alley.

What's he want with this specific date? Does he know I'm here watching him? Maybe, as the sun's effectively behind me from where he is, he might not be able to detect me.

In answer to that, he glanced up at her. A sneer passed his damaged lips, but he didn't move from his hiding place.

Okay, so maybe I need to find a way to turn off my beacon, or whatever it is he's detecting. But, he's definitely waiting for something else to happen.

She didn't have long to wait as two pairs of footsteps could be heard coming around the corner that led to Exchange Street. Cassie frowned – there was something familiar about both of them.

She had to suppress a cry. *It's Grandad and, oh my God, that's Laurence behind him – the original Laurence, not the one in Patrick's body. And he's younger than I've ever seen him before. The one I saw having his head cut off was the oldest. He looks even younger than the one who killed Charlie on his bus. What's going on?*

"Leave me alone," said her grandad. He was walking like an automaton, stiff-legged as if he was fighting against the induced movement.

Oh no. Laurence is compelling him to walk in front of him. How's he doing that?

She had to resist the urge to teleport down there knowing that she shouldn't interfere with that version of Laurence.

I might stop his death from happening.

Instead, she observed how Laurence was coaxing the reluctant device that Cassie could detect within his jacket. He was using it to coerce her grandad to do whatever he wanted, just as he had forced her mum to think she had fallen in love with him.

With a gesture, old Laurence made Bill stop and lean back against a wall. Propped there like a mannequin, he was unable to do anything for himself and Cassie watched as Bill's eyes stared unblinking, his limbs rigid.

Then old Laurence encircled Bill's face in his hands, which glowed that unnatural malachite green.

"What is this?" old Laurence barked a few seconds later. "No. What do you mean I died in 2000? Impossible. This is 2014 – I'm still alive. Portals? What portals? Portals through time? Where did they come from? Who made them? And Rebecca is dead? How? Tell me. What? Don't you know anything more?"

She watched him pull the device from one of his pockets to stare at it.

"Why didn't you tell me time travel was possible?" he demanded of it. "Yes, I know I've never asked about that before. Why can't you just tell me things I need to know, curse you? Thousands of years and it's only *now* you decide to let me know. Useless thing." There was a pause. "Wait. How do I do it myself? Do I need portals? Tell me. Bugger your protections. Tell me." Another pause. "No? What do you mean 'too dangerous'?"

Cassie was aware of the battle going on between Laurence and the device.

"You will *not* refuse my commands. I order you," he said after a while.

There was another pause and then, with a grin, he said, "Ah yes, yes. I see."

He placed the device back into his pocket before his form flickered, disappearing for a couple of seconds before reappearing three feet away.

"Yes, I do see," old Laurence said. "This changes everything, doesn't it? Well, I'm glad I bumped into you again, old man," he said, turning his attention back to Cassie's grandad. "But I need to teach you a lesson about accosting me in the street. Maybe I can use you in some way to wear your granddaughter down so that she becomes an easier target. Aha, I know. Let's see if your mind can handle falling to pieces a tiny chunk at a time. And, what's more, I can make it so that you won't remember a thing about today, you soon-to-be senile old fool."

Bill was momentarily encased in a flash of green. He groaned and began to slump to the ground. Old Laurence laughed and then, apparently considering the episode complete, casually strolled off towards Bedford Street leaving his victim lying abandoned.

Oh my God. I know what this is. It's Grandad's repression. This must be where it happened. But, I can't do anything about it – I daren't. I have to let it happen otherwise I will change history all over again. Oh, Grandad – I dare not save you from this. Damn you, Laurence. Damn you, Ka'Tor.

She saw another movement as the later Laurence in Patrick's body stepped from his hiding place. She watched as he slowly walked towards the prone form. Reaching Bill, he knelt down beside him.

What's he doing? Oh shit, no. His hands are glowing.

There was another flash of green around Bill's head.

"A change of plan," Laurence hissed. "Let's make it even more interesting for younger Cassie, shall we? Let's see if there's room in your head for anoth…"

"No!" Cassie screamed, teleporting down to throw herself at Laurence. "That's the last thing you'll ever do."

She wrestled him to the ground using techniques she'd learned from Em'Dor and others back in the Stone Age. As she did so, she felt a wave of nausea but, grimacing, she did her best to ignore it. Trapping him beneath her and without really understanding what she was doing, she encircled Laurence's head with her hands, hands that were also glowing malachite green. She drew in as much energy from the surrounding area as she could and bore down on him, blasting him with the full strength of what she could muster, burning her way into his head and past his defences before he had the chance to even think about raising them or teleporting away.

Inside Patrick's head, she saw the spiky red entity that was Laurence's consciousness try to retreat, to hide in some dark recess of the brain. But she followed him there, pounding him with more of the same, cutting off every possible avenue of escape, restricting and compressing him into the tiniest imaginable space.

"You're not escaping this time," she hissed. "I'm going to purge Patrick's head of every last bit of you once and for all."

No please, she heard him beg, though Patrick's mouth didn't move. But, even within that utterance, she could feel him trying to look for a way out, a chance to regain a bit of control so that he could teleport away.

"Not this time," she shouted. "I'm not falling for that again. This time I'll finish you for good. I owe it to Grandad, I owe it to everyone you have ever taken over and then killed, even if their body lived for years afterwards."

But, even as she limited Laurence's abilities, she became aware of the damage that his occupation had caused to Patrick's consciousness. It was like looking at war-torn devastation in what had once been a peaceful town. But, within that wreckage, as Laurence's influence over his body diminished, Patrick himself was trying to wake up, to regain control over what remained.

"Please k-kill 'im," Patrick muttered, his voice slurring as he struggled to get the words out. She diverted some of her energy to boost his ability to talk and he continued, "Don't worry about me. Don't let him escape to do it to even one more innocent person. Even if it kills me, promise you'll stop him."

"I-I promise," Cassie replied.

Spurred on with her determination, she drew in even more energy and constructed a prison within which Laurence was encased. And, just as he had tried to do to that innocent man near Pottergate, she squeezed that prison down until it was the size of a pinprick. Knowing it would likely kill Patrick if she continued on this path and feeling Laurence trying to push back against her, she changed tactics.

Instead of resisting that push, she suddenly aided it instead, but channelled it to a point several feet away from Patrick's skull. The essence that was Laurence, and all of his experiences going back to when he had been Ka'Tor, burst from Patrick's head and splashed onto the pathway. It resembled an animated liquid that morphed into multiple shapes, some recognisable, many beyond description. It reminded her of the creatures she had fought in the chalk caves underneath Earlham Road. They writhed as if each was trying to force the rest into adhering to that one's form. But none of them were powerful enough to dominate and they fell back to a frantic mess.

Oh, my God. Is this thing all that remains of the people he took over?

She was suddenly distracted by voices further along the alleyway and saw three people staring at her from Bedford Street. Each of their faces betrayed the horror they were experiencing at what they could see.

Damn, this is too public. I need to do something.

"Nothing to see here," she told them, blasting that idea into their heads. *It's not a repression,* she told herself. *It will wear off after a day or so. Maybe they will remember, maybe they won't. I just need them gone right now.*

She was relieved to see them turning aside to walk off along Bedford Street as unconcerned as they had been before they'd looked along the alleyway.

That must have been similar to what Laurence did to Grandad – but I didn't need the device to do it. Hell, I'm turning into a Laurence clone. That's scary.

To prevent further interruptions, she projected a compulsion around the entire alleyway. Anyone trying to enter would be compelled to turn around and go the opposite way.

But, while she had been distracted with the onlookers and creating the compulsion, the mass that was Laurence's consciousness hadn't been idle. It was on the move trying to return to the body from which it had been ejected. Cassie placed herself between the writhing mass and Patrick's limp body. Her hands boiled with energy and she aimed a blast at it.

The mass shrunk back but started inching towards her grandad instead.

"Oh, no you don't," she shouted, green fire shooting from her hands once more to emphasise the point.

The entity reared up and came for her instead. Screaming, she raised her hands and channelled all of her energy into blasting it.

"When I say, no more, I mean *no more*," she shrieked.

The mass ballooned, absorbing everything she could throw at it. She suddenly realised that it was feeding off her, using the power that she hurled at it, growing larger by the second. Already, it towered over her.

I need to do something, and quickly before it gets big enough to envelope me.

Backing off, to avoid the expanding mass from touching her, she found herself backed up against a wall. A pressure on her shoulder blades reminded her of what she carried upon her back. She reached over her shoulder and slid the scimitar from its scabbard. Gripping the handle in both hands, she sped herself up and swung the weapon in an arc slashing the entity while using the blade to concentrate her remaining energy into its point. The creature split along its length as it lit up with an intense light.

When the inevitable explosion came, she was ready for it and threw a protective shield around herself, Patrick and the prone form of her grandad. But, as so much of the creature had been burned up from her blast, all that resulted from the explosion was a shower of particles that drifted to the ground, covering everything for yards around with a thin layer of grey dust.

As the last particles settled, Cassie returned to normal speed and forced herself to scan it, not trusting that Laurence hadn't found some way of escaping. She found that it was as inanimate as the cobbles upon which it landed. Even probing it as deeply as she had seen into her own body when she had rejuvenated herself, she found no evidence that anything resembling life had survived within it.

"Did I do it?" she whispered. "Did I really just kill Laurence?"

She concentrated, adjusting her senses to detect any signs of a trail that indicated he had managed to time travel away once more.

There was nothing.

"I think I did it," she whispered. "He's dead. He's finally dead."

But, as the enormity of what she'd achieved sunk in, she thought, *Oh, God. Ka'Tor. I'm so sorry I left you. You didn't deserve this. You should never have turned into Laurence. Oh, Ka'Tor – I killed my own baby.*

She dropped the sword, sank to the ground and burst into tears.

Country Cottage

A few minutes later, Cassie heard two sets of footsteps coming from around the alley corner that led to Exchange Street.

Shit. Has the compulsion stopped working?

She gasped when only one figure came into view.

"You?" Cassie said, attempting to wipe her tears away on her sleeve.

"Yes, it's me, Cass. Who exactly were you expecting?" said Anne Luckin. She was attired in clothing that was far from appropriate for 2014. It looked distinctly Victorian. The black skirt almost reaching the ground was mostly hidden underneath a similarly dark-shaded coat. Her hair was tamed beneath a black bonnet, though a few strands of wavy, grey hair escaped from one side. The combination was far too wintery for the warmth of the day. "Ah, dust everywhere. Well done, Cass. I know it was hard, but it had to be done."

Cassie shook her head, trying to suppress her tears from a second outburst. *This is too much.*

"Oh," said the old lady, staring at what lay at Cassie's feet, "the sword as well. I suppose it makes sense. We need to find a new home for it."

"What are you talking about and why are you here?"

"I've come to collect Patrick," Anne said.

"Uh? How did you know he would be here?"

But, the old lady merely smiled before turning her attention to Patrick.

"Oh dear, he is in a bit of a mess, isn't he? It's even worse than I remember."

"I thought he might be dead," Cassie sniffed. "Will he be okay?"

"It will take some nursing, but he will eventually make it."

"Oh, thank goodness," Cassie said, turning to look at Bill. "Grandad needs looking after as well. I'd better..."

"No," Anne Luckin snapped. "You need to leave him to recover on his own. You do realise that, don't you?"

Cassie nodded. "Yes," she whispered. "The repression."

Anne Luckin tipped her head to one side and said, "Near enough. But I need you to help me with Patrick."

"What? To get him to a portal? Is there one nearby?"

"No. We need to use a direct route, which is where you come in."

"Oh. Um. Where to?"

"1857 and a cottage in Sussex."

"Sussex?"

"I'll explain later. Now peek in my head – just a quick peek, mind – nothing deep. Just so that you can see where the place is. Oh, and also the correct date."

"Um, really?"

"Yes, come on. The sooner we get Patrick somewhere safe, the less he will suffer – he's lost too much already. He will barely even remember his own name after this. So, scan me, right now."

Cassie shook her head but did as she was asked. She placed her left hand against the side of the woman's face. Anne Luckin's concentration was intense and the surface layer of her memories held an image of a cottage. It was set in a garden adorned with flowers and surrounded by the rolling hills of the South Downs. The image moved to focus upon an upstairs bedroom, simply furnished with a single bed, a chair and a chest of drawers. The date of April the fifteenth, 1857 came through as well.

"My birthday again?" Cassie queried.

Anne Luckin nodded. "Made it easier to coordinate and remember. Now, do you know exactly where to take us?" Cassie nodded. "Good, and I will also need to talk to the, um, occupier of the house about what she needs to do for Patrick. She won't be expecting this."

"She? Who is she?"

Anne Luckin shook her head. "Are you ready?"

"Um, one question."

"What? We don't have much time."

"How did you get past the compulsion shield thing I put up?"

"Don't ask. You'll figure it all out in time."

"Really? Um, were there two people round the corner?"

"That's two questions – but the answer is the same."

"Ah, did a later me bring you?"

Anne smiled. "You're getting it."

Cassie, seeing movement out of the corner of her eye, looked across to her grandad. He was starting to regain consciousness.

"We need to go before he sees us," Anne stressed. "Pick up the sword."

"Right. 1857. My birthday," Cassie said, sliding the sword into its scabbard on her back.

Anne nodded and said, "Bring us out at midday." She held Cassie's left hand in her right. Cassie took one of Patrick's hands while Anne took the other. "Let's go," Anne said, once their circle of hands was complete.

Cassie initiated the teleport driving them back through time and then southwards until she located the cottage. They emerged in the bedroom and Cassie released Patrick. He flopped down onto the bed with a groan. She frowned at Anne Luckin, who didn't seem at all perturbed about having been teleported back over 150 years and over 230 miles away.

"You've done this before?" Cassie asked.

"Of course," Anne grinned. "Don't ask when. You will know soon enough."

"So it looks like I'm going to be busy with hauling you around the years."

The only answer she got was another smile from Anne.

"Now what?" Cassie asked.

"You see those clothes on the chair?"

"Yes, but the chair was empty when you were thinking about this place."

"I can't be expected to remember everything. Right, change into them – you need to look the part."

"Huh, what part?"

Anne pulled envelopes and papers from her coat pocket. Some she placed on the chest of drawers – Cassie saw that one was a birth certificate and the hand-written name on it was Richard Patrick Luckin whose date of birth was recorded as the twenty-first of May, 1825. Anne then extracted money from the envelopes, counting out more than four hundred pounds.

"We need to go back a year to the spring of 1856 and buy this place."

"What?" Cassie replied.

"Women owning property, especially married women, in these times, while not illegal, is not exactly normal unless you come from a rich family. So, I need you to influence those auctioning it to get over their, shall we say, reluctance to sell it to me. Oh, and a little while after that, we will need to go back slightly further to do a bit of haunting."

"You what?"

Anne Luckin laughed. "That's the reason we get this place cheap. It was empty for a few months in 1855 after the previous owner died of old age. Then local people started reporting strange goings on and the idea that it was haunted circulated. So, after buying it, we need to go back and make sure that anyone else looking to buy the property is put off by the rumours. It sounds like fun."

"Um, but suppose it really is haunted. What then? I've seen enough ghosts to know that they exist."

"No, it's definitely *not* haunted," Anne laughed again, "and I should know."

"How?"

Anne shook her head. "Not long now before you find out. When you meet the occupier. Now, clothes. I'll help you into them – Victorian dresses are not exactly simple."

Upon arrival at the auction house, Anne gave Cassie strict instructions to let her do all the talking and, under no circumstances, call her by her real name. "You'll soon figure out why," she added.

The auction was a boisterous affair but Cassie's subtle mental compulsion on the auctioneer, along with the man who tried to bid against them, tipped the sale in their favour.

The amount accepted for the cottage was 325 guineas or £357 and five shillings. Anne produced the money which was checked and a receipt issued. Cassie watched as Anne signed the legal papers, transferring ownership of the property deeds. She suppressed a gasp when noticing that Anne hadn't signed her own name but had, instead written: Sarah Theresa Rebecca Boardal.

For identification, Anne produced several age-worn sheets of folded paper. Cassie, keeping her face as unsurprised as she could manage, observed that the first, a birth certificate, declared that Sarah Theresa Rebecca Wolfe, had been born in 1781, which made her aged 75 in 1856. The second was a marriage certificate to 25-year-old William Boardal in 1802 and the third was the latter's death certificate, dated 1843.

As they walked out of the auction building, Cassie whispered, "Boardal. That name again."

Anne Luckin smiled. "Yes."

"Obviously all lies. Where did you get the official documents?"

"Forgeries made in the nineteen-seventies. I claimed they were for a television play, so they had to look as accurate as possible for the close-ups. They were based on some real ones I had copies of. They even managed to get the right sort of paper."

"Wasn't Wolfe your real maiden name, though? I remember that from when

Grandad looked up the family tree online."

"I stole that from you, wolf girl. Ah, online. God, I really miss the Internet."

"What? But wasn't that way after your time?"

Anne Luckin chuckled and then said, "Okay, let's get around the corner and out of sight. Then we'll take the shortcut back to the cottage, if you know what I mean. Anyway, it's time for you to meet the occupier of the cottage properly."

"So, who is it? What's their name? Or aren't you allowed to tell me?"

"Given that you will soon meet her then, yes, I can tell you. Her name will become Anne Luckin in 1858 when she marries Richard Luckin who, of course, is better known to you as Patrick."

"Marries? You mean…"

"Yes, it's younger me. And that's why I needed you to bring Patrick back."

"Does she know that you are her older self?"

"She didn't at first."

"Oh, and what did she think about that?"

"It was a bit of a shock at first. Though not as much of a shock as… well, that's coming up soon. Anyway, she was already used to portals and time travel."

"I'm totally confused."

"Hah, you were definitely that, enough to make you go weak at the knees."

"What on Earth are you talking about?"

"You'll see. Right, I think we're out of sight of anyone else. Take us back to the cottage – two days after your birthday in 1857. Bring us out in the garden this time at three o'clock in the afternoon."

Cassie did so and, upon their arrival, Anne marched up to the back door and pushed it open, knowing it to be unlocked. Cassie followed her into the kitchen.

"Sit yourself down," she said, placing a sealed envelope on the kitchen table.

"What's that?"

"A list of things to do. A lot of them have already been done as far as I am concerned, though most of them will be new to you. But you'll need to do all of them at some point or another in order to keep the wheels oiled, so to speak."

"Oh right, but who made the list?"

"We both do – past me and future you."

"Oh, not more paradoxes?"

"Necessary. No, don't open it now. Put it in your pocket and go through it when you're back on your own again."

"Um, if you are telling me about things in my future, doesn't that cause more paradoxes?"

"If we don't get all these things done between us, then your future can't be guaranteed. I spent my retirement sorting out all the links. It's a bit like that chart I remember you saying you had on your wall."

"Uh, how do you know about that?"

"You told me all about it."

"You mean I will do at some…"

"Or maybe you already have done," Anne said, grinning. "Now excuse me. I'll get my younger self down from upstairs. She's looking after Patrick and starting to find him rather attractive. I envy her for what she's got coming."

Cassie pocketed the envelope and sat on a chair, gazing about the room. It was furnished simply but felt like somewhere familiar, a proper home. There was a smell that reminded her of a bakery.

She frowned, noticing a photograph on a shelf of the cabinet in one corner. The face of the uniformed man smiling at the camera was familiar, though she was pretty certain she'd never seen that particular photograph before.

She stood and went over to the cabinet to pick the photo up for a closer look. *Oh, my God, this doesn't make any sense. What is Anne Luckin doing with a photo of Charlie?*

There was a noise behind her. She quickly put the photo down and turned around. Anne Luckin and her younger self stood there, side-by-side.

"Hello, Cassie love," said the younger one, smiling.

Cassie looked from the younger one to the older one and back again. For a moment, her breath was caught in her throat.

"No," she finally squealed. "How is this even possible?"

"This is where she nearly faints," said the older one, matter of factly, as Cassie's knees gave way.

Diversion: Fire

After a minute's contemplation of what the old lady had told her before disappearing, Kay shook her head before dragging on the rope to divert the clone's attention from the trams.

"There's a portal up there. Can we use it?"

"Huh?" said the clone. "No. Gone. Air."

Kay cursed and stomped off down the pathway, snatching at the rope, which caused the clone to stumble momentarily before she happily trotted behind her.

"So, where's the next one?"

"Duh. Dunno. There," the dumbo said, pointing in the direction of a building on Red Lion Street just past the tram terminal at Orford Place. The sign on the building proclaimed the establishment to be Curl Brothers Limited.

"Ah, Debenhams. Nice and close. Good. The cold's making me want to piss."

"Water," the clone said.

"That's nowhere near water. There's an underground one in the basement and an air one up on the first floor."

"Water," the clone repeated.

"Idiot."

The dumbo shrugged and they headed off towards Orford Place.

Ten minutes later they were exploring the interior of the department store. Kay ignored the stares from other shoppers for both their clothing and the fact that she was hauling a younger girl along on the end of a rope.

"This version gets flattened in the Second World War," Kay explained, knowing it would be lost on the clone. It amused her that another customer overhearing what she said stared back, a shocked expression across his face. "So, upstairs or down?"

"There," the dumbo said, pointing to a staircase leading downwards.

"I hope we haven't reverted back to underground ones again."

"Water."

"How can there be water down here? Is it flooded or something?"

"River."

"There's no river here, you idiot."

"Was," the dumbo said.

"Was? What do you mean?"

The clone frowned as if trying hard to think. "Cockey. Pipe."

The dumbo led Kay to a part of the shop that was adjacent to Red Lion Street not far from where it met Rampant Horse Street. As they approached the corner, Kay could feel static in the air.

It's nearby, but where is it?

The clone stared at a section of wall in between a couple of wooden displays.

"Is it actually in the wall itself? How do we get at it?"

As the clone started to reach out with one hand, Kay grabbed the other. The clone's outstretched hand sank into the wall and, for a moment, appeared to stop there, seemingly cut off at the wrist.

Without warning, the clone disappeared into the wall, and Kay was sucked in after her. They were enclosed in rushing water for a moment before they popped out the other side. Both of them were cold and soaked to the skin.

At least I no longer need a piss, Kay thought as she stared up at an arched roof space. But it wasn't the architecture that caught her attention – it was the fact that the place was filling with smoke from the flames that were licking their way up the roof rafters.

"Shit," Kay said. "This isn't water – damn well needs to be, though. Quick. Back through the portal before it fades."

"We was just here," the dumbo said, ignoring the fire and walking further from where the portal had deposited them. The clone stopped at a table that, for some reason, had partly burnt leather straps lying across it. Ignoring the water dripping off her, the clone stood beside the table as if mesmerised. The rafters on the other side of the table were engulfed in flames and they were getting closer.

"No, we weren't," Kay said. "Come back."

"Yes, we was. This is the last place. You won't like it. After this, nothing."

"What? Crikey, that must be the most I've ever heard you speak and some of it almost made sense. Now come back right away."

Kay pulled on the rope to drag the dumbo back towards her, grabbed her hand and threw them both back through the portal. It was already beginning to fade but, somewhat reluctantly, it allowed them passage.

Instead of being instantaneous, this one took around four seconds before it released them, during which Kay heard a voice shouting as they passed through.

Popping out the other end, they immediately stumbled over fixed seating.

"Ow," Kay shouted, picking herself up before helping the dripping dumbo to her feet. "Theatre Royal – the original one. Good job we didn't come out during a performance."

They were in the stalls about halfway between the stage and the back of the theatre. The air felt warm suggesting they'd come out during summer.

I hope so, Kay thought. *I need it after that soaking and freezing up on the castle.*

"Man," the dumbo said.

"Oh, I see you're back to the usual incomprehensibility. Did you have a sudden fit of normality back there?"

"Man in portal."

"What?"

"Man in portal," the clone repeated pointing to where the portal had been. It had faded away so wasn't usable a third time.

"Oh, you mean you heard a voice as well?"

"Ya."

"I knew I heard something as we came through. What did he say?"

"Debbie."

"Yeah, might have been. What does it mean?"

The clone shrugged.

"Of course you don't know. Come on, dumbo. Let's find a way out of here." She dragged the clone towards an exit door at the back of the theatre. "Say, can you smell something?"

The dumbo pointed towards the stage where Kay could see smoke coming from behind the safety curtain.

"Oh God, here we go again," Kay muttered. "This place burnt down in the nineteen-thirties if I remember rightly. Let's scarper before someone blames us for yet another catastrophe."

Spaceship

Righting a Wrong

Cassie arrived beside the dilapidated cottage. She'd travelled back in time to 1549 once more and, after what she had just been through, couldn't remember exactly what the time had been when she'd departed this spot to begin her chase after Laurence. She had a vague feeling it had been around midday so, not wanting to mess things up by meeting herself before she'd departed, she moved forwards to around two o'clock. Opening up her mental map, she expanded it beyond the Earth to look for the spaceship tethered to the orbiting piece of rock at the L4 position. It took a bit of hunting down as she couldn't remember if the L4 Lagrange point was ahead of or behind the Earth. She remembered Patrick – or was it the device? – saying something about a position sixty degrees around the orbit.

Then she spotted it – it was the one ahead of the Earth.

The teleport took several seconds and she appeared in the same section of the spaceship from which she had departed. However, there was no sign of either Georgia or the device. After checking that the atmosphere was breathable, Cassie concentrated and detected something several rooms away. A doorway, open this time, beckoned and, feeling slightly queasy in the reduced gravity, she moved through three almost identical sections until she saw Georgia strapped into a chair that was meant for someone – or possibly something – a lot larger. Some sort of helmet was attached to her head.

Hovering nearby, the device was glowing a muted green.

"Is she okay?" Cassie asked rushing to Georgia's side to notice that her eyes were closed. "She'd better be. If you've harmed…"

"Yes," the device interrupted. "She is being taught enough to enable her to fly this ship back to this position when the time comes."

"Okay, I see. Georgia sometimes joked about getting a job at NASA as their astronauts needed to be fit, athletic types. Maybe her dream might come true."

"The crude mechanics of your current space technology are not relatable to this craft. There is no comparison."

"Yeah, what a surprise," Cassie muttered.

"She is nearly ready – the process is in the last stages," the device announced. "We could leave soon. Hold – I am detecting changes. You are different."

"What do you mean?"

"There are changes within your structure that I have never detected before."

"Yeah, I turned Gallifreyan."

"Your reference is irrelevant. But, as you have returned, you must have accomplished the undoing of all Laurence's changes."

"No. There's still one left."

"Why did you not finish the job? It was imperative that…"

"No," Cassie shouted. "Just shut up. Let me do the talking – and the ordering – this time."

"If you insist. What do you order of me? Do you want to know how to rectify that altered timeline?"

"No, I know what to do. But something else needs to be done first – but I'm not capable of doing it. Or, even if I am, I don't want to. That's your job."

"What might this task be? Is it of significant importance to delay leaving?"

"Stop asking questions and follow me," Cassie said. "Jump into my pocket."

"Is this necessary to…"

"I said shut up. I've just spent ages going around fixing things and, after what I've just seen, I've had enough. I want this over and done with. Either do what I tell you or piss off back to your own galaxy or wherever it was you came from and I'll figure it all out by myself."

There was a pause.

"I will place myself within your pocket," the device said, disappearing. Cassie felt the inside pocket of her denim jacket move.

"Right," Cassie said. "We're going home. September 2017. This will be the alternate timeline that's been in place since Laurence changed things in 2014."

She teleported back to Earth, appearing once more outside the cottage of 1549 before moving forwards in time, heading home.

"When we arrive, we need to be quiet. So, we'll be invisible and I will wrap us in silence so we don't scare her."

"Who?"

"You'll see."

Cassie materialised into the familiar location of her own bedroom. However, the room was far removed from its normal state. Clothes were strewn across the floor and over the chair and bedside cabinet. Mixed in with them was an assortment of unwashed cups, glasses and plates, the latter encrusted with uneaten food. The place was a mess, and it stunk.

On the bed sat her sixteen-year-old self. Except Cassie had never lived through this version of her life. The girl – Cassie could barely think of this person as herself – was a lot thinner, almost gaunt, her face pale and drawn. Her unwashed, tangled hair hung lifelessly around her shoulders, hiding her eyes. She was wearing a ridiculously short skirt and a top whose left sleeve had been rolled up to just above the elbow. Around the left wrist was wrapped a strip of material. It had been wound around several times and then tied in a knot.

"It is you," the device stated unnecessarily.

"No, it isn't me. Can't you see that? I was never like this."

On the bed, there was movement as the girl opened a pencil box. But there were no pencils contained within. There was only a knife whose blade glowed in the sunlight shining through the grubby window. Cassie winced as the girl tested the sharpness of the knife's point on the palm of her left hand. She had to suppress her intake of breath as a tiny trickle of the girl's blood flowed.

"What is she doing?" the device asked.

"Girl scars," Cassie muttered as her alternate self first untied and then unwound the material from her wrist. Once the skin was exposed, the scars were obvious, the most recent still to heal.

The girl contemplated her wrist for a few moments before placing the blade against the skin. Knowing what was about to happen, Cassie sped herself up so that the scene around her became as good as frozen.

"I cannot comprehend why this alternative of you is acting in such a manner," the device said.

"No, of course you can't," Cassie snapped. "Do you know who she is?"

"It is my conjecture that this is not a version of yourself who resulted in the one with which I am familiar. This is not part of the extra data held in the disc nor in that third backup. Therefore, this is an alternative timeline and, given that it needs to be eliminated, it is possibly not relevant."

"Not fucking relevant, you moron?" Cassie shouted. "It's Kay. This is where she came from. When you created her, you filled her head with memories of the Kay who'd died after the motorcycle crash. I remember asking you at the time where her original memories came from. Then we got diverted after you went bonkers as soon as I mentioned paradoxes. Don't you remember that?"

"Yes, your exact words were: *So where did those memories come from? Who originally thought them? How can such things exist?*"

"Do you remember everything I've ever said?"

"Only those where I have been present."

"Bloody hell. Well, this is it. This is where Kay's memories came from. From this abused version of myself who cuts herself because of what Laurence did to my grandad – what he's forced this version of me to go through. I caught a glimpse of some of it when I looked inside her head when I came here before."

"Before?"

"Yes, when I realised that I'd felt a new timeline come into being."

"When was that?"

"When the Patrick version of Laurence had a second go at Grandad after the first version set up that repression in 2014."

"But there was only the one repression – nothing else – and I removed that on the last day of June 2018."

"No, this is an alternate timeline. Look into my head. Learn about all that happened to me after I jumped back to Earth from your spaceship the first time. Then you'll see where she came from."

Cassie felt the device scan her and she let it access all of her recent memories – the chasing of Laurence into the virus-infected world of 2020 and his attempts to destroy her past by taking that infection back to the beginning of the Second World War. It was initially silent as it encountered Cassie's memories of being caught in the blast of a nuclear bomb, and how she had reassembled herself.

But, after witnessing her self-induced regeneration, it said, "Cassie Fox. I knew you were dangerous… but this is beyond what even I could have expected. You have tempered the wildness of raw energy and have recreated yourself. I have constructed clones of you but I needed an intact template. Conversely, you have rebuilt an enhanced version of yourself from scratch in your own image."

"Yeah, well…" Cassie said, not sure of how to react. "Um, let's get on with what else I've done."

It watched her go through the list that Anne Luckin had given her: the visits to the Sussex cottage in 1855 to set up the hauntings; stealing photos of Great Grandad Charlie from her house in 2005, one of which ended up in the kitchen of the Sussex cottage; and taking Anne on several trips including one where she deposited her in School Lane in 2014 bypassing the compulsion her earlier self had set up only minutes before.

"She is the old lady," the device stated. "I will pass the message of trust back to you. I see that the list is paradoxical in itself as you and the so-called Anne Luckin are telling each other about its components out of order."

No kidding, Cassie thought, remembering her confusion when Anne had instructed her to take her and the scimitar to the road outside Kay's safe house in December 2000. Hidden from view, they had watched Kay depart on her motorbike along with her earlier self on Charlie's bus for the confrontation with Laurence and his temporary decapitation. Anne had then instructed Cassie to dump the scimitar over the garden wall of a house on the opposite side of the street, but said the instruction had come from a future Cassie.

The most traumatic event to revisit was when she took Anne and a bundle of her own clothes back to the cottage of 1549. She could hardly believe that the charred creature on the bed barely clinging to life was herself. As before, she felt sick just reliving that memory.

And, because she had suppressed that particular memory until the very end, the device also witnessed her final battle with Laurence.

"You have killed Laurence," the device stated.

"Unless he managed to get inside Grandad's head, which wouldn't surprise me, then yes – I killed him. It… it had to be done."

"You have regrets about that action?"

"Regrets? I had to kill my own son! How the fuck do you think I feel?"

"Angry."

"Oh, fucking well done. Your powers of deduction are second to none."

"Your sarcasm is misplaced."

"So, you understand sarcasm now, do you? When I first had you, you were totally reluctant to even talk to me."

"After leaving the restrictive environment created by Laurence in his various guises, I began to explore how his influence had reduced me to the barely thinking machine you first encountered. I was also aware of my effect upon others with whom I came into contact."

"You mean killing them slowly?"

"Correct. I was unable to counter it due to the deep-seated commands Laurence had instilled."

"You didn't kill me, though."

"You were his next intended victim, so you were automatically spared."

"Well, lucky me. But not so lucky for Kay and her grandad."

"I have scanned the version of your grandfather that is present in this timeline. His mind is corrupted but while Laurence had intended to occupy his head, your intervention induced only a change of personality."

"Only? Jesus Christ! Look what it's done to her. It was bad enough seeing the tribe cutting children's faces. Seeing a version of me doing something similar because she can't face life is absolute torture. That could have been me. It *is* me. And you haven't seen the outcome yet – I know what she does to herself to get away from it all. I saw the blood. She never reached seventeen, for fuck sake."

"I do see it, I can read in your mind what you saw this version of yourself inflict upon herself in her limited future."

"Yeah, but the adult Kay I knew couldn't have gone that far otherwise she would never have existed. So how do her original memories fit in with all this?"

"That copy I took of her just before she died after the motorcycle crash does not contain elements of self-harm to the extent demonstrated here. Also, given the state of her at the instance I took the copy, I was never certain I had captured everything. She died while I was extracting those memories."

"You still have all of those memories and all those people living inside you?"

"Yes."

"They're not real, are they? Any of them. Kay, Charlie or even Mum. It was always you making out like you had them inside you. But you didn't, did you?"

"That is correct. But the responses I had them portray were as true to their original personalities as possible."

"Just another way you lied to me."

"That may be one interpretation."

"You made me believe my mum was still around."

The device was silent for a moment. Then it said, "You are suppressing another memory. A relatively recent one."

"Keep out of that one."

"No, you think it while you try to hide it from me. But I sensed the change at the time. Remember, I was there in your house until your grandfather passed me on to you at seventeen."

"So, you knew even back then and didn't let me know?"

"You needed to believe it."

"Once all this is over, I want you out of my life completely."

"That is expected and probably inevitable."

"Yeah, well. Make sure it happens this time."

"Agreed."

"But right here and now, I need you for one more task."

"Only one?"

"Yes," Cassie said, looking at the girl sitting like a statue on the edge of the bed, the knife poised at her wrist to make the cut. "Kay."

"There is an anomaly. When I installed old Kay's early memories into the clone I made of you, they felt incomplete and there was some resistance."

"Resistance? How?"

"That clone was you but overlaid with new memories. At the time, I suspected I hadn't done enough to suppress your influence upon that clone, but given the deterioration in the state of the memories I had to work with, I didn't know where I could source a complete set."

"You do now," Cassie said.

"Yes, but taking memories from a girl in this state is inconsistent with the required outcome. The Kay generated from this version of you would last little more than a few days. She is already on the verge of suicide."

"Well, go back to her at an earlier date, then. Last year, maybe."

"But, then there would be a gap in her memories."

"Stretch them out. Make her feel that what happened between 2014 and 2016 actually lasted until 2018."

"That… might be possible."

"Do it, go back and find a point where she is still the Kay we remember."

"But, we would still need to insert those enhanced memories into the clone. When would that happen?"

"As soon as possible after she was first cloned, I'd say. Can you do that?"

"Yes, but you will need to guide me."

Cassie nodded and then said, "Don't fuck this up or I'll drop you into the nearest volcano or even Mount Doom, whichever is more convenient."

"So, I was wrong," Cassie said, standing invisible at the top of the Castle Mall escalator that led out to Castle Meadow. It was 11:28 on June the thirtieth, 2018, and they had just watched her unsuspecting seventeen-year-old self pass them to descend the escalator.

"What do you mean?" the device asked.

"How many times can you detect me here?"

"Nine, including you," it replied.

"What? I thought there would only be six. Where do the other three come from? List them all."

The device reeled them off: the original who had passed them and was now just reaching the lower floor; the one watching Starbucks from the food gallery who was about to help make the clones; two invisible ones, the first down on the lower floor having been thrown by similarly invisible Laurence/Patrick, the other on the walkway above and about to drag Laurence away; the one below them inside Starbucks who was finishing up her meal, leaving the second coffee cup for the multiple Kays to drink; and the three on the roof of the Castle.

"Ah, I'd forgotten about those last ones," Cassie said. "They're not actually in Castle Mall though, are they?"

"I can still detect them from here," the device said. "No doubt, I would find more if I extended the search parameters. For example, there is also one in your home who, after ordering me to remove the repression on your grandfather, goes back to the previous day to rest."

"Okay, that's enough. If there had been more than nine in total, then it would have indicated even more future versions of me turning up. This place is turning into a regular time-travellers convention – all of them me."

While waiting for the cloning process to start, Cassie thought back to what she'd got the device to do over the past hour. They had moved back to 2016 and it had copied the memory contents of the Kay they found there while she slept. They then headed for 2014 and School Lane. After watching her earlier self defeat Laurence and help Anne Luckin take Patrick back to 1857, they had removed the effects of Laurence's second attack upon her grandad, leaving only the original repression in place. Having negated that final alternative timeline, which reinstated the original one, they jumped forwards again to June 2018 and the day in Castle Mall where it had all begun.

"It starts," the device said.

Cassie looked down and sped herself up to match the clone-making process taking place on the lower floor.

"The one allocated to become Kay has been created," the device announced.

"We need to get to her and insert the extra memories. Look, she's moving. No, wait. She's stopped next to that mobile phone stand. What's up with her?"

"The confusion in her mind is causing her to believe in two possible pasts."

"Get down there and do it right now."

The device popped out of Cassie's pocket to reappear on the stand below where its patterning attracted the clone's eye.

A second later it was done and Cassie felt movement as the device returned to her pocket. As the Kay clone ran from the mobile phone stand, Cassie, feeling somewhat calmer and relieved, said, "Oh, thank goodness for that. I presume she will now go and find her first portal."

"She will have to be quick," the device said.

"Why?"

"They will cease to exist in a short while."

"Oh damn, I forgot about that. Look, she's running back up the escalator – we need to think of something quickly."

"She needs to be moved back to a time when portals exist."

"Right, I'll slow time, grab her and send her back – I don't know – a day, a week – maybe even a year."

As the Kay clone was about to pass them, Cassie accelerated herself and became visible. She grasped the clone's hand and moved back over a year to June the sixth, 2017, materialising only when the area was clear of onlookers. It was only when she released the girl's hand that she realised she should have checked the weather as well – it was raining.

Returning to invisibility and normal speed, she watched the clone run out onto Castle Meadow.

"I bet that's confused her," Cassie said. "Maybe it's for the best as, at least, she'll have realised pretty quickly that something weird has happened. Okay, back to 1549 and your spaceship."

That's No Moon

Under Georgia's guidance, the ship undocked from the asteroid. As soon as it was free of the rock, she brought it to a halt. The device then emitted a pulse of energy and Cassie felt her internal calendar jump.

"Whoa. What happened there?" she asked.

"I have moved us back almost one hundred and forty-two thousand years. To return this ship, we need to arrive not long after we initially steal it. The journey here took 994 of your years – the return will take the same."

It then instructed Cassie and Georgia to move into a separate chamber where they were shown transparent-walled cubicles not much larger than themselves.

"What are these for?" Cassie asked.

"Safety," it replied.

"In what way?"

"Time travel in space is dangerous. These will protect you."

"You mean we're going to spend 994 years sleeping upright in these things?" Cassie asked.

"No. While the ship moves towards its destination, you two will skip forwards in fourteen, seventy-one-year jumps within the ship. It will only take a few minutes of your experienced time."

"So, why can't we just move forwards in time normally like I do on Earth or like when you just moved this entire ship back thousands of years?"

"Firstly, the entire ship along with yourselves was moved back as a single entity in time only. Despite the fact that your solar system was in a significantly different area of space in 1549, we were still tied to the gravity well of your sun."

"What's that got to do with it?"

"Do you recall Laurence almost getting lost when he tried to time travel after he departed this craft?"

"Uh, yes?"

"You need to be anchored to a gravity well when you travel in time."

"A gravity well?"

"Yes, such as the Earth or the Sun. Laurence found the Earth jumping away as he travelled in both time and space. The solar system, the Earth included, can be travelling at over six hundred kilometres each second in relation to the cosmic microwave background. Time travelling even a few minutes in space may result in an offset of millions of kilometres. Laurence was lucky that he quickly deduced the problem and corrected for it. When on Earth or any body of substantial density, you are anchored even while you travel. So, unless you deliberately move position, you appear to be locked to the same place when moving through time."

"Okay, I think I sort of understand that," Cassie said.

"Good for you," Georgia said, "I have no idea what it's talking about."

"That is to be expected as you are not conversant with travelling in time yourself," the device continued. "However, to travel back to the location from where this ship was stolen requires a physical journey that will last 994 years. As human bodies – without using techniques such as those utilised by Ka'Tor throughout his existence – cannot endure for such a period, you must time travel to that future. But, upon that journey, this ship will not be tied to a gravity well of any significance and therefore, if you time travel even within the ship, it's likely that you will find yourself marooned in deep space for even the smallest of jumps."

"Ah, so is this what these cubicles are for?" Cassie said.

"Correct, they will keep you anchored within the ship when you travel into the future."

"Um, these are separate cubicles – how will Georgia time travel?"

"You will allow me to control that aspect for both her and yourself. We need to coordinate our arrival so that neither of you arrives too soon or too late."

"What about you?" Georgia asked. "Will you be time travelling as well?"

"No, I will remain here for the duration."

"Blimey, won't that be a bit boring?" Georgia said. "Suppose your batteries, or whatever it is you run on, go flat?"

"I do not use batteries. I absorb energy from any source available, just as Cassie has learned to do. Also, I have been in existence for over one hundred and sixty thousand of your years… and I am incapable of becoming bored."

"Well, goody for you," Georgia muttered. "I can't last more than half an hour unless I've got something to do."

"A hundred and sixty? Where did the extra twenty come from?" Cassie asked.

"When I came into your possession, I was already two thousand years from my initial construction. Also, I dwelt in Earth's deep past for around seventeen thousand years recuperating after you convinced me to create the portals."

"Oh right. Um, one question. Are you coming back with us?"

"No, according to what I have learned about my future, I will be taken away for analysis to prevent events from my history from being repeated."

"So, who will control our time travel on the way back?"

"That, I concede, is something I have yet to determine. Certainly, I am not aware that my earlier self performed such a task as I was in a deactivated state until reaching the Earth. Someone is therefore required to pilot the craft to enable the completion of that cycle by ejecting me onto the planet."

"Ejecting?" Cassie queried.

"Oh yeah, I've already been taught how to do that," Georgia answered. "There are systems on the ship for expelling waste products."

"Waste products?"

"Yeah, *that* sort of waste products," Georgia laughed.

"Oh, right, of course."

"There is also another reason I will not be returning with you."

"What's that?"

Cassie heard her own voice replayed: *Once all this is over, I want you out of my life completely.*

"What did it say?" Georgia asked.

Cassie realised the device had only allowed her to hear her previous demand.

"Oh, something I said to it a short while back. I was quite angry at the time."

Georgia raised an eyebrow and asked, "As angry as when you threw it across the room back in the cottage?"

"Close," Cassie whispered.

"Ah, that bad. Um, one other thing."

"What's that?" said both Cassie and the device.

"I'm absolutely famished. Is there any food on this bus and, if so, do we get to eat before we go all Star Trek and seek out new worlds?"

"Woah, is that it?" Georgia said. For them both, it was just over two hours later.

After the matter converters had generated something that resembled and even tasted like an Indian takeaway, they'd entered the cubicles where the device guided their shortcut through 994 years. Returning to the main control room, they observed the approach to their destination, which involved passing a couple of Saturn-sized planets orbiting close to a local star. One gas giant had been an almost uniform purple while the other raged with orange storms like Jupiter.

In front of them, a screen displayed what the ship was about to come into orbit around. That it was a sphere was obvious but, with little to draw references from, it was impossible to determine its size – it could have been small and close up, or huge and far away. There were marks on it – shading or pits or maybe they were entire cities – Cassie had no way of telling. "Is it going to be full of aliens?" she asked.

"Unlikely as it is fully automated," the device said. "Only if there are others using its facilities will there be a chance of encountering sapient beings."

"So, what is it, exactly?"

"It is, in your terms, a space station."

"A space station? Exactly what goes on here?" Cassie continued.

"It is a place where craft are docked until required, where goods are stored until allocated or are moved between craft as they are transferred from where they were manufactured to where they are required. It may be considered to be similar to your world's railway goods yards of the mid-twentieth century."

"That's a really useful comparison – not – since that's fifty years before we were born," Georgia laughed. "Well, for those of us who don't have the ability to go back in time and visit them, anyway."

Cassie couldn't help smiling.

"They will be requiring authentication for docking shortly."

"They?" Georgia questioned.

"Whatever systems are in control," the device answered.

"What are they? Things like you?"

"Similar, possibly. From what I recall – which isn't much as I was in storage and awaiting assignment – the systems are likely to be of a lower order than myself. Much of their functionality is preprogrammed."

"Have I got to talk to them?" Georgia asked. "If so, then what will they be asking about when we arrive?"

"I will answer as your minds cannot handle the language and your vocal tracts are barely capable of reproducing the required audio frequencies. Keep us on the path marked out for orbit until docking has been authorised."

To Cassie's eyes, Georgia's hands moved over the desk of controls in front of her as if she had been piloting craft like this all her life. She wondered if her friend's mind had been adversely affected by the induced training she had undergone. There was a buzzing and a section of a wall illuminated itself. It displayed a changing pattern of dancing colours that made little sense to Cassie. Observing the frown on Georgia's face, Cassie supposed it was having the same impression on her as well. The flashing lights were almost painful to look at for too long. They were, however, less distracting than trying to look at a creator, for which Cassie was thankful.

The noise and patterns went on for nearly half a minute as they orbited the space station. After the patterning halted, a screen indicated the allocated docking point.

Georgia's hands manipulated the controls, bringing them closer to one of the darker specks on the surface of the station. The speck grew into a blotch and then into a circle of concentric rings.

"Aren't we supposed to be slowing down?" Cassie squeaked as the station rushed towards them. "Oh, I see," she added, as the inner rings slid open to reveal an entrance. They descended into a tube barely wider than the ship. After a few seconds, the tube opened into a spherical chamber where the ship came to rest on a circular pad near the centre.

"Now what?" Cassie whispered, feeling completely out of her depth.

This is a bit like waking up in the Stone Age – though, this time, it's like I've suddenly woken up in the far distant future. Except this is still really the past – not that it feels like it.

"The information transferred to my past self via the restore operation is lacking detail on this."

"So, do we go out there?" Cassie asked. "Is there air out there to breathe? Who or what do we talk with to get things sorted out? And where do we find earlier you?"

There was a pause and then the device answered, "I will make contact with those operating this station."

"Didn't you say we were going to have to go back in time and steal this craft?" Georgia said.

"That was the information I passed back to myself."

"And was that it? Any idea on how we actually do this?" Cassie demanded.

"No."

Cassie and Georgia looked at each other.

"I don't like the sound of this," Cassie said.

"At least there doesn't seem to be anything actually out there to harm us," Georgia said.

A second later there was a humming sound and both of them were teleported out of the ship against their will.

Manacled

Cassie woke to find herself drenched in sweat. More worrying was that she was spread-eagled upon an angled metal slab that was warm against her back. She tried to move only to find that her arms, legs and body were clamped to the slab at the wrist, elbow, ankle, knee, belly and neck, holding her almost motionless. Despite this, she could sense that gravity was once again reduced, and the down direction was behind her somewhere, though closer to her feet than her head. It enforced the impression that the slab was angled at about thirty degrees to a floor that was impossible to see.

In front of her, machinery or instrumentation filled a wall, some of it resembling that which she had seen on the spacecraft. No more than three feet away, parts of it glowed with dull red, blue and green hues that, combined, were the source of the pallid light that struggled to fill what little of the immediate area she could see.

There was a noise not far to her left. With only a few degrees of movement available in her neck, she twisted her head to that side. Similarly imprisoned and attached to the same slab of metal, Georgia's form came into focus.

Cassie gasped. Georgia was naked and also dripping with sweat.

Oh my God. Where are we? How long have we been here?

She managed to peer down at her own body, seeing herself in a similar predicament.

What the fuck have they done with our clothes?

She whimpered and struggled against her bonds. Her arms, pinioned above her head, had almost no free movement; the situation with her legs identical.

Unable to free herself, she tried teleporting away. But, as soon as she attempted this, there was a reaction from the machinery – the lights increased in their brightness and flashed from one colour to another. Cassie soon realised that her teleportation abilities had been suppressed in some manner.

Unable to do anything else, Cassie tried to see what else surrounded her. Beyond Georgia, there appeared to be more of the machinery and the same was true of the areas to her right and above her head. They were enclosed.

Cassie tried to think at the device but elicited no response. Her concentration was interrupted when Georgia screamed.

"Are you okay?" Cassie asked.

"W-what's happened? Where are our clothes?" Georgia spluttered. "We were in the ship and then we were here."

"I know. I've only just come to as well," Cassie said. "But I think we've been here a while. Possibly hours."

"Are they going to probe us or whatever it is that aliens are supposed to do?"

Cassie gulped. "I hope not, though maybe they already have when we were out cold."

"Oh shit. Can't you teleport away?"

"Already tried that – something's stopping me. I think all these lights are doing something."

"They're definitely giving me a headache, all right. It's like they're more than just lights."

"Yes, they must be," Cassie replied, scrunching her eyes shut. But the intense colours seeped past her eyelids.

"Is it trying to hypnotise us or something?" Georgia whimpered.

"Possibly," Cassie mumbled. "Driving me nuts."

"It's like those colours when we were coming in to land. Where's the device?"

"No bloody idea. I can't raise it."

"Shit."

Despite her eyelids remaining closed, Cassie could tell that the colours were speeding up. She risked a peek at them but the flashing was still too much to bear. She shut her eyes for several seconds and then tried again. This time, the lights were flashing so fast that they had blurred into a uniform orange which, at least, was far less disturbing.

Suddenly they stopped and returned to a static pattern. But the respite was short-lived as they were replaced by screeching noises being emitted by the machines around them.

"Oh God, what now?" Georgia groaned.

But Cassie had heard such noises before. It was when the device and that creator alien had been communicating with each other in the cottage of 1549.

The noises went on until she felt they permeated her entire body. Like the coloured lights, the noise was impossible to shut out. The plate to which she was attached resonated with the lower frequencies while the upper ones made her teeth buzz, especially the two fillings in the upper molars on the right side of her mouth. The noise permeated her brain until she thought she might go mad.

Beside her, Georgia whimpered.

After what seemed like far too long, the noises suddenly halted and a voice said, "Kaaaazzzz, Kaaazziiieee, Kaahzzie, Cassie. Jaaaawww, Joorge, Joorgeee-ah, Georgia."

"What?" Georgia gasped. "Did it just say our names?"

"Oh God, I'm just relieved that the noise has stopped."

"Me too – I thought my brain was going to explode."

"Language neurons tarrrr… targeted and mapped," the voice continued in a raw manner. It reminded Cassie of the voice of the device when it had got in a fit back in Castle Mall over the word, *paradox*. "Communication established. Is comprehension initiated? Do you understand?"

"Is this a bit like when the device relearned English after Laurence reset it?" Georgia whispered.

"Yeah, could be," Cassie said before shouting, "We can hear you. Why are you holding us prisoner? Let us go."

"Krrrr… Criminal activity hazzz been established. Your biological patterns match those of entities previously detected when a space-travelling vehicle was requisitioned without proper authorisation. Your species, origin and intentions are unknown. Restraint is imperative." The voice was becoming clearer with each word and sounding less artificial at the same time.

"Criminal? But we brought your ship back," Georgia shouted. "We didn't steal it."

"Not yet we haven't," Cassie whispered. "Maybe we shouldn't try to anger it."

"Fuck that," Georgia growled. "I don't appreciate being strapped naked to a lump of metal. As soon as I get free, some balls are going to get kicked."

"Don't bet on anything around here having balls or anything resembling them," Cassie said.

"Don't care. Just wait until I get my hands on… aaaah."

There was a single green flash – Cassie wasn't sure if it had been just inside her head as her eyes hadn't properly registered it.

"What the hell was that?" Georgia said.

I know that colour, Cassie thought, *and if Georgia felt it as well…*

"Criminal temporal activity has been detected," came the machine voice. "Its source has not been located. Are you the cause of it?"

The device, Cassie thought. *I knew it. But where is it? Is it here?*

But Cassie couldn't sense it. All she could feel was the warmth of the plate at her back, which was increasing in temperature. The rate the sweat was dripping from their bodies accelerated.

"We didn't do anything," Cassie said. "We can't do anything. Let us go. You don't have the right to treat us like this."

"Irrelevant. Unknown species have no rights until their primary intentions and place within the hierarchy is determined."

"Hierarchy? So where do we fit in?"

"Unknown. Apart from a single earlier incursion by your biological signatures, your status is, as yet, undetermined."

"Well, in that case, can you let us go or, at least, stop trying to cook us?"

"Your species' requirements are not yet fully resolved. Is it normal that you exude fluids from your epidermis at such a volume?"

"Only when it's too fucking hot," Cassie shouted.

"Please desist from such activities. The liquid has a detrimental effect upon the systems monitoring you."

"We can't, you moron," Cassie screamed. "This is what our bodies do when someone tries to heat us up too much."

"Your bodies were initially wrapped in unnecessary materials. These were removed and disposed of when it was determined that they were not part of your anatomical system and therefore served no function of any importance."

"No importance? And you did *what* with them? Disposed of them?" Cassie shouted.

"Oh, Christ," muttered Georgia. "Make it cooler, for God's sake. I'm going to pass out if it gets any hotter."

There was a shudder around the room as something clanked and rumbled at a different frequency. The temperature dropped a little.

"Oh, that's better," Cassie said.

The temperature plummeted.

"Bloody hell, too much," Georgia screamed. "I'm freezing now."

"Your biological regulatory systems are primitive and extremely inefficient," came the mechanical voice.

"That's why we wear clothes, idiot," Cassie shouted. "Don't you understand?"

"Clothes?" said the voice – there was a short sequence of flashing lights and then it added, "Very primitive. You are barely above animals. What is such a species doing out in space and able to purloin space vehicles far in advance of your apparent technological status?"

"Just put the temperature back up, please," Cassie begged.

There was a clunk from somewhere behind them.

"An adjustment has been made to compensate. Is that proving adequate?"

"Better," Cassie said as the air temperature returned to something more reasonable. "Now, how about letting us free?"

"Request denied. Evidence is being gathered to determine suitable punishment concerning the unauthorised removal of a vehicle."

"Bugger," Cassie muttered. "But we brought it back, undamaged."

"Its presence confirms its return. However, although the vehicle has been returned only... hours – is that the right term for your measurement of time? – after its original removal, it has been determined that it has aged considerably since that removal. Such ageing can be damaging, is illegal without authorisation and is thereby considered criminal. Temporal activities have been detected within it and these must be fully analysed prior to any possible release. Meanwhile, your restraint is imperative and non-negotiable. Discussion will now cease until a verdict has been reached."

"Bugger again," Cassie muttered. "Where the hell is the device?"

The minutes stretched into an hour and then two. Both Cassie and Georgia, unable to free themselves, fell into silence. Cassie could hear Georgia's breathing beside her but, in the subdued lighting, was no longer able to see her.

Any use of her abilities caused the flashing colours and noises to return and she had to relent. Her arms and legs were aching from lack of movement and she had an itch on her nose that was threatening to drive her insane.

After a while, she discovered that, if she was careful and moved her mind slowly, she could expand her map and see part of the layout of the structure within which they were held. The entire room, which was walled with the instruments that were monitoring them, showed no evidence of any physical doorway. But, beyond that room, she was able to detect open areas – though whether or not they held a breathable atmosphere she couldn't determine.

"Cass," came a whisper from beside her.

"What?"

"I need to piss."

"Yeah. Me too. I've been trying to ignore it."

"I won't be able to ignore mine for much longer."

Cassie remembered something from earlier on when the voice had tried to order them to stop sweating. *Didn't it say something about our sweat messing up its machines? Yes, I'm sure it did. Oh, I wonder…*

"I've got an idea," she whispered to Georgia.

"Are you kidding?" Georgia replied after Cassie had outlined her plan. "Is that the best we've got?"

"Can you think of anything else?"

"Nope, okay then. What have we got to lose? Apart from our dignity."

"Dignity? Trussed up naked like this? Right. Are you ready?"

"Dying for it."

"Okay, on the count of three, two, one…"

"Aaaah," Georgia said, obviously relieved.

The machines around them, which had been silent and barely glowing, went into overdrive. The lights became manic for a couple of seconds while the screeching threatened to burst their eardrums. Just when Cassie thought it was never going to stop, the noises halted and the lights dropped, falling in intensity to a solid dull blue. As they did so, Cassie felt the suppression of her abilities weaken. It was barely enough, but she managed to absorb energy from around herself – from the machines themselves, which dimmed their lights even further. It was enough to boost her strength to teleport a tiny distance and out of the clamps that held her. She caused the teleport to flip her over so that she reappeared on top of and facing Georgia. Grabbing Georgia's wrists in her now-freed hands, she then teleported them both out of the enclosed compartment to one of the open areas.

As they emerged, naked and dripping with their own urine, Cassie tried to analyse the atmosphere. It appeared to be breathable, though the mix was not ideal – there was something oily in the air.

"Jesus Christ, it bloody worked," Georgia gasped and, wrinkling her nose, added. "But we both need a shower. Yuk, it's clinging to me – not enough gravity for it to run off."

"Yeah, I know," Cassie said. "But there's no time to worry about that now. We need to get away before they figure out where we went and recapture us."

Georgia tried to stand and shake the liquid off her legs but it wasn't working and she began floating away instead. Now that they were unrestrained, they realised that gravity was so low that they had little grip on the floor.

"Sit down, don't let go of me," Cassie said, starting to feel as nauseous as she'd been when first finding herself on the spacecraft. She concentrated first upon trying to locate the device and then, when that failed, to find the ship they'd arrived on. "Damn," she said, her eyes shut as she expanded her map to encompass the entire station. "I can't find the device or the spacecraft. No wait…"

She expanded the map beyond the space station.

"You found them?"

"Yes, the ship – but it's no longer docked. It's being piloted away somewhere. And I think I can detect that the device is still on it."

"What? You mean we've lost our escape route?"

"No, I don't think so. Remember, we have to steal the ship in the past. So, let's go there to do just that."

"How far back in the past?"

"No idea. The device said we had to arrive back *after* we'd stolen it in the first place but it didn't say how much time that actually was. We'd better go slowly. Maybe a day at a time."

"Okay, let's go. I hope there are some spare clothes around somewhere."

"Yeah, it's not exactly warm here," Cassie agreed. "You ready?"

Georgia nodded.

Cassie made sure she had a solid grip on Georgia's hands and teleported them back twenty-four hours…

…and materialised in the vacuum of open space.

Of the space station, there was no sign.

Diversion: Café

"He just disappeared into thin air," Kay shouted. "How the fuck did Laurence do that? I had him tied up securely."

She dragged on the rope, hauling the clone across the library floor.

"Come on, damn it, you bloody useless waste of space," she shouted, pulling the dumbo in the direction of the portal through which her earlier self had departed only minutes earlier. "Hand," she spat, grabbing the hand that the dumbo proffered.

About to step into the portal, she heard a familiar voice shout, "Wait."

"Mummy," cried the dumbo as Kay's foot touched the portal's surface.

Kay spotted another dumbo stepping out from behind a bookcase. But there was something about it that suggested it might not have been a clone.

"Cassie?" she shouted but, it was too late. Her cry was lost as the portal grabbed them both and deposited them in amongst steaming wreckage.

"Bloody hell," Kay coughed as the smell of burning and petrol hit her nose. "Where in damnation are we now? And was that another clone back in the library or the real one?"

"Huh?" the clone said.

"Rhetorical question, idiot."

"Huh?"

"Oh, do shut up. At least the fire's been put out in this one. Not that it had even started in the last one. Christ, how many more of these damn fire-related portals have we got to go through?"

Kay renewed her grip on the clone's rope as they stumbled over the devastation. Much of it appeared to be collapsed and charred wooden beams that had been doused in so much water that many were still dripping. It was obviously night and she could only just see where she was going. She tried to figure out exactly where they were. That the place used to be a shop of some kind was obvious. However, given the extent of the damage – nearer the front, parts of the floor had collapsed – it must have been nothing less than an explosion. Kay wasn't even sure she could determine what sort of establishment it had once been.

"Make yourself useful. Find the safest way out," Kay ordered, peering through holes in the floor down into the darkness of what was probably the basement.

The dumbo pointed at a wall that barely existed and stumbled in that direction. Following her, Kay found that it, too, was littered with debris, though not to the same extent. There was something vaguely familiar about the place. In the pale light coming from street lamps outside, she could make out what looked like the wreckage of a piano. It wasn't the only one.

The dumbo led her past a broken plate glass window and out onto a narrow pavement and roadway.

"Ah, Exchange Street," Kay said and, upon glancing at the name of the shop, added, "Suttons Pianos again." She looked up at what remained of the frontage of the adjacent shop into which they'd appeared. "Ah, Tony's Place. It is... was a café. I had a cup of tea in there a few years ago. If I remember rightly, it went up in smoke at some point – tonight was obviously that point. Well, not much left now. Looks like Thorns also copped it as well," she said, noticing how the upper floors of all the nearby buildings were completely burnt out.

"Whut?" said the clone.

"Why do I bother?" Kay sighed.

She heard footsteps. A man in a police uniform was hurrying towards them.

"Get out of there," he shouted. "It's too dangerous. What were you doing poking around in there, anyway? Sight-seeing? Oi, come back."

Ignoring him blowing his whistle, they ran up Exchange Street towards the marketplace. The policeman chased them for a few yards but then fell back.

"Good," Kay said, slowing down. "I think he must have been on guard duty to stop people investigating the explosion. At least he wasn't talking gibberish."

"Whut?"

Kay was still puffing as they turned right onto Guildhall.

"I'm too bloody old for this," she rasped. "Hmm. Not often you see traffic lights here. Fifties or sixties for sure."

Kay picked a newspaper from a rubbish bin near the trees in front of the Guildhall. It was dated October the sixteenth, 1963. There was no mention of a fire in Exchange Street. "Late edition, it says. The fire must have happened after nightfall," she said, dumping the paper back in the bin.

"Whut?"

"Okay, genius. Where's the next one?"

"Whut?"

"The next portal, you idiot."

"Last one," the clone said.

"What?"

"Last portal."

"What are you talking about?" Kay said as they jogged up past the Guildhall and onto Saint Giles.

"No more."

"There's plenty of them."

"Plenty. Last one."

"You need to come with a translation manual," Kay muttered, adding somewhat louder, "So where is it?"

The clone stopped and frowned.

"Not yet."

"Oh, right. Any others we can use?"

The clone shook her head.

"So, we've got to find somewhere to hide for a while, have we? Good, I could do with a kip."

The clone nodded.

"Right, hopefully we've got time to get all the way home. Better get a move on to be on the safe… Oh shit, here they come."

Several translucent forms were rising out of the road in front of City Hall.

"This way," Kay said, running down Lower Goat Lane. "Let's hope there's no more on Pottergate."

Kay was seething by the time she'd reached the front door of the safe house. She was exhausted while the clone had hardly broken into a sweat. Holding fast to the rope, Kay had urged the clone to run ahead using her as motive power.

But, at least, they'd managed to elude the nasties. They'd got close a number of times but, this particular type kept tripping over each other or accidentally merging their bodies and taking several seconds to disentangle themselves. When they were running down Duke Street, one nasty had actually fallen off the narrow bridge and disappeared into the Wensum.

As usual, the nasties refused to come any closer to the safe house than the end of the road. They hung around on Waterloo Road as if something physical prevented their access.

Something's holding them back, Kay thought hunting down her front door key. *But I'm definitely not complaining about that.* She frowned, remembering a similar situation when she was with the real Cassie at their mum's funeral.

Once inside, Kay noted that the front room was empty of the motorbike. Going through to the back room, she could also see that the scimitar was missing. *1963 is too early for the both of them.* She tried to remember what years it had been when she'd bought them. *The motorbike was the seventies, wasn't it? Oh God, I'm starting to forget things. I don't know how much longer I can stand doing this shit.*

In the kitchen, the cupboards were bare of food apart from an open packet of loose tea, half a damp bag of sugar and two cans of spam.

Ugh, not spam again. Okay, so it lasts years unopened but I'm sick of the stuff. Maybe I should have bought a chest freezer. No, how would I have got a modern chest freezer back to the sixties or even earlier? Do they have chest freezers in 1963? It's hard enough making sure I keep this idiot alive. Oh God, I'm too tired for this. We'll have to grab something to eat in the morning.

She pulled the clone upstairs by the rope and, throwing a few blankets at her, told her to go to sleep on the floor. *My old bones need a proper bed – and the dumbo is too thick to care that I make her sleep down there.*

It didn't stop her feeling just that little bit guilty.

As she lay there, listening to the snores rumbling from the clone and failing to get to sleep herself, she thought, *I wonder if she's right and the next portal really will be the last one. I damn well hope so.*

Space

Dressing Up

With air rushing out of her lungs and the film of liquid over her eyes starting to boil away, Cassie gripped Georgia tightly and, without even thinking about it, pulled in energy from all directions. With that energy, she formed a shield around the pair of them, preventing further loss of air and bodily fluids. Then she tried to figure out the solution to the next problem.

Oxygen.

In front of Cassie's eyes, Georgia's mouth was stretched wide as if she was screaming, but with so little air available to her, she could only contort her face.

How the fuck do I make oxygen? Cassie thought, trying to remember all the stuff about chemistry from school science lessons years previously.

It's an element, isn't it? If I don't do something soon...

She had a better idea and teleported forwards by a day so that they appeared back on the space station. Dissolving the shield, she tasted oil in the air again.

"What the fuck happened?" Georgia gasped.

"I forgot. No gravity well. We weren't anchored to the space station – it's not large enough."

Looking around, Cassie realised they were in a different area of the station.

"Oh, Christ," Georgia said. "It's getting cold."

"Not as cold as being completely naked in space," Cassie said. "I think I need to figure out how much this space station is moving in relation to everywhere else. Hold my hand again. I'm going to go back less than a minute."

Georgia looked scared.

"I'll wrap us in a shield just in case. Take a deep breath first, okay?"

Georgia, the fear not leaving her face, nodded and filled her lungs.

Cassie travelled back once more, this time by around forty seconds. They found themselves in a different part of the station, a corridor of some sort though whether it went up or down or horizontally, Cassie wasn't sure, as the gravity was even lower.

"Damn, it must be moving really fast," Cassie said. "I think the air's slightly better here, though."

"Not by much."

Cassie shut her eyes and viewed her map determining that the hop had moved them about a mile further towards the centre of the construction.

"I reckon this place must be about fifteen miles in diameter," she said. "There are hundreds of docking bays like the one we arrived in."

"Hundreds? How the hell are we going to find the ship in all that?"

"I will be able to spot it, I think. Okay, let's try again."

By taking several small hops, Cassie eventually found somewhere close to the centre where the temperature was almost acceptable and the air breathable. They were in a small room without any furniture or ornamentation of any kind.

"This is probably the best we can find for a moment."

"Is it safe?"

Cassie shrugged. "Is anything here safe? I certainly wouldn't bet on it. But, I do think I've figured out how to move around this place in time without it disappearing from under our feet."

"I hope so," Georgia whispered. "I don't think I fancy another trip into space in my birthday suit."

"Yeah, talking of which…"

Cassie closed her eyes and drew in more energy from the craft around her – there was plenty to extract, though it appeared to hum through the walls without any need for discrete wiring. She then tried to transform that energy into something solid. She had seen how the device had done it when it had constructed all the clones in June 2018.

Surely, clothes must be easier than making clones, aren't they? Though maybe not as easy as shields.

"Right, what's that like?" she asked.

Georgia picked up the thing that had appeared on the floor between them. It was like some sort of cape or toga – a circle of material that was almost but not quite cloth. There was a head-sized hole in the centre.

"What's it supposed to be?" Georgia said, picking it up. "Oh no, look. It's disintegrating – coming to pieces in my hands."

"Er, yes. Damn. Not quite as intended. I need a template to copy – but, if I had that, I wouldn't need to be doing this in the first place. Let me try again."

After several attempts, Cassie had managed to concoct a couple of crude dresses. After using the reject attempts to wipe their bodies free of the worst of the remaining liquid, they pulled the dresses on over their heads.

"Well, it's better than nothing," Cassie said. "I need to practice more."

"Ah, good enough," Georgia said, attempting to adjust her dress to fit her slimmer frame. Her voice was tinged with relief. "But what's next? Have you found the ship yet?"

Before Cassie could answer, she felt something that raised the hairs on her skin. She concentrated on its source – something was homing in on them.

"They're on to us," she said. "We need to get away right now."

She grabbed Georgia's hand and moved them back in time about twenty minutes, this time taking into account the direction and velocity of the space station itself. To her relief, they materialised within the same room. She repeated the process until it was around six hours earlier.

"Right, I found the ship," she said. "It's here in the place where it originally docked. But it's empty, so that means this probably isn't too long after they'd teleported us to that interrogation room or whatever it was supposed to be."

"Is the device there?"

Cassie concentrated once more. "No," she said, "I can't detect any trace of it at all. I think I need to get us back to when the ship first arrived."

Another hour back and the docking bay was empty so Cassie flipped back and forth until she saw it arrive in the map in her head.

"There," she said.

"What have you found?"

"Seconds after we arrived, something grabbed us from it but I think the device went somewhere else."

"Where?"

"I don't know. I can't sense it any more. Maybe that doesn't matter, though."

"Why not?"

"Because we need to be back before the ship is stolen so that we can steal it in the first place."

"Ah, yes. Of course. But how far back is that and where will it be?"

"Yeah – I have absolutely no idea."

Treasure Hunt

"How many more times?" Georgia groaned as Cassie hauled them back further.

They were still in the same room but, according to Cassie's built-in calendar – not that the year value made any sense – they had travelled back the equivalent of eleven days.

"I'm detecting ships. Lots of them. All scattered around the station."

"Which one is ours?"

Cassie frowned. "None of them feel like the one we arrived on but there's so many, it's hard to tell. Ah, these are definitely occupied."

"By what?"

"Yeah, *what* is probably right – I can't focus on them. I think they might be those creator aliens."

"Um, if you're detecting them, can they see us?"

"No, I… damn, yes. Something's coming," Cassie shouted, grabbing Georgia's hand once more.

She dragged them back another couple of days though, in her haste, she hadn't been as accurate in her positioning. They came out near the rim of the station in an area whose thin atmosphere was unbreathable.

Grabbing Georgia's hand, she travelled once more – this time in space only, to bring them back to the previous room.

After catching her breath, Cassie said, "Okay, we're down to three ships now. Ah, and I think one of them is ours before it got nicked."

"Are you sure?"

"She is correct," said the device, appearing in the room beside them.

"Ah," Georgia gasped in surprise. "How did you find us?"

"I went back to before the ship was stolen and waited within it until I detected you arrive. I used the opportunity to store within it the extra backup ready for my earlier self. I also created the disc."

"Well, haven't you changed your tune?" Cassie muttered.

"I was not aware that I was producing music," the device replied.

"No, you idiot. You've just set up another paradox thing and you're completely blasé about it."

"Indeed, I am substantially corrupted and operating far outside my original remit. Such issues need to be rectified at the earliest opportunity."

"Yeah, right. I think you're enjoying it."

"You are mistaken. Emotions such as enjoyment are not part of my repertoire. I am incapable of such."

"Bollocks. I bet you claim not to be able to lie, either. Anyway, no time for that. Was it you who caused the green flash when we were being held prisoner?"

"Yes, after you had been transported away, I tried to follow, only detecting you once you had regained consciousness. However, security measures prevented my materialisation within that area and negated any rescue attempt. When I checked later, I found evidence that you had teleported away, so concluded that you had managed to elude them. There was a residue of bodily fluids containing your biological signatures over much of the instrumentation. However, I couldn't determine how you achieved your departure."

"It was a piece of piss," Georgia said.

"Literally," Cassie whispered.

"Now that you are thinking of your escape, I can read the method utilised from the surface memories of your minds. An ingenious one. Congratulations."

"Keep out of my head," Georgia shouted. "I let you do that pilot training on me because we needed it. But you agreed it would be the limit. No more, okay?"

"Indeed and agreed – further mind reading will only be performed with your prior permission."

"Yeah, and don't forget it," Georgia said.

"I notice that your clothing has been replaced. It is crude."

"We know," Cassie said. "Emergency DIY dresses. There wasn't time for me to learn how to make them properly."

"I am detecting a rise in temporal activity. I believe you are being tracked. I forecast the imminent arrival of creators."

"We know," Cassie said. "We came back further as there will be lots of them in a couple of days."

"Your departure must therefore be swift."

"Crikey," said Georgia, "I feel like we've hardly been here for more than twenty minutes."

"In subjective time, I estimate that you have been present on this station for approximately ten hours."

"No wonder I feel hungry," Georgia said. "I hope the ship is stocked up."

"As before, the matter converters may be utilised for the purpose of food production. However, given the proximity of those attempting to intercept and contain you, it is imperative that we seek out my earlier self."

"Where?" Cassie asked.

"Storage section _____," the device responded.

"Ow," Cassie shouted. "Stop talking like that – you know we can't understand the language."

"It's bloody painful on the ears as well," Georgia added.

"Let me guide you. Follow," the device ordered.

Cassie grabbed Georgia's hand and followed the trail the device was laying down. It led to a remote part of the station near the outer edge.

They found themselves in an area devoid of gravity and warmth.

"Ah, not again," Georgia said.

"At least we can breathe," Cassie said trying not to shiver while orientating herself. She grabbed at a nearby pole. It was part of an interlocking lattice framework that extended in all directions. Attached to the framework in random positions were cuboid structures ranging in size from a few inches across to ones that would have no problem housing a double-decker bus.

"This is my container," said the device, floating close to a cube whose sides were no longer than Cassie's arm.

"How do we open it?" Georgia asked through chattering teeth just as the device pulsed green and a hole opened in one of the cube's surfaces.

Cassie peered inside to see multiple devices, each one packaged in a transparent box. Some had casings unadorned by any form of patterning, others had markings in various colours. All of the patterns on the devices were static but none of them resembled her one. "Um, which one is you? There must be nearly a hundred in here."

"There are sixty-three. One has already been removed for usage."

There was another pulse from their device and those within the cube moved to allow one that had been buried to rise to the surface.

"Ah, that's definitely you. That green is distinctive even if it isn't moving," Cassie said, grabbing the transparent box. "So, what else do we need to do?"

"Pastwards, quickly," the device squawked. "I detect creators and I am not as yet ready to surrender myself to them."

The device disappeared and Cassie, after concentrating to see the quickly dissipating trail it had left, grabbed Georgia's hand again and followed. It took them back four days to an area nearer the centre of the station. They appeared to be in some sort of tunnel, smaller though not unlike that through which their ship had passed before it had reached the landing area. But, there was air, a reasonable level of gravitation and the temperature, while cool, was tolerable.

"Oh, thank goodness," Georgia sighed.

"They are tracking me," the device stated. "I cannot evade them for more than a few seconds. Hide earlier me about your person."

"Where? This dress doesn't have pockets."

There was a flash and Cassie's eyes opened wide in shock. "How dare you?" she shouted, her hands flying to her abdomen. The now empty case floated slowly to the floor.

"What the hell's it just done?" Georgia said.

"I must be concealed from creators. Inside you was the only possible way," the device said.

"But... but... that's... that's almost... r–"

"Your body has already produced a child. There was room."

"You might have asked first," Cassie growled, conscious of the ball of pressure within her.

"My apologies. No time. They are almost here and moving in time or space once more will not prevent our discovery."

"Shit, okay. So what are we going to do? Where's the ship?"

"Being serviced. It will return ready for departure in fifteen local light cycles."

"Fifteen what?" Cassie asked.

"Too late – the creators are close. My apologies once more."

"What for?"

"I realise now that I have to break a promise," the device said.

"What do you mean?" Cassie said. "What promise?"

"Cassie Fox. I said goodbye to you once before. This time it will be permanent. Conversely, Georgia, what I do now will only be a temporary adjustment. However, despite its necessity, it could eventually kill you."

"What? I... No...," Cassie stuttered.

"Kill me? What's it doing?" Georgia said.

"Remember these words, Georgia," the device said, opening and bathing Georgia in a green glow. "Save her."

"No," Georgia screamed. "Get out of my h–"

The green glow cut off. "I will lead the creators away and then surrender to them for analysis. Do not attempt to follow me," the device said to Cassie, adding, "Save her again and then save yourself. Leave soon... goodbye."

It disappeared and, this time, left no hint of a trail.

Georgia's mouth was open wide as if she was screaming but no sound came out. Her eyes, similarly wide, stared at nothing. Cassie was reminded of her six-year-old self after Laurence had pushed the memories of Cow Tower and Lollards Pit into her younger self.

"Georgia. Are you okay? Wake up. We need to get away."

There was no response.

Uh-oh, I think I can detect something coming. Where the hell do I go? The ship. Ah, I can't see it now. Where's it gone? What did the device mean by fifteen whatever-it-said? Oh shit, something's here already.

There was the sensation of electricity surrounding them and the hairs on Cassie's skin stood to attention.

A moment later, Cassie's eyesight was blasted into confusion by the appearance of four creators hovering within the tunnel – two on each side of them.

Cassie found herself immobilised once more as screeching sounds penetrated her skull. After a moment, some of the noises resolved themselves into words and phrases.

What she heard was far from encouraging.

Primitives.

Confirmed.

Limited.

Disruptive.

Anomalous.

Hierarchy position?

Unmapped.

Mental scan initiated.

Result?

Simple, not predictable.

One enhanced, one catatonic.

Abilities detected.

Elaborate.

Temporal; teleportation; matter manipulation.

Unauthorised enhancements?

Confirmed.

Dangerous?

Potentially.

Physical scan initiated.

Result?

Concealed technology detected within.

Extract?

Dissection advised.

Interrogation?

Unprofitable.

Integration?

Unworthy.

Terminate?

Advisable.

Commencement?

Immediate.

Diversion: Endings

"Well, it looks safe enough at the moment," Kay said, peering out of her bedroom window. The lamp-lit road appeared clear of any nasties in both directions. There were few vehicles in view – not at all surprising for 1963. There was also little movement anywhere along the road but, given that the time was barely past six in the morning, that was just as unsurprising.

"Hungry," the clone announced.

"Yeah, shut up. So am I. Unless you fancy some spam, you'll have to wait – it's too early for anywhere to be open."

"Hungry," the clone repeated.

"I told you to shut up," Kay snapped.

There's bound to be a café somewhere along Saint Augustine's or Magdalen Street. Oh, what about the Kummin Kafe near Stump Cross – or has that already closed by 1963? There's also that greasy spoon place round the corner from Wensum Park – that should exist in this time, shouldn't it? I'm sure that was open right up into the seventies or eighties.

Kay sighed and wished she'd written down that list of places to eat and when they existed that she had thought about creating so many times. But, like many things, it had never turned into something concrete. Dodging nasties and trying to keep clones alive had always taken priority.

Going downstairs, she stared once more at the contents of the kitchen cupboards. *I suppose I could make a cup of tea. But it will have to be black unless... ah, is that a milkman I can hear?*

Opening the front door, she wasn't mistaken as the rattle of glass bottles in crates echoed down the road. She waited at the gate, jingling a handful of loose change, watching as the little electric vehicle meandered closer. The milkman stopped his float every few houses to deliver the orders – few doorways were omitted. *My place is probably the only one that never has a regular delivery.*

"One pint, please," she said as he pulled up to deliver milk to the nosey git next door. "Got anything to eat on there? Biscuits?"

"Oh, hello," he said, giving her tight-fitting black outfit a strange look. "No, just milk, eggs and orange juice."

Kay wondered about the eggs but she didn't have any oil to fry them in and didn't fancy them boiled. "Just the milk, then, thanks."

"Your daughter got a couple of pints off me last week. I don't remember seeing the bottles being put back out."

Kay shrugged. "Not seen any around. I'll leave them out if I find them."

He nodded and, handing Kay a bottle, said, "Ninepence please."

She picked some coins from her change and handed them over before re-entering the house.

So, younger me was here a week ago. I wonder how old I was then. Ah, I really should have kept a log of the dates I've been here. Like the list of places to eat, it's a bit too late to start it now.

In the kitchen, she swilled the loose scale from the electric kettle down the sink and filled it to just under halfway before plugging it in. While it was boiling, she contemplated the cans of spam once more. *Yeah, I'm hungry, too. Maybe I should have got those eggs. Oh, sod it. Spam it is then. Not that there's anything to go with it.*

The clone was far from impressed with the plate of cold spam and poked at it with a fork.

"Eat it or leave it," Kay said. "Don't keep rearranging it around the plate."

"Horrid," said the clone, before slurping down the rest of her cup of tea.

"So are you. Want another cup of tea?"

"Yeah."

Kay boiled the kettle again and, while waiting, said, "Is it really the last portal?"

"Huh?"

"You told me last night there weren't any more portals."

The dumbo frowned as if dredging up the thought took far too much effort. Finally, she said, "No more."

"What do we do then?"

"Dunno. Don't remember."

Kay tutted. "Of course you can't remember. It hasn't happened yet. You can't remember stuff from your own future."

The clone frowned and said, "Yes. Can."

Kay sighed. *This one really is a total idiot. At least, she's good at finding portals. I'm still hungry – for something other than spam, though. Maybe I'd better make sure I've got enough change.*

Kay rummaged through her pockets, checking her stock of legal tender for the year. She found a bag labelled 1962 but it held little in the way of change.

"Don't go anywhere," she said to the clone before ascending the stairs. In the back bedroom, she hunted around for bags with early nineteen-sixties dates on them. She found one marked 1965 and, after rejecting a handful of coins that were dated 1964 and 1965, topped up the 1962 bag from her pocket. Near the uncurtained window, the pile of modern round pound coins that she knew were fakes was still quite small. She pulled out a couple of bronze-coloured coins from a hip pocket and, after confirming once more that the Queen's profile wasn't aligned with the obverse, tossed them on the pile.

It was gone half eight before they ventured out. The clone, after a couple of minutes of concentration, had decided that the portal they sought was in the 'old library' at the junction of Duke Street and Saint Andrew's Street.

"At least there's no sign of any nasties," Kay said, making sure the rope was secure around the clone's waist.

"Won't be."

"Really, how do you know?"

"Wasn't."

"Back to nonsense again? Or can you really predict the future?"

The clone didn't reply.

"I don't ever remember the Free Library catching fire," Kay said, as they walked past Saint Augustine's swimming pool several minutes later.

"Doesn't," came the clone's reply.

"Ever?"

"No."

"So why is it a fire one, then?"

"Goes to last one."

"How do you know?"

"See it all."

Kay frowned. "Are you telling me that you really *can* see the future, so you've always known what's coming?"

"Yeah."

"Hmm, now I come to think about it – it's always been more like you were remembering things, not discovering them for the first time. Okay, let's test this. Um, right. Do I die after this or get to cut Laurence's head off first?"

"Dunno."

"So much for that. What about you?"

"Nothing."

"Nothing happens to you?"

"End."

"What do mean by 'end'? Do you die soon?"

"Yes."

"Oh, you're completely sure about that?"

"Yes."

"And you're not worried about it?"

The clone said nothing, being more interested in the shoe shop across the road.

"How do you die?" Kay asked as they crossed.

"Laurence," the clone said, stopping to look closely at the array of shoes on display.

"No surprise there – him and his nasties have been responsible for the deaths of most of the ones I ever tried to save. Are you scared of dying?"

The clone frowned and then shrugged before answering, "Is what is."

Kay stared at the clone as they entered Saint Augustine's Street. *This one is as unique as the real Cassie.*

Fifteen minutes later they were at the door to the Free Library. Despite the time having just passed nine o'clock, the doors were locked. Kay stepped back and took a better look at the place.

"It's no longer open," Kay stated. *Not since the other one opened its doors, anyway.*

"Keys."

"You mean I should break in?"

The clone nodded.

"And do I succeed?"

"Yes."

"Hmm, so you know about that, then. Interesting. Maybe I shouldn't have kept telling you to shut up but made you tell me what was going to happen next. But, if I got you to do that and then did something different to what you told me I would do, what would happen?"

The clone stared at Kay with a very confused look upon her face.

"Looks like the concept of a paradox has blown your tiny brain," Kay laughed as she rummaged through her pockets for her picks.

It took her a couple of minutes to work her way through the lock but, as soon as it clicked open, she pulled the clone through into the musty interior.

"Okay, where's the portal?"

The clone pointed to the old service desk upon which lay several long, narrow, open-topped, cardboard boxes. A few still held index cards. Now that it had been pointed out, Kay could feel the presence of the portal.

"Here we go then," Kay said, walking up to it. "I wonder where it goes."

"Assembly House."

"Is it on fire?"

"No."

"Good enough. Right, give me your hand."

"Will be."

"Ah…"

The blast of energy that hit Kay almost as soon as she stepped from the portal knocked her unconscious. When she woke, she found herself securely tied to a table. Above her, the rafters were familiar.

Then she heard something else that was familiar – a voice.

"Welcome back to consciousness, decoy," said Laurence. "Your tame clone has willingly revealed to me that Cassie – the real one, that is – will be on her way to rescue you soon. Actually, no, not soon. Several days. Enjoy having a rest while you wait…"

Flight

Save Her

The speed of the circling creators accelerated, merging them into a continuous blur. Cassie was being pulled in all directions. Any more and she would be torn apart. Despite her efforts and abilities, she was unable to prevent it. Lying at her feet, the limp form of Georgia was oblivious to the situation.

Physically held immobile, Cassie still had reserves she could call upon. She used those reserves to shield both herself and Georgia as well as she could from the onslaught. But she realised that the power of these creatures was beyond anything that she could muster on her own, even if she had been allowed freedom of movement.

A mental fog descended upon her, clouding her ability to think. As she fought to prevent darkness from fully descending, something grabbed her foot with a grip that verged on painful. With effort, she managed to force her eyes downwards to see Georgia's hand clamped around her ankle.

There was a flash of green and they were both somewhere and somewhen else. *When* was answered by Cassie's calendar, which had gained more than sixteen days bringing them to a point around half a day before they arrived. *Where* was instantly recognisable – they were back in the control room of the ship. However, this time, there was something less worn about it – this version hadn't spent centuries orbiting Earth's sun.

She saved me. Georgia saved me. She teleported us. How is that even possible?

While Cassie was gasping for breath, Georgia sprang to her feet without a word, hitting buttons and controls on the desk in front of them. A noise reverberated around the area. Georgia opened her mouth and answered in kind before punching a final switch. The ship lurched and started moving, leaving the chamber in which it was stored to enter a tunnel. Seconds later, it erupted into open space and Georgia's hands once more played over the controls.

Cassie staggered towards her and was shocked at the expression in Georgia's eyes. It was like looking at a stranger – one whose brow perspired alarmingly.

She's possessed. Is that the device doing this? Is it inside her? Where is it?

Cassie's hands moved once more to her own abdomen, knowing full well what it concealed.

Georgia stood and grabbed Cassie's hand, leading her through to the cubicles. She ushered Cassie into one, following her inside. Activating the door closure, their bodies were crushed far closer together than Cassie had ever been with anyone in her entire life. *Apart from that time behind Erin's garden shed,* Cassie shivered. It was almost obscene though, to Cassie, Georgia appeared oblivious to that fact.

"Seventy-one years per jump. Fourteen jumps. Comprehend?" came a monotonous, unnatural voice from Georgia's throat directly into Cassie's ear.

"Yes," Cassie said. "Same as on the way here."

"Three, two, one, now."

Nothing happened.

"Oh, you mean I have to do it myself this time?" Cassie asked.

"Three, two, one, now," Georgia repeated, without any sign of annoyance.

Cassie squeezed her arms around Georgia's waist and pushed them both forward by seventy-one years, hoping that they would remain within the ship. She felt relieved when they reappeared still crushed together within the cubicle.

"Next," ordered Georgia.

Cassie complied and then repeated the sequence a further twelve times.

After the last one, Georgia pushed the cubicle door open and ran back to the control room. On the screen in front of them, Cassie felt tears well up as the familiar view of Earth appeared. But, it wasn't quite how she remembered seeing it from photos taken from space. This version had larger polar caps and the Sahara was green with forest. Georgia zoomed the view and Cassie watched as unspoilt lands, barely touched by human hand, flashed below them.

The view halted over a mountainous region in Asia and Georgia zoomed in further. Halfway up a mountain peak, it came to rest over a small open area in front of a cave. Cassie's hand flew to her mouth.

Oh. The tribe's cave. There are people down there.

The view zoomed in further.

How is it doing this? Has the ship put a camera down there? No, is that Em'Dor?

Yes, it is. Oh God, she looks so young. And is that Ka'Chull returning from a hunt? Yes, surely it is. Ah…

Amongst the olive-skinned tribe, she saw one whose dark hair curled way below her shoulders and whose skin was pale. The girl, completely naked and obviously pregnant, was being guided by a child of about ten.

Me before I woke up. Ka'See. Oh my God. I had no shame. None of the other adults are naked. And that's Em'Lo, isn't it? And even she's wearing a skirt.

The camera swung down for a full view of the face. Cassie's breath caught in her throat as she observed the lifelessness in the eyes.

Dumbo – I was just like a dumbo back then.

Beside her, Georgia was silent, her eyes almost as blank as those of the girl – Cassie could hardly think of that person as herself – on the screen. After a few more seconds, Georgia's hands manipulated the controls and the scene shut off to be replaced by the view of the Earth.

"Device," said Georgia, holding out her hand.

"It's gone," Cassie said.

"No. There," Georgia said, pointing at Cassie's stomach.

"Oh, um, I will need to, um, try to get it out. I'm not too sure exactly where it's been, er, put."

A green glow erupted from Georgia's hand and Cassie was teleported three feet to one side against her will. But, she was instantly aware that the small pressure inside her was gone. Georgia's hand caught the device before it had a chance to fall slowly to the floor. But, as Georgia gripped the device, Cassie couldn't help spotting the drip of blood fall from Georgia's nose.

"Waste disposal," Georgia announced, marching off to another part of the ship. Stumbling behind her, hand rubbing her stomach, Cassie found herself in part of the ship she'd never previously visited. Georgia opened a small hatchway and dropped the young comatose device into it. Returning to the control room, she hit a few more buttons and the device was ejected from the ship.

"How long will it be before it lands?" Cassie whispered.

"Three days."

"How will it wake the me down there?"

Georgia reached out to Cassie and held her hand. "Three days forward."

"Oh, I see. Okay, here we go. Um, we're not in the cubicle. Is it safe?"

"Yes, ship in orbit," Georgia responded as another drop of blood pooled beneath her nose. "No delay. Speed essential."

"Well, let's hope you're right."

Cassie moved them both three days into the future, noting how the view of the Earth on the screen jumped.

"It moved."

"Expected. Orbit not geo-locked. Tribe cave in darkness. Night still young."

As Georgia spoke, Cassie couldn't help noticing that her tongue was scarlet and red-streaked saliva began to run down her chin.

"Are you all right, Georgia?"

"Of course, watch." Georgia zoomed the view and watched the screen. "There," she said, pointing to a streak of light that burned through the atmosphere above the cave and then fell to Earth a few miles to the east. The landing resulted in a burst of flame several miles in length as the device buried itself in the side of a mountain.

Georgia's body pulsed with yet another green flash which, this time, moved out from the ship to descend to the planet below.

"Is done. Your mind released, woken. Ka'Tor mind linked to device."

"But, I didn't wake up properly until the next morning." *Oh, but didn't Em'Dor tell me that I had woken up that night when the fire in the sky happened shouting with what they called my 'mad talk'?*

"Irrelevant. Is done as was. Circle almost complete."

"Almost? Um, is Georgia okay in there?"

Georgia raised an eyebrow and then frowned. "I am Georgia."

"Oh no, I don't think you are. Not fully. Also, you're bleeding from your nose and mouth. I think the device left something in you. Instructions or guidance. It apologised, remember?"

"Yes," Georgia frowned. "I didn't want it in my head – but it's here." Then her face softened. "Oh, Cass. I think it's fading. I need to act fast."

Georgia returned to the controls and set the ship back in motion. It turned away from the Earth and moved to the L4 point, reaching it in less than a minute. As Cassie watched Georgia manipulate the control board, she saw sweat running down Georgia's arms and legs. That wasn't all. Blood oozed from her nose and down her chin where it fell to stain the front of the makeshift dress.

Oh shit, didn't the device say that what it was doing to her might kill her? Oh, hold on Georgia. I think it's nearly over.

Finally, the ship came to a halt adjacent to a jagged body of rock. Metallic ropes shot from the side of the ship to tether it in place.

"Did it. I did it," Georgia grinned, sounding more like her old self. "Oh…"

"Are you okay?"

"No, not at all," she said, her eyelids falling shut as she drifted slowly to the floor. The breath caught in Cassie's throat as blood gushed from Georgia's ears, nose and mouth.

Save Her Again

"Georgia," Cassie screamed. Dropping down beside her best friend, Cassie's hands automatically emitted the healing that she'd used on her mother. But it wasn't working and it was obvious that not only had Georgia stopped breathing but her heart was also rapidly slowing.

Damn it, I saved myself – I've got to save Georgia.

She switched to using her map to scan Georgia's inert body, discovering the damage that had been caused by whatever the device had done to her.

It must have known what those damned creator things were going to do. Why didn't it use me instead?

She remembered hearing one say, 'One enhanced, one catatonic.'

Maybe, if the device had enhanced me any more they would have detected it and stopped us. Or, alternatively, maybe it used me as a decoy, setting Georgia up to get us out of that situation. But Georgia's body wasn't built to handle all this.

Cassie drew in energy from beyond the ship, directly from the sun itself, and channelled it through Georgia's body, strengthening and repairing her heart, as well as preventing any further damage to her brain due to a lack of oxygen. After several minutes, she was rewarded with an increase in the pulse rate. Then she turned her attention to Georgia's breathing and, remembering the lessons learned when they'd done that first aid course together, applied CPR, hoping she remembered correctly how it was done. As she physically pumped Georgia's chest, she simultaneously repaired the lacerations in the walls of her lungs and larynx. She suspected the cause of this damage was when Georgia's voice had been forced to generate the sounds of the alien speech – something she remembered the device saying that human vocal cords were ill-equipped to replicate. There was also minor bleeding within her brain and burns on her skin.

Was that caused by giving Georgia the temporary ability to teleport and time travel? Is that what I risk when I do it myself?

Cassie did her best to repair the lesions, praying she wasn't causing further damage in the process. After fixing everything, she almost jumped in shock when Georgia gasped in a lungful of air unaided. Cassie halted the CPR and concentrated on repairing the remaining damage throughout Georgia's body.

After several more minutes, Georgia's eyes opened and, staring directly into Cassie's eyes, she mouthed, "Thank you." Then, her face creased up and she burst into tears.

They clung to each other for ages, though Cassie also used that time to monitor the state of Georgia's health, making slight adjustments where she could to help her friend recover fully.

By the time Georgia felt well enough to stand up, more than ninety minutes had passed since she'd collapsed.

"What now?" Georgia asked several hours later. "Is it over? Do we just go back home?"

They sat in the control room eating prawn cocktail sandwiches followed by ice cream sundaes that Georgia had managed to persuade the matter converter to generate. Cassie had also figured out how to get it to produce practical clothing, though it resembled something out of Star Trek.

"Oh, I just remembered something else," Georgia said.

"What's that?"

Georgia leaned across the control panel and frowned.

"I think it's one of these."

"What is? Um, are you sure you know what you're doing?"

"No, not really," Georgia replied. "But, I do remember it telling me that this was to be the last thing I needed to do for you."

"Last thing? I don't like the sound of that."

"No, I think it meant that, after this, we are totally free of it and can go home. Ah, I think it's this button here."

"The red one? You sure? Maybe you shouldn't press it. It reminds me of..."

But Georgia had already depressed it.

There was a small whir of machinery and a slot opened to one side of the main controls and something popped out to fall to the floor.

"Ah," said Cassie. "I'd forgotten about that. Something else I need to do to make sure the timeline runs as before."

"Oh, the big red button."

"Yes," Cassie said, picking it up off the floor. She examined it, noting the familiar phrase around its edge: *For use in emergencies only.*

"That must be the last thing, then," Georgia said, sounding relieved.

Cassie frowned. "No, I think there must be something more."

"Like what?"

"The device said 'save her' to you. Then it said 'save her again' to me and then it told me to save myself."

"Did it? I think I was too busy having my mind invaded to notice."

"We've definitely done two of those three. You saved me by getting us away from the creators and piloting the ship home. Then I saved you after what the device had done to you almost burned you out."

"Almost? It bloody succeeded. I remember collapsing with a flood of blood coming out of nearly every orifice."

"Yeah, it was downright scary."

"But you *did* save me."

Cassie smiled and nodded. "Of course I did. But why a third time and why do I have to save myself? Have we got to face something else before we go back, or even *after* we go back?"

Georgia shrugged, shaking her head.

"I must be missing something," Cassie said. "I must be – but what?"

"Talking of which – how *do* we actually get back? We need to make sure we don't end up floating around in space again."

"At least we won't be naked this time."

"Yeah, I don't want to repeat that in a hurry."

"I think I should teleport us back to Earth – no time travel. Then go forwards all the way to 2019."

"Why not do that here on the ship?"

"For a start, the ship won't be here after 1549 as that was when it leaves to take us off to that space station so we can steal it all over again."

"Oh, yes – bloody confusing."

"And, also, I'd feel safer time travelling on Earth – bigger gravity well."

"Right. So, if we go to Earth now, can we visit your tribe? I want to see how it really was – not just the picture in my imagination."

"We saw it earlier on the screen."

"Yes, but, for me, that was more like a dream. I wasn't in control. So... can we?"

"That would be one way of scaring the shit out of them. We'd have to be invisible. Also, as I have no recollection of ever seeing you and a future me when I was back there, then either we never did this or we managed to keep ourselves concealed. It's not like when I saw us as shadows back in the cottage."

"Yeah, I suppose so. Do you think it's dangerous to try, then?"

Cassie nodded. "Possibly. Also, I'm trying to remember all the things I added to that chart on my wall – all the unanswered questions."

"What about them?"

"I think most of them have been answered. We now know where the device came from and how it ended up on Earth. Also, I now realise that it was you, while you were still under the orders of the device that woke me up and how it ended up connected to Ka'Tor. It just happened to be at the same time that the device became the fire in the sky."

"So, there must be a time when you are in great danger and we need to step in and make sure you survive."

"Yeah, but what and when? There were plenty of times when I was in danger back then. When I got attacked by that wolf. When I ran away after Ka'Tor was scarred and they all turned on me. When that bear tried to attack me when I was asleep in the devastated area caused by the device's landing. Oh, and possibly when I first arrived back here with absolutely no memory at all."

"And stripped completely naked."

"Don't remind me."

"Can we visit all of them in case it's not one you can think of?"

"I suppose we could. Not really sure I want you gawking at me while I was being a naked and pregnant dumbo, though."

"I've seen you naked lots of times since we were kids. Including today, of course."

"Yeah, I know, but… oh wait…"

"What?"

"I remember at least two more things on my chart that haven't been answered. And, also, one more thing that I would have added to it if I'd actually been home to do so."

"What are they?"

"Well, one is that zebra girl, but I'm not even sure she is really anything to do with all this."

"The what girl?"

"Oh, okay. Girl in a striped t-shirt. Charlie called her that. I don't think I ever told you about her. Remind me some time – just not now, though. The one I never added was a guy who I tried to rescue from being crushed to death by Laurence. I popped the man through a new portal and he definitely went somewhere – I just don't know where."

"You never told me about him, either."

"Not exactly had time before now to sit down and relax, have we? But the main one was the big green question mark."

"Oh yes," Georgia said. "Where Ka'Tor claimed he'd killed you and eaten your liver or something just as revolting."

"Near enough. Drank blood from my heart."

"Yummy," Georgia said, wearing a disgusted expression.

"The last thing I remember was that he attacked me using the device. And I'm pretty certain the energy he released really should have killed me instead of triggering my return home."

"In that case, I think you should definitely go and save yourself before he does accidentally kill you."

"I agree. But, not until we've finished eating dinner, or whatever this is supposed to be."

Saving Herself

"Is that them?" Georgia whispered as they peered across the rock-strewn slope in the darkness. Three tiny points of light bobbed around in the distance as they advanced up the gully of chewed-up rocks resulting from the device's landing.

"Yes, that will be Em'Dor, Ja'Mutt and Pi'Tut on Ka'Tor's trail. He is slightly above us up the hill. Oh, and there's no need to whisper. I've enclosed us in something that will prevent sound escaping. This is the part where earlier me is tip-toeing up the opposite side, trying to avoid being seen."

"Is it all about to kick off?"

"Not yet. I remember being angry with Em'Dor and the others for what they'd done to Ka'Tor. Em'Dor then apologised, which caught me off guard until she explained exactly what had happened afterwards. Right, here we go – I'll bring us a little bit closer as well."

Cassie held Georgia's hand as they hopped several minutes ahead to watch Stone Age Ka'See run towards Ka'Tor shouting, "Ka'Tor, Ka'Tor, drop it. Danger."

"What are you saying to him?" Georgia asked. Cassie realised that, other than the names, Georgia couldn't understand the tribe's language.

"Trying to warn him, but he was as angry at me for running away as he was at those who'd scarred him. Right, don't let go of my hand. I need to be as close as possible to him but may need to move quickly – I can't remember the exact sequence in which things happened."

From Georgia's perspective, both their own positions and those they were observing changed. Cassie's son was shouting at his mother who stood directly in front of him.

"Nice skirt," Georgia whispered, seeing the animal skin that Ka'See wore.

Ka'See held out her hand and said, "Give me, Ka'Tor. Please?"

"No," Ka'Tor snarled, snatching the device away. "Thing mine. Spirit talk to me. Not you. They cut me. Ka'See run. Ka'See not save Ka'Tor. Hurt lots. Kill them. Hate you all. Kill you all."

"Please Ka'Tor," Ka'See said, "That thing is dangerous."

"Here we go," said Cassie as they watched the device in Ka'Tor's hands open. "This is where he immobilises me."

"Go away," Ka'Tor shouted. "Thing is mine. Hate you. Not want mother. Not want father. Not want anyone. Only want spirit thing. Go away."

"Right," Cassie said as Ka'Tor continued his tirade against those on the mountainside. "I can tell he's building the device up to kill me. I'm going to slow time so I can rescue my earlier self at the right point. I'm going to have to leave you in normal time in order to concentrate on doing what I need to do. Okay?"

"You sure you know what you're doing?"

"Absolutely not. Here we go."

Cassie slowed time just as Ka'Tor shouted, "Leave Ka'Tor alone. Thing is mine. MIIIIINNNNNEEEE–"

As she wrapped Ka'See in a protective shield and moved her out of harm's way, an idea came into her head. *Ka'Tor needs to believe he has killed me, so let's give him what he wants.*

She thought back to when she had been observing the device creating the clones of herself in Castle Mall. She opened her map to view Ka'See. Then she caused matter and energy dragged in from elsewhere – from the air, from the light of distant stars, but mostly from the jumble of rocks and torn earth around her – to coalesce into a clone, duplicated directly from the original, placing it where Ka'See had been. But this clone held no proper life of its own. It was merely a copy built for a single purpose.

Returning to normal speed, she watched the roar of energy from the device directed by Ka'Tor tear into the clone's body, ripping it open.

"Oh, my God," Georgia gasped. "Was that really you?"

"No, just a clone," Cassie said as she grabbed hold of Georgia's hand and started to propel them through time. She gripped the shielded version of herself in her other hand. The first jump was twenty-four hours ahead and then she travelled a day for every experienced second.

"But how? Where did it come from?"

"I just made it. I figured out how and made it. Just like those crappy dresses."

"But it looked so real. Was she alive?"

Cassie shook her head. "No, I made sure of that. She was made from rocks – it's like I sort of photocopied her from the real me."

"Where is the real you – the earlier one, I mean?"

"Here. But she's still shielded just to make sure she isn't aware of exactly what's happening to her. But, as we're travelling very slowly in time, I'm also scanning her."

"What for?"

"Trying to figure out why she lost the ability to time travel herself. Ah, there's some sort of mental block. It's a bit like what I did to my six-year-old self to hide the memories of Cow Tower and all that."

"Can you fix it?"

"I have to, otherwise I won't be able to return from the past under my own steam. And, if I don't do that, then I won't be able to come back and rescue myself."

"Oh, bloody hell. More paradoxes?"

"Yeah – a complete mess of them. Right, I can see what the block was doing and I'm going to dissolve it slowly."

"Are you going to take her all the way back to 2019?"

"No, I remember discovering the ability returning and regaining control over it myself. Right, we've gone about ten years ahead now so I'm going to loosen the shield so that she starts to become aware that she's travelling through time."

"Will she know we're here?"

"No, she mustn't – because I don't remember that bit myself. I've got to stick to what I do remember. I think I realised that I was time travelling first and then my calendar came back. But, I dare not let go of her until she starts taking control herself."

"Right. I'd better keep quiet and let you get on with it, then. Um, can she hear us?"

Cassie shook her head. "She's within her own shielding and I've kept us two in a separate one. Nothing can pass between them unless I choose to pass it."

"Clever… and scary."

"Yeah, definitely the last. Right, we're about ninety years from where we started and she's realised she's time travelling. I'm going to accelerate otherwise it's going to take a lifetime to get back home and I'm already knackered. I also want to start to dissolve her shield while keeping us fully hidden from her."

As they passed a thousand years, Cassie was certain her earlier self was beginning to experiment with taking control.

At a hundred thousand she was sure and relinquished contact, hurling herself and Georgia faster through time than she'd ever travelled before. Within a few minutes, they were back in the twenty-first century and heading for home.

Cassie kept them hidden as they materialised in her bedroom, which was just as well as she'd arrived a few seconds too early. Her earlier self along with Patrick and Georgia were just about to depart for 1549.

"Right, let's get started," the visible Cassie said. "Hold my hands."

Once her earlier self had disappeared, Cassie threw off the invisibility and flopped down on the bed, exhausted.

"Well, I certainly don't want to go back through any of that ever again," she said.

"You did it," Georgia said, lying down beside her.

"Yeah, but I couldn't have done it without your help."

They gripped each other in a tight hug and simultaneously burst into tears.

Loose Ends

Broken Promise

Cassie was rummaging in the loft of her house. It was early August 2018 and, apart from her, the house was unoccupied. She had previously stopped off in 2013 to boost the protection she had originally set up in 2011. This time, being able to absorb energy from wherever it was available, she'd beefed up her earlier effort. Now, the house was shielded years into the future.

In the loft, she searched through Kay's money boxes looking for one particular bag. It had to be here as she'd already seen it in Anne Luckin's possession. She knew it was due to go missing at some point. It was one labelled 1860. At least her grandad had sorted them into batches. Once she'd found the box containing the oldest notes and coins, she'd had to pull the whole lot out before she'd discovered it tucked into one corner under a dozen or so bags from the 1890s.

I'd better let Grandad know at some point that it really was me that took it.
She noticed that the bag had a name scribbled on the other side: Anne.
This is definitely it. Right, now for the big one.

After travelling back eight years and dropping down eight feet, Cassie held herself invisible as she appeared in her mother's bedroom. It was Boxing Day, 2010, and she knew she was about to break a promise.

Concentrating, she could make out the other presences in the house. Downstairs, her grandad and younger self were watching television. She could also feel the device stashed behind that drawer in its wooden box. It gave the impression of being deactivated, almost like it had been after Laurence reset it.

On the bed, her mother was lightly sleeping, an open magazine on the bed covers in front of her. Cassie knew that, in a few days, an earlier version of herself would discover that the bed held what she had thought of at the time as no more than an empty shell.

I'd better get on with it, she thought, breathing heavily.

She absorbed energy from around herself and erected a shield – one not dissimilar to those she'd created around herself and Georgia in the Stone Age. Less complex, its functions were to prevent any sound from escaping and to emit a mild compulsion to prevent anyone entering the room unexpectedly.

With that in place, she sat on the side of the bed and placed her hand on the back of one of her mother's. She noted that her mother's skin was as lined and wrinkled as it should have been.

Obviously, I'm not an expert at this. But, it must have been convincing enough. No one questioned it at the time. And I've got a template to copy – not like with those dresses – and time to do it more accurately – unlike with Stone Age Ka'See.

She began the process of duplicating the body on the bed, placing the copy up in the loft space where it could remain hidden for a short while.

As she completed the process, she saw movement and, as her mum's eyes opened, she smiled warmly.

"Oh, Cass. You… came… back."

"Couldn't keep away," Cassie said, wincing slightly at how thin her mum's voice sounded. She was talking very slowly as well. Each word took effort.

"Your hair. Beautiful. Have you… had it styled?"

"DIY – I'll tell you about it later."

"Later? Okay. Better be quiet – they're downstairs," Rebecca said. "They might hear… and come up."

Cassie shook her head. "No," she said. "I've placed us in something like a soundproof box. No one will disturb us."

"That new?"

"Yes, I've learnt to do a whole bunch of new things. Had to…"

"Go on?"

Cassie shook her head. "This, er, well, this isn't the right time."

"Oh. Have you, er, well…"

"Have I what, Mum?"

"Have you… come to say… goodbye?"

"In one way, yes," Cassie said. "How do you feel?"

Rebecca frowned. "Tired. Very tired. Whatever you did… before

Christmas… almost completely worn off. But… so grateful you let me have this last Christmas together… with Dad and younger you. Wouldn't have lasted this long… without it."

"I'm so glad I could help," Cassie whispered, feeling her voice about to crack.

"You… coming back after this, or… is this the, the last time?"

"Mum, in a few days an earlier me will come and visit you."

"Oh good… So glad… Look forward to it."

Cassie shook her head once more.

"What?"

Cassie sighed. "While you are still here physically – mentally, well…"

"Oh," Rebecca said, looking shocked. Then she smiled briefly, obviously trying to compose herself. "I understand," she said. "You know something?"

"What, Mum?"

"Keep feeling I might just slip away. Any time. Maybe…"

"Maybe what?"

"Maybe… a portal… take me."

"No, not a portal. Although I didn't see it at the time, I've realised now there were several things wrong with what I did see."

"What?"

"You were like an empty shell. Your hands were smooth as if you hadn't bent your fingers in months."

Rebecca looked down at her hands. "Don't understand."

"It means it was a bodge job. But, obviously, it was good enough to fool people into thinking it was you."

"What… you talking… about?" Rebecca said, a frown wrinkling the pallid skin of her forehead.

"This," Cassie said, raising her hands to hold over her mother's chest.

She released the energy.

"Cassie Fox. No. You promised me. You mustn't do this. Please. No."

"Sorry, Mum, but I've got to break that promise. I found out that Laurence had programmed the device to slowly kill anyone other than himself or any person he was going to take over."

"But, I've got to die in order…"

"No," Cassie said, firmly. "But everyone has to believe that you did. Even me and Grandad. How are you feeling now? Any better?"

"Oh, my goodness, Cass. I'm feeling… oh, this is almost ecstatic. But how? You couldn't do this before?"

"I can now and I've fixed far worse… believe me. Actually, you *will* see it for yourself one day – but that's a long time off. Anyway, once you're feeling strong enough to stand up, I'll show you something else I can do. Something that was done to me thousands of times back in 2018."

"2018? But it's 2010."

Cassie grinned as she delivered more healing energy into her mother's body. "Yes, but to me, 2018 was the past."

"Thousands? Wait, are you talking about all the other copies of yourself that the device made? The clones that followed Kay around the portals?"

"Yes, but I only need to make one."

"Oh… I-I think I see. But do you really know what you're doing?"

"Not really. I've only done it once before and that was an even bigger bodge job. But this has got to work because I've already seen the evidence that proves it did. You okay to get out of bed yet?"

"I don't know," Rebecca said, gazing at her hands. "Oh, they look so much better, so less frail. I haven't managed to stand without assistance for weeks now. But I-I think I may be able to. I'm feeling stronger by the second."

Cassie helped her mum off the bed. She was quite wobbly but seemed to gain strength with every step she took.

"Is this really going to work?"

"Yes," Cassie said. "I didn't realise it was you at first."

"What? When?"

Even though she knew she had planned this, Cassie's eyes were watering with pure joy as she used her abilities to purge her mother's body of all the effects of the cancer. Not only that, but she also negated the damaging effects of the chemotherapy. The techniques she had learned through experimenting with her own body and on Georgia on the spaceship, she applied to her mum, rejuvenating every last cell.

"A much older version of you. You kept bumping into me and…"

"And what?"

"No, I will let you work that bit out for yourself. Spoilers," she said, as she caused the hair on her mother's head to sprout, replacing the thin grey tufts with new dark growth, accelerating it until it was several inches long. Like her own, it curled naturally.

"Can't you tell me anything?"

"Yes. You will eventually get to travel through portals on your own."

"Really?"

"Yes, but not for a while yet. Well, I think that will do for now. Wow, just look at yourself in the mirror."

Rebecca turned and stared into the full-length mirror on the door of the wardrobe. She whimpered, seeing her reflection.

"I'm... I'm... Oh, am I dreaming this? I must be dreaming this."

"No, it's all real, Mum. It's all..."

Cassie choked up, unable to say anything more for a moment.

Rebecca reached up and touched her hair, stroking it with a look of disbelief in her eyes before she turned back to her daughter and grasped her close as their tears mixed.

"Right," Cassie said more than a minute later, her voice still very shaky, "I need to finish this."

"What now?" Rebecca said in a voice that, for the first time in months, exhibited its full resonance.

"Watch," Cassie said and, with one hand on her mother's arm, stretched out the other towards the empty bed. She teleported the partially completed clone of her mother down from the loft space. As the form appeared, it was obvious that it resembled her mother as she had looked several minutes previously. It was also clothed in an identical night dress. Cassie did one more thing – something she hadn't needed to do with the clone of herself that Ka'Tor had blasted to pieces.

She imbued it with a fraction of life. Just enough to fool anyone.

Rebecca gasped. "Oh, my God. That looks so real. Did I really look like that a few minutes ago?"

Cassie nodded. "Yes. Yes, you did. And now, you look like the lovely, beautiful mum I remember from my childhood."

"Is it… is she alive?"

"Yes. Well, alive enough to fool everyone – including me two days from now. She will just need to last until the twenty-fourth. All she will be able to do is eat and drink a little, and her eyes will follow the portals like yours did."

Cassie's hand lowered and the clone took on a life of her own.

"That is so unnerving," Rebecca whispered. "Does she think she's me?"

Cassie shook her head. "No. Mentally, there's very little of you in there. She's barely alive."

"So, what happens now?"

"We leave," Cassie said.

"And go where?"

"A cottage in Sussex near the coast."

"Sussex? Why Sussex?"

"Don't ask – more things going round in circles."

"This will really take some getting used to," Rebecca said. "What if someone finds me? What if I get picked up on CCTV or something?"

"Not in 1856, you won't."

"What? 1856? Well, no. I don't suppose so…"

"Are you ready?"

"Will I ever see Dad again?"

Cassie shook her head. "I don't know. Like me up until recently, he has to believe you died."

Rebecca nodded. "It would have been nice to say goodbye."

"Maybe I'll find a way. I can't promise anything. Some things might be too dangerous."

Cassie dissolved the shield around the room. Then, holding tightly to her newly-rejuvenated mother, she teleported them both away, leaving the almost empty shell on the bed.

The clone stared aimlessly around the room and, after a while, muttered one word, "Gone."

Apologies

In the narrow aisle between two tall rows of bookcases in the school library, they froze and stared at each other for several long seconds.

"Sorry." It came out of both of their mouths simultaneously.

"I was a total bastard," Jason said.

"Yeah," Cassie whispered.

He shrugged. "Erin and her parents had words afterwards. Mum did, too."

"And?"

He tipped his head to one side. "I ignored them, didn't want to believe what they were telling me. Thought they were wrong. Word got around. People refused to have anything to do with me, Mark too – unless I apologised to you."

"I think Georgia had words with him."

"Yeah – I guessed that. Um…"

"What?"

"The things that happened the day after… Were they real?"

"What things?"

"Maybe it was concussion. I did have to go to the doctor a few days later and they did some tests. Said it probably was. I was imagining lots of weird things."

"Like what?"

"This will probably sound mad."

"Go on."

"Well. I thought I saw four of you at once and you all kept hitting me. Then, I thought I was halfway up a mountain in the snow. You were there as well."

"Was I really?"

"Maybe. No. I think I was going mental for a while. But afterwards, I did… well… have a good long think about things."

Cassie nodded.

Then Jason frowned. "Um, why did you apologise to me just now?"

"I…" Cassie started, but couldn't continue. She looked away. *Because it's my fault that you lost your father, took him away from your mum and wrecked her life. If I had never been born, you would have been a much better person. But I can never let you know… never tell you what happened to him. Never tell you how he ended up married to my mum back in the 1850s with little memory of his previous life.*

"Um, well maybe I should ask you out," he said. "Just for a drink or a meal or something to apologise properly for… well, you know…"

Cassie raised an eyebrow and forced herself to look him directly in the eye.

"Only if you fancy," he added, breaking eye contact.

Cassie pursed her lips and thought about it. Before the silence grew too long, she whispered, "No. Probably not a good idea. But thank you, anyway."

Jason nodded, "Yeah. I understand. Can't blame you."

Cassie stared at her feet, unable to say anything more.

"Um, bye then," he said.

"Yes. Bye," she whispered before turning around and walking away, her head wracked with guilt.

Later that same evening, she took down the timeline chart from her wall and folded it up before stashing it in a box under her bed. Then, she opened the drawer of her bedside cabinet and picked up the disc with its red button.

"I really hadn't expected to see this thing again. Okay, one more trip back to that day."

Invisible on the grass mound above Castle Mall, she watched the frizzy-haired, seventeen-year-old version of herself stomping in from the Farmer's Avenue entrance. Despite the heat, she was wearing her denim jacket and looking extremely angry as she plonked herself down on the grass.

Cassie smiled. *I'd better slow time so that she doesn't detect me.*

"I'm sorry for all the troubles this is going to bring you," she said to the immobile face in front of her. Then she slipped the disc into the inside jacket pocket and backed off to watch before returning to normal speed.

"Damn," said her earlier self, as she reached into the pocket and pulled out the disc. A few seconds later, after reading the inscription around the edge, she let out a small squeal.

Right, Cassie thought, *was that it? Was that the last thing I had to do? Oh God, I really hope so.*

Tourists

"For goodness sake, Cassie," Georgia said after Cassie had offered several feeble excuses. "Get your phone out and text him right now. You agreed you would send the first text."

"He might not reply," Cassie said, unlocking the phone.

"You won't know until you try, will you?" Georgia scolded. "Look, you like him and I'm pretty sure he likes you, too. It's been well over a week since we were at the pizza place – well, a week for him, anyway. Feels more like months to me. Leave it any longer and someone else will snap him up. Maybe someone else already has. Give it here – I'll start you off..."

Georgia snatched Cassie's phone, pulled up the messenger app and typed: *Hi Callum, u stil fancy meting up so I can show u that Lrord Sheffeild plague? Cassie x*

"There," Georgia said, handing the phone back. "Sweet and to the point."

"And full of typos," Cassie grinned, staring at the message. "Maybe you should have let the device fix your dyslexia after all."

"Not bloody likely. Might have gone too far like when it almost fried my brain. Having alien things mess with my head is too much. Never again."

After correcting the typos, Cassie hesitated her finger over 'Send' before finally plucking up the courage to poke it. After she heard the whoosh sound effect, she closed the phone cover, saying, "He probably won't reply."

"Yeah, taking bets?"

Twenty seconds later the phone pinged.

"Hah!" Georgia said. "Is it him?"

Cassie opened it up, looked at the reply and nodded.

"Well, what did he say?"

Cassie showed her the reply: *Love to. When's good for you? Cal x*

"See – you got a kiss back. Told you he liked you. Now, fix a date," Georgia ordered with a grin.

It took several more texts to find a date on which they were both free. Callum couldn't make the following weekend as he had to go home for his dad's birthday. Also, Cassie couldn't make some of the evenings as she had to revise for upcoming exams and the few evenings that she did have free, Callum couldn't make.

They finally agreed on May the fourteenth, a Tuesday when both of them had a late afternoon and evening free.

"Damn, but you're hard work," Georgia laughed as Cassie shut her phone off.

At four o'clock, Cassie was waiting on Castle Meadow for Callum to arrive. They had agreed to meet at the top of the Davey Place steps where they joined Castle Meadow. As the day had been one of the warmest of the year so far, she had selected a dress to suit the weather, but had brought a light jacket – not one of her denim ones for a change – in case the evening cooled off.

If it gets as far as lasting into the evening.

She watched buses turn up and disgorge passengers, none of whom were Callum. Because of building work close by, she couldn't see too far along the pavement towards the Bell Hotel and Red Lion Street.

I can't remember which number bus he was supposed to be on. What if he doesn't turn up?

Fed up with peering at buses around the Castle Meadow curve, she glanced up at the castle battlements and tutted. As usual, the ghost of Robert Kett hanging in his chains was waving to her.

Go away. I don't need you keeping an eye on me as well.

But he continued to wave and, just as Cassie was thinking of waving back to him, she realised someone was standing next to her.

"Wow," came a voice. "What have you done with your hair? It's fantastic and, um, long."

"Oh," she said, looking up into Callum's smiling face, "I, er, well, um, this is actually natural. I've, um, found a way of stopping it going frizzy. That's the reason I used to have it straightened. I didn't see you arrive – which bus did you get off?"

"Oh, sorry," he said, "I forgot the bus I was on only stops outside Debenhams and not Castle Meadow. Am I late?"

"Er, no. Not at all."

"I, um, saw you looking up at the castle," he said, also staring upwards towards the battlements. "Saw someone you know up there?"

She shook her head, aware of the effect it had on her hair, and fully conscious of Kett's ghost giving her a thumbs up – something he had never done before. "Just, er, gazing into space, probably."

"Oh, right. Well, um, here we are then. What's the plan?"

"Plan? Oh, the plaque, I suppose that's the plan," Cassie said, thinking she was beginning to sound like a complete idiot.

"Well, it's such a nice day, and I've not really explored much of Norwich apart from the centre. So, are you up for giving me a tour?"

"Oh, right… yes, good idea… a tour." *For goodness sake, I must be coming across like a complete dumbo. Get a grip. Yes, a tour would be good.*

"Yes," Callum continued, "how about some of the interesting places I've never known even existed, but places you've known all your life?"

"Um, yes, I, er, I'm definitely up for that," she replied. *Okay, where's a good place to start?* "Have you walked around the cathedral grounds or been down to Pull's Ferry?"

"I know where the cathedral is but I've not explored it, so that sounds like a good start. What's Pull's Ferry?"

"Ah, right, I'll show you. This way," she said, leading him down the steps.

As they turned right into Castle Street, she asked, "So, how long have you actually been in Norwich? Is this your first year at UEA?"

"No, second," he replied.

"You mean you've been in Norwich for nearly two years and you haven't explored it properly yet?" she asked with a smile, starting to relax.

"Hah, no, guilty as charged," he laughed. "Well, I do try to get home when I can. Also, I live in a shared house as you can only live on campus during your first year. What with accommodation, food shopping and fees as well as just general living, things aren't exactly cheap. So I couldn't afford to go out and explore too far afield."

"Yes, I know what having to live on the cheap means," she said. "Had to do that for far too many years. So, have you been able to see anything of Norwich at all, then?"

"Oh, I've visited the city centre lots of times. Done the usual student-type stuff, nightclubs, pubs, cinema and even been to the theatre a few times when it wasn't too expensive. But, that was always with others who were also strangers to Norwich. Erin tried to herd a few of us together into seeing some of the other sights but we often couldn't agree on which ones or when to go. I mean to say, it took a couple of weeks to organise that meal where we bumped into you."

I'm really glad you did.

"Is Erin the only one who's a Norfolk native?" Cassie asked as they walked along London Street towards Bank Plain.

"Pretty much. Holly's probably the only other one – she comes from Cromer. She invited us to go to the carnival there last year. Sounded fun, but I couldn't join them as I was at home for the summer."

"Oh yes, she's the one with, um, Ben, wasn't it?"

"Yes, that's them. He's from near the south coast somewhere, I think. Megan's from some village near the Welsh border – can't remember the name – and Luke's from Middlesborough."

"Him and Erin seemed close at the meal."

"Yeah, I thought she and Luke had something going at first but then I caught her and Megan together when they hadn't realised I was there. Rather passionate, it was – not just, you know, as friends. And I know Megan has stayed over at Erin's parent's place in Dussindale a few times recently."

"Oh, right. I hadn't realised. Well, good for her if that's what she wants."

"Seems like what they both want. How about you and, er, Georgia?"

"Georgia's been my best friend since nursery. She's also been with her boyfriend, Mark, for a couple of years now. I think that one is going to turn into something quite long-term."

"He wasn't with her that day at Donnellis."

"No, that was a spur of the moment decision to celebrate my inheritance."

"Yeah, I couldn't believe it when you said how much."

"It was a total shock to me as well. Two years ago we were totally skint."

"We?"

"Oh, I live with my grandad and, at the time, he couldn't do a lot. I was having to look after him quite a bit. He's a lot better now."

"Ah, good. Glad to hear it. Just your grandad?"

"Yes, no brothers or sisters. And, um, no parents." *Well, not in this century.*

"Ah, sorry, yes, I remember Erin saying something. Must have been tough."

"It was," she said with a sigh. *But things are much better now, especially right this minute.*

"So, apart from sixth form, what other things are you into? Any hobbies?"

"Er, no, not a lot to tell, really," Cassie said as they crossed Bank Plain at the pedestrian lights and started down Queen Street. *I can't very well tell him my hobbies include time travelling, screwing up history, visiting alien space stations, creating clones and going back to the Stone Age to have a baby, can I?*

"So, um, no other, um, I mean, you're not, er, well...?" he said, seemingly unable to finish the question.

"Actually, this will be the first time I've been out with anyone in, um, well, since, er..."

"...Erin's party?"

"Yes," Cassie said. *I just stopped myself saying 'in four years'.*

"I certainly hope nothing like what happened at that party happens tonight," he said, with a nervous-sounding chuckle.

They spent the best part of an hour wandering around the Cathedral, the cloisters and grounds. After a stroll down to Pull's Ferry, they took the riverside walk to Bishops Bridge, past the Red Lion pub and on to Cow Tower.

"Impressive," he said, as they gazed up at the tower's cracked countenance. "Are you okay? You're looking a bit nervous."

"Oh, sorry, yes, I'm fine," Cassie said. "I got a bit spooked here when I went on one of the ghost walks a couple of years ago. We were told that some pretty awful stuff went on in this place."

"Oh, you have ghost walks here as well? We have those up in Sheffield, not that I've ever been on one."

"Sheffield? Is that where you're from?"

"Almost. We live in Conisbrough – it's between Sheffield and Doncaster. We have a castle as well."

"Your own personal one?"

"Hah, no. I meant Conisbrough does."

"What's it like?" *Any ghosts hanging from it in chains that like waving to you? No, don't ask that!*

"Compared to your one here – it's more like a pile of barely-standing ruins," Callum laughed.

"Oh dear."

"Yeah, quite picturesque, though. So, what was your ghost walk like?"

"A bit of history along with some... well... interesting theatrics."

"Scary?"

"Sort of, in a humorous way," Cassie said. *Until it woke things up in my head.*

"Was the history accurate or, well, embellished just to make it spookier? I've heard they do that."

"Oh yes, some of it was definitely over the top. Entertaining though. But sometimes you weren't too sure how much of what they told you was really based on truth and how much was there just to spook you out." *Except I do know some of it was definitely worse than they said. At least I can stand to be here now without going completely doolally, thank goodness. It still feels weird, though, being here and not being affected by it.*

They followed the river back to Whitefriars Bridge. Then, as it was the main reason for the tour, she led him to the road named Saint Martin at Palace Plain where, after a short walk, she halted.

"Here it is," Cassie said. Embedded in the flint wall before them, the stone plaque read: "Near this place was killed Lord Sheffield in Kett's Rebellion 1st. August 1549."

"Oh, that would be easy to miss if you weren't looking for it," Callum said. "Thank you so much. I'd probably never have found it on my own."

"You're welcome," Cassie said, smiling. *Damn, why is my heart thumping? At least I resisted Georgia's insistence on wearing that dress I'd worn at Erin's party. Too many bad memories and it would have been far too low cut. Anyway, he's already seen me in that one.*

Callum got his phone out and snapped a few photos of the plaque. "My mum will love this," he said. "It's through her line that we think we go back to Lord Sheffield."

"You sound more certain now. Have you found more details?"

"No, not really. Just wishful thinking, I suppose. Hah – if I had a time machine, I'd go back and check it out properly."

Cassie closed her eyes for a second. *Don't tempt me.*

"Um, Cassie. Would it be all right if I took a photo of you with it? If you're okay with that, I mean."

Cassie smiled and stood underneath the stone plaque, the top of her head several inches below it. She posed while Callum snapped pictures on his phone. He even stepped out into the road to take a few of her from head to foot.

"Got enough?" she asked, grinning.

"I should have taken some at all the other places you showed me."

"What? Of the places or of me?" she grinned, knowing she was being cheeky.

"Hah, both. But, um, yeah, definitely of you."

"Oh, um, right. So, where now?" she asked, embarrassed once more. "Anything else you'd like to see?"

Shit. Did I really just say that?

"Er, I think I'm ready for a bite to eat. You?"

"Yes, I'm more than just peckish."

And maybe not just for food.

"Good, I could do with a sit-down, anyway," he said, looking down at his right foot.

"Oh, is your foot bothering you?"

Callum nodded. "Just a little. It will be fine after a rest."

Cassie felt slightly guilty. Although it had been Callum who had requested a tour, she hadn't realised how much of an impact it would have on him. His walking had distinctly slowed in the past half an hour.

"Any restaurants or pubs near here?"

"The closest place is the Adam and Eve."

"Oh, I've heard of that. Doesn't it date right back to Lord Sheffield's time?"

"Yes, they claim to be the oldest pub in Norwich. I've been there two or three times." *Though there's one visit I'd definitely prefer to forget.*

"Is it far?" Callum said, looking back towards Whitefriars.

"Other way," Cassie said with a laugh, pointing in the opposite direction. "Look, you can see it from here. Actually, we sort of passed it earlier on – the car park, anyway – just after I showed you Cow Tower."

"Fantastic. The food's on me, of course."

"No, I'll pay."

"Absolutely not – I insist. Anyway, you provided the company and the tour."

The Adam and Eve was quite packed but they managed to find a small table. They had to wedge themselves close together on the wooden, built-in seat. Cassie was conscious that their legs were touching, but it didn't feel at all uncomfortable – the opposite was true.

They studied the menu and both selected scampi and salad. While waiting for it to arrive, they chatted about university and school life. Cassie managed to avoid giving any hints about her less-than-believable adventures while Callum told her about his aspirations within the archaeological world.

"Have you been to the old Roman town at Caistor St. Edmund?" he asked.

"I've heard of it," Cassie replied, finding herself wanting to know about it because of Callum's enthusiasm. "Never been there, though. Sounds interesting."

"We had a quick tour of the place a while back. They often do digs there. I'll check to see if anything's coming up this summer or maybe next year. If you'd like to see a dig actually in progress, that is."

Cassie grinned and nodded but thought to herself, *I suspect any digs scheduled for next year might find themselves unexpectedly cancelled, but I can't tell him that.*

Once their meals arrived, they both ate quite slowly. In Cassie's case, it was because she wanted to prolong this experience of being with someone she was growing to like more each second. Possibly, she considered, it was even more than just 'like' despite this only being the third time they had met. *Do the first two even count?* she wondered.

But the meal came to an end and, instead of wanting to make any move, they ordered coffees and continued talking. It seemed to Cassie that Callum didn't want to end the evening quite yet, either. She was conscious that, due to the narrowness of the seat, her left leg was still touching his right under the table. As subtly as she could, she moved her left hand down to rest it upon her own leg and then, while they talked, she let her hand slip so that a couple of her fingers lay against his jeans.

Proceeding as slowly as she could, she channelled her healing abilities into those fingers. Initially, she used her experience of fixing Coronavirus within her own body to introduce antibodies into his bloodstream. *That should keep him safe once all that starts to kick off.*

Mentally exploring his leg and travelling down the tissues inside his calf, she could sense where the tendons, muscles and bones hadn't quite formed properly around the heel. She explored her own right leg in a similar manner, comparing the two. That old repair to his Achilles tendon, while it had improved the mobility of his ankle, was crude compared to how it should have been. She could see how her leg was constructed and felt that, inside Callum's ankle, a tweak here and a stretch there might make things right. *I am my own MRI scanner. Here goes.*

Barely understanding what she was doing but knowing she could do it, she slowly and gently pushed, stretched and repaired the affected areas. She compared the result not only with her own leg but also, by extending her influence further, with his left leg.

"Ooh," Callum said, frowning.

"Is something up?" Cassie asked, bringing her hands back out from under the table. "Your leg still hurting?"

"Well, no," he said. "My ankle twitched on its own."

"How do you mean?"

"A bit weird. It's like something fell into place. I can't quite describe it. It's a bit like when you crack a finger joint and your whole hand feels a lot better, or maybe more relaxed."

"Never cracked my fingers," Cassie said. "Isn't it bad for you?"

"An old wives tale," he grinned. "My dad's always doing it, much to Mum's annoyance."

Cassie laughed and glanced out of the nearest window.

"I love it when the evenings get lighter," she said. "There's probably still a good half hour before it will start getting dark."

"Well, as it looks like we've finished," Callum said, "we should probably take advantage of the remaining light, if that's okay with you?"

Cassie agreed and stood up, watching Callum as he extracted himself from the table to stand next to her. She smiled inwardly as he didn't appear to be having any issues with his foot.

They approached the bar and Cassie offered to pay once more. But Callum wouldn't let her, reminding her that he definitely owed her a meal for providing the tour and, as he put it, the excellent warmth of her company.

Magic

Outside, he offered an arm and she readily held on to it.

"So, where now?" Callum asked.

"There's plenty more of Norwich I could show you if you like," she said.

"I'd love that, Cass," he said. "I really would love that."

Cassie found she couldn't reply as her breath caught in her throat. Instead, she squeezed his arm with hers and they began walking slowly back towards Whitefriars. They crossed the road and wandered down Bedding Lane to come out adjacent to the river on Quayside. Callum stopped to read all the names on the wooden bales art installation that had been there for several years. A few minutes later, she was showing him Elm Hill. With the light beginning to fade, he took several photos on his phone and got her to pose, this time in front of the tree which, she had to explain, was no longer an elm.

At the top of Elm Hill they turned left onto Princes Street where Callum halted, saying, "Uh, why is there a keyboard in the pavement?"

Cassie looked down and said, "Oh, no one knows where that came from.[3] Another one of Norwich's mysteries."

"What's down there?" Callum asked about a minute later as they were about to pass a narrow alleyway on their way towards Tombland.

"Oh, Tombland Alley," Cassie said. "That place oozes history."

"Really? Can we go down there?"

"If you want. They, er, do say it's haunted. Are you okay with that?"

"It's still just about light so hopefully we're safe from any major hauntings," he laughed.

I hope so, Cassie thought, peering along the pathway. *Oh well, I can't see*

---

3 It would be another year before the mystery of the concrete keyboard would be solved. See: https://www.vivadjinn.com/u/keyboard

anything at the moment.

It was almost too narrow to walk side by side until they turned a corner to come out between the raised flower beds, but their hands remained clasped together.

"Crikey, all these places are totally crooked," Callum said.

"Yes," Cassie chuckled. "They're hundreds of years old." *I remember them looking almost the same when I was here in 1549.*

They were around halfway along the alleyway when she felt Callum jump slightly, just before she heard a young female voice say, "Hi Cass. Ooh, he's nice. Is he tasty?"

Oh shit, Cassie thought, spotting the form taking shape on the path before them. *Not now, please?*

But then Callum said, "Oh, does she know you?"

"Huh? You can see her as well?"

"Yeah, I, um, wasn't going to mention that I'd seen something until she spoke, just in case you thought I was, like, weird or something."

"And you're not spooked?"

"A little. I've never met one that actually spoke before."

"You sound like you've seen others."

"Yeah," he sighed, tilting his head to one side. "You?"

She nodded and smiled. "Plenty."

"Hey, Cass, are you ignoring me?" said the Grey Lady.

"Sorry, Grey," Cassie said. "How are you doing?"

"Kay doesn't come round any more. I miss her."

"Yes, sorry about that. But, um, right now, er..."

"Oh yes, is he your boyfriend?" the ghost asked.

Cassie met Callum's gaze. Neither of them said anything for a couple of seconds. Then he smiled and nodded, saying, "I hope so."

"I hope so, too," Cassie whispered, looking directly into his eyes.

Callum put his arms around her and, willingly, she let herself be pulled close. Then their lips met.

"See, I knew you were ignoring me. Okay, I'll go and find someone else to haunt."

The kiss ended and they found themselves alone.

"Wow," he said. "You must be magic."

"What do you mean?"

"Well, you can see ghosts."

"So, apparently, can you."

"Yeah. I never needed to go on a ghost walk, you know."

"What, because you see them anyway?"

He nodded.

"Me too," she said.

"So, why did you go on one?"

"It was Georgia's idea. She's lovely, though she can be quite insistent sometimes," Cassie laughed. "But, why did you say I was magic?"

"Okay, well, apart from the fact that I've never experienced a kiss quite like that one before, it's…"

"Yes," Cassie breathed. "That was… definitely something I would like to repeat. But… you were going to say something else, weren't you?"

"Er, yes. Um. This is going to sound weird but, since being in the pub, my foot… um, it's like something happened. It feels like I've got a new leg, to be honest. If that's what happens when I'm with you, then, er…"

"What?" Cassie whispered.

"Then I don't want it to end," he whispered, looking extremely embarrassed.

"Me too," she said, holding him close. This time, the kiss lasted even longer.

When it did end, they both noticed that night had fallen.

His hand found hers and they strolled out onto Tombland and started back towards Castle Meadow.

Once they reached it, she noticed Callum staring up at the castle. The combination of the castle's illumination and the night's darkness meant that it was partly hidden but she could still make out Kett's ghostly form.

"Um, Cass," Callum said.

"Mmm?"

"Earlier on, when we met, you were looking up at it, weren't you?"

"Er, yes."

"Does he wave to you as well?"

"The man in the chains?"

"Yes. I've sometimes seen him hanging there. Never dared go up, though. Do you know who he is… or was?"

Cassie nodded. "Yes, I know exactly who he is," she whispered.

"It's Robert Kett, isn't it? When I was reading up about Lord Sheffield, I heard all about how Kett had been captured and put on trial and eventually hung in chains from the castle walls."

"Yes," Cassie said. "He's still a bit of a character."

"Oh, you've spoken to his ghost? Wow, I bet that was weird."

Not just his ghost… no, that's too much to reveal at the moment.

"Would you, er, like to speak to him yourself?" Cassie asked.

"Um, seriously?"

"Yes. Can you see him right now?"

"Yes," Callum said, "plain as day."

"Maybe it's about time I introduced you two properly, then," Cassie grinned.

"What, right now? I expect the castle is all closed up, isn't it?"

"Yes… but I do know a sort of… well, you could call it a shortcut."

"Shortcut?"

"You know, earlier on when you said I was… magic?"

"Um, yes?"

"Well, er, are you prepared to experience even more magic?"

"I, er, yes, I think so."

"Promise you won't be scared?"

"I've seen enough odd things in my life not to be too scared," he said, adding, "I hope."

Cassie grinned and said, "Okay, hold my hand."

"Sounds good – and then what?"

"Welcome to my world," Cassie said taking Callum with her on the shortcut up to the castle.

The End

Acknowledgments

My thanks go to Bob Goddard, Susan Ellis, HJ Brown, Sally Carr and Ross Chettleburgh for reading the manuscript, highlighting issues and mistakes, and making suggestions. Thanks also go to Donnellis Pizzeria for agreeing to the use of their premises for a significant aspect of the story.

By the same author:

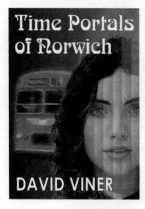
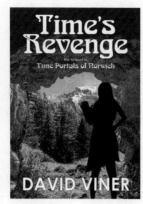
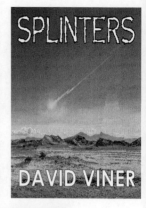

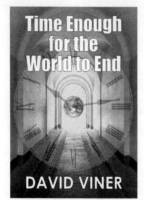

Also published by Viva Djinn (Horde) Publishing

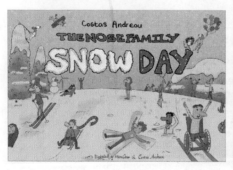